PI

UNC
TERRITORY

A Mad Max Mystery

"Mad Max is at it again--another "uppity woman" who can't leave well enough alone. Just the way I like it. Uncharted Territory is a well-crafted mystery, with a nuanced plot, and plenty to chew on."

—MOLLIE COX BRYAN,
Agatha Award Finalist for *A Cumberland Creek Mystery Series*

"Auntie Mame and Miss Marple combine in heroine Mad Max as Ashton takes a genre bending look at the aftermath of Katrina when the storm surge wiped out a lifestyle and left evil behind."

—FIONA QUINN,
contributor to *Virginia Is For Mysteries* and *Chaos Is Come Again*

"Mad Max Davies sees how the other half lives as she and her family begin a new adventure that takes them far from home and into the darker side of society. A good read with some unexpected twists."

—KRISTEN HOUGHTON,
author of *For I Have Sinned: A Cate Harlow Private Investigation*

"The last place most people would leave home to heal from personal loss would be post-Katrina Mississippi, but this is plucky and determined Mad Max Davis in a genre-bending tale of murder, suspense, chaos, and triumph."

—MICHAEL MURPHY, author of *Goodbye Emily*

Uncharted Territory
by Betsy Ashton

© Copyright 2016 Betsy Ashton

ISBN 978-1-63393-051-3

This is a work of fiction. The characters are both actual and fictitious. With the exception of verified historical events and persons, all incidents, descriptions, dialogue and opinions expressed are the products of the author's imagination and are not to be construed as real.

Published by

◄ köehlerbooks ™

210 60th Street
Virginia Beach, VA 23451
212-574-7939
www.koehlerbooks.com

For Jene —
fellow reader, fellow
writer & corporate
goddess. ♡ — Betsy

UNCHARTED
TERRITORY

A Mad Max Mystery

Betsy Ashton

Betsy Ashton

VIRGINIA BEACH
CAPE CHARLES

I write for myself and for a stranger.

Sofia Starnes
Virginia Poet Laureate, 2012-2014

CHAPTER ONE

Mississippi, September 21

IN PRE-DAWN DARKNESS, I eased the RV door open and tiptoed down four steps to bare earth. Coffee cup in hand, I turned three hundred and sixty degrees. A strong northern front had blown through overnight, sweeping the humidity out to sea and leaving a crystalline sky behind.

An underlying stench of death and decay, however, lingered.

Johnny, Emilie, and I had settled into our new home the day before. While we waited for the rest of the family to arrive, I watched large birds ride thermals in lazy circles over a distant bayou west of our compound. I didn't know what kind they were, but they were always in the same place. Black and large, they added to the ominous emptiness. I hadn't had time to drive across the gray wasteland to find out what was going on.

A slamming trailer door and boot steps on packed earth announced Johnny's arrival from the other side of my RV. He walked up, smiled, and stared at the rising column of birds. Clad in jeans, boots, and a clean T-shirt, he was ready for work.

"Good morning, funny man." I tilted my face for a kiss.

"Back atcha, pretty lady." He kissed my cheek.

"Do you see those birds?" I pointed. "More of them today than yesterday."

"Yes. Something's dying over there."

"Dying?"

"Yes." Johnny tugged my left earlobe.

"Not dead?"

"Buzzards circle until an animal dies. Then they land."

"Whatever it is sure has attracted a crowd." I hugged Johnny but kept staring at the birds. Day one, and I was already spooked by the alien landscape.

More flocks formed near the unseen bayou. Birds landed and rose.

"That's not all that's attracting crowds."

What did he mean by that cryptic remark?

Johnny clapped a ball cap on his head and walked to the cook tent for breakfast before leaving for the job site, kicking up tiny puffs of dust in his wake.

Before I came down to Mississippi, I hadn't expected such unbroken flatness, such a lack of color. Nothing taller than a car or trailer or pile of rubble. No flowers. In fact, nothing green except a few battered live oak trees. Had Charles Dickens written about spoiled lands instead of broken people, this landscape would have made a perfect subject.

When I reflected back over the past few months, I could never have foreseen the changes I would make in my life. I never figured I'd be taking my grandchildren into a war zone.

At least it seemed like one to me.

CHAPTER TWO

New York City, week of August 15

WHO'D HAVE THOUGHT Queen Elizabeth and I would have anything in common. I mean, we both endured totally sucky years. Her *annus horribilis* in 1992 brought public humiliation to the Royal family when both of her sons divorced their wives. In the past twelve months, my only daughter, Merry, suffered a severe brain injury, which altered her personality. The grandchildren and I were learning to cope with her new behavior when she was murdered. Her husband, Whip, was arrested for the crime.

No Royal eloquence for me. No *annus horribilis* but, without a doubt, mine was a shit-eating year.

Was it any wonder I fled my son-in-law's house in Richmond for my apartment in New York City? Time spent with my closest friends, the Great Dames, would help me heal enough to keep my promise to my grandchildren and return to full-time child rearing.

"To Maxine Davies, our dear friend and fellow life traveler." Eleanor, the alpha Great Dame, began the now-familiar toast.

"We'll miss you and think of you often." Grace held her stemmed glass high.

"You understand, dear, we don't associate with—" Rose added.

"—trailer trash!" Raney finished.

Five well-manicured hands raised crystal glasses and clinked rims.

I rolled the tartness of the pomegranate martini around on my tongue. "How many times do I have to tell you? We won't be living in trailers. They're RVs."

My friends didn't approve of my plans. They understood why I had to be involved in raising my grandkids, but they believed we'd all be better off if we weren't road warriors. A huge chunk of me agreed.

"They have aluminum siding and wheels, don't they?" Raney knew the answer.

"Yes."

"They move. They're trailers." Raney thrust her chin out in a comic imitation of me when I was being bullheaded.

I shook my short, highlighted hair and gave up. Time to quit when I couldn't win.

"I am sorry you could not convince Whip to be sensible and change his mind about where he works." Eleanor raised a perfectly plucked eyebrow. "Life would be so much easier if he would work in Richmond."

"What does Whip have against putting down roots and living at home?" Grace peered at me over her reading glasses. She glanced back at her cards and twisted a lock of newly hennaed hair. A classic tell, as poker players would say. She held a good hand.

After my son-in-law was exonerated of Merry's murder, we argued long and hard about his pigheadedness about living in Richmond. I wanted him to work close to home where the kids could continue in their schools. He could be home every night to help with homework and be the dominant influence in their lives. Nothing Emilie or I said changed his mind.

We quit the battle after Emilie asked me to stay with her and her brother, Alex, to help them grow up. I accepted the fact Whip was happiest living in some remote area building roads or tunnels or bridges. I dragged two concessions from him.

One, he had to accept jobs in the States, because I wasn't about to haul two kids to a series of foreign countries. I had to be able to return to New York City monthly to fulfill a myriad of obligations.

Two, I would choose how we lived. Not wanting to set up house in a series of tents, cheap motel rooms or crummy rental houses led to my current solution: RVs. Trailer trash or not, this was the most sensible solution.

"If you brought the kids here to New York, we'd see you all the time." Rose gnawed at her lower lip, removing her lipstick, something she did when she wasn't getting her way.

"I have to stay with the kids, no matter where they are. Besides, I need to be needed."

"We need you too." Rose had the last word for a while.

Eleanor topped off our glasses. The Great Dames, five friends who met once a week at one of our apartments for bridge and 'tinis, ranged in age from Eleanor at around seventy to me in my mid-fifties. Well, late fifties. We were half plastered. No wonder. We'd been playing cards in Rose's apartment in the Dakota and sipping all afternoon. I'd had enough to drink but held out my glass anyway.

I found it nearly impossible to think I wouldn't be seeing these close friends all the time. All widows, we enjoyed disposable time and income, not the least of which we poured into our apartments.

Rose's made my mind itch. I'd been sitting in this embodiment of formal decorating for a dozen years without acknowledging its elegance. French, mostly Louis XIV, and not a reproduction. Though Rose's apartment was spotless, a whiff of decay wafted on the air-conditioning. Far too many objects in too small a space. Lemon furniture oil, Chanel, and martinis couldn't mask centuries-old musk.

Grace dealt a new hand. I missed the next bid.

"Earth to Max."

I made a stupid bid, and Raney and I ended up losing the hand.

"Pollygees, Raney, pollygees."

"Seriously, Max, are you going ahead with this crazy scheme? After last year, I thought you'd stay home." Grace handed the deck to Rose, who shuffled with gusto.

"I hoped to, but I promised Em and Alex. After all those years of being a road warrior and leaving the family management to

Merry, Whip wants to be a more hands-on father. Since he can't do it without my help, we'll all be living in RVs."

"I don't understand why you choose them over us." Rose was ever the center of her own universe. "We're your best friends, after all. Besides, if you don't stay here, how will you find an acceptable husband?"

CHAPTER THREE

New York, week of August 15

AROUND SIX, ELEANOR, Raney, and I wobbled off to our favorite Thai restaurant a few blocks away. Rose and Grace, who had apartments in the Dakota, were in for the night. Eleanor lived over on Sutton Place, and Raney and I were in the lower eighties on Park.

"You are changing, Maxine. I was surprised when you did not rise to Rose's comment about finding an acceptable husband." Eleanor's elegant diction set her apart from the rest of us Dames. She had never lost her aristocratic British accent, even though she had lived almost sixty years in the States. "In the past, you would have torn her apart."

"I wanted to. She's been riding me for a year, ever since I told her my friend, Johnny Medina, wasn't Spanish royalty but a Mexican-American from Albuquerque."

We dodged a group of mothers with strollers the size of condos rolling four abreast in front of the Plaza Hotel. Raney glared at them when they forced her to step into the gutter. She glanced up at the mounted policeman who shrugged.

"When she made her latest snarky remark, I bit my lip. She can be so opinionated, but I didn't want to get into it today."

"I doubt she would agree."

"About being opinionated?"

"Yes. She craves excitement. If you married Spanish royalty, she would have a year's worth of gossip to share." Eleanor waved her hand and scattered Rose's words on the sidewalk where we walked over them.

"Well, I'm not marrying anyone."

"Does she believe everything that comes from her mouth?" Raney asked.

"Her prejudices are deeply ingrained. I doubt she knows how she sounds to others." Eleanor linked her arm through mine. She steered me around two elderly men arguing in Yiddish at the corner.

"I doubt she cares." Raney, who loved Rose as much as I did, had no illusions about our friend's opinions.

"I don't get it. She keeps harping on me to remarry, yet we're all widows. She isn't on your backs all the time." I'd given up trying to understand Rose's motivation. Except when she was hounding me, I enjoyed her company. She played a wicked good bridge game.

"She used to be. You're her latest target," Raney said.

"I wish she'd stop. I'm weary of her nagging."

"She does not want to see your point of view." Eleanor squeezed my arm. Slender and elegant, she was inches taller than me.

"I'm happy as I am." I shrugged off Rose's barbs as I'd done often. "I may be bad luck for husbands. After all, I've buried three. I don't want to go through that again."

"You care a lot for John." Eleanor refused to use a nickname for anyone.

"I do, indeed."

My granddaughter, Emilie, called Johnny a friend with privileges. I wasn't sure she understood what the phrase meant, but I did. It fit. Johnny and I surprised ourselves at how comfortable we were with each other. Opposites in many ways, we nonetheless had a great deal in common. We came together to solve my daughter's murder and stayed together because we had fun.

"Why is he special?" Eleanor had listened to me talk about Johnny for a year.

"He makes me laugh."

I pulled open the door to Thai Palace. Steamy warmth carried the aroma of curry, hot pepper sauce, and fresh basil onto the sidewalk. We sat at the only open table.

"I haven't seen you this excited in a long time." Raney glanced at the menu.

"I can't wait for Em and Alex to come home. Peru is too far away." I didn't look at the menu. I knew it by heart.

"I am pleased Whip wants to be more involved in their lives, although his stubbornness compels you to make the life choices he is unwilling to make." Eleanor unwrapped her napkin and separated fork and knife into soldier-straight lines beside her small appetizer plate.

"He's missed too much of their childhood already. His work and travel are out of sync with raising children. And he was in jail for months. He's never stayed home with the kids, has he?" Raney scattered her silverware on one side of her plate.

"It's not part of his DNA." I stared out the window for a moment. "Yet, when you see him with the kids, he's an amazing father."

Eleanor twitched her fork into better alignment. "He is not a good-time parent, is he?"

"Good-time parent?" Raney asked.

"Someone who is only there to take kids to the park or movies."

An interesting question. Whip, rough around the edges and more comfortable with men than women, was a tough but fair disciplinarian.

"No, he isn't, but no matter what he says or how he feels, he can't raise the kids without help. We'll go where his job takes us."

I brought a small porcelain cup to my lips, inhaled the tea's delicate bouquet, and glanced out the window again. A fire engine roared past, lights flashing and siren screaming. I couldn't watch Raney stir sugar into jasmine tea.

"Will Johnny be working near you guys?"

"I hope so. We're not sure where we're going, because Johnny and Whip haven't talked about which project to take. Johnny will go with us if Whip needs another supervisor."

"It would be nice if he were nearby." Eleanor poured a bit more tea into her cup.

"Won't that be awkward, what with the kids around?" Raney winked.

"You've got that right."

"But recreational vehicles." Eleanor returned to her concerns about my temporary housing. "Are you certain they are safe?"

"As safe as anything. Besides, RVs were the simplest solution. The kids and I can personalize our space to give it a feel of home."

I leaned a little to one side when the waiter served lemongrass soup and placed spring rolls in the middle of the table.

"Think of it as camping out, not living in RVs. We won't be doing anything silly like sleeping on the ground or in tents. Anyway, I've camped before."

Raney choked on her soup. "The last time you *camped* was on a five-star safari in Kenya."

"Tanzania."

"Whatever. You had an army of helpers doing everything for you."

"What's your point? I was camping."

Reggie, my last husband, had surprised me with the trip for one of my zero birthdays. We hardly roughed it. Living in RVs wouldn't be roughing it, but we wouldn't be living in luxury either.

"It'll be different from anything I've ever done. It could be a mound of giggles. Or it could be a total disaster. I won't know until I take the first step in this new lifestyle."

"I wish you could have stayed in Whip's house or at least in Richmond." Eleanor nibbled on the end of a crispy egg roll. The door behind her opened and closed as diners finished and left, replaced by a never-ending flow of hungry people.

"We couldn't stay in the house because Em had screaming nightmares about the aftermath of Merry's murder."

"Your life would be much easier in Richmond." Raney sided with Eleanor.

"It would, but it's out of the question. At least Whip assured me we'd stay stateside. No international jobs."

The waiter bustled over and removed empty soup bowls. Our entrees would be out soon.

"Will he keep his promise?" Eleanor trusted my son-in-law only so far. She'd seen him change his mind almost as often as I changed my big-girl panties.

"No choice. He backs out, I bring the kids here in a New York minute."

"I hope he breaks his promise." Raney and I were closer than sisters. She spoke from her heart, not from malice. She grinned, but she was serious at the same time.

She wanted me home. I wanted me home too.

"Can you believe how fast I sold the house? When I listed it, I expected nothing but ghoulish lookie-lous drawn by the shooting drama. I got lucky."

"Location, location, location, huh?" Raney had been on the phone with me every day, listening to my house-selling escapades.

"Whip's was the only house for sale in Riverbend, one of the most desirable suburbs outside of Richmond. Didn't hurt to have no competition, thank you very much."

"How are your grandchildren enjoying Peru?" Eleanor waved for another pot of tea.

"Oh my God. They're having way too much fun. They loved their first visit. After Whip got out of jail, we decided going back would be therapeutic."

I drained the last of the tea in the old pot. Our waiter returned with our entrees and three sets of chopsticks. I opened mine; no one else did.

"Alex, of course, is running rampant throughout the construction site. He lords it over everyone. Gets into trouble as a matter of routine. He's our regular little Captain Chaos. Charlie, the boss, encourages his hijinks. She's positively fallen in love with him."

"I can see him now." Raney dug into her Pad Thai.

"We e-mail, text, and use these little web cameras to talk to each other every day." I tried a bite of my green chili chicken and spooned on more pepper sauce. Thai food wasn't Thai food if it didn't bring tears. "Their therapists have cameras, so the kids can continue with their weekly counseling sessions."

"Electronic therapy." Eleanor glanced around the crowded restaurant. "What will you think of next?"

"It's easy today to maintain continuity with their doctors, and when they come back to Richmond, they'll find the sweetest new town house waiting for them."

"Kids need a home," said Raney.

"Whip doesn't realize he's doing to the kids what was done to him." I lifted a bite of chicken with my chopsticks.

"How so?" Raney stabbed noodles with a fork.

"His father was in the army. They moved all the time. Whip hated being rootless." Outside a large family was trying to corral octopus-armed children. Their whoops carried through the window.

"Yet, he demands you play the role of army wife and follow him." Raney's face clouded.

"Yes and no. He didn't demand. He maneuvered me into a corner until I volunteered. I'm not happy about the situation, but the kids come first." Whip had indeed out-maneuvered me, but I let him.

"How long, Eleanor, do you think it'll be before Max throws in the towel and brings the kids to Richmond or New York?" Raney turned toward Eleanor. "Want to bet?"

"I do not bet. Maxine will make the best of the situation, regardless of what that will be."

"The children will be gypsies." Raney nailed one of the problems I hadn't yet solved.

"Too true. At least they'll have their own rooms in Richmond. The RVs will provide more stability than a series of motels or rented places. They'll have two homes, plus my apartment."

"I see." Raney shook her head. She didn't agree but knew any further discussion would be wasted.

Eleanor raised an eyebrow before taking a bite of sea bream.

"Are you prepared for Whip and the children to return to the States?" Eleanor worried about all the planning that went into uprooting my life.

We were tired from the day and sleepy because of our full stomachs, but we weren't quite ready to go home.

"Almost. I have everything in place but the tutor. Whip wants the kids homeschooled. I'm so not getting suckered into that. I need someone who's qualified, someone who'll fit in with the family."

I'd been advertising and interviewing for weeks but hadn't found anyone remotely suitable. Not only did the tutor need the academic credentials to homeschool Emilie and Alex, she had to be willing to live like the rest of us.

"I might know someone, a retired gentleman at church who needs something challenging to keep him from getting bored. I could introduce you."

Hmm. A man, huh? A male teacher might knock some sense into my wild child. "That'd be wonderful."

"What about your mantra?" Raney asked.

"You mean, 'I'm through raising children, and I'm never living in the South again'?"

"There is another? It has guided your life for years. Can you up and walk away?"

"I don't have a choice, at least for the foreseeable future. Funny, isn't it? You know me, the one who thrives on order and predictability. Heck, now I don't know where I'll be going. Or when."

"Well, you do love adventures. Being with the children full-time will be another one." Eleanor said.

"It will."

"I hope you do not run into any—"

I held up one finger to silence her. Eleanor nodded before fishing in her purse for her wallet.

I pulled my wallet from my oversized bag and put a bill on the table. "What could possibly happen living near a construction site?"

"Nothing will happen as long as you have your canary in the coal mine around."

"Canary? Are you talking about Em, my early warning system?"

"I am," Eleanor said. "Having someone with her psychic gift will come in handy again."

I hoped Eleanor wasn't right. True, Emilie was a powerful warning system, but I wanted her to rest her gift and enjoy being a kid again.

"If I know you, Max, you'll find something so you won't be bored." Raney tossed her money on top of the pile.

"I'll have Alex to provide all the adventure I need. He causes trouble just by getting up in the morning. Captain Chaos is drawn to trouble like iron shavings to a magnet." I stared at two tea leaves and one twig floating upright in my cup. What were they trying to tell me?

Two couples edged forward to claim our table before other diners could. The waiter brought me a doggie bag and a separate check.

"I'm a parent and a grandparent. Anxiety comes with the territory."

We left, but not before four people slid into our chairs, which hadn't had time to cool off.

Eleanor caught a cab and headed across town. Raney and I walked up Park, enjoying the cool dry Indian summer evening. I turned my face skyward and breathed the crisp air. I ignored the exhaust fumes from the fleet of yellow cabs racing down Park. We waded through pools cast by streetlights.

I kissed Raney and walked four more blocks to my apartment. I smelled my misstep before I felt it. Swearing under my breath, I hopped to the curb to scrape fresh dog poop from the bottom of my shoe. So much for the "pick up after your dog" citywide ordinance. Idiot.

Images ricocheted like silver ball bearings in a Pachinko machine. My radar registered shadows emerging from Central Park, pedestrians hurrying home in the dark, laughter from a passing car and taxi horns.

One shadow broke free and jaywalked her way across Park. I paused, set a sack with the extra Thai dinner atop a mailbox and climbed the steps to the door of my apartment building. My doorman ushered me into the lobby with, "Have a nice day, Mrs. Davies?"

"I did indeed, George." I headed toward the elevator. "Thank you for asking."

"I wish you wouldn't encourage the homeless."

George, my stereotypical New York doorman, watched out for the widowed and divorced ladies in his building.

"There but for the grace of God. We're all one misstep from disaster."

"We surely are. Oh, I put several boxes in your foyer. Be careful you don't trip over them."

That must be the kids' laptops, monitors, and Alex's PlayStation. Maybe the iPods and speakers for each RV and the bus.

I unlocked my door and kicked off my soiled shoe before I dropped my keys in the basket on the foyer table and put my bag inside the hall closet. I reached into my pocket for my phone when it buzzed.

Caller ID revealed Johnny Medina. I flipped it open. "Hey, funny man."

"Hey, yourself, pretty lady. How were the Great Dames?"

"In rare form. We played cards and drank too many martinis. I just got in and am all full of Thai food." I settled into an easy chair in the den and propped my feet on a large ottoman. "You'd have been bored."

"No doubt."

"We gossiped, kvetched about local politics, and deplored the general state of the world."

"Spare me!"

"Are you still coming to New York in two weeks? The Dames demand to check you out." I'd been trying to get Johnny to the city for months, but his workload never seemed to give him enough time. Odd, though, if I flew to Richmond for a weekend, Johnny found himself free. I was pretty sure he was allergic to Manhattan.

"I bought my ticket."

Progress.

We chatted about stuff and nonsense. Had you asked me two decades ago if I'd be fascinated with the nitty-gritty of running my husband's company, I would have rolled my eyes like Emilie. In order to be effective as chairman of the board of Davies Industries, however, I dug into design specifications and patent applications, financial statements and balance sheets. Immediately following Reggie's death in an experimental plane, I stuck my nose into every crevice and secret of what was now my company. The other board members expected me to be a figurehead.

Fools.

They didn't know me when I took over, but they sure as hell learned about me. As chairman, I was anything but a walkover figurehead.

This time around, Johnny and Whip gave me a crash course in running a heavy construction company. They discussed every aspect of setting up a project. I was glad my company didn't have the same layers of logistics to manage.

"What's left on your list?"

"The teacher."

I told him about my latest series of failed interviews, injecting all the drama I could into what was a trial by slow torture. Given a choice, I'd opt for water boarding.

Johnny howled at my description of a candidate I called Tootsie.

"You should have seen this bimbo. Short skirt, very tight blouse—"

"Knockers?"

"Stop that! Yes, she had a good rack."

Johnny laughed again.

"Anyway, when I introduced myself as Max Davies, you could have tasted the girl's disappointment." I grinned at the memory of the crestfallen look on the applicant's face.

"So, she thought Max was a man, huh?"

"You've got that right." I punched a pillow into shape.

"So much for being a trophy wife."

"She was hideous. I doubt she could remove her eye makeup without an ice scraper."

"That was the end of Tootsie?"

"I couldn't get away from her fast enough."

"Let's hope you'll be lucky soon. I miss you."

"I miss you too, funny man." I walked barefoot into the kitchen for iced water. "Enough of my problems. Have you and Whip decided where we're going?"

"I like a dam removal project in eastern Washington. So does Whip."

"That could be fun. The only place I've seen in Washington is Seattle. It'd be nice to be closer to my son in Portland, too. When'll you know?"

"In a few days, pretty lady. We'll play in New York before we head off to the wilds of the Pacific Northwest. Hey, one more thing. We have to ride the Cyclone together."

Johnny and I loved roller coasters as much as Whip and the kids. We bonded over screams and queasy stomachs.

"I figured we'd spend a day at Coney Island."

"To ride a historical wooden roller coaster is too good to pass up."

"Oh, so coming to see me isn't seducement enough to get you to New York?" I pretended to be insulted.

"That's not what I meant."

"It's all right. I'll get even."

"Sounds good to me."

We hung up with air kisses.

CHAPTER FOUR

New York, week of August 22

I SLEPT LATE one morning about a week after my bridge date, which meant I didn't wake up until six. I lay in my darkened bedroom thinking about how we defined ourselves by our careers, by whom we married, by the stuff we collected and displayed. Most of what I lived with was Reggie's stuff. Some of it was even my second husband's stuff.

Sleepless around two in the morning, I remembered how free I was when I cleared out Whip's house. Each decision lifted burdens from my shoulders. Whip gave me carte blanche to get rid of whatever I wanted, but "leave the garage to me."

Gladly.

"Oh, and don't toss my favorite T-shirt. It's hanging on a hook in the closet."

Oops. Too late. I thought it was a rag, which it was, and threw it away. Oh well.

Alex balked at getting rid of anything.

"Your new room isn't as big as your old one. Can we get rid of things you never use?"

"What if I want them again?" Alex's anxiety approached the wail point.

"Let's at least start with the clothes you've outgrown." I grinned at the shaky Skype image of a very dirty boy, his spiked hair full of dust.

After much less than-subtle persuasion, Alex agreed his old toys could be donated. "None of my computer stuff. Okay?"

"Okay."

I almost asked about his computer, but that would lead to pleas for a new one. The old one would stay in Richmond; new, smaller laptops would conserve space in the RVs.

I'd whimpered over my daughter's clothes, the photos of happier times on the chest of drawers, and Merry's remaining jewelry. I'd inhaled her scent lingering on dresses and coats in her closet. I'd washed and ironed everything before filling bags to donate to a battered women's shelter. I'd given Darla, Merry's best friend, dibs on her shoes. I'd kept her handbag collection. Merry spent more on handbags than I did, and I was extravagant. She'd never had a chance to carry the yellow Prada or the Jimmy Choo, the last bags she bought on the day of her accident. I'd set aside photos and jewelry for Emilie.

Wrapped in the memory of how liberating it felt de-cluttering Whip's house, I walked my apartment, room by room, with a freshly critical eye, a notebook, and a packet of sticky notes. Reggie had purchased this large apartment years before we met. When he gave me a blank check to redecorate, I chose formal furnishings to match our lifestyle. While I loved the apartment, it no longer was mine. Truth be told, it was Reggie's. This place, my space, harassed my psyche.

I might have been planning to live in an RV while I helped raise Alex and Emilie, but that didn't mean I was giving up my apartment. I had to have a place to call mine. After all, taking care of the kids had a limited time frame. When they were older and off in college or when Whip decided to work and live in Richmond, my job would be done.

Should I sell? Move? Out of the question. I'd never find another apartment with such spacious rooms and such a perfect location with a view of Central Park at a price I wanted to afford. No, the apartment was great; the stuff in it wasn't.

I left sticky notes on everything I wanted to change. The den housed the most not-my-stuff. Dark green paint, two sailing-ship oils, books, books, and more books. Most of the books could stay, but little else. I couldn't wrap my brain around how to change it. I put a sticky on the door.

Something was missing. In the middle of another restless night, I figured it out. My entire apartment was too serious, as if I were living someone else's image of who I was. Nothing made me smile. I didn't have a single bit of whimsy on display.

On the top shelf, far in the back of my walk-in closet, a battered teddy bear from my childhood hid behind a pile of shoeboxes. One button eye was gone, as was much of the fur on the belly, but the lop-eared, half-blind bear represented many happy hours when I was a young child. I put it in the middle of my bed.

With the first culling behind me, I put several CDs on the stereo. *Celebration* came up in the shuffled rotation. I danced to my favorite Kool and the Gang song, willing to celebrate anything after the bleakness of the previous year.

Years earlier Raney and I had used the same decorator. I found his card and dialed his number before I thought about the impact my plans might have. Ben had been all too happy to use rich colors from formal manor houses—dark green den, red dining room, wallpapered bedrooms. I hoped he'd be as happy to have a different challenge.

"But you can't, Mrs. Davies," Ben wailed. "You can't erase my masterpiece. You can't."

I could all but see Ben having a fit of histrionics, wringing his hands and weeping. I heard a struggle and his partner, Corey, came on the line.

"Ben's collapsed into a sodden puddle." Corey covered the mouthpiece. "Stop it right now. I'm sorry, Mrs. Davies. What did you say to him?"

"I told him I wanted a new look. He went off the deep end."

"Like what?"

"Like clean, comfy, light colors, less stuff, squishy furniture. A place where my grandchildren can relax. Where I can too."

"I'm your man. Let me glue Ben back together. A Cosmo or two should do it. When do you want to meet?" I heard a partially muffled comment. "Ben, will you be quiet?"

We agreed on a few days out. I'd taken the first steps toward changing my internal and external landscape. Emotional pounds lifted from my shoulders. I wanted to blend the best of my past with the best of my present.

I puttered around my apartment, marking items for transfer to storage. With time on my hands before I could meet Corey to plan the face-lift, I rooted through the safe in my bedroom for insurance photos. What with inheriting half a century of art collected by two rich husbands, I hadn't a clue what I owned. I sat on my balcony with a cup of hot tea on a small table beside me. Red and gold trees in Central Park promised autumn's impending arrival. I thumbed through an inch-thick stack of glossies.

Where did I get all this stuff? And such expensive stuff at that. I was bored to tears with Reggie's dark European paintings and large oils of ships. Sailing had been one of his passions. I admitted I loved our modern sailboat, but the seventeenth-century ship portraits on storm-ravaged seas hanging throughout my apartment depressed me. Maybe I should have a yard sale, courtesy of Sotheby's. I sorted the glossies and set aside photos of a small Cezanne and a couple of Picasso sketches I wanted on the walls.

Where was the modern art? Reggie had collected a number of pieces as an investment with no intention of hanging them. Had he bought anything I wanted on the walls?

I found the insurance rider at the bottom of the safe. Sure enough, it included a Kandinsky, an early Jackson Pollock and several paintings from less well-known artists. The colors and lines lifted my spirits. One of the modern pieces would fit with Richard du Lac's Two Sisters, the oil I bought the day Merry was injured. It hung in my bedroom where I could see it as soon as I awoke. It reminded me of the promise of happier times.

Two prints stuck together. I separated them, taking care not to damage them, and clapped my hands. I'd rarely bought art after Reggie and I married, but early on I fell in love with a bold oil hanging in a café in Lafayette, Louisiana. Reggie called the painting kitschy. I didn't care; I bought it anyway.

George Rodrique's blue dog paintings now sold for over twenty thousand dollars. I'd paid less than five hundred. He might not have liked my taste in paintings, but Reggie would have approved of the return on my investment. I put Blue Dog #3 at the bottom of the stack. I couldn't wait to show the photos to Corey. We were going to have such fun shopping in my vault.

CHAPTER FIVE

New York, week of August 22

"HI, GUYS." I grinned into the camera. I missed hugging the kids, but I was getting used to this new means of communication. I no longer minded its delays and jerky movements.

"Do you have blinking red pompoms on your head?" Emilie leaned closer to the camera. This from the girl whose hair was streaked yellow and orange. Pink was passé.

I patted my blonde hair before I tweaked the pompoms. They danced back and forth. "Do you like the new look?"

"I double-dog dare you to walk over to Auntie Raney's wearing them." Emilie collapsed into giggles.

"I'll do it when you come to visit."

"Yippee!" Alex shouted and tried to elbow his sister out of camera range. "Can we come to New York as soon as we get back?"

Emilie slid out of the frame, mouthing, "Boys."

"We'll see. Tell me what you did today." The pompoms blinked on and off. I admired my reflection. I couldn't feel serious wearing such goofy things.

"Charlie and Dad took us horseback riding to an abandoned village yesterday. I found some old bones." Alex bubbled over about his latest adventure.

"They weren't bones," Emilie said off camera. "You found pieces of wood."

"Well, they looked like bones." Alex hated to be corrected by anyone, especially his sister.

"How's the hunt for a teacher coming?" Whip moved Alex aside to enter the narrow picture. He was as dusty as his son. No matter if the work was physically difficult, Whip was happiest on some remote construction site where being dirty at the end of the day didn't matter.

"Don't get me started. Why are people incapable of understanding the written word? Particularly when it's a want ad for a teaching position? In the past two weeks, I've had applications from five young women who wanted to be nannies in uptown apartments."

"Wish I could help." Whip's expression, though, said *better you than me.*

"So do I. Wait 'til I tell you about my interview with Mrs. Doubtfire yesterday."

I'd arranged to meet the applicant at a midtown teahouse. On paper she was almost too well-qualified. In person she could have been a tackle for the Pittsburgh Steelers. Her physique didn't exclude her, but her behavior did. She let me know almost before we finished introducing ourselves what her minimum requirements were.

"Her own room with a sitting room and a big-screen television, access to the kitchen and any food in it, three-day weekends, two weeks off each quarter, a car if we weren't going to be in the city, taxi allowance 'since I won't drive in this insane traffic,' private hotel room when we travel."

The Peru group laughed. Charlie walked through the picture behind Whip, flapped a hand and passed out of sight.

"Tell me you didn't hire her," Emilie said as soon as she could breathe. She leaned over her father's shoulder. "If you did, me and Alex—"

"Alex and I."

She stuck her tongue out. "*Alex and I'll* behave like complete and total brats. We'll run her off in a day."

"I knew at hello she wouldn't work. The more she talked, often while chewing, the more revolted I became. Terrible manners and crude language. I admit I judged her first by her looks, but that judgment held up."

I peered around my den. Was the perfect teacher hiding among the thousand-plus books on the shelves? Had I missed her in the shadows?

"If I can't find a qualified teacher, we'll have to stay in Richmond."

Whip shook his head. "Out of the question."

I glared at him. He wasn't manipulating me into being the kids' teacher. Two roles, parent and grandparent, were more than enough. "What if I can't find someone? Are you going to homeschool them? Or do the kids not go to school?"

"You'll find a way."

"Yeah, sure." My frowny face was in direct conflict with my bouncy headgear. "What gets me is the deplorable lack of basic knowledge. Even among the barely competent candidates, all college grads, mind you, they don't speak grammatically correct English. Either they know something about math but nothing about civics and world history, or vice versa. I haven't found anyone with a well-rounded traditional education. I haven't gotten as far as talking about living in an RV with any of them."

"We don't have to go to school," Alex yelled from off camera. "We can learn everything we need over the Internet."

"And a whole lot more you don't need." Whip stopped that line of thinking.

"Eleanor knows a man in her church that might do. I haven't seen his résumé or met him yet." I crossed my fingers.

"A man, huh?" Whip was interested. "Could work."

"Maybe he'll keep Alex focused." I worried about Alex picking up too many bad habits in Peru. Whip was too lax for my comfort.

"I'm focused," came Alex's shout from behind his father.

"Yes, on everything but your schoolwork." Whip grinned at his son.

"Anything else going on I should know about?"

"We're going to stay in the States. Tops has a project in the Pacific Northwest that looks hopeful."

"The dam job?"

"How did you know?"

"Johnny told me. Let me know when you're ready to leave Peru. I need a few days to get to Richmond and stock the town house."

"It shouldn't be longer than a couple of weeks. That okay?"

"Sure is. I can't wait to see you guys."

"Love you, Mad Max," Emilie signed off.

"Bye," from Alex.

"See ya," from Whip.

Another wave and a flash of red hair from the ever-moving Charlie before the connection faded.

CHAPTER SIX

New York, week of August 29

EVEN THOUGH I was nervous as if I were on a first date, I was late to Eleanor's. Usually so punctual you could set your watch by me, I was fixated by the television coverage of Hurricane Katrina. Warnings before it made landfall promised this storm would be bad. Never in my wildest nightmares did I foresee the New Orleans levees breaking and an entire city being drowned. Eleanor opened the door.

"I'm sorry, but I couldn't tear myself away from what's going on in New Orleans." I gave my handbag and sweater to Joyce, Eleanor's longtime maid, and hugged my friend. "Now I understand why people can't look away from a train wreck."

"What those poor people in the Super Dome are enduring is inexplicable. I never thought I would see our own country treat people in desperate straits this abominably."

Eleanor tucked my arm through hers and led me into her sitting room. A tall man stood looking at a bookcase, his hands locked behind his back.

"Certainly not," I said.

The man turned to face me.

"Stuart, may I introduce Maxine Davies."

"Maxine, this is Stuart Duxworth-Ross."

We shook hands; we made no attempt to hide the fact we sized each other up. Mr. Duxworth-Ross was a head taller than I was and wiry lean, with gray eyes, caterpillar eyebrows, a trimmed beard and fading red hair. Dressed in a navy blazer, tan slacks and a white shirt, the one out-of-the-ordinary touch was a yellow polka-dot cravat instead of a tie. Eleanor motioned for us to sit and offered coffee from an urn on the butler's table.

"Joyce will serve lunch in half an hour."

Aromas of fresh baked bread and homemade tomato soup filled the brownstone.

Since it was dominating the airwaves, we talked about hurricane-ravaged New Orleans before turning to a variety of social topics from childhood obesity to the war in Iraq to the deplorable state of education in the US. Although I learned very little about Mr. Duxworth-Ross himself, the more he talked, the more interested I became. His diction and grammar were Queen's-English perfect.

When Joyce called us to lunch, we moved into the dining room. She put bowls of soup and egg salad sandwiches in front of each of us. I waited until she left before turning to the reason we were together.

"Mr. Duxworth-Ross, I believe Eleanor's told you I'm looking for a teacher to homeschool my two grandchildren."

"She has. Please, call me Ducks. It's less of a mouthful." His smile revealed white, slightly overlapping front teeth.

"With pleasure. I'm Max, Maxine to Eleanor, who loathes nicknames."

"Yes, I learned." Ducks grinned. "The hard way."

"My grandchildren went through a year of hell." I gave the barest information about Merry's accident and murder, its aftereffects on Emilie and Alex, where they were in school, and their current escapades in Peru.

When I paused over a bite of sandwich, Ducks asked, "If I may be nosy, are they in therapy?"

Well, that was refreshing. His first question was about the children. Prior applicants talked about their personal requirements and ignored my grandchildren's needs. I filled in more blanks about how they were continuing therapy through technology.

"Ah yes, the e-couch. How very wise."

"Alex's bounced back with the resiliency of an eleven-year-old. Em still has nightmares, but she's learning to fear them less. Her doctor says they'll get better but may never go away." I crunched a homemade crouton in the soup. Yum. Dark rye.

"And she's how old?"

"Almost thirteen."

"Did she see her mother killed?" Ducks set down his empty coffee cup.

"No. She didn't."

"Right. I'll want to hear more later. It'll help me know how to approach her the first time." Ducks earned more points by keeping the focus on Emilie. Thus far, he'd asked for nothing but the right kind of information to access her state of mind.

I lifted a spoonful of soup. Hot enough to singe my tongue. I held the spoon for a few moments. "I assume, Ducks, you're a teacher."

Ducks looked startled. "Right. You don't have my CV, my curriculum vitae. It's what you call a résumé."

"I'll want to see it as soon as possible. Did you bring a copy?"

"No. I wanted to meet you first. Now, to answer your question. I was a teacher. I taught math, science, and English in England for fifteen years. I was headmaster across the pond before coming to the States in the same role at a progressive private school in Massachusetts. Even as headmaster, I continued teaching math and physics."

"What made the school progressive?" Eleanor, a semi-retired university professor, had a keen interest in education at all levels.

"Year-round classes were radical at the time. We gave the students two weeks off a quarter." Ducks put his spoon down. "I adopted it from the Japanese school system. As a private academy, we didn't have to satisfy an elected school board, just a board of directors."

"What else did you try?" Up to now, nothing disqualified this urbane man.

"We live in a global society, yet we're sorely inept at using our own language, let alone a second one. I introduced teaching math in Spanish and history in French. We even had an option of Mandarin for social studies."

Imagine taking a class in a different language. Not taking the language per se, but using it to study a subject like history or economics. How cool was that?

"How did combining math and language study work?"

"After a few bumps, very well."

"I would be happy if children in New York City could read English when they graduated." Eleanor had little faith that the current system educated students.

"I agree." Ducks held up his cup. "Any chance for more coffee?"

Eleanor pressed a buzzer. In a few seconds, Joyce arrived with a fresh pot.

"Which languages did you teach?" I motioned toward my cup for a refill.

"Well, I don't speak Chinese, but I'm fluent in Spanish and French. Not too bad in German or Italian. Some Swahili."

"That is quite a range," Eleanor said.

"I can't pretend to be fluent in Swahili. My level is conversational at best." Ducks dropped two sugar cubes into his coffee and stirred. "Have your grandchildren started language studies?"

"Em started Spanish last year. Alex begins this year. They're pretty good in conversational Spanish, since the laborers in Peru don't speak English. I don't want to think what they're really learning, though." I shook my head.

Alex's bad manners had morphed into an art form since he wasn't under my scrutiny. I had so much work to do. If that continued, I'd need lessons in parenting. I had no clue what the current trends were. I was way old school.

"If you approve, I'll use Spanish textbooks to teach everything from algebra onward. Science too. We'll study history and social studies in French."

"What about electives?" I stirred cream into my coffee, my spoon making soft clinks against the thin porcelain cup.

"Like what?" Ducks sipped more soup.

"Economics. Ecology. Civics. Science. English and American literature. Computer science."

"Certainly. There are plenty of books and study plans we can use. Shouldn't be a problem. Anything else?" Ducks's calm put me at ease.

"Em loved her after-school creative writing class." I'd picked her up twice a month. She read me everything she wrote. Some of it was damned good. Some needed a lot of work.

"Brilliant. I play with a bit of writing myself."

Okay, we had the basics out of the way. Down to one more issue. "Several teachers I interviewed wanted to teach to the New York Learning Standards exams. What do you—?"

"State-legislated ignorance! This obscene overemphasis on testing has reduced education to a mockery of what it was a few decades ago. It wasn't all that good then. Preposterous!"

Eleanor and Ducks argued the demerits of standardized testing with a vehemence that shoved me to the sidelines. The more I listened, the more I liked what he said, but I couldn't jump to conclusions. Not with my grandkids' education at stake.

"Okay, we agree students can learn more than the basics. How would you challenge Alex and Em? They still have to pass the exams, after all."

"I pushed my students to do more than they thought they could. I'd do the same with your grandchildren once I assessed their strengths. I like to build on what they already know and what they like." Ducks outlined a rigorous program incorporating traditional subjects with more unconventional ones. Computer science for Alex, creative writing for Emilie. Plenty of exercise as well.

We talked for another half hour before I had to leave to meet Corey at my vault. As I reclaimed my sweater and bag, I gave Ducks my card and asked him to e-mail me his contact information, résumé, and a list of references both in the US and England. My gut told me he was the real thing, but my gut wasn't enough. If his references checked out, he'd have to pass Emilie's gut too.

"One more thing. We won't be staying in New York City or in Richmond."

"Eleanor mentioned trailers." Ducks winked at our hostess.

"By the way, how long have you been in the States, Stuart?" Eleanor jumped in before I could deny the RVs were trailers.

"Twelve years. I became a citizen two years ago, so you don't have to worry about my status. I'm legal."

I shook Ducks's hand, kissed Eleanor, and walked through the sunshine to the corner to hail a cab.

"I think I found our teacher." I could hardly wait for Whip to get on the satellite phone.

"Duxworth-Ross. A Brit? Is he stuffy?"

"Well, he speaks the Queen's English and has excellent manners, but stuffy? Not in the least. Very passionate about teaching. I have to check his references. I want you, Em, and Alex to talk with him as soon as possible."

"Let me know when." Whip smiled. "By the way, have you talked to Johnny today?"

"Not yet. Why?"

"Change of plans."

"Where?"

"Going to Mississippi." Whip gave me nothing but a destination. How the heck was I supposed to plan for a state, not a town or a city?

"Katrina?"

"Yes."

"Mississippi? Why not New Orleans?"

"We build roads. We're going where we can get to work right away. I have no idea what they're going to do in a submerged city." Whip's excitement about the new job indicated how even a small piece of the massive reconstruction would net huge profits for his company.

"Gotcha."

"Johnny's going down tomorrow to scope out the conditions."

There went Johnny's trip to New York. Again.

"It's gonna be primitive. The tidal surge wiped out most everything. If you don't want to come, I'll understand."

"Get real. I'll coordinate with Johnny."

"He'll know better after he gets there." Whip turned to speak to someone out of my sight. "Gotta go. Good luck with Ducky."

"Ducks. I doubt he's ever been called Ducky."

"Ducks, then."

I sat alone in the silent den after I powered off the laptop. Ducks intrigued me. I wanted to know more. He'd better send his résumé the next day. I was running out of time.

CHAPTER SEVEN

New York, week of August 29

I READ EVERY report I could on the destruction in Mississippi. The media's near-total immersion was New Orleans, but whole towns in adjacent states vanished. Just plain disappeared. No trace except piles of rubble and twisted, broken homes. Anguished interviews with Mississippi's governor, Haley Barbour, offered little beyond the number of dead and missing. I studied background material on towns I'd never known about before the storm: Bay St. Louis, Pass Christian, Biloxi, and Gulfport.

Okay, I knew about Biloxi and Gulfport but not Pass Christian or Bay St. Louis, or any of the other small towns no longer there.

Johnny and I talked at least once, sometimes twice a day. Between calls, I measured the back of my Land Rover and every box and suitcase accumulating in the living room. How much could I take with me? How much should I ship to Whip's office? Amid the dislocation of moving into an RV and swatches of materials and paint chips from Corey, plus selected glossy photos from the vault inventory tacked to the walls, my apartment was my own personal disaster zone.

No matter how many times we spoke, my last call of the night was with Johnny.

"Hi, pretty lady." Johnny sounded as weary as me.

"Back atcha, funny man. What've you been up to?"

"Cleaning my old camping trailer. You can't imagine the mess four men left it after we went pheasant hunting last season." Johnny laughed.

"Do I want to?" I perched on a chair next to a large cardboard box, a roll of packing tape at the ready to seal it as soon as it was full.

"Probably not. Anyway, I'm ready to go."

"Are you driving down without me?" I'd looked forward to traveling with Johnny. I didn't want to find my way through the desolation alone.

"Only for a couple of days. Whip wants eyes-on reconnaissance before we drag everything to the work zone." Johnny's recliner squeaked in the background.

"I'm glad I won't have to go by myself." I alternated between excitement of our new situation and dread of what we'd find there. I propped my elbows on my knees, phone to my ear.

"When we go, I'll drive my truck and haul the trailer. You can drive one of the RVs and tow your car. Whip'll bring the other RV and tow his truck. Feel better?"

"Yes."

"We have to get as many people under roofs as possible. In a pinch, my trailer can sleep four. Those who don't have shelter will sleep in tents. It won't be pretty, but most of the guys I've talked to know the drill. My first crew will arrive over the next few days."

"Where will we set up the RVs?"

"In a church parking lot."

"Really? Why there?" I eyeballed the box. Too big for my beast. I'd have to ship it.

"It's supposed to be flat and kind of paved. I'll know soon enough."

"Let me know as soon as you can. I need to give the coordinates to the bus company for delivery."

"Gotcha."

"Why can't we put people in the church basement?" The most logical solution would be to appropriate shelter wherever it existed. If local people weren't already camping out in the church, we should be allowed to do so.

"Don't know."

I needed to see the destruction to understand.

"We need more contractors and laborers. We'll be hiring like crazy." Johnny's recliner squealed again. It needed oil, but I wasn't about to comment on a man's chair.

"That's good, isn't it?"

"It is, if we can find workers. When I checked in with the general contractor, he said he's leaking men."

"Leaking?"

"So far two guys bolted without warning."

Men walking away from a good-paying job made no sense. "Bolted? You mean, they up and left?"

"That what's strange. There's tons of work. Paying top dollar. No reason for them to jump to another job. Everyone's paying pretty much the same."

"Better conditions elsewhere?"

"I doubt it. If it's true, we may have trouble keeping people."

"I know it's going to be primitive, but I have to be sure the kids'll be safe." I picked at the ragged edge of the tape.

"Everything's going to be chaotic for a while until we understand what's going on. You might want to delay coming down for a few weeks." Johnny said. "If I thought you'd be in any danger, pretty lady, I wouldn't let you come."

"Then we'll be fine, funny man. I'll call you in the morning."

CHAPTER EIGHT

New York, week of August 29

I RAN ERRANDS most of the day after lunch at Eleanor's. I laid in supplies of dried foodstuffs, my kind of condiments, spices and other seasonings, and gobs of silly junk from the party store. We'd need games, CDs, and DVDs. Books too. I sagged with relief when I returned late in the afternoon to find Ducks's work history and a dozen references in the US and England in my inbox. *Please let him be as good as he seems.*

A glance at the clock told me it was too late for overseas calls. Since I wanted to reach the five English references as quickly as possible, I left messages saying what I wanted to talk about and that I'd call the next day. I had time to catch some of the Massachusetts people. My first connected call was with Ducks's last employer.

I peppered him with questions. "How did he relate to the students? How did he get along with the staff? Was he too strict? Not strict enough?"

An hour later I hung up. The director of the Newman Academy could be the head of the Stuart Duxworth-Ross fan club.

"Upright, a great teacher, a good motivator, strict but fair, better educated than most of the staff. If I had had my way, Ducks would still be at my academy."

"Why did he leave?"

"He came into an inheritance and resigned to travel. If he ever wants to return..."

Inheritance? It hinted he didn't need a job. It also fit with Eleanor's impression he'd welcome something challenging to fill his time. I understood how too much leisure time could be stultifying. If he worked out, he'd be up to his butt in alligators from early morning to late at night trying to keep up with the kids.

I reached a former student in Maine. Another Ducks fan. She studied with him from sixth grade until she graduated and thought he was the best teacher she'd ever had.

"What did he teach you?"

"History and math."

I switched languages. She was as fluent in Spanish as me, albeit with a Continental accent to my American one. We talked for almost half an hour until I could no longer ignore the call-waiting beeps. Before I hung up, however, I asked if she knew any students who didn't like her favorite teacher. She gave me two names, one man, one woman, and their phone numbers. Would they give a more balanced view?

The missed caller ID was an English country code. I punched redial and reached a former student who was most anxious to talk. It wasn't too late for him to give me an enormous list of grievances against Ducks, who didn't have a hyphenated last name when he taught in England. The former student hated being taught in French and Spanish. He hated math, history and English. His parents sent him to boarding school because he failed everywhere else. Ducks was his last chance.

"Did you graduate?"

"I did. Headmaster Ducks didn't let any of us quit."

"Is that why you don't like him?"

"I don't like him because he made me work my arse off and wouldn't leave me alone."

Uh oh.

"What do you mean?" I'd heard rumors about boarding school behavior.

"He kept on me to get my homework done, wouldn't let me slack off on the rugby pitch. Even forced me to be a house advisor."

"What did you do after graduation?"

"I entered the London School of Economics, left in six years with my MBA and now work in banking." He laughed. "I still hate math."

"Would you send your children to study with the headmaster?"

"Would that I could. My eight-year-old takes after his old man, I'm afraid. Short of finding another Headmaster Ducks or locking him up until he's thirty, I'm not sure what to do."

I relaxed with a glass of wine and called Ducks. He threw questions at me. Two struck home. Could I put him in touch with the homeschooling coordinator in Richmond, and did they have a program for advanced placement courses?

"If you think I'll work out, that is," Ducks said.

CHAPTER NINE

New York, week of September 5

I OPENED MY apartment door a second before a startled Ducks had a chance to knock.

"My doorman called to say you were on your way." I shook his hand. "Come on in."

"I'm not used to having a stranger call me by name." Ducks stepped into the foyer.

"I hope it wasn't too creepy." I hung his jacket in the hall closet.

"Not at all. How did he know who I was?"

"I gave him a pretty good description."

"Right."

Ducks followed me to the den, where the laptop was set up to call Whip and the kids. I opened the connection and introduced the two men. "When you're done, will you come into the living room at the end of the hall?"

I pulled the door closed and headed for the kitchen to check on the chicken cacciatore. I inhaled aromas of tomato broth and tons of garlic and fresh herbs. I stirred and tasted, adding some fresh ground pepper. My stomach growled. *Ah shoot. I forgot to invite Ducks to stay for dinner.*

An hour later, the den door squeaked. I walked into the hall with an empty glass in one hand and an open bottle of Beaujolais in the other. I burst out laughing. Ducks wore my red pompoms. They clashed with his mop of rusty hair. I led him to the living room.

"I couldn't resist." Ducks removed the headband as soon as we sat down. "These yours?"

"Uh huh. They're a nice diversion." I poured wine and raised my glass. We clinked rims.

"Emilie nearly had hysterics when I put them on."

"Did she double-dog dare you to wear them on the street?" I sipped my wine.

"She did. How did you know?" Ducks turned off the pompoms before trying the wine. He smiled his approval.

"She dared me too."

"Will you wear them?"

"Of course." What would my doorman, that oh-so-formal man, think when I exited the building in them?

"Why?"

"Because after my daughter's murder, I vowed to be zanier than I'd been the previous year."

Ducks nodded. "Zany is healing."

"When I was a child, I loved *The Carol Burnett Show*." I hadn't connected the dots before, but she was one of my heroes. "She gave women permission to be goofy, even silly."

"I've seen reruns. She was funny. Did you identify with her?"

"Sort of. She was liberating for those of us who were uptight at a time when outrageous behavior wasn't condoned by society." I was too keyed up to fuss any longer with goofy head gear or a comedienne with the best Tarzan yell ever. "So, what do you think?"

"Is Alex always so excitable?" Ducks perched on the edge of the love seat and leaned forward, wineglass clasped between his hands.

"What do you mean?"

"He jumped from subject to subject."

"He's showing off. He gets nervous when he meets new people. Don't forget, he's been under his father's care for a couple of months. Discipline and manners aren't high on the list of things Whip worries about."

"Right." Ducks set his glass on the marble-topped coffee table. "What does he like to do?"

"A little of this, a lot of that. Why?"

"He talked about hiking and horseback riding with someone named Charlie." Ducks raised a bushy eyebrow. "He told me his sister's in love with the Frito Bandito."

That was my Alex, always trying to get the better of his sister. "The Frito Bandito's a local Peruvian Indian who provides security for a fee. Em thinks he's hot. Charlie's the site boss, Alex's first true crush."

"And this 'Charlie—'"

"—is one Charlotte Bridget Lopez-Garcia."

"Brilliant." Ducks laughed.

Was he relieved Charlie was a woman? People who hadn't met her assumed Charlie was a man. Once you'd met her, you had no more doubts.

"Alex said he likes computer games."

"Yes. We let him play those we approve." I rattled off a list. "I can beat him in several. Paintball too."

"He says he's a wiz on the Internet. True?"

"Oh, he knows his way around the Web." I refilled our glasses.

"Did he really help catch his mother's killer?" The way Ducks framed his questions gave me insight into my grandson's overactive mind.

"He found unsolved murders everywhere the killer had worked. He helped prove the man who murdered my daughter was a serial killer." Oh, great. To an outsider, I must have sounded crazy. Serial killer, indeed.

"What does Emilie like to do?" Ducks smoothed his beard.

"She didn't tell you? Usually, she chatters on about her interests."

Ducks shook his head. He leaned back, legs crossed at the ankle, but every bit as intense as when he sat down.

I gave him the Emilie for Dummies version of her school activities: soccer, swimming, tennis, and creative writing. I left a lot out. "She does well in school. Loves studying and reading."

"Who's Dracula?"

That came out of nowhere. "My daughter's murderer."

"Even though she said he can't hurt her, she's still afraid of him." Again, his hand went to his beard. "She's fragile."

"He can't hurt her. He's dead." I picked up my wineglass but didn't sip.

"I see."

"She spent months living in fear he'd come for her. She needs a lot of healing."

Much as I tried not to worry, her well-being was my number one project. I trusted her instincts about people having colored centers; colors gave clues to feelings and behavior. I assumed she wasn't alone with her gift.

"I think she trusts me. I can help."

"Good." Whew. One huge hurdle passed.

Ducks frowned. Silence grew from a few moments to several seconds. I let him think. Was he worried the kids might be too energetic? The interview had gone down rabbit holes I didn't expect.

"Let's see if I can describe Alex. He needs guidance and discipline to get him back in the habit of studying. How were his grades?"

"Decent to pretty good. Pretty good in math and computer science. Decent in English, civics and general science. Not good at all in history. Overall, a B average with peaks of brilliance when he got excited about a subject. He'd pass Charlie with an A plus."

"No ADD?"

Another good question. We'd had Alex tested. He was excitable, but no attention deficit disorder. I understood how he'd given Ducks that impression.

"When he's unfocused, he's like a bouncing ball. Impossible to follow. When he's focused, though, the world could end, and he'd be oblivious. He sleeps like the dead. Nothing wakes him."

"I'll make sure he gets lots of exercise. It'll help him concentrate." Ducks reached for his glass. "Can we go back to Emilie?"

"You spent the most time with her, didn't you?"

"Of course I did. She's amazing. She's thrilled about staying with her father. She talked a lot about you, too, if you're Mad Max." He ran a hand over his beard again, smoothing whiskers that didn't need to be smoothed.

"Guilty."

"Are you a Mel Gibson fan?"

"More Tina Turner." Note to self: buy a Tina Turner wig before the next call to Peru.

"Right."

"If you don't mind, it's getting a little late." I scooted toward the edge of my chair. My stomach complained on cue. A timer pinged a warning from the kitchen.

"I've stayed too long." Ducks set his glass on the coffee table and stood.

I held up one finger. "That's not what I meant. I have chicken cacciatore with rice and salad in the kitchen, all of which will be inedible if they sit much longer. Will you join me? I want to hear more about your conversation with Em."

"You can replay it later."

I had the decency to blush. "Busted. I should have told you up front I wanted to record the session. That was rude."

"At first I thought you didn't trust me. I almost turned the record function off. Then I changed my mind." Was Ducks angry or amused to have beaten me at my own game? "I have nothing to hide."

"I'm sorry. I wanted to listen to the questions you asked. Please understand I'm fiercely protective of Em."

"I can see why." Ducks followed me into the kitchen.

We carried serving bowls into the dining room where I'd already set the table.

"I can help protect her."

"Does Em agree?"

"She does."

"That's good enough for me."

Over coffee and sherry, we returned to my oh-so-rare granddaughter.

"Does she have any idea how powerful her gift is?"

Had Emilie told Ducks she was psychic? No, she'd never tell a stranger. Something in Ducks made her feel safe. "She most certainly does. She struggles to control it."

"Who's guiding her?" Ducks took a sip of sherry. "She can't control her gift without help."

"Dr. Schwartz at the University of Richmond."

"Angela Schwartz? I've read her books. She's good, but she's a seer. Emilie's a sensitive, probably an empath. Still, Dr. Schwartz has done terrific work on ESP and second sight."

How much did he know about this stuff? There was much more to Mr. Ducks than red hair, bushy eyebrows and a British accent. "It's difficult. She feels so strongly at times, I'm afraid she'll be overcome."

"She could. Dr. Schwartz is terrific at working with special kids, though. I had a boy at Newman who was different. I wish I could have sent him to her." Ducks's fingers toyed with a fork.

"Was he paranormal too?" I was used to Emilie's ability to sense things I couldn't.

"Beg yours. Emilie's not paranormal. She's normal for her. Different from you and me. I've studied people whose sensitivities aren't the same as the rest of us." The fork came to a rest.

Had Ducks studied Dr. Schwartz's works because of the boy? Or, could he have similar capabilities? Before I could ask, I caught a guarded look. Ducks blinked slowly one time.

"I could see how hard she's trying to develop coping skills. I've been there before." Again the guarded look and the single blink.

I made up my mind. "Do you want to take on the challenge of Alex and Em?"

"I passed the job interview?"

"Indeed you did." I leaned back and relaxed. At last. I had my teacher.

"You haven't listened to the recording, you know."

"Does Em want you?" I raised my small glass and inhaled the sherry's bouquet. Dry and a little smoky. Perfect.

"Yes."

"That's good enough for me."

"I'd love to work with them. It'll be rollicking good fun."

Ducks and I raised glasses and clinked rims to seal our deal.

"Can we meet tomorrow? Get all the paperwork done?"

"I'll take you to lunch." Ducks leaned back in his chair. "Do you know Le Bistro, a little hole in the wall in SoHo? Makes the best French food."

I knew it well. Eleanor, Raney, and I had lunch there the day of Merry's accident. Ducks helped clear the table before leaving. I retired to the den with a splash more sherry to listen to the entire interview.

After going through the recording once, I called Johnny. I was as excited as Alex when he talked with Ducks.

"Should I be jealous?"

"Not at all, funny man. Ducks is so not my type."

"And I am?"

"Most assuredly."

Sometime after one in the morning, I had listened to the conversation two more times end to end. Emilie's last comment puzzled me.

"Don't worry. It won't matter to us."

Now what the hell did that mean?

CHAPTER TEN

New York, week of September 5

I ARRIVED AT Le Bistro on schedule with a file of photos and a contract. My old friend, the owner of the restaurant, brought me a cup of coffee before I was settled.

"Tell me what I need to know." Ducks leaned forward, eager to begin his new adventure.

First, I handed over a series of names and phone numbers.

"Ah, the homeschooling coordinator and head of the advanced placement curriculum. Right." Ducks pushed the paper to one side. He wanted to reach them for textbooks and lesson plans.

I produced three pictures of the two monstrous RVs and a converted bus.

"Brilliant! I won't be roughing it in a tent on rocky soil." He stared at the bus photo, all but drooling.

"Oh, we'll be roughing it, just not sleeping on the ground. We're going to Mississippi near the Gulf Coast. Cell coverage's iffy on its best day. Most amenities either blew or washed away."

I'd read every press clipping I could find that described the aftermath of the hurricane. Not much was left.

"My friend Johnny calls it a food desert. We'll have to plan meals in advance and make do with what we can buy inland or what I bring from New York."

"I've lived in worse conditions. I spent six months on sabbatical working with refugees in West Africa. No running water, no electricity, and rotten food." Ducks spread the pictures across the small table. "We were much better off than the local population. I felt guilty complaining when I needed a wash. We carried buckets of water from the river for bathing."

"Why not bathe in the river?"

"No crocodiles in a bucket."

Our food came. Ducks tapped the picture of the bus. "Please, please, tell me they didn't repaint this."

"I hate to disappoint you, but the company's contract with John Madden called for the bus to be repainted. Alas, the Madden Cruiser is no more. Here's what it looks like today—boring burgundy and gray." Nothing on the outside identified its former user. Everything inside, however, was pretty much the way he had left it, except for two or three fewer big screen televisions.

Ducks made a face before shrugging his shoulders. "Probably for the best. Still, it would have been a grand giggle."

"It'll double as the classroom." I should have had the company paint the outside yellow. That would have been more appropriate. I handed over photos of the RVs. "Whip and Alex will be in one, Em and I in the other. That leaves you with the bus."

"Are you sure? From what I can see, it's the largest beast." Ducks peered at the interior. "It has the biggest kitchen too. Am I to cook as well?"

I looked up in time to see one caterpillar eyebrow raised in question. Was he teasing me or had I somehow insulted him?

"No. Your contract is for teaching and keeping the bus clean. I'll be doing most of the cooking with help from the kids. We'll have grills for Whip to use outside as much as possible. We'll eat as a family most nights, if that's all right with you." I hadn't thought this through. "We'll have to make up the rules as we go."

"Indeed. I like the idea of eating as a family." A wistful tone entered Ducks's voice, only to disappear as quickly as it came. "I'm glad to take my turn. I know my way around a stove."

"Good. My friend Johnny doesn't cook. Anything." Johnny puzzled me when it came to food, because he loved eating. Could he be as allergic to kitchens as he was to Manhattan?

"Really?" Ducks dabbed his mouth with his napkin. "I find that hard to believe."

"He reminds me most fires start in kitchens. I accused him of being afraid to learn to cook. His response was he was being prudent. And so the discussion went." I threw my hands in the air.

Ducks laughed. "Brilliant. I can't wait to meet your Johnny. We're going to be fast friends."

"Oh, you will be. He's very funny."

"That's good. Without a sense of humor, how can we make sense out of life?"

The café owner brought our meals. We ate in silence for several bites. I tucked into my salad Niçoise.

"Feel free to put me in the rotation. Don't ask me to fix anything English, though. I loathe boiled vegetables." Ducks sliced a bit of beef paillard, dipped it into sauce Béarnaise, and ate it.

"Even mushy peas?" My favorite pub meal was a pint of lime and lager, fish and chips with malt vinegar and mushy peas. To the uninitiated, mushy peas had the consistency of baby food.

"Especially mushy peas." Ducks pulled a face. Had he been in the States so long he'd lost the taste for this oh-so-British dish?

"We'll get along fine. I boil water and pasta and stir fry everything else. You can forget locally grown food. What truck farms there were drowned in the tidal surge. Southern Mississippi has few markets left standing. We'll have to be creative with spices, sauces, and condiments."

Ducks held up another photo. "I like the way you outfitted the RVs."

They were equipped with bedrooms at the back. The kids' spaces each had a bed over a desk. IKEA to the rescue. Each vehicle had laptops, a PlayStation, iPods and flat-panel TVs with DVD players, plus a satellite dish for live television and Internet access.

"We won't want for entertainment, will we?" Ducks pulled a small notebook from his jacket pocket. He made a few notes. "Do we have athletic gear, old-fashioned board games, books?"

"Yes and yes and hmm. Better bring your own books. I doubt we'll find any libraries with dry shelves." I drew on everything Johnny had told me about living in nothingness and destruction. I found it impossible to imagine. "Do you need a laptop?"

"I'm set." More scribbles filled a second page.

"Just checking. Finding a Best Buy in the hurricane zone might be impossible."

"At least I don't have to sleep in a bunk. I'm a bit too tall. My feet would be propped up on the wall."

"And I'm no fool. I grabbed the bedroom. I'm done with climbing ladders to get into bed."

"Did you have bunks as a child?" Ducks pressed a carrot on the back of his fork.

"No, but the upper berth on my sailboat can only be reached by a ladder."

"You have a picture of you on the deck of a yacht in your den, don't you?"

"That's the Direct Deposit. Reggie bought her right after we were married. We sailed her all over the world."

Ducks's hand paused in midair. "Reggie? Maxine Davies. You're Reginold Davies's widow."

"Guilty as charged."

"I followed his adventures when he was in the press. Quite a man."

"Indeed, he was."

We finished our lunch in silence. My head was bursting with information and precious little time to process it.

"How will you get everything to Mississippi?"

I gave him a copy of the current plan Johnny and I had concocted. "How about you? You're more than welcome to make it a convoy. Ride with us if you don't have a car. Meet us if you do."

"I'll meet you. My car's too small for any but the barest necessities, though."

I pointed to one of the papers in the growing pile beside Ducks's coffee cup. He should feel free to ship large boxes to Whip's office. The address was in the stack. He could drop off smaller things at my apartment for me to bring in my car.

"Do you have a bike rack? I'm rather an avid rider."

"Sure do. Drop it off."

I couldn't think of anything else. I didn't know enough to know what I didn't know. We went over the terms of his employment, salary, and time off. Ducks signed the contract and tax form. We shook hands. I wanted to do back flips across the restaurant. My last major headache was behind me.

#

Over the next couple of days, Ducks dropped off three soft-sided duffle bags, two guitar cases, and his bicycle.

"Too much?"

"I don't think so."

"Do you need help loading this?"

"No, thanks. Two of the maintenance men in the building volunteered."

I raised a hand to my forehead and rubbed my temples. Jeez, I hoped it all fit. If not, well, that was what UPS was for, wasn't it? I handed Ducks the coordinates for the church parking lot where we'd be camping.

"I'll be off in a couple of days. Do a little sightseeing along the way. I'll be there in a week and a bit." Ducks opened my apartment door and walked to the elevator. "Ta."

"Drive safely."

A cheery flip of the hand was all I saw before the elevator door whooshed closed.

CHAPTER ELEVEN

New York, week of September 12

AFTER A WEEPY send-off dinner with the Great Dames, I left the underground parking garage a bit after dawn and pointed the nose of my overstuffed Rover west across the George Washington Bridge and south onto I-95. Skyscrapers glowed pinky-gold in the rising sun. Rays glinted off car windshields, making them appear cleaner than they were.

My excitement about starting a new adventure when the season was changing grew as New York City faded in my rearview mirror. Soon enough, I'd be in Richmond with Johnny. Right after that, I'd be reunited with my Peruvian travelers. Whip had wrapped up his job and was on his way to the airport in Lima.

"I missed you, pretty lady." Johnny kissed me.

"I missed you too, funny man." I hugged him.

We headed out for a late dinner at Capitol Ale House downtown, where we relaxed in a corner with glasses of wine and beer.

"Unimaginable destruction and miles of nothing. Debris piles everywhere. You drive through the rubble, come around a corner and find a large swath of dirt scrubbed clean."

"What about trees?"

"The old oaks survived. No plants, grass, or bushes. Nothing green." Johnny swallowed a sip of beer.

"Nothing green? Oh my." He had to be exaggerating, didn't he?

"I shouldn't have taken a detour into New Orleans. I felt like a damned voyeur." Johnny covered his eyes with one hand. "Believe me, you don't want to be there. That city's so sad the air itself smells like it's dying."

"I can't imagine."

"I'll take Mississippi any day. It may feel empty at first, but it isn't." Johnny nodded at our waiter, who held up two fingers to indicate he'd be over in two minutes to take our food order. "Vast stretches of nothing. When you look ahead, you see a battered stone building in the middle of a patch of dirt that might have been a parking lot. Some rickety shacks survived with such heavy damage I can't figure out how they made it through the wind, rain, and tidal surge."

What would it be like to lose everything? I'd had fears of being homeless and penniless for years. Oprah Winfrey, one of the richest women in the world, talked about being afraid she'd lose all her money. She maintained a stash of cash in case she ever needed it. She called it her bag lady money.

The idea of being destitute was ridiculous, both for her and me, but primal terrors weren't easily rationalized. I'd have to watch my reaction to loss because I didn't want to channel my anxiety to Emilie—as if I could prevent her from knowing what I was feeling.

"We should be in good shape, though. We built an expandable fenced compound in a church parking lot for the cook tent, sleeping tents, portable toilets, and the trailers. Even a shower tent, just like they have in the military." Johnny ticked off points on his fingers.

"Jeez, not you too. They're not trailers. I should never have told you about the Great Dames' toast."

"Even though you won't be sleeping in a trailer, I will. As will most of the crew, if they're lucky." He shook his head. "The area can be expanded when more crew members get in. I want everyone living inside the chain link fence."

"Why?"

"It's just safer. We carry our tools in our trucks. Harder for someone to steal them if they're inside a fence."

"I see." I returned to one point that didn't feel right. I fiddled with my silverware. "What about the church? I still don't get why they won't let some of us camp in the basement. Or in the church itself."

Johnny howled. "You'll get it when you see it."

"Okay, but if someone talked to the minister, I'm sure he'd open his doors." Nothing in what Johnny said made a lick of sense.

"I haven't met Pastor Taylor yet, but I know he won't open his doors to the workers."

"Seems rather unfriendly, don'tcha think?" I sipped my wine. Why was Johnny dead set against asking the pastor to help? "When do you want to leave?"

"First thing Sunday morning. Can you be ready?"

"I can."

"Are the RVs here?" Johnny flipped his menu closed.

"Yes. I spoke to the dispatcher yesterday."

The waiter ambled over; we placed our orders.

"And the bus?"

"The leasing company's delivering it."

"I can't wait to see it." Johnny, like Ducks, had visions of the old Madden horse trailer.

"Don't get your hopes up. It's been repainted." As Ducks would say, I had a grand giggle at the looks of disappointment on both men's faces. Alex hadn't seen the bus yet, but he'd howl his disapproval to the heavens about the paint job.

"Ah shit! Is the teacher going to live in it?"

"Where else would a teacher live but in a 'school' bus?" The image appealed.

"Poor guy. Nothing like living in your home office to keep you tied to your job."

Ducks wouldn't be able to get away from his day job. None of us had ready escape routes. No popping home for a weekend unless you were local. Or had your own private plane. Which I did.

We headed back to Johnny's apartment for the night.

#

I met Whip, Emilie, and Alex at the Richmond airport the next afternoon. Alex blasted through the doors from the concourse and threw himself on me.

"Look at you. You must have grown another foot." I had the red pompoms on because I liked the way people gawked. Some smiled; other looked sideways, embarrassed by the batty old lady with the funny headband.

Alex looked down. "Nope. Still only two of 'em."

"Brat." I ruffled his unspiked hair.

Emilie was next and all but knocked me off my feet. She, too, was taller and very tan. Her hair, no longer yellow and orange, was almost back to its original light brown, albeit streaked lighter by the intense Andean sun.

"You wore them." She pointed to the blinking accessory before breaking into laughter.

Whip, the man who wasn't a hugger until after his wife died, swallowed me with his arms and gave me a kiss on the cheek. We grabbed luggage and hurried to my car.

"Way cool." Alex slid into the now-empty back seat of the Rover. "I didn't know you had one of these."

"There's a lot you don't know about me." I backed the car out of its space.

"Are we taking this to Mississippi?" Emilie asked. "It seems kinda old."

"She may be an old beast, but she's reliable." I paid the parking fee.

I drove Whip and the kids to their new home. Emilie and Alex raced through the town house and tried to figure out who had the bigger room. Emilie did, but Alex's looked bigger. I made coffee, and Whip and I sat down at the dining room table. The town house wasn't as roomy as the old house, so we couldn't have kitchen talks like we did when we were figuring out how to handle Merry's infidelity. We had tons of details to get through before I left.

"Johnny and I are leaving at oh-my-god-it's-dark-hundred on Sunday." I checked off another item on my list. "I unloaded the Rover and stowed gear, food, and supplies in my RV."

"Gotta get into the office for a few days to wrap up the paperwork on Peru." Whip relaxed and looked around his new home. His smile told me I'd made the right decision. "I'll try to leave by midweek, maybe a day or two later."

"I can take the kids. I'm driving the girls' dorm. There's plenty of room."

"The girls' dorm?" Whip asked.

"Em and I are sharing one of the RVs. Hence, the girls' dorm. Get it?"

Whip nodded. "Alex and I are in the boys' dorm?"

"What else?"

"Can't wait to see the trailers."

"Gad! Even you think we'll be trailer trash." I looked up in time to catch Whip's wink. "Can you go with me tomorrow morning to check everything out? I shipped a mountain of boxes to your office. Can you fetch them on your way to the dealership?"

"Can do."

Emilie and Alex dashed back to the living room after checking out their bedrooms. Alex threw himself on the couch and grabbed the remote. He turned on the television and shouted, "Yippee, cable."

"Use your indoor voice, Alex. You have neighbors on the other side of the walls."

I couldn't help smiling. Alex had picked up tons of bad habits in Peru. They had to go. Beginning now.

"Yes, ma'am." Alex turned the volume down on the television too.

At the ungodly hour of eight in the morning, I piled travel-lagged kids into the Rover and drove to the RV dealer to show them their new homes-away-from-home.

Alex galloped to the boys' dorm. Inside, he stopped short and stared at his IKEA-inspired study-sleeping area. Like a shipboard cabin, Alex's desk and bookshelves were underneath the bed. His space was all metallic pipes and shelves, very rugged and masculine. His eyes bulged when he spied unopened boxes under the desk.

"A new computer? And a new PlayStation? You're the greatest, Mad Max." He tugged the first box into the passageway.

"Don't open them. Your toys will be safer in their shipping cartons."

I left Alex itching to unpack his electronics; he didn't give a darn about his clothes and personal items. Emilie and I walked over to the girls' dorm. Emilie's personal space was all blond wood and brightly-colored squishy pillows. She stowed her boxes and bags. When she climbed into her bed, she discovered a beat-up toy, a Puss in Boots, propped against pillows. At one time it had been her mother's favorite.

"Wow. I never imagined you'd give this to me. Thank you." She hopped down and threw her arms around my neck. I caught a glint of a tear. A gentle warmth flowed through me.

Johnny and Whip pulled up with two truckloads of boxes. I played foreman: those boxes in that RV, this stack in this one. The kids marched them to their respective dorms and stowed them in empty cabinets. We'd have plenty of time to unpack in Mississippi.

The final thing I wanted Whip to do was check the tow bar assembly. If Johnny wasn't around when I needed to unhook the Rover, I had to know how the darned thing worked.

"I want to go with you, Mad Max. We haven't had much time for girl talk. I have a lot to tell you."

Alex wanted to ride with his father.

CHAPTER TWELVE

On the road to Mississippi, September 18 and 19

EARLY SUNDAY MORNING, Johnny climbed behind the wheel of his truck. I did the same in the girls' dorm. We headed west out of Richmond and angled across southwestern Virginia toward I-81. I half turned my head toward Emilie.

"So, today we're taking our first decisive steps into the unknown."

"It's going to be fine, Mad Max." Emilie grinned, teeth flashing white against her tan. "Think of it as the first day of the rest of our lives."

I groaned. Emilie knew how much I hated that cliché. "I can't believe you said that."

"Gotcha." She semi-reclined in the captain's seat next to me, worn out from the non-sleep sleepover at her best friend Molly's and last-minute rushing around. Within half an hour, she zonked out, head rested against the side window.

What had she and Dr. Schwartz talked about at their last face-to-face therapy session? She'd tell me when she was ready. Or not. Teenage girls needed their secrets. I could respect that. I had mine too.

Three hours into our trip, state troopers shunted all traffic off I-81 onto a rural road. The southbound interstate was closed by a massive tractor-trailer accident. We crawled through rundown hamlets where small frame houses with giant satellite dishes butted against the pavement. Old-fashioned clotheslines sagged under the weight of oversized bib overalls drying in the sun. On several front porches, refrigerators stood next to beat-up couches. Beside a once-blue house, an old couple sat in ancient metal patio chairs. The woman swatted flies, while the man threw a ball for a dog. I waved. They stared.

Our detour lasted for several miles before state troopers allowed us back on the interstate. We pulled into a truck stop for lunch and stretched cramped legs. We studied the map and talked about how far we'd get the first day. Johnny wanted to be at the site in two days, so we'd press on until I was too tired to drive.

"This may sound silly, but can we stay overnight at a Walmart?" Emilie squirted ketchup on her pile of fries. Sometimes she had weird ideas, but this one made sense. Walmart was known for being camper-friendly.

"Okay by me. How about you, Max?"

"Why not? The parking lots are clean, well-lighted spaces. Isn't Walmart camping part of life on the road?"

"Besides, we can shop." Emilie grabbed a napkin to make a list of what she couldn't live without.

"Do you know I've never set foot in a Walmart?" We didn't have them in New York City. Walmart shopper jokes on the Internet tainted my impression. Like Johnny and Manhattan, I was allergic to the concept of Walmart.

"Boy, are you in for a treat." Johnny led us back to our vehicles. "Or a shock."

Emilie stayed awake after lunch as we wound our way into Tennessee. She told me all the gossip from the sleepover at her best friend's house, what courses her friends were going to take, and which boys the girls thought were hot.

"You'll be ahead of your friends if Mr. Ducks keeps to his curriculum."

"What's it going to be like?"

"What's what going to be like? Homeschooling?"

"No. Mississippi. I mean, the hurricane did a lot of damage and killed a lot of people. I don't know if I can handle what I'll feel."

Was this what she and Dr. Schwartz discussed? How to deal with cosmic pain? I felt the warmth again. "I don't know how I'll handle it either."

"You? You're worried?" Emilie stared at me.

"Of course. Johnny's described what he saw, but I have no idea what it'll be like."

"Wow."

"What? Did you think I was superwoman?" I took my eyes off the interstate long enough to tug a lock of hair tinted pink. The sleepover included a makeover.

Emilie was once more my way-too-old granddaughter. "Can we not feel the hurt and pain?"

"Can you not breathe?"

We stopped for the night in a Walmart on the south side of Nashville. Three other RVs of varying age and size were grouped at the outer edge of the large lot when we pulled in an aisle away. After dinner in the dorm, Johnny and I went outside to walk around.

Emilie disappeared into the store. "It might be my last chance to shop for a long time."

No sooner had we stepped outside than a couple about my age wandered over, a bottle of wine in hand.

"When you pulled in, I figured we'd be neighborly. I'm Hank Scott, and this is my wife, Valerie."

"Max Davies."

"Johnny Medina."

We shook hands. I went back into the RV to root out plastic glasses, since I hadn't unpacked anything better. I unearthed some folding chairs. We arranged ourselves on the pavement in the still-warm evening.

"We're Care-A-Vanners." Hank, a tall lean man with thick gray hair, poured the wine.

I glanced at the label. Top shelf. Hank's philosophy matched mine: Life was too short to drink bad wine. Or eat bad chocolate.

Even if we were living in a trailer and drinking from plastic glasses in a Walmart parking lot.

"What's that?" Was there an entire subculture roaming our highways I knew nothing about?

"We live in our RV year round. When I got tired of cleaning eight-thousand square feet of house, we did something radical. We downsized and acquired wheels." Val nodded toward her RV, which was as big as mine. "We can go anywhere we want."

How weird would it be to have no house by choice, not by chance? "Ours is temporary. It's the best solution we have right now for housing."

"We love the freedom of being able to unhook and go on a moment's notice, but after a year, we got bored with too much leisure time." Hank sniffed the wine before taking a sip. The plastic glass didn't dampen his enjoyment.

"Being aimless left us without a sense of purpose. When the Mississippi River flooded in the mid-1990s, we headed out to help." Val, an athletic brunette of about sixty, grinned. "I filled about a million sandbags to shore up a levy. The Care-A-Vanners began there. Other RVers worked with us. We exchanged e-mails and phone numbers."

Before they knew it, they had over forty names of people who wanted to volunteer. Hank contacted Habitat for Humanity to see where it could use help. "Now, we're an official part of their program."

"We've built a community of road people like us, Max." Val had a list of new best friends.

"We'd never have met them in our old life." Hank stretched his arms over his head.

"You can say that again." Val turned to wink at her husband.

What was their old life like?

"As you might guess, we're on our way to Gulfport, where Habitat's central coordinating office is. We don't know where we'll be working until we get our assignments."

Johnny said we'd be out along highway ninety between some place destroyed and some other place wiped out.

"Join us." Hank stood and stretched once more. He yawned. "We always need more hands."

"I may do that," I looked toward the big box store. No Emilie.

"I'm not sure we qualify, though, as Care-A-Vanners, I mean."

"Why not?" Val handed me a card with their phone numbers. Johnny and I pulled out ours.

"We all have permanent homes. We don't live in the RV all the time."

"You're healthy, aren't you?" Hank asked.

"Yes."

"You have two hands, don't you?"

"Yes."

"You qualify." Hank called over his shoulder. "See you in Mississippi."

"Thanks for the wine."

"Next time you see us, we'll be under hard hats."

Val looked at my linen slacks. "Did you bring clothes you don't mind ruining?"

What was I thinking? I couldn't wear Manhattan casual from Bloomingdale's in a disaster zone. I shook my head.

"Go inside and shop. When this is over, you can toss what you buy today."

I tucked Val and Hank's phone numbers in my pocket. They might be fun to look up if or when we had cell coverage. Johnny kissed me and headed toward his trailer. I walked into Walmart to find Emilie. I steeled myself for my first exposure to the butt of too many late night talk show jokes. It wasn't what I expected. Clean, well-lighted, with wider aisles than any store in Manhattan, and massive.

I pushed a shopping cart down aisle after aisle. In the clothing section, I tossed cotton shorts, denim shorts, jeans, T-shirts, sweatshirts and other disposable clothes into the cart. I added a couple of pairs of cheap sneakers. The more I ambled through the store, the more things I added to my basket. Books, board games, CDs, and DVDs. Soccer balls and nets, volleyballs and a net went into the cart.

When I hit the toy section, my cell buzzed.

"Where are you?" Emilie asked.

"Head to the toy section."

"You're inside?"

"I am. Shocked?"

By the time Emilie turned into the right aisle, I had a hula hoop spinning around my waist. My granddaughter almost wet herself laughing. "You're wild."

"What did you expect? *Mad* has multiple meanings."

On our second day on the road, we drove straight south through Alabama toward Mobile. By midday, we met our first belts of abject poverty that had nothing to do with natural disasters. Emilie couldn't take her eyes off the broken-down trailers and ramshackle houses along the highway.

"I had no idea how poor some parts of America are."

I'd seen poverty abroad and homelessness in New York, but Emilie had never seen how poor, poor could be. Tough object lesson. "People distinguish between poor and po.' Seems like this qualifies as po,' don'tcha think?"

Emilie didn't answer. She stared straight ahead. I wondered where her mind was.

Johnny left us after lunch to be sure everything was set for our arrival.

"Turn right at Mobile on I-10."

An hour into the next leg of our journey, Emilie turned to look at me. "Do you ever think about Mom?"

The question blindsided me.

"Every damned day. What about you?" I wanted to hug her, but I had all I could do to keep the RV on the road.

"Sometimes I can't remember what she looked like before her accident." A tear hung on her lower lashes. "I look for memories of her, but I can't seem to find them."

"I know what you mean. I want to forget what she was like after the accident and remember how she was before."

"What did Auntie Eleanor mean when she gave you a 'doo-wop'?" Emilie twisted toward me as much as her seat belt would allow.

Ah yes, my "doo-wop."

"Auntie Eleanor meant Mom's accident gave me a second chance, a do-over, to heal the estrangement between us." I'd had great hopes of healing a long-time rift with my daughter.

"Did you?"

"At first I told myself I could. This time we'd have a normal mother-daughter relationship." I made no effort to hide my pain. Why bother? Emilie would feel it. "I told myself so many lies I almost believed them. Unfortunately, I ran out of time."

A lone tear leaked down my cheek.

"It would have worked."

Emilie had a bead of sweat on her upper lip. She was in her secret place where she sought answers to questions for which I had no clue. When she returned to the present, she asked one more question that I didn't anticipate.

"What did you do with the money? I mean the money you took from Mom's safe deposit box right before she died."

I knew precisely what she was talking about. "I put it in college accounts for you and Alex."

Her smile challenged the sun for brilliance.

About a hundred miles east of our destination, the land changed. I noticed the lack of underbrush first. Smashed flat buildings left behind piles of timber and rubble. A few tattered live oak trees stood like wounded sentries. Gray-brown dirt piled head high with debris. I expected Spanish moss to hang in ghostly curtains from oak branches, but the moss had been shredded by the hurricane-force winds.

I followed the GPS off the interstate and groped my way along no-longer-marked state and county roads, many of them barely passable. Were they this bad before Katrina? We came upon a sign for a small town. Just the sign. No town. I was doing about twenty miles an hour, because dirt and debris covered the road—where there was a road. Large chunks of pavement had washed away.

"Will you pull over for a minute?" Emilie was pale.

"Are you ill?"

"No. I want to get out and look at something."

I stopped where the edge of the road should have been. Not that it mattered. With no other cars in the vicinity, I could have parked crosswise and bothered no one.

Emilie waved a hand. "What do you see?"

On one side of the street were battered trees, dirt swept free of grass and shrubs, piles of rubble, plastic grocery bags, a broken pink bicycle in a tree, sheet metal, ubiquitous white plastic chairs on their sides—the detritus of American civilization. On the other side, nothing. What was she seeing that I was missing?

"What is it, dear child?"

"Steps."

We were on what had been a residential street. Rows and rows of concrete steps marked where houses once stood. Steps leading to empty slabs.

Emilie opened her door and climbed down. She pointed at something on the ground a dozen yards ahead. Propped against a step to nowhere was a mud-caked teddy bear that had lost its child. She picked it up, shook the dirt off, and carried it back to the RV. It sat on her lap for the rest of the trip.

I drove away feeling guilty because we had luxurious accommodations compared to the people from this small, destroyed town.

When I pulled up to a chain link fence, Johnny waved me through and pointed to the rear of the site. He unhooked the Rover and backed the RV between the school bus and his trailer.

"The homesteaders circled the wagons."

I had been told time and again we were camping in a church parking lot. When I looked for the church, more concrete steps led upward to another slab of nothing. No wonder Johnny howled when I suggested putting people up in the church.

No church. No basement, just a rapidly filling parking lot.

CHAPTER THIRTEEN

Mississippi, September 21 and 22

JOHNNY RETURNED TO the compound covered in dust and sweat from the first day supervising his road crew. About the only thing recognizable was his gleaming white smile in a dirty face. He waved in passing and headed to the shower tent. When he re-emerged scrubbed pink, I met him halfway with a cold beer.

"What did you mean this morning about more than birds attracting a crowd?" I waited for and accepted a kiss. His cryptic statement rattled around in my brain all day while Emilie and I straightened out our RV.

"I talked with the men after we got in. Some have seen guys following them. Everything's in such a state of flux that we should stay alert. It could be nothing more than people looking for homes or family."

"But you think it could be something more?" I leaned against Johnny's solid chest.

"I didn't say that. I'm going to keep watch until I know what's going on." He kissed the top of my head. "You should too."

"I agree. I don't want to live with fear hanging over my head like a cloud filled with broken glass again." I wrapped my arms around my body, chilled in spite of the late-day warmth.

Johnny dropped an arm across my shoulders. "Don't worry, pretty lady. I won't let that happen."

#

Men emerged from tents and trailers and moved toward the heads and cook tent as I finished my second caffeine injection of the day. The fenced area where we'd set up our construction camp had a great deal of open space.

"Everything will change within a week when more of the crew arrives," Johnny said.

Whip and the teacher weren't in yet, although the bus, which would serve as the classroom, was parked next to my RV. The area on the other side of the fence might have been barren, but a small community formed inside the boundary.

Emilie and I'd introduced ourselves to each worker the night we arrived. In the morning, I nodded to individuals I recognized. Once they spent the day working in the sun, they walked to the showers looking like dust-covered zombies. They waved or lifted their hats each time they saw me, but none had ventured to our side of the compound.

A separation developed between our side and that of the workers. Thus far, Emilie was the only child inside the perimeter. I hadn't thought to ask Johnny if the workers would bring their families. Regardless, I wasn't going to let the separation linger more than a day or two. We were too small a collection of neighbors to be merely nodding acquaintances.

CHAPTER FOURTEEN

Mississippi, September 25

A SMALL TAP at the RV door demanded my attention.

"Señora, I'm Pete, the cook."

"I remember you. We met yesterday."

"Do you have any bandages?" He stepped back when I opened the door.

"Come on in. Are you hurt?" I didn't see any visible blood.

"Not me, señora. One of the workers has a large cut on his head."

"Do you need help?" I turned back into the RV when Emilie materialized behind me with our small first aid kit. We followed Pete to the cook tent, where a wiry young man pressed a wet towel to his head. I pulled the towel away. A deep cut ran through a purpling lump behind his right ear. I swabbed and cleaned the wound.

"You need stitches."

The bleeding slowed, but the wound seeped.

"Can you put those little strips of tape over it?"

I pulled the wound's edges together. "You didn't get this bumping your head on your truck door. What happened?"

"A man hit me with a bat. I went to the ATM about twenty miles away to be sure my wife got my paycheck."

The man winced when I pushed the tape into place.

"Did you see anything we could use to identify him?"

"All I remember was he was black and had no hair. I don't remember anything else." He shook his head. "He ran off when I yelled."

Emilie raised an eyebrow.

A man attacked by a bald black man with a bat? An ATM that might be a magnet for attacks?

"We're going to need a bigger first aid kit." Emilie led the way back to our RV.

Emilie went back to reading a novel, leaving me to putter around the kitchen. So little to clean. So much time on my hands. I sank into a chair and rested my chin on my hands. The stillness and emptiness outside highlighted how many challenges I faced. In that moment, I felt more alone than I'd felt in decades. I reached for my cell and called Raney.

"I don't know how I can stay here, Raney." My brain was foggy. Today was another IV caffeine drip kind of morning. I tucked the cell under my chin. "I feel out of sorts."

"What happened? Did you step out of bed into a whole pile of Mondays?"

"It's not Monday."

"You know what I mean." Just like Raney to put her special spin on my woes. "What's bothering you?"

"I never thought Mississippi would be so, well, flattened. All I've seen is destruction and rubble. No sign of people." Nothing in my life prepared me for living amidst devastation, not when I was accustomed to noise, hustle, cars, and people everywhere.

"You'll have to fix that. You need people around you." Raney turned down the stereo until it played softly in the background. She was in a Bach frame of mind. I leaned more toward *The End* by The Doors.

"We have some great guys in camp, but they work all day. Besides, I don't have much in common with them."

"Get out of the damned trailer."

"It's not a trailer," I said on autopilot. I laughed.

Raney had done it again. She'd gotten me out of my funk.

"I doubt I'll find anyone who just wants to have coffee." I missed the social side of my life in Manhattan more than anything else. "My gut tells me when people come back, they won't be in the mood for idle chitchat. More like cleaning up and starting over."

"Kind of like what you're doing."

Wasn't that the truth? I was starting over or, as Alex insisted, rebooting my life. I had Eleanor's "doo-wop" to live out.

"What about the teacher? Can't he help?" A new CD clicked on in the background.

"Maybe, if the kids give him free time." I knew almost nothing about the man I hired and who would be living as part of our extended family. Getting to know him could be a blob of color in a monochrome world.

I told Raney about the undercurrent of menace running through the camp, about the possibility that men were following us, and the attack at the ATM.

"Please don't tell the other Great Dames." I didn't want to worry Eleanor. And I didn't need any of Rose's "I told you so" high-minded comments.

Raney closed the balcony door against a sudden yowl of a police car's siren. "You think I won't worry?"

"You can handle it."

We hung up after I promised to work on gaining new situational awareness. Some situation. No people. Plenty of human detritus.

CHAPTER FIFTEEN

Mississippi, September 27

EMILIE BLINKED SLEEP from her eyes and padded into the kitchen area for coffee before heading for a shower. With limited water in our holding tanks, we were forced to bathe quickly. We named the exercise a *minuture* shower, as in "one minute you're in, one minute you're out."

One week in my new environs. One week, and I was bored out of my flippin' skull. It didn't take long. I could clean and organize our living quarters so many times. I could write in my journal every day, but each entry would sound like a teen-aged whine of "I don't have anything to do." If I didn't explore our greater surroundings, I'd go stark raving nuts.

In the post-Katrina desolation, Mississippi was less populated than the Sea of Tranquility. I hadn't seen any local residents driving past our encampment, but I couldn't find people when I hid inside an RV.

Whip and Alex were still on the road, so after breakfast Emilie and I hopped in the Rover. We spent an hour driving through debris fields and barren ground. A shack or two stood, but each looked abandoned. We found a metal building, a large but tattered tent, and a brick church, but no humans. When we finished our first venture outside the compound, Emilie pointed to a structure of sorts about half a mile to the east.

"Someone's over there."

"Wonder who it is."

She shrugged and stared at the barely organized pile of trash.

From a distance I couldn't tell if the figure was a boy or a man. Whichever, he was furtive as a skunk. Did he have anything to do with the men who were missing from the road crews? A day after we arrived, Johnny told me about the unrest among the crews along the highway.

"A worker from a crew a few miles up the road vanished, truck, paycheck, and all. That makes three we know about," Johnny said.

"'That we know about'? Do you think it could be more?"

"I don't know. I don't have the entire picture yet. Until I do, I'll station one of the guys at the front gate to provide some safety."

"I hope he has a gun." I didn't want to live in fear, but a guard on duty would make me feel better about Emilie and Alex living in this wilderness.

"If he does, he'll keep it hidden."

I pretended to feel secure, but I was on edge.

Emilie reemerged from the RV. "Let's take a bike ride to the beach before everyone else arrives."

"Good idea."

We dressed in bike shoes, T-shirts, hats, and sunblock. Emilie wore a pair of Daisy Dukes she bought at Walmart. I had on more age-appropriate bike shorts. Emilie wanted to find the Gulf; I wanted to find other humans. We didn't take suits and towels, because I didn't think we'd have time to swim. We accomplished Emilie's goal. We found the Gulf. We didn't accomplish mine. We didn't find anyone lounging on the sand.

We were halfway back to the compound when a dirty pickup clattered along the broken roadway and passed us too close for my comfort.

Emilie glanced at the driver then away. "Not good."

###

The next morning, I perched on a folding director's chair outside the girls' dorm, cell phone once again tucked against my shoulder. Emilie was off for a jog.

"It's creepy here, Raney."

"Creepy? How?"

"It's too darned quiet at night. I mean totally quiet. No traffic noise. Few natural sounds either. No light except moonlight. Pitch black."

"For someone who loves the Manhattan bustle, silence would feel unsettling. What else?" Raney knew me too well. My angst had to be driven by more than an absence of sound.

"No people. Em and I've done a bit of exploring, but we've seen only one truck that wasn't owned by the workers." I sipped some water. "Em's reaction to the driver was, 'Not good.'"

"Do you think you're in danger?"

After the troubles of last year, all I wanted was peace and serenity. "Too soon to tell."

"You need to re-establish your radar. You need a different kind of screening process from what you have here."

"I guess."

"I know."

CHAPTER SIXTEEN

Mississippi, week of September 26

"HOW DID YOU know where to begin when you first went to Kosovo, Eleanor?" I never knew when a call would go through or how long I would stay connected. I'd seen a temporary cell tower about twenty miles to the west, but not all calls connected. When I had Eleanor on the phone, I went straight to the reason I called: I needed confirmation I'd made the right decision coming to Mississippi.

"Overwhelming, is it not?" After the fighting ended, Eleanor, an economist and war historian of international stature, had led a team of advisors into the war-ravaged country to develop a strategy to rebuild the shattered infrastructure. "When we arrived, the capital city Pristina was little more than bombed-out buildings, head-high piles of debris and unexploded ordnance. We could not move freely. It was too dangerous."

"There's nothing but rubble here, too." I failed to keep the despair from my voice. "At least there are no shells lying around."

"After we had a chance to get settled, we realized we had to break the project into a series of tactical steps." Eleanor's team concentrated on reconstructing a central bank, which adhered to international rules, regulations, and responsibilities.

"I wish I knew where to start."

"Maybe you are looking too far away." Eleanor's decades of studying and teaching war and its economic aftermath could serve as guidance in our domestic war zone.

"What do you mean?"

Eleanor advised me to find one thing I could do to help. I could leave the kids to Ducks and the highway work to Johnny and Whip. "Do not try to change everything all at once. Everything is too hard."

"Em told me to look closer to my feet." I recalled her words after we left the town of steps.

"Wise child. Look smaller. When you take the first step, others will follow."

"You make it sound like that old movie with Bill Murray."

"Which one?" Eleanor had little interest in movies.

"The one about the agoraphobic." I searched my brain for the title. "*What About Bob?*"

"And what, my dear, made you think about that?"

"Because Bob's psychiatrist got him out of the house by taking baby steps."

"I see."

"Anyway, I wish you'd send a strategic team in to create a redevelopment plan." I rubbed my throbbing temples. "Each project, be it roads, bridges, rail, housing, electricity, or water mains, feels independent of all others. If anyone has the big picture, no one's sharing it with me."

"We should treat our citizens and their needs the same way we treat other countries."

"Indeed."

"Follow Emilie's advice. Look closer to your feet."

#

So far, Johnny, Emilie, and I were the only family members residing in a bare lot surrounded by chain link fencing somewhere in totally flat, east-of-Jesus Mississippi. Whip called to say he'd arrive in a day; Ducks was perhaps another day behind in the "and a bit" part of his week-long journey somewhere near the western edge of Florida. He wasn't sure where the heck he was.

"My GPS keeps sending me down roads that don't exist."

"So did mine. Keep heading west. If you reach the Mississippi

River, turn around." We hung up.

"I wish Dad and Alex would get here." Emilie worried about her father. "I'll feel better when they're with us."

"Me too." I washed the breakfast dishes and wiped down the countertop. Dust accumulated on all surfaces. "Do you want to go back to the beach? It might be your last day off for a while. School starts as soon as Mr. Ducks arrives."

"I don't think so. I want to do some reading. Take a run later." Emilie looked out the front window of our RV. I'd parked it with its tail pointing east, its nose west.

"Something's all wrong over there." Emilie pointed to an ever-increasing column of birds over the distant bayou.

"You can say that again."

The birds unsettled me, although I didn't see them swooping down to hook talons in my hair like they did in Hitchcock's movie. Since we'd arrived, more columns of buzzards had formed.

"I don't like this one little bit." I put the last clean cereal bowl away.

"Uncle Johnny needs to take a look."

"You mean, you don't want us to go explore?" I folded the dishtowel and hung it on a rod. I reached over and tapped the tip of her slightly freckled nose.

"I'm not Alex."

Emergency sirens shattered the midmorning silence in the empty camp. With nothing to muffle the wails, the vehicles could have been right outside the camp's perimeter rather than a few miles off. Blue and red lights flashed. I looked out the window but made no move for my car keys. I wasn't going to chase ambulances.

Two vehicles, huh. No, wait. Three. Not good.

Emilie set her novel aside. "Uncle Johnny found someone dead."

"How do you know Uncle Johnny is involved?"

Emilie gave me her favorite du-uh glare. Why did I bother to question her? If she felt Johnny was involved, he was.

"Three ambulances?"

"If my count's right." I called Johnny's cell.

"Hey, pretty lady." A distracted voice with our standard greeting.

I couldn't respond with "Hey, funny man." This wasn't the time to joke around. "Did I see three ambulances going toward the buzzard column?"

"Yeah. I came over this morning. It took me a while to find the bodies." A siren screamed in the background. "Gotta go. Sheriff's here. I've got to call you back."

My cell buzzed an hour later.

"Bad news?"

"Not good. Two bodies and one almost body."

"Almost body?"

"I'm coming back."

"Come to my dorm. I'll have coffee waiting. Lunch, if you want it."

"I doubt I can eat."

Emilie had overheard my half of the conversation. "He found the missing men."

I'd told her what the men were whispering. I wanted her to put her three-hundred-sixty-degree situational awareness to good use. We couldn't be too careful. If we were in a dangerous environment, she was part of my early warning system. I'd missed it when she told me about feeling someone was evil last year. I'd dismissed her feelings until her mother was murdered. I wouldn't do it again.

"He found bodies. I don't know if they're the missing men or not."

A pale and drawn Johnny clomped up to the dorm, pulled off muddy boots and wet socks, rolled up his pant legs, opened the door, and fell into a captain's chair.

"You stink." I kissed his cheek and set a cup of coffee on the side table.

"Thanks. I resemble that." Johnny twisted his neck to relieve stress. Four pops indicated success.

"Have you been walking through garbage?"

"Close."

Emilie puttered in the kitchen area, fixing sandwiches. He

reached for his cup.

"Our men?"

"One might be."

I waited for him to collect his thoughts. His hands trembled when he raised his cup to his lips.

"Only one?"

"Yeah. One had been in the water for a few weeks. Its clothing was ripped, but I think it was wearing a dress."

"A woman?" I sat beside him. "A Katrina victim?"

Emilie perched on a chair opposite, mustard-smeared spatula in her hand.

"Could be. One was still alive. Not one of the workers, though. He'd never done manual labor in his life." Johnny's cup rocked when he set it down. Luckily, it didn't tip over.

"How could you tell?"

"His hands were manicured."

"Oh, dear God. How did you find them?"

Johnny ran his hands through his hair, standing it on end. He'd followed one column of buzzards. About a mile off the road, he'd found the bodies piled on top of each other partway out in a muddy swamp.

"A bayou?"

"More like slimy mud."

"You marched out into the muck? Without thinking? What if there were alligators or water moccasins nearby?" I couldn't believe he'd do something so irresponsible.

"I didn't see any." He had the decency to look contrite.

"One Captain Chaos in this family is enough."

"I'll think next time." Johnny must have seen the skepticism on my face. "What?"

"Like hell you will."

"I'll try."

"Back to the bodies. How do you think they died?" I sipped coffee. Cold and bitter. I gave up on it for the day.

"Both men had been struck on the head, so they were most likely murdered. Or soon-to-be murdered. I don't think the manicured man will make it." Johnny glanced at the cup but didn't touch it. "The woman could have been hit by flying debris or could have been the flying debris and hit something."

"And you know this how?" I grew more uncomfortable with each new revelation.

I glanced at Emilie. She internalized Johnny's words but hadn't escaped to her secret place.

"I had plenty of time before the sheriff showed up."

"What did he say?"

"Nothing. Just stared and sneered." He pulled a card out of his shirt pocket. "Sheriff Forrest Hardy. Wrote a number on the back. 'Next of kin can claim the remains as soon as the autopsies are done.' Like he's going to do autopsies. He'll eyeball the remains, get someone to sign the death certificate, and wash his hands of the whole disgusting mess."

"You didn't like him." Emilie set a sandwich beside the untouched coffee. "The sheriff, I mean."

"Not as far as I could throw him. He acted like he was annoyed he had to drive all the way out into the swamp for a dead greaser."

"Greaser? The sheriff said that?"

"He did. He used other epithets too. He was happy someone was getting rid of the illegals so he didn't have to run them off himself."

"You're not an illegal." The sheriff's attitude made Emilie angry.

"He doesn't care, Em. I'm Hispanic. He doesn't like us. Anyway, the sheriff's useless as...Let's say he's plain useless." Johnny picked at the sandwich.

Just what we needed, a racist sheriff who didn't want to enforce the law. "Do we have a deeper problem?"

"We might." Emilie was inside her secret place.

Johnny wrapped his sandwich in a napkin and walked barefoot to his trailer for dry socks. He left me without a kiss or further word to ease my worries.

"Alex is going to be, like, totally pissed." Arms wrapped around my waist.

"How so?"

"He missed the first bodies." She leaned back and grinned at me. Her face didn't register a hint of joy. "I didn't."

"Brat."

CHAPTER SEVENTEEN

Mississippi, week of September 26

THE BOYS' DORM appeared at the front gate around three. Almost before Whip finished backing his RV into place, Alex dashed between the dorms right into the path of a pickup. The driver slammed on his brakes but skidded on dirt and gravel.

"Hey, kid, watch out."

I ran after Alex and yanked him out of the way. "You're damned lucky, young man, that truck wasn't heavier."

Alex, showing enough good sense not to answer, tried to turn away.

"I'm not done yet. You could be a grease spot right now."

"I know," came a mumble.

I reached out to put a finger under his tucked-in chin. He'd look me in the eye if it killed him. "You may have run wild in Peru, but here we use trucks and heavy equipment instead of laborers."

Alex stared at the red and yellow behemoth earth movers nibbling away at chunks of the destroyed road.

"What the hell were you thinking?"

"I wasn't thinking."

Whip ran over and pounced on Alex like a duck landing on a June bug. His face was thunder-cloud purple. "One more time, kid, and I swear I'll tie you to the back of the RV until you're twenty-one."

Alex sulked.

"Follow me."

Father and son disappeared into the boys' dorm.

Emilie ambled over and put her arm around my waist. "What's holy-crap boy-child done this time?"

"Holy-crap boy-child? Good name. Yours?"

"Charlie's. She used it mostly when he wasn't around, although she's been known to call him that to his face." Emilie bit into her afternoon apple.

"Bet he loved that."

"Ya think?" She gave me a hug before retreating into the dorm.

Five minutes later, Whip opened the door. "Unpack your clothes and put them away. You'll stay inside until I release you. No electronics. Got it?"

Alex didn't answer.

"Do you hear me?" Whip shouted over the growls of heavy equipment.

Alex must have agreed, because Whip stomped across the space between the girls' dorm and the school bus. On my first day in Mississippi I'd set out chairs because we needed an outdoor gathering place. Whip threw himself into one. It creaked under the assault.

Elapsed time from arrival to Alex's first time-out: less than fifteen minutes.

"If it weren't damned politically incorrect, I'd beat the shit out of him like the Colonel did me."

Whip's father believed a good beating taught never-forgotten lessons. I'm not sure it worked. "Why are we always threatening to hit him?"

"Don't know. I get scared when he runs out without looking. He's totally irresponsible." Whip looked more worried than angry. He rubbed his temples with the heels of his hands. "I can't lose him like I lost his mother. Why won't he think?"

"Because Captain Chaos is eleven."

###

Whip ambled over to Johnny's truck, where three men talked across the truck bed. He planted one booted foot on the rear bumper and lost himself in guy stuff. My men shared updates on the project. I carried bags of groceries, paper products, and other supplies from the girls' dorm and put them on the counters in the boys' dorm, ignoring Alex, who was in a parental time-out. I wasn't going to let him wiggle out of his silent punishment by talking to me. Emilie was off on a jog under strict instructions to stay on what passed as main roads.

"Don't worry, Mad Max. I won't be out of sight of the compound."

"As if you could find someplace to get lost." I gave her a gentle push and watched her pink hair bob down the road. "Be back in an hour."

Late in the afternoon, after Alex finished his time-out, Emilie helped him unpack the boys' dorm. I enjoyed a quiet respite outdoors with a favorite book when a howl came from inside the dorm.

"That's not fair. You got to see dead bodies, and I didn't." Alex's plaintive wails carried through the screen door.

"I didn't see the bodies. Uncle Johnny did." Emilie skipped out of the boys' dorm and over to the gathering area.

"Guess you told your brother about Johnny's little trip into the bayou." I turned my book face-down on my lap.

"Yup. He's not too happy about having missed it." Emilie winked.

"Double brat."

Where was our wayward Ducks? Pickups and dump trucks trickled into the compound, while men gray with dust queued up at the showers. I was about to send out the cavalry when a commotion at the gate brought men running. Before I could get up to see what the fuss was, a car horn blasted, a dorm door slammed, and Alex whooped. When I walked around the front of the RV, my chin dropped.

A 1967, mint-condition, British racing green, ragtop XKE blocked traffic. Ducks was on the premises.

CHAPTER EIGHTEEN

Mississippi, week of October 3

THE INSTANT DUCKS stepped from the "Jag-you-wawr," Alex leaped across the open area and tried to climb inside. Ducks grabbed him around the waist.

"Alex!" My grandson wasn't going to forget his recent time-out for impulsive behavior. Twice in one day was two times too many. I marched over and dragged him aside by his arm.

"You know better, young man. Your mom and dad taught you to ask before you touch someone else's property." I nudged him to be sure I had his undivided attention. "Now, let me introduce you to Mr. Ducks. You can apologize and ask him to show you his car."

Damn. What was wrong with him? He'd have to relearn common sense and basic civilized behavior. Back to Parenting 101.

Alex shuffled over, shook Ducks's hand, apologized, and asked if he could look at the car. Ducks accepted the apology and waved to the gawking laborers. Satisfying everyone's curiosity at once was more efficient than having people come by one by one.

I backed away and bumped into Whip.

"What'd Captain Chaos do now?"

It took less than ten seconds to give Whip an update. "I handled it."

Whip joined the growing crowd around the XKE.

"Not at all like your Jag, is it?" Emilie walked up.

"No, but I always wanted one like this. It's gorgeous." For years I'd lusted over the classic lines of the '60s-era two-seater.

Em grinned. "So, why don't you buy one?"

"I don't need it."

No wonder Ducks wanted me to bring his things. His car had room for little more than a fantasy. I introduced him to our growing community of workers and family. He spoke to the workers in Spanish and earned their respect. After dinner, he, Whip, and Johnny talked late into the night.

Ducks took twenty-four hours to settle in, giving Alex and Emilie one more day of freedom. Johnny and Whip left early each morning and returned in time to shower before dinner. I worked at the breakfast table in my dorm, putting together weekly menus and struggling with the unfamiliar logistics of running a large, extended family in a wasteland. Now that we were all together, I had to get serious about establishing a supply line to the nearest stores and a shopping routine.

I spent a fair amount of time writing in my journal, sending e-mails and texts to my friends and trying to get phone calls to stay connected. Satellite dishes provided Internet access. I'd already dismissed snail mail; I doubted a post office operated within a fifty-mile radius. Maybe more. Anything we ordered would have to be delivered to my apartment or shipped to Whip's town house to be transported to the compound when one of us went home.

On our way down, Emilie and I found a Walmart about sixty miles from the site. At least I could stock up on fresh food and essentials, although it'd take an entire day to shop. If I forgot something, though, we'd have to do without until the next week's trip to town. No running down to the corner store for milk and bread. No corners. No stores.

Johnny's truck returned right after noon. He backed up to the gathering area, hopped out of the cab, and dropped the tailgate. Ducks and Alex came out of the bus and helped unload two redwood picnic tables with benches and two canopies with mosquito netting.

"Now, we can eat outside together, if we want."

"Where did you get these?" Ducks told us he hadn't found many stores open to the east.

"One of our guys told me a Lowe's reopened in Gulfport. I slipped away early. We need some place to hang out at night." Johnny pulled off his gloves and banged dust from his jeans.

"Mosquito netting, huh? Funny. I haven't seen a *single* mosquito since we got here. Or a *married* one, either."

Johnny chucked me under the chin, kissed my forehead and climbed back in his truck.

"What do you say? Should we set up the canopies and break these in?" Ducks gestured at the tables.

"Sure."

It took an hour of wrestling with the stubborn canopies to set them up. It would have helped if the instructions hadn't been written in gibberish. I pulled the director's chairs inside the netting.

Ducks disappeared into the bus. He re-emerged with a fistful of papers and a spiral notebook, a pen tucked behind one ear.

"Which child is a morning person?" Ducks asked as soon as he sat down. He spread a calendar and lesson plans across the table.

"Em. She gets up right after I do."

"Which is?"

"No later than six." I looked at a page filled with tiny writing.

"I'm an early riser. I'll ride my bike before starting Em's classes at eight."

"Sounds good. I'll roust Alex out by nine." I made a note to begin the process a little earlier, because my grandson was a notorious bed slug.

"Great. I'll start his classes at ten." Shifting class times to take advantage of each child's biorhythms should promote learning to the best of their potential. "I prefer to alternate teaching with quiet study, plus plenty of exercise."

"I like the exercise part. I brought soccer balls and nets, skates, volleyballs, and the bikes. I can look at Walmart for whatever else we need."

"They play soccer?"

"Both are very good. Em's been playing since she was seven. Alex started a couple of years ago."

"Brilliant."

"Have you seen Alex?" I stopped in the middle of preparing dinner. I hadn't seen my grandson in a couple of hours. "Last time I saw him he was rolling his bike through the gate."

"He's okay." Emilie tore lettuce for a salad. "He just rode farther than he planned and forgot about the time."

Must be another of her feelings. If she didn't sense Alex was in danger, I'd have to be patient. When he got hungry enough, he'd show up.

Alex returned just after Whip and Johnny emerged from their after-work showers and sat at one of the tables.

"Way cool." Alex said. "Where did you get these?"

Johnny gave him a quick recap of his race to Gulfport.

I was annoyed Alex was late. I threw a cloth over the table and laid six place settings. "Go wash up."

"Okay."

I carried bowls of food to the table. Whip forked steaks onto a pre-heated grill. Emilie followed with a pitcher of lemonade for her and Alex.

"Where did you go?" She asked when Alex reappeared with a freshly scrubbed face and hands.

Alex rode out toward the beach where he met a couple of local boys. I hadn't seen anyone Alex's age, although Emilie said a couple hung out at a battered shack about a quarter mile east.

"How old were the guys?" Ducks asked.

"Older than Em, I think."

Whip pulled seared meat from the grill and passed plates around. He heaped pasta salad on his plate right next to a thick rib-eye. Emilie and I split a steak with enough left over for a sandwich the next day.

Alex cut a huge hunk of meat and crammed it into his mouth. "Both guys were kinda weird."

"Weird? How?" Ducks asked before I could.

"One's all goth."

"That's so last century." Emilie gave an exaggerated eye roll.

"The other one didn't say anything. He's retarded."

"You don't know that, Alex," Whip said. "Don't call people names."

"This second boy could be shy." I reinforced Whip's lesson. "Maybe when you get to know him, you'll like him."

"I doubt it." Alex stared at his plate.

"He's harmless," Emilie said from inside her secret place.

During dinner I shared some of my concerns about the overwhelming tasks ahead of the displaced people who once called this place home. I filled everyone in on Eleanor's advice about looking closer to our feet to find something to fix.

"She's told me about her work in Kosovo and other war zones," Ducks said. "We've had many conversations after church. I'd follow her advice."

"I wonder," Johnny said, "if it's harder to build a civilization from scratch or rebuild one after it was destroyed."

"It's gotta be easier to start from scratch," Whip said after a few moments.

Emilie joined in. "If you don't know what you've lost, you're grateful for everything new. But if you know what's missing, you have expectations of getting everything back the way it was."

"Good point, Em." Ducks polished off his steak and swung around to straddle the bench. "Have we seen angry frustration from those who lost their homes?"

"Only in New Orleans." Alex said. "Plenty of news stories on television about rioting and people killing each other."

"You're right. Anger is boiling over there. People who have nothing could be willing to do anything to improve their lives." Whip's words sounded ominous.

I listened to the men discuss the overwhelming problems facing our country in Katrina's aftermath. Would we begin experiencing thefts and attacks, like the residents of New Orleans were facing daily? Would the region descend into lawlessness? Would attacks on the road crews increase in frequency? In intensity? Would the police run or stand and help? Were all police as disinterested as Sheriff Hardy, with his prejudice against Hispanic outsiders?

If anything threatened the kids, I'd turn into a raging three-toed bitch kitty to protect them.

Regardless of what happened that was out of our control, we had to understand the spirit of the place. Or the spirit of what this place used to be. We might be able to influence what it became.

A flood of warmth bathed my body. Something soft brushed my cheek. I was used to Emilie's way of reassuring me. The touch on my cheek was new. I looked at the men, but no one gave any hint of responsibility.

The next day Whip and Johnny drove their trucks to the work site, shotguns on racks in the rear windows.

Our first weekend together brought perfect beach weather. The kids and I finished our chores and rode our bikes five miles to a clean, mostly white sand strip. Ducks disappeared into New Orleans, and my men were out on the road putting in overtime. I brought towels, a blanket, and sunblock and looked forward to a swim. I warned the kids about getting sunburned.

"We're still brown from Peru." Emilie was having nothing to do with my warning.

The water was warmer than anything the kids had experienced off the Outer Banks where I'd taken them on vacation the previous summer. Even though I slathered them with lotion, I lost track of how much time they spent in the water. We all swam, and when I grew tired, I went back to my blanket. Emilie soon joined me on her towel. She lay on her tummy and asked me to rub the scent of summer on her back.

"We need boogie boards," came a shout from the water's edge.

"Great idea." Perfect way to get more exercise too.

A dirty tan pickup backfired its way along the sand close to the road. It slowed when it passed us. It repeated this down and back two more times. The passenger aimed a finger like a gun at us.

The next day I frowned at a slightly crisped nose tip where I hadn't applied enough lotion. The bottom of Emilie's feet got burned, disproving a myth. And Alex? His shoulders and ears were blistered and sore. He promised to be more careful next time.

One thing had struck me while we were lying in the sand. The day was gorgeous, but no one but us was on the beach.

Where were other children?

CHAPTER NINETEEN

Mississippi, week of October 3

WHEN I CALLED The family to dinner, the atmosphere around the table was weird. No other way to describe it. The day began with heavy cloud cover and got worse. An aluminum foil sky hung over the compound, driving the air from lungs, but no rain fell. I struggled to breathe. The humid air was like inhaling wet cotton.

I set the table, all the while paying close attention to the group dynamics. Alex was his normal chatterbox self, oblivious to everything but what was important to him. Emilie and Ducks were preoccupied and silent; secretive looks passed between them but no words. Whip and Johnny were brooding lumps, worried enough to spook me but not about to tell me what was going on.

I clapped a large colander on my head before walking to the common area with a tray of food.

"What are you wearing, Mad Max?" Alex looked up long enough to register my odd hat.

"Just something to keep the aliens out of my brain."

"Not working, is it?"

I wanted to smack my grandson but settled for a groan instead.

"Okay. Enough of this silent crap." I plunked a salad bowl on the table and held it. I'd pass it after someone filled me in. "Talk."

"Something odd happened on my bike ride this morning." Ducks ran a hand over his beard. "I headed toward the bayou to check on those birds. I was almost there when a ratty pickup crowded me off the edge of the pavement. Two guys in the cab shouted at me in Spanglish that if I knew what was good for me I'd go back where I came from."

Johnny and Whip glanced at each other. A ratty pickup? I'd seen one recently. Emilie played with her food; Alex chomped his hamburger.

"When I answered in English, they started to drive away but stopped."

"What'd they say?" Whip leaned over to stab an ear of late summer corn. We wouldn't be getting much more.

Way too casual. What the hell was going on? I looked at Emilie who bobbed her head an inch up and down. Johnny discovered his plate and refused to meet my questioning frown.

"They wanted to know if I was Mexican, as if I look Mexican." Ducks shook his head.

"Not a chance." I slathered mustard on my burger. "There were two of them?"

"Four, actually. Two in the bed, two in the cab."

That didn't sound good. Had our two original men in the truck at the beach turned into a pack of human predators?

"Were Goth Boy and Spot in the truck?" Emilie had an edge to her voice.

Ducks looked at her and nodded. If I hadn't been staring right at him, I would have missed the exchange.

"Goth Boy?" Johnny hadn't heard Emilie use the nickname before.

"I met him a few days ago. Talks trash and wears dirty black clothes." Alex wiped ketchup off his chin. "All Marilyn Manson."

"He was in the cab with an older guy I'd never seen before. I'm pretty sure one of the boys in the bed was Spot, but he kept his face turned away."

"Spot?" Johnny flipped a second burger onto a bun.

"He has really, really bad zits, Uncle Johnny." Emilie pointed at her own smooth cheeks. "He's the one Alex thinks is, um, slow."

"Gotcha." Johnny smiled for the first time since he sat down.

"What about the fourth guy?" Whip pushed his plate aside.

"I've never seen him, either. Older, maybe mid or late twenties, black. Very muscular like he lived in a weight room."

"Did he have tattoos?" Alex's eyes widened.

"He did." Ducks tried to eat, but Alex kept interrupting him.

"I'll bet he was in jail." Alex's vivid imagination pushed reason aside.

"I don't know about that. The driver was mid-twenties, also black. He had a shaved head."

"Crap," Whip said.

Alex finished his corn. His eyes sparkled. "Maybe they broke out of jail."

I could no longer keep my mouth shut. "Just because a man has tattoos doesn't mean he's a convict."

"I know, but…"

"No buts. You watch football and basketball. You know most players are covered with ink." I couldn't let this teaching moment pass.

"It's just, like, it's much more fun if they're convicts." Alex thrust his jaw out.

I thought only the women in my family inherited the stubborn jaw. Not so. Convicts running around on the loose was fun? Probably was to an eleven-year-old. I shut up.

"Were you scared?" Alex's eyes all but bugged out of his face.

"I wasn't scared, but I was bloody well pissed. When they ran me off the road, they almost wrecked my bike." Ducks drew his eyebrows together in a single continuous red caterpillar. "It wouldn't be easy to replace out here."

"Hate to think what they'd have done if you'd been Mexican."

Why the hell did Whip have to say that? Nothing like overstimulating Alex's already vivid imagination. I tried to send a *shut up* message by glowering at Whip. A glower doesn't have any effect if the gloweree isn't looking. I wasted my time and a perfectly good silent warning.

"Are they the guys who've been spying on us in the afternoon, Mr. Ducks?"

"Who's spying on whom?" Johnny wiped his buttery hands on his napkin.

Alex reached for the last piece of corn but drew back his hand. "Does anyone else want this?"

No one claimed it. The boy was learning, even if some of the lessons took longer than others. Alex buttered the ear and crunched the juicy kernels.

"I've seen the boys before," Ducks said, "but not the men. The kids have followed Em, Alex, and me when we go out together."

"They hang out over in that shack. They watch us a lot during the day," Alex said over a bite of steak. He jerked his chin toward the east.

"So, Goth Boy and Spot were in the truck." Emilie stared at her plate before raising her eyes to meet mine. Not good, her look said.

"Spot's, like, really spooky. He pops up everywhere. He rides this rickety old bike, but mostly I see him hiding behind those trees." Alex pointed at the remaining live oaks half a mile away next to the tumbledown shack. "Goth Boy watches us too. They're both creepy."

"Spot follows me when I go running. But don't worry. He's harmless."

I didn't like the sound of that. Emilie hadn't mentioned anything about being followed. I guaranteed we were going to talk about this later. "Can you remember anything else about Spot?"

"Dirty. Like he hasn't had a bath in forever. Like he lives in that shack or sleeps out in the open. He always wears the same filthy jeans, T-shirt, and sneakers." Emilie closed her eyes for a moment. "He's kinda got a beard, but it's not very thick. Not like yours, Mr. Ducks."

"He's not much more than fourteen or fifteen." Ducks stacked Alex's empty plate atop his. "I tried to talk to them once, but Goth Boy dragged Spot away."

"Stay away from them." I put on my sternest face. I fussed with empty bowls to keep my hands busy.

"Don't worry. I am," Emilie said.

"What do you remember about the truck?" Whip turned to Ducks.

"Faded yellow, maybe light brown at one time. Ninety-five or ninety-six Ford F-150. Dent in the passenger door. No license plate."

"Gotcha." Johnny smiled for the first time since he sat down.

"What about the fourth guy?" Whip pushed his plate aside.

"I've never seen him, either. Older, maybe mid or late twenties, black. Very muscular like he lived in a weight room."

"Did he have tattoos?" Alex's eyes widened.

"He did." Ducks tried to eat, but Alex kept interrupting him.

"I'll bet he was in jail." Alex's vivid imagination pushed reason aside.

"I don't know about that. The driver was mid-twenties, also black. He had a shaved head."

"Crap," Whip said.

Alex finished his corn. His eyes sparkled. "Maybe they broke out of jail."

I could no longer keep my mouth shut. "Just because a man has tattoos doesn't mean he's a convict."

"I know, but..."

"No buts. You watch football and basketball. You know most players are covered with ink." I couldn't let this teaching moment pass.

"It's just, like, it's much more fun if they're convicts." Alex thrust his jaw out.

I thought only the women in my family inherited the stubborn jaw. Not so. Convicts running around on the loose was fun? Probably was to an eleven-year-old. I shut up.

"Were you scared?" Alex's eyes all but bugged out of his face.

"I wasn't scared, but I was bloody well pissed. When they ran me off the road, they almost wrecked my bike." Ducks drew his eyebrows together in a single continuous red caterpillar. "It wouldn't be easy to replace out here."

"Hate to think what they'd have done if you'd been Mexican."

Why the hell did Whip have to say that? Nothing like overstimulating Alex's already vivid imagination. I tried to send a *shut up* message by glowering at Whip. A glower doesn't have any effect if the gloweree isn't looking. I wasted my time and a perfectly good silent warning.

"Are they the guys who've been spying on us in the afternoon, Mr. Ducks?"

"Who's spying on whom?" Johnny wiped his buttery hands on his napkin.

Alex reached for the last piece of corn but drew back his hand. "Does anyone else want this?"

No one claimed it. The boy was learning, even if some of the lessons took longer than others. Alex buttered the ear and crunched the juicy kernels.

"I've seen the boys before," Ducks said, "but not the men. The kids have followed Em, Alex, and me when we go out together."

"They hang out over in that shack. They watch us a lot during the day," Alex said over a bite of steak. He jerked his chin toward the east.

"So, Goth Boy and Spot were in the truck." Emilie stared at her plate before raising her eyes to meet mine. Not good, her look said.

"Spot's, like, really spooky. He pops up everywhere. He rides this rickety old bike, but mostly I see him hiding behind those trees." Alex pointed at the remaining live oaks half a mile away next to the tumbledown shack. "Goth Boy watches us too. They're both creepy."

"Spot follows me when I go running. But don't worry. He's harmless."

I didn't like the sound of that. Emilie hadn't mentioned anything about being followed. I guaranteed we were going to talk about this later. "Can you remember anything else about Spot?"

"Dirty. Like he hasn't had a bath in forever. Like he lives in that shack or sleeps out in the open. He always wears the same filthy jeans, T-shirt, and sneakers." Emilie closed her eyes for a moment. "He's kinda got a beard, but it's not very thick. Not like yours, Mr. Ducks."

"He's not much more than fourteen or fifteen." Ducks stacked Alex's empty plate atop his. "I tried to talk to them once, but Goth Boy dragged Spot away."

"Stay away from them." I put on my sternest face. I fussed with empty bowls to keep my hands busy.

"Don't worry. I am," Emilie said.

"What do you remember about the truck?" Whip turned to Ducks.

"Faded yellow, maybe light brown at one time. Ninety-five or ninety-six Ford F-150. Dent in the passenger door. No license plate."

"Sounds like the beater is the one that one of the missing men drove." The men warned Johnny to be on the lookout for this truck right after we got here. It belonged to a man that had disappeared a couple of days before our arrival. His body hadn't turned up.

Emilie and Alex cleared the table. Ducks half rose. I held up a finger and pointed to his chair. He blinked once before returning to his seat.

"Okay, what's going on?" I wasn't about to let the men weasel out of satisfying my curiosity.

"What do you mean?" Johnny's fake innocence earned a napkin draped over his head.

"Don't give me that crap. Two guys in the same pickup cruised past us several times at the beach. They've threatened Ducks. And you two." I pointed at Johnny and Whip. "You came back from work and were little pods of brooding isolation until Ducks told you about his strange encounter."

I walked around the table and sat next to Johnny. "Do you think the stolen truck is linked to the bodies you found?"

"Most likely."

"Is that why the men are all jumpy?"

Normal evening sounds included chatter and laughter from the workers' side of the compound during the dinner hour, followed by guitar music and singing later. This night all we heard were low murmurs. The camp was unnaturally quiet.

"Yes." Johnny opened his second Coors.

"And this is why I see shotguns in your trucks?"

Johnny and Whip glanced at each other. Both men walked to their trucks and returned with shotguns. Johnny's was an old wooden stock Mossberg; Whip's pump-action was newer.

"I loaded bird shot in one side and slugs in the other." Whip looked at Johnny. A nod from the older man was all the proof I needed that they felt threatened.

"Why bird shot and slugs?" Ducks asked.

"If bird shot doesn't stop someone, slugs will," Johnny explained.

"Permanently." Whip snapped his jaws shut.

"Any similarities among the missing men?"

"All vanished after payday. Could be someone is robbing them and driving them off." Johnny made sweat circles with his can on the tabletop. "Could be someone's killing them without bothering to drive them off."

"Were they all Hispanic?" Ducks fit more pieces of the puzzle together.

"All but the truck owner. He was Chippewa." Johnny continued playing with his beer can.

"But they all look Hispanic." Ducks picked at a speck of dirt on his jeans. "That's why they asked if I was Mexican."

Ducks wore a safety helmet when he rode. With his red hair covered and his head lowered, could he be mistaken for a Latino, even from a distance? No flipping way, not even if you shut one eye and stared directly into the sun with the other.

"Probably." Whip nodded.

"Do we have racists running around loose? Maybe trying to chase strangers away?" Ducks walked toward the bus. It was his turn to help with the dishes.

"Could be. We're strangers. The problem could be us versus them, not necessarily black versus white or Hispanic versus white," Johnny said. "This was pretty much a closed society before the storm. We've upset the balance of nature. Someone doesn't like it."

"Has anyone talked to the police?"

"About what?" Johnny's neck artery pulsed. "Some guys clearing out after getting paid? We have no proof anything's wrong."

"We have two dead bodies." I remembered that the sheriff said something about someone doing him a favor. Was he involved with the missing men? Was he killing them? Or encouraging the attacks? I shook myself to chase the bogeyman away.

"Don't you or the kids ride your bikes, run or skate alone." Whip rose. He headed toward the dorm. "I don't want anything happening to you."

Johnny put his arm around me. I got the message.

###

I shut the door to my bedroom before I dragged a locked box from under the bed. Inside was my new thirty-eight caliber revolver. I'd upgraded after I realized my trusty thirty-two-caliber snub-nose had all the stopping power of a fly swatter.

I had a concealed carry permit from Virginia but not from New York. No way could you get one if you lived in the five boroughs. I tucked the gun into my shoulder bag. I figured if anyone found it, I'd plead ignorance. Regardless, I'd be able to protect myself and the kids if need be.

CHAPTER TWENTY

Mississippi, week of October 3

I'D BEEN IN Mississippi long enough to be bored out of my flippin' skull. Cooking and cleaning and writing and reading weren't hacking it.

Just before dawn, I sat in the gathering place, sipped coffee, and listened to the stirrings of the still-sleeping camp. A sliver of light in the east obliterated stars for another day. They'd return, but as they winked out, I lost old friends.

Lights popped on in the boys' dorm and the bus. Ducks emerged in bike shorts and a tight shirt, hard-soled bike shoes clicking on the metal steps from the bus door. Bed-head hair disappeared under a helmet. He pushed his bike toward the gate. Without a word but with a flap of his hand, he pedaled off alone in spite of Whip's warning.

Whip emerged moments later, ready for work. Another door opened. Johnny walked by and didn't acknowledge me sitting in the dark.

I was homesick. I missed the Richmond suburbs. I missed the canyons of New York. I missed the noise of a city crowded with too many cars. I was like Goldie Hawn in *Private Benjamin*: I wanted to wear sandals. I wanted to do lunch.

I missed color. My Technicolor worldview wasn't compatible with a monochromatic landscape. I wanted one tiny flower, even a weed. Barren earth and piles of man-made rubble troubled my soul. I made a mental note to buy flowers every week for the dorm. Anything to hint of nature's rebirth.

I even missed Starbucks, or at least the concept of Starbucks, where people could laze away an afternoon, reading and chatting with friends.

Most of all, I missed people. Lots of people. Our small camp of workers was friendly in a distant sort of way. Though I knew each worker by name, we didn't socialize. Even on weekends, those who stayed in camp kept to themselves. I hadn't talked to a single person face-to-face, outside of my extended family, about anything important.

Early morning in the camp was never silent. People belched, sneezed, coughed, and farted. I heard it all. A mosquito buzzed past my ear and made the mistake of landing on my arm. Slap. Gotcha.

My first mosquito. Hope I didn't kill the last one on earth. No chance of that, but they should be everywhere. I was in the South, after all. It was autumn, but it was still warm and humid. I shouldn't complain, but it seemed darned odd not being serenaded by high-pitched whines day and night.

Now that I thought about it, I hadn't seen many insects of any kind. The first flies appeared at our dinner table as soon as we arrived. Ants carried provisions to their nests. They had to rebuild after the flood exactly like the people did. Now, a mosquito scouted for food. Squashed on my forearm, it wouldn't be reporting back to the swarm that dinner was served.

What else was missing?

Birds. On the way down, our RV startled flocks of seagulls, which squawked skyward. On any coast, gulls were ubiquitous. Wherever they could scavenge for garbage or dead animals or fish, there they were. Crows followed. Of course, there were the buzzards. After a disaster like a hurricane, scavengers ate well.

With no voles or mice in evidence, no cats prowled. In the alleys near my apartment and in Central Park across the street, I often caught glimpses of feral cats slinking about on the hunt. No stray dogs, either. The landscape had been scrubbed clean.

When I scouted the area during our first days here, I found a few structures had survived Katrina. A couple miles up the road was a battered brick church without its cross and steeple, which probably landed in Tennessee. A twisted message board said Catholic services were held monthly. A heavily-damaged building, scoured to bare metal on its southern side and wearing a bright blue FEMA tarp instead of most of its roof, stood alone at the edge of an empty field. Johnny had told me tents were popping up, and Habitat for Humanity was building homes.

That must be where Valerie and Hank and the rest of the Care-a-Vanners were. I needed to look them up. They were my kind of people.

CHAPTER TWENTY-ONE

Mississippi, week of October 3

JOHNNY WALKED BACK from the cook tent. When he spotted me in the gathering area, he stopped long enough to kiss my cheek.

"Whatcha going to do today, pretty lady?"

"It's time to pay a call on our landlord."

"Don't get into any mischief."

"Do I ever, funny man?"

"Not enough recently. See you at dinner."

Johnny got about halfway to his truck when he turned. "Those boys are still hanging around."

"I don't trust them."

"Me neither." Johnny walked off.

"I'll ask Em if she feels they should be watched."

"They should." The words drifted toward me on a gentle morning breeze.

After Ducks's encounter with the men in the stolen truck, I needed information. From my childhood experience the clergy was far more connected to local events than they acknowledged. At least my childhood priest was. Pastor Taylor, the Baptist minister and owner of the parking lot where we lived, might know something. I hoped so. I needed to feel less unsettled.

I pulled up beside the battered metal building about a mile farther inland from the Catholic church. What had once been a warehouse now served as church, youth center, and living quarters, according to Johnny.

"Wondered when you were goin' to stop by and say hello. After all, you're campin' in my parkin' lot, aren't you?" A disheveled man held out his hand. "Name's Hodge Taylor."

"Maxine Davies, but everyone calls me Max."

"Come on in, Miz Davies. I've watched you drive past several times." The pastor sounded like his ancestors had been in the South since before the War. "Glad you found time to be sociable."

"How...?" I stopped. "Of course. Strange woman in the area, Land Rover with New York plates. You're right. I should have come over earlier. I have no excuse except I've been busy being busy. I'm sorry."

"Well, you're here now. Rest yourself." Pastor Taylor waved me toward a metal folding chair. "I'm afraid this is all I have. Katrina stole most else."

"That's not a problem." I sat.

"Would you like some sweet tea? I just made a pitcher."

My expression gave me away. I'd tried sweet tea once and nearly spit it on the floor.

"Or water?" Did I see a twinkle in his eye?

"Water, please, if I won't be insulting."

"You won't. I find Northerners don't take kindly to our favorite beverage." He handed me a bottle of chilled water.

"I've tried it, but I don't like it." I opened the water and sipped.

"Always order *un*-sweet tea in a restaurant. When we have restaurants again, that is. You'll be safe."

While we settled into get-acquainted small talk, I took a good look at our landlord. Middle-aged, thinning hair, glasses, medium height, twinkling eyes, and sun burnt.

"I'm curious, Pastor Taylor, where are all the families? The kids?"

"Elsewhere."

"Elsewhere?"

"Look around, Miz Davies. Aren't too many places left to live in. Where have my families gone? Everywhere but here." The twinkle left his eyes. "For too many, their whole world is gone."

I could empathize with his pain. Had there ever been such a mass exodus of displaced people in the US before? It was our own Diaspora.

"Will they come back?"

"It's home, so, yes, most will. It's hard to imagine right now, what with no public services or housing." Pastor Taylor's face had the thousand-yard stare of someone on a first name basis with loss and grief. "I haven't found most of my families. Some drowned in the storm. Some fled to safer areas. Others went to live with relatives out of state. A few I have no idea about."

I could understand his sadness. After any disaster, natural or man-made, people scattered. Tracking them could be a full-time effort. Even then, many stayed scattered.

"This is poor country, Miz Davies. People didn't have much before. Now they have nothin'." Pastor Taylor looked around his metal building. "Most shopped at Goodwill until they earned a bit of change. Then they went to Kmart or Walmart."

"Would jobs bring families back?" Like Johnny and Whip, I wanted more local people rebuilding the roads. "Good paying jobs?"

"Sure would help."

"There's plenty of work in highway construction. My son-in-law will hire as many people, skilled and unskilled, as you can send his way." Hadn't he seen the "Help Wanted" signs on every remaining post and tree?

"Good to hear. Thought you might be importin' laborers."

"We are, but only because no local men or women turned out."

"I'll spread the word." Pastor Taylor walked to a long table and poured himself another glass of sweet tea. "You're sure you won't join me?"

I shook my head and raised a half-full bottle of water.

"It's such a Southern thing, like two first names, callin' everyone Miz or Mister, usin' a family name for a given name. Take mine. Hodge is my mother's family." Pastor Taylor chuckled and returned to his chair. "Now, what did you come for, Miz Davies?"

"I'm looking for information." I lifted the water bottle, and a drop of condensation fell on my knee.

"What kind of information?" Pastor Taylor didn't so much as squirm on his uncomfortably hard chair, while my backside cried out for a cushion.

"I'm a fish out of water here, but I get the feeling something's all wrong. It makes me worry about my grandchildren's safety."

"I've seen the girl out jogging."

"That's Emilie."

"She has pink hair." One eyebrow raised.

"Today. Who knows what color it'll be tomorrow."

"Then the holy terror on the bike is your grandson."

"Alex has more energy than his skin can contain. The bike should be a safe way to burn it off." I paused. "Now I'm not so sure."

"There's trouble about. That's for certain."

"A couple of boys have been following my granddaughter." A hint of worry grew into a frown.

"Tell me about them."

I did in as much detail as I could remember.

"I know them. Your Goth Boy is Danny Ray. His family's been here for generations. He's got a record for minor crimes, mostly stealin'. You know, nuisance stuff. He thinks he's a vampire."

"That explains the Goth look. Is he a member of your church?"

"Danny's not a member of anythin'. He quit school at fifteen and has been hangin' around the outskirts of civilization ever since." Pastor Taylor's face was set in rigid planes. "Damned fool kid."

"How about the other white boy? My granddaughter calls him Spot. He has bad acne."

"Odd you say 'white boy.'"

"Goth Boy and Spot are hanging around with two older black men. They harassed my homeschool teacher the day before yesterday. When he was out riding his bike early in the morning, they tried to run him off the road before asking if he was Mexican."

"Is he? Mexican?"

"Red-haired Englishman."

Pastor Taylor nodded. "I've seen him out and about. He rides very fast."

"He does. That's why I never ride with him."

"I've never known either boy to run with blacks. Mostly, blacks and whites keep to their own kind, but with all this disruption, maybe it's not strange they're runnin' together."

"Overt racism?"

"Not really, Miz Davies. It's just the way things have always been. Anyway, Spot's Jake Montgomery. Never been tested that I know, but I'd guess he has a mild form of autism, prob'ly Asperger's Syndrome. Always behind in school, slow to talk, not retarded, but his brain works different from ours. Not the same kind of outsider as Danny Ray."

Was this who'd been stalking Emilie? A kid looking for a friend? How did these two boys end up left behind when the storm hit? "Do you know anything about their families?"

"Jake was lost soon as he was born. No one knows who his daddy was, but his mama was the town drunk. Kept a still and sold white lightnin' for cigarette money." Pastor Taylor walked to the open doorway and leaned against the jamb. He looked off to the east.

"Did she mistreat the boy?"

"Not unless you call ignorin' him mistreatment. But no, I never knew her to hit him much, if that's where you're goin'."

"It was."

Pastor Taylor gave me a pretty clear picture of the dysfunctional nature of the Montgomery household. Even when he tried to help get Jake tested, his mother slammed the door in the pastor's face. "She didn't truck with any fancy stuff. Called me all sorts of names. Anyway, Jake's always been harmless."

"Let's hope he stays that way."

"You can say that again." Pastor Taylor uttered a near silent tsk tsk. "Danny Ray, on the other hand, well, he's got a mean streak in him a mile wide, but I haven't known him to hurt anyone. Intimidate, maybe, but not do any physical harm. Like I said, we're in new times. No tellin' what he could get into or who could influence him."

I didn't want either boy to turn to violence.

"These boys're feral, Miz Davies. No one cared for them before the storm. When the warnings sounded, Danny's mother lit out. Jake's mother ran with her two daughters. I don't know if she abandoned the kid, or if he wasn't home when she left."

Could such mothers exist? Oh, wait. My very own daughter found it inconvenient to be a mother. Merry told me right before she was murdered.

"I'd be beside myself if I couldn't find one of my grandchildren."

"Best to keep your granddaughter away from them."

"I'm trying to."

Pastor Taylor gave me something new to worry about. Life had taken yet another difficult turn. I picked up my overly large shoulder bag.

"One more thing, Pastor Taylor. Several of the laborers have gone missing."

Pastor Taylor frowned. "Missin'?"

I told him what little we knew about Johnny finding the bodies and some men not returning to work after a weekend. "We know one of the bodies was one of our workers."

"And the others?"

"One was a woman. Might have been a local. The other is unknown. White male, thirty something, very well groomed."

"I'll check with the sheriff about the woman. The man might have been one of the workers in a Gulfport or Biloxi casino."

I slung my bag over my shoulder.

"I'll ask around."

"Please be careful."

"I will. You too."

"Thank you for your hospitality." We exchanged cell numbers before shaking hands.

Why the hell couldn't I have a normal life without danger and drama? For a year maybe. Or a few months. Even a few weeks. Tomorrow.

That night, half a dozen men came to our side of the compound. They'd appointed Pete, the cook, as their spokesman.

"Abuelita, bad men are around. We've seen them." Pete twisted his ball cap between his hands. He spoke in Spanish. "We've talked together. We all have children at home. We'll watch over yours like they're our own. We'll help keep them safe."

I walked to Pete's posse, shook each man's hand and thanked them. I swallowed hard to clear the lump in my throat. The men nodded and returned to their side of the camp. I held Johnny's hand.

"Abuelita?"

"Little granny."

"I know what it means." I was puzzled by its usage.

"Granny is a term of respect not of age. They gave you their word of honor. Nothing will happen to Alex and Em if they can help it."

I put my head on Johnny's shoulder and wept.

CHAPTER TWENTY-TWO

Mississippi, week of October 10

ALMOST TWO WEEKS passed before we heard anything definitive from the sheriff about the dead people in the bayou. When he called, we learned the second man didn't survive. The coroner ruled the cause of death for all three was blunt force trauma to the skull. Big whoop! Johnny's original observations told us that. More outrageous, the coroner ruled the deaths accidental. Accidental, my ass. If they were, how did three bodies end up dumped in stinking mud in the same spot on top of each other?

Johnny, Whip, and I drove over to a makeshift office to make arrangements to send our worker's body home to his family.

"Someone's killing your illegals." The sheriff threw out an unsubstantiated claim.

"'Illegals?' I count one dead construction worker." Johnny's tone was even, but I heard the threat behind his innocuous words. "And a dead woman of who knows what race and a well-groomed white man."

"Don't give me any lip, asshole. All you greasers are illegal as far as I'm concerned. We didn't have no crime around here until your kind showed up." The sheriff's lip curled. "Take your bodies and git."

"Let's set the record straight, Sheriff. One is a worker. We'll take care of it."

"Take what you want. I'll dump the rest."

Dump? Wasn't that what had happened in the first place? Cold sweat slicked my breasts.

"I resent you calling these men working to rebuild *your* *fucking* highways illegals. Our workers are American citizens." Whip's red face attested to the difficulty he was having controlling his temper.

"You watch your mouth." The sheriff's face was mottled with rage. Three alpha males faced off and struggled for supremacy. One had an unconcealed gun on his hip. "I don't give a rat's ass if they've been here since before Columbus. They're greasers. We don't want 'em here."

"But..." Johnny strove for a cooler tone. He almost achieved it. "What are you going to do about our murdered friend?"

"Not a goddamned thing. Coroner says it was an accident. Don't see anyone getting murdered 'round here. Don't care if your kind gets killed."

"So, you aren't going to investigate the missing men, either?" Whip asked in order to have everything spelled out.

"Hell no. They're doing me a favor by getting the fuck out of my county. Git out of my office if you know what's good for you."

I climbed into the back seat of Whip's truck. I couldn't wait to get away from that awful Dodge Boy. I waited until we were miles down the road before throwing a pink and purple hissy fit. I think I scared the crap out of Whip when I drummed my feet on the truck's floorboard. Not the smartest thing to do when the driver's already wound tighter than a yoyo.

"How can that jerk say he doesn't care if you get killed? And no crime before Katrina? Get real."

"Sheriffs in these small towns are all alike, Max. They're elected. They strut and posture and bluster about solving crimes, but they do diddly-squat." Johnny turned to look at me. His cheeks were drawn, leaving a scar from a childhood knife fight more prominent than ever. "Hardy'll pretend to take a tough stand to keep his job when he comes up for re-election. Until then, he'll do as little as possible."

"Not all that much different from the dipshit district attorney in Richmond who tried to convict me of murder." Whip had gone through hell after he was wrongly charged with murdering his wife, my only daughter.

"But..."

"He looks at me and other Latinos and sees little people he can intimidate. Hell, he might encourage his guys to hassle anyone who's DWH." Johnny smiled at me, a smile that didn't reach his eyes.

"DWH?"

"Driving While Hispanic."

"But racial profiling's against the law." I was so angry I shook the car. Or, maybe it was the rough road. Either way, the car shook.

"Apparently not around here."

Johnny shifted to face forward. He stared out the window at the dead landscape rattling past us. Whip missed missing a pothole. My teeth chattered.

"You don't think he's behind the killing, do you?" I was shocked at how controlled these two stubborn men appeared.

"No, but I'd bet a hundred bucks he knows who is." Whip ground his teeth. "Someone other than Sheriff Hardy has to prove it."

"None of this makes any sense. We're here helping, and this small-town piss ant sheriff wants us driven off." My state of mind redefined puzzled. I was sorrowfully confused.

"If it doesn't make sense, then we don't have all the facts." Johnny sounded calmer than Whip, but the pulse in his jaw told a different story. "We need to get them."

"Oh no. No, no, no. We are so not going to solve another crime. Not this one." I was on the verge of a major tantrum. I stamped my foot again.

Whip held up his right hand. "Settle down. Could be that's how it's done here."

"How can you be so goddamned calm?" I wanted to rage at someone. Whip wasn't helping by being as stoic as a rock.

"I sure as hell am not going to turn away. If the sheriff won't help, we'll find someone who will." Johnny sat up straighter.

"Just not us. Okay? Okay?"

Neither man said "okay." I stared out the truck window. I

was as sick as the barren land.

I didn't want any of us working on another murder case. If we had to get involved, though, I had a small bit of evidence in my pocket. I'd recorded the entire conversation on my cell phone. I hoped my recording was clear. If we ever had a chance to challenge Sheriff 'I don't do racial profiling, but if I did, I start with you' Hardy, I had proof he discriminated against Latinos. Probably broke a federal law or twenty.

"First thing, gonna put all the crews on high alert," Whip said.

"Like Homeland Security? We went from yellow to orange?" I blinked hard to control my tears. My hopes for a normal life without drama blew right out the open truck window.

"Don't want it to go to red."

Whip and Johnny dropped me at the dorm before driving back to the gate to talk with our guard, Sampson. As I opened the door, I glanced over at Sampson, who pulled up his shirttail to expose a gun in his waistband. Well, well. We did have an armed guard. If the sheriff played ostrich about murder, it wouldn't surprise me if he encouraged local troublemakers to increase their intimidation. Troublemakers like the black men seen with Spot and Goth Boy.

I paced the empty dorm until I de-fumed enough to be civil. I went over to the bus to report in and found a note on the door: "Max, I'm at the beach with the kids. They needed to kick around a soccer ball."

Good thing they weren't here. I was so pissed off, I'd say too much. I picked up my shoulder bag and went calling.

"Come in and rest yourself, Miz Davies. You got a world of thunder on your face." As before, Pastor Taylor waved me to my favorite folding chair and brought a bottle of chilled water. It didn't take me long to begin my rant about justice and racism.

"Now hold up a minute. I missed somethin'." The pastor held up a hand. "I'm pretty sure I can't listen as fast as you talk. You take a deep breath and start from the top."

"I told you about the three bodies found out in that bayou."
The pastor nodded.

"One was from our crew. His head was bashed in." I took the advised breath. "Help me understand something, Pastor Taylor. Do all sheriffs around here behave like a Dodge Boy?"

"Dodge Boy?" The pastor scratched his head. "Big fat blowhard? Good one, Miz Davies. I see you've met our illustrious Sheriff Forrest Hardy."

"I have." I picked at the label on my water bottle with a thumbnail. "I wasn't impressed."

"Forrest's the only one who's impressed with himself. He's as mean as a snake and twice as wily. Be sure you give him a wide berth. He'll cause your workers no end of grief if anyone gets crosswise of him. You didn't..."

"Shoot my mouth off?"
The pastor grinned.

"Pastor Taylor, we barely know each other, and already you have me nailed."

"Well, you're a woman of strong opinions, Miz Davies. Such women can be hard for us Southern men to take."

"Sometimes just me being me pisses people off." I knew my weaknesses. I couldn't always control them. "Rest assured, I waited until we were way down the highway before I had a tantrum. Unless the sheriff bugged Whip's truck, he couldn't have overheard what I said. I'm not going to repeat it, because I wasn't polite."

I relaxed for the first time all day thanks to Pastor Taylor's unflappable demeanor.

"You know, you remind me much of my dear momma, rest her soul."

"Your mother?" I wasn't that much older than the pastor.

"She used to say 'To get ahead in life, a woman has to be two-thirds lady and one-third bitch.'"

I laughed harder than I had in days. "My second mother-in-law turned the phrase around. 'You have to be one-third lady and two-thirds bitch.' Either way, it fits."

When I regained my composure, Pastor Taylor stood. It was time to leave, but he surprised me. "Have you met Pastor Washington over at the AME tent yet?"

I shook my head. I'd stopped by several times, even left a note in an envelope with my personal card with my name and number on it, but I had yet to hear from him.

"It's past time you met. I'll warn you, though. Roland can be tetchy."

CHAPTER TWENTY-THREE

Mississippi, week of October 10

I PULLED THE Rover to a stop in front of a battered tent.

A pear-shaped black man with a shaved head raised a hand to his eyes. He squinted into the sun. "That you, Hodge? Whatchu doin' with dat woman?"

"Now don't be like that, Roland. I came to introduce Miz Davies."

"Not to be rude, Miz Davies, but why'd I want to know you?" Pastor Washington barked a deep, dry-rasp of a cough. He planted fists on wide hips and stood his ground.

"I told you he can be tetchy. Roland, meet Maxine Davies. Miz Davies, this is Pastor Washington."

We shook hands. I looked into untrusting dark eyes under thick brows.

"You left notes for me."

"I did."

Pastor Washington dug into the rear pocket of tired khakis and pulled out my card which was crumpled and dirty. "Why'd you think I'd want this?"

I'd blown it. Back in New York, I left cards with people I met. My ingrained habit didn't play well in Mississippi.

"I meant no harm, Pastor Washington. I left it in case you wanted to contact me."

"If I wanted to talk to you, I'd have driven over to Hodge's parkin' lot. Hard to miss where you're livin'." He stuffed the card back in his pocket.

"Point taken."

"Why don't you invite us in?" Pastor Taylor reminded the black clergyman I was a guest in his house of worship, even if I was unwelcome.

We followed the cough under the tent and onto a concrete slab where we sat on more folding chairs. Did all churches around here come with folding chairs? Was it a Kmart special?

"You sound bad, Roland."

"Gave up cigarettes ten years ago. I'm allergic to mold and dust. Nothin' much else here since the waters receded and the mud dried up. So, I cough."

Pastor Taylor summarized the threats against Ducks, the dead bodies and Sheriff Hardy in a couple of succinct sentences. Pastor Washington's face darkened further.

"Forrest Hardy's got less sense than pond scum. That man's a danger to hisself and everyone 'round him."

"I agree, Pastor Washington. I'm worried. Someone's stalking our crews, trying to drive off anyone they think is Mexican."

"Prob'ly." The black minister shrugged. "Prob'ly. Lots of folks don't cotton to outsiders comin' in and tellin' us what to do."

"I don't know about telling people what to do. We came down to help rebuild your roads." I kept my tone even.

"By yourselves, from the looks of it."

"If you mean because we're from elsewhere, that's right. No local men or women answered our calls for workers. We'll hire them on the spot if they'll raise a hand."

Pastor Washington said nothing. I was pretty certain he didn't believe me.

"I'm worried about the safety of my grandchildren. I need to know they aren't in danger. Can you help?"

"They look Mexican?"

"Well, not Em. She has pink hair today."

"Seen her out runnin'. Pretty little thing."

"Thank you. Alex, my grandson, is deeply tanned, but his hair's so sun bleached no one would mistake him for anything other than he is."

"What would that be?"

"A bloody pain in the ass, to quote his homeschool teacher. His sister calls him holy-crap boy-child."

For the first time since I stepped out of the Rover, Pastor Washington stopped frowning. White teeth flashed in a damp face.

"I got one like that. Sent him up north with his grandmama until we got some place to live. Call him 'Rascal.' He's eight."

"Captain Chaos is eleven, going on zero if he doesn't behave."

"Miz Davies, you have a way with words."

"Thank you." Not content with a small victory, I opened an imaginary can of worms, grabbed a fork, and ate. During my discourse about the missing workers and three dead people, I mentioned the two black men driving the stolen truck. Pastor Washington's smile vanished so quickly I was no longer sure I'd ever seen it.

"You sayin' black men's doin' the killin'?"

"That's not what I'm saying, Pastor, but one of our men was murdered. His head was bashed in. Two men and two teens are running around in another missing man's truck. The teens have been following my grandchildren. I'm afraid."

"The boys are our feral teens. Jake Montgomery and Danny Ray." Pastor Taylor stepped in.

"Damn. Not those two. I hoped the storm took 'em inland."

"If it did, they're back. One of the men they're with is covered with tattoos and heavily muscled. The other has a shaved head and earrings."

Pastor Washington's brows drew closer together. He nodded but remained silent. I wasn't going to get any support from this quarter. Jeez.

When I dropped Pastor Taylor off at his church, he said, "Roland's okay, but he's suspicious of white folks. Took me most of a year to get to a first-name basis."

"Does he dislike all white folks or Northern white folks in particular?"

"Yes."

"Both, huh?"

"He calls Yankees 'three one twos.'"

I thought for a second. "Chicago area code?"

"That's right."

CHAPTER TWENTY-FOUR

Mississippi, week of October 10

I DROVE ALONG an unrepaired secondary road, avoiding the worst potholes, finding the best packed dirt. I was no calmer after my visit with the two pastors than I'd been before. This broken land attracted broken people who preyed on weaker people. Well, they weren't going to prey on me or my family. No way, no how. I patted the new friend in my handbag. *Mess with me, you jerks, and you'll find out just how good a shot I am.*

Raney was right. Getting involved in something outside my insular family would be one way to shake off my funk. Sitting around talking with Johnny and Ducks and Whip was fine, but it wasn't enough. I didn't see a warm let's-have-a-cup-of-coffee relationship developing with either pastor. Habitat for Humanity might do the trick.

I had no trouble finding the site because the partially constructed houses were the only new structures in the area. Besides, signs were everywhere: parking, main construction tent, supply tent, mess hall. I pulled the Rover in beside a maroon-and-white RV and hopped out. A sheriff's cruiser slowed before moving along the broken road.

I filled my lungs. Wonderful. Raw lumber. No rot or decay. Nothing but the clean smell of pine. Electric saws whined;

workers pounded nails into boards.

I hadn't realized how late it was. I'd spent more time with the pastors than I planned. It must be close to quitting time. People were standing around chatting.

"Max?"

I hadn't expected to hear my name. I recognized Val, the woman we'd met in the Walmart parking lot. We both waved.

"I knew you'd find us." Val gave me the kind of impulsive hug strangers who were kindred spirits gave each other. "You had that look about you."

"What kind of look is that?" I warmed to this woman.

"Rich bitch who can't sit around doing nothing all day. Just like me. You're a born volunteer." Val put her arm around my waist to steer me into the complex.

"I was going to call you, but I figured I'd stop by."

"Hank's here somewhere." Val looked around and yoo-hooed at her husband. "I told you Max would show up."

"Welcome to Hope Village." Hank pulled off a dirty work glove and shook my hand, two old friends who had recently met. "Where's Johnny?"

"Working. He and my son-in-law are rebuilding route ninety."

"I have to run, Max," Val said. "I need to check on dinner."

"Before you leave, Val, you need to know something's happening to the road crews." I took all of a minute to paint the ugly picture of attacks and threats. "One of our guys was murdered, and several others are missing."

"Tell the leader. I'll spread the word among the Care-a-Vanners. We'll keep a sharp watch for these guys." Val gave me another hug.

"Lock your doors. Oh, and don't expect any help from the local sheriff. He doesn't like us, and all but told Johnny he'd be glad if we all went away or died." I hated sounding angry, but I was pissed as hell.

"You poor dear," was all Hank said.

Before I knew what was happening, Hank led me to the main construction tent. He was less forceful than Val but every bit as effective. He had a live one and wanted to introduce me to the Habitat leader.

I spent half an hour with the leader, Gayle Hollins, telling her about myself and the children. Alex was far too young, but she needed painters for the finished houses badly enough to bend the rules for Emilie. I agreed we'd show up on the coming Saturday. We exchanged cell numbers.

When a truck honked its horn, the village buzzed with renewed energy. Voices shouted. People cheered and clapped.

"Thank God, they're here." Gayle ran out of the construction tent before I could figure out what was happening. A heavy-duty pickup towing a large shiny trailer pulled up beside several RVs. Painted on the side of the trailer was God's Pit Crew. Three more trucks followed.

"These guys are from a church in southwestern Virginia. They came down a couple of weeks ago, right after we did." Hank had been lingering outside the construction tent to see how I made out with Gayle. "They have a complete workshop in the trailer. I can't tell you how grateful we are for their skilled hands. Come on over. If it's the same guys, you've got to meet them."

Hank introduced me to eight men in about as many seconds. I forgot every name except for the driver, "Ronny Howard, like the actor." He looked nothing like the kid who played Opie in the old *Andy Griffith* Show. What stuck in my brain was his accent. It was so unintelligible I'd rather have my ears removed with a cheese grater than listen to him for long.

"I have to get back to our compound. See you Saturday."

Hank slapped me on the back. I was one of the guys.

Okay, one down. Emilie was taken care of. What did I do with Alex? Should I ask him? Yes.

When I pulled into our compound and parked the Rover, a boy slipped behind a pile of debris outside the perimeter. Spot, the left-behind who never had a chance.

After signing up at Habitat and having warned them to be careful, after learning we had an armed guard at the gate, I should feel better. I didn't. I'd plain old run out of interest in the day.

One worker came back from working on a side road. He'd been pelted with rocks and bottles by two guys in a ratty truck. He had a deep cut on his forehead. I sat him down at the picnic table and fetched our replenished first aid kit. I cleaned the wound and put a butterfly bandage over the cut. It wasn't deep enough to require stitches, but he had to keep it clean. I handed him a tube of antiseptic salve.

"They got me with a beer bottle, Abuelita." He held up a paper bag. "I didn't touch it. I don't know if it'll ever be useful, though."

I sent him off. I waited outside the dorm absentmindedly counting the returning men.

"Only the guy with the cut was hurt." Ducks crept up behind me. I tried to jump out of my sneakers. "The others are safe."

"How do you know? Did Em tell you?" I crammed my heart back in my chest.

Ducks shook his head. As I entered the dorm, I felt a feather brush my cheek.

You're one too, huh? I didn't speak aloud. I didn't have to. Warmth from Emilie and an attack by the mysterious feather confirmed my suspicion: I had two different kinds of spooks watching out for me.

CHAPTER TWENTY-FIVE

Mississippi, week of October 17

EVEN THOUGH I didn't feel personally threatened, I needed Raney to give me a second opinion on whether I should keep the kids in Mississippi. Would being in a dangerous environment be detrimental to their healing so soon after their mother's murder?

"You should stay unless you and the kids are in physical danger," Raney said.

"We aren't yet, but I never anticipated how hard it would be living without civilization."

"This is more of your doo-wop. What a great object lesson for Alex and Em."

I needed to keep reminding myself I had a do-over, Eleanor's doo-wop, on raising kids, but this parenting gig caused me to over-examine my actions. I was no longer the spontaneous woman I was before Merry's accident.

"I've never known you to be a quitter." Raney threw down a challenge.

I was no quitter. Not when each of my husbands died. Not when Merry was injured. Not when she was murdered. Not now.

"Look, you woke up this morning, didn't you?"

That was obvious. "Yes."

"That gives you another chance to change something."

She was right. I'd taken a few small steps forward on a path into uncharted territory. Time to take a whole heck of a lot more.

I'd warned the two Baptist preachers, but I had one last church to visit. I stopped at St. Anna's before setting off for my weekly excursion to town. A recovering Catholic, I grew up in a solid fieldstone church. I'd visited cathedrals in Europe and loved the empty spaces filled with God light pouring through stained glass windows. St. Anna's was a humble, single-story brick building, damaged but not destroyed. It was locked.

A rectory or manse stood beside the church, half hidden from the road. I knocked. After a full minute, a pale but pretty child of around ten opened the door. Her dark eyes grew round when she saw me.

"Mama." She half shut the door.

A youngish woman appeared and sent the child inside. In heavily accented English, she told me to go away.

"I'm looking for Father Alvarado. Is he here?" I switched to Spanish.

The woman shook her head. "Not for a few weeks. Come back."

With that, she turned and shut the door. The deadbolt clicked.

Well, then. So much for being friendly.

When I was little, Catholic churches were unlocked and a spiritual leader or servant of God was always available. This woman exuded no warm-and-fuzzies. I was pretty sure she wasn't the traditional servant of God. Still, I'd found a child.

Where there was one, could there be more?

Try as I might, I couldn't stop thinking about the little girl at St. Anna's. I used the windshield time driving to civilization and back to create any number of scenarios about her and her mother. I had no idea how old she was; I guessed she was closer to Alex's age than Emilie's. She didn't act very socialized. Maybe she and her mother had recently arrived in the country. Maybe they didn't speak much English. Maybe the child was shy. No, it was more than shyness. Something deeper.

I took Emilie over after classes a few days later to get her read. We made some cookies, well, cookies from a mix, as an excuse to go calling. I rang the doorbell and waited.

"Why are you interested in this girl?" Emilie looked around the porch for signs of life. Nothing. No plants or chairs. No wreath on the door. No welcoming signs of habitation. The storm could have blown it all away, but I didn't think so. Nothing personal had ever graced this porch.

"I don't know. Partly because she's the only child I've seen." I rang the bell again. "It's something else. I want to know what you feel."

I was about to give up when the woman unlocked and opened the door. I introduced myself and Emilie and told her we were her new neighbors living in the Baptist church parking lot down the road. I made myself so nicely neighborly and pushy she had little choice. She edged aside to let us in.

The woman led us into a cool, dark living room and went to fetch a pitcher of iced tea. The drapes were tightly drawn, without even a sliver of light coming through. The room was as dark as dusk, even though it was mid afternoon on a bright sunny day. Emilie and I accepted glasses of what I hoped wouldn't be sweet tea. I steeled myself to be polite and took a sip. Hark! Regular tea with a sprig of mint and a slice of lemon. She still hadn't told us her name.

"Thank you for letting us stop by. My name is Maxine Davies, and this is my granddaughter Emilie."

"I'm Isabella Sanchez de Jesus." Mrs. Sanchez stumbled with English. "I, um, hope the tea is all right."

"It's delicious, Mrs. Sanchez." Emilie responded in Spanish.

The woman relaxed a little when she realized Emilie spoke her language, though she remained on guard.

I asked where her daughter was, saying I wanted our two girls to meet. "Are there no other children here?"

A flicker of wariness appeared before the woman stood and walked to the hallway. "Marianna, please come here."

A few minutes later, Marianna stood in the doorway. She wore a shabby yet clean, pressed dress. Who put dresses on young girls today, anyway? The child could have been from an earlier time, mid-fifties or earlier. She smiled and looked at Emilie.

Her expression was far older than her years. Had she seen more of the world than a girl her age should have? Was she an old soul in a too-young body? Emilie had a similar look about her, but my granddaughter's was the result of her mother's murder and her special gift. That didn't seem to be the case with Marianna.

Emilie smiled, introduced herself and held out the plate of cookies. Marianna entered the room and perched on the edge of a chair. She looked at her mother for approval before she reached for a cookie. We didn't stay long. I'd accomplished my goals—learning their names and exposing them to Emilie.

#

We hadn't been back long before I trotted over to the bus. I planned to run my impressions past Ducks when he gave a cry of anguish. The door was open. I ran in.

"Ducks? Are you all right?" I headed toward the back of the bus.

Ducks emerged from the bathroom. I stared at him before bursting into laughter. He had one, not two, bushy red eyebrows. I peeked around him. Sure enough, the other one lay like a dead caterpillar in the basin.

"I forgot to change the shoe on my razor." He held up an electric shaver. "Now I'm lopsided."

"Give it to me."

He handed it over, sat on the commode and let me even out his other eyebrow, whimpering all the time. "Thank goodness you didn't shave it completely off. You'll be lean for a while, but your brows will grow back."

"Do you think Alex will notice? He'll ride me unmercifully."

"Is water wet?"

That night the nuclear family ate under the cloth gazebo, all except Ducks, who fled to New Orleans in an effort to forestall Alex's teasing. Netting and citronella candles kept the recently-arrived ravenous mosquitoes at bay. Barely. I swatted at flying things, real and imagined.

Alex was overflowing with energy as always on a Friday night. With no school the next day, he wheedled his father into taking him to the beach Saturday.

"We're going to swim and throw Frisbees. I'm going to ride my new boogie board."

"We're going to paint." Emilie was as excited as Alex about Saturday's activities. "We get to help people get new homes."

"I'd rather play." Alex, ever stubborn, wasn't about to admit he wanted to work with us.

Emilie chattered about our visit to Mrs. Sanchez and her shy daughter, but she seemed to be holding something back. From experience, I knew she'd talk about it when it was time. She was my granddaughter; no one could pry something out of me until I was damned good and ready. I sat lost in thought. For a moment, it felt like unfamiliar territory. Johnny brought me back to reality with a question.

"What was their last name?" Johnny shook hot sauce into his jambalaya and stabbed a chunk of andouille sausage.

"Sanchez de Jesus. Odd combination," Emilie said.

"Sometimes Brazilians born out of wedlock are given the mother's family name followed by 'de Jesus,' kind of like 'child of Jesus.'" Whip said. "Do other Latin cultures do the same?"

"Not a Mexican and Mexican-American habit. Could be Central and South American." Johnny forked a piece of chicken into his mouth. He stirred his jambalaya and moved some objects to one side.

"So, Mrs. Sanchez was illegitimate?" Emilie seized on one possible reason for the family name.

"Not necessarily. The name could have been handed down in the family for several generations. Don't assume either she or her daughter is illegitimate," Johnny said.

I leaned closer and looked at the pile of objects on the side of Johnny's dish.

"What?" He'd been caught doing something he wasn't supposed to.

"You don't like carrots?" I pointed a finger at his dish.

"I'm a grown-up. I don't have to eat carrots if I don't want to." He stuck his chin out to tease me.

"You'd better eat them if you know what's good for you." Alex laughed. "She'll make you sit there until you do."

"Wanna bet?" Johnny threw down a challenge.

"Yup." Alex tucked a slice of carrot into his mouth and chewed.

I frowned and pointed. Johnny poked an orange-colored sliver and carried it to his mouth, held his nose and chewed.

Emilie came in to kiss me good night and snuggled down beside me before climbing into her bunk.

"Marianna's bright orange inside." Her gift of seeing people's internal colors helped her analyze their state of mind. "She's darker around the edges, though."

Her mother's colors changed from bright to dark after she fell under her killer's control.

"Mrs. Sanchez is dark yellow. That's not good."

"Do you know what it means?" I hugged my granddaughter.

"Not yet. I may have to ask Dr. Schwartz or Mr. Ducks." She kissed my cheek before scrambling into her bunk. "Don't worry. You're still pinky orange. You'll figure out what's going on."

I will? The familiar warmth embraced me. Emilie pulled her curtains closed. I will.

I prepared my clothing for the next day's work. When I picked up a jacket I'd worn on the trip down, I stared at the card Val and Hank gave me at Walmart. I went straight to my laptop and opened Google. Hmm, way more to them than I thought when we met.

Emilie and I rose early Saturday, grabbed a quick breakfast and headed to Hope Village. Emilie was too excited to sit still; I was curious to see how much progress the Care-A-Vanners and God's Pit Crew had made. Where two houses stood less than a week ago, two more were ready for painting. Three were well along and would need painting by the following weekend.

"Watch the Pit Crew." Gayle met us when we got out of the Rover. "I've been doing this a long time, but I've never seen a bunch of guys work as quickly or as hard as they do. They want to finish eight houses before they go home in a few days."

"From the looks of this place, they'll make it."

I led Emilie to the main tent and got her registered. Gayle pointed us toward the supply tent, where we picked up brushes, rollers, trays, and gallons of paint. One of the Care-A-Vanners walked us to the next house ready for painting, showed us where to begin and how to do the work.

Halfway through the morning, Val poked her head in the room.

"Why don't you and Johnny come over next Saturday? We have potluck suppers. You could get to know everyone."

"Sounds great."

After my snooping on Google, I wanted to get to know the Scotts a whole lot better. Johnny and I would have a real date with adults outside our family.

"You're lucky. Someone's already done the ceilings." Val glanced upward. "You don't have to worry about splatters either. Last thing we do is lay the carpet."

With that, Emilie and I went back to work. We worked in companionable silence until we finished the first bedroom. We broke for water and an apple for energy.

"Something's wrong with the Sanchezes." Emilie played with her water bottle. "I don't feel good about them. They were so uncomfortable around us. Almost like they were afraid to talk to us."

"I agree. That house is full of secrets." I polished off my apple and wished for a second one.

"Mrs. Sanchez doesn't want anyone getting too close to Marianna. She's, like, totally protective." Emilie drained her bottle. We walked to the food tent and brought back two more and a couple of apples in our pockets. "Even more protective than you are."

I swatted her butt with a paint rag.

"Did you notice how scared Marianna was? She wouldn't say anything without her mother's approval." I gulped ice water.

"Like I said, their colors are all wrong. I need to get to know her. I wonder if they'd come to the beach with us." Emilie stretched and headed toward the second bedroom.

"It's worth a try." My radar was going off big time. I'd seen that look of wariness before.

With an hour free before I had to finish dinner, I plopped in a chair outside with my journal and an "un" sweet tea. Whip and Alex hadn't returned from the beach. I documented my concerns for the Sanchez family, all the while trying not to remember where I'd seen her haunted look. I'd finished my daily entry when Ducks emerged from the bus. He ambled over, snagged a chair with a foot and pulled it close.

"Mind if I join you?" He pulled his pipe from a pocket. "If I'm not interrupting."

"Not at all." I closed the journal before setting it on the table. "Hey, aren't you supposed to be hiding out from Alex in New Orleans?"

"I didn't go after all. I couldn't stop thinking about the Sanchez family. I rode over to the church and stopped. No one answered when I knocked. You and Em are right to worry about that child." Ducks opened his tobacco pouch and filled his pipe. "Something's off."

"And you know this because Em told you? Or is it something you feel?"

I hoped I didn't get the single warning blink. Instead, Ducks relaxed and leaned toward me, elbows on knees.

"As you've guessed, I have some of the gift too. Mine's different from Em's. It's also not as well developed."

Oh great. I had two spooks around. "Better developed than mine, I bet."

"Because I no longer fight it like you do."

I was used to Emilie's weirdness. She no longer freaked me out. Ducks, too, was part of a select group. "Is this what Em meant at the end of your interview?"

Ducks's eyes hooded and a single blink followed. "We all have our secrets, Max. The one I'm ready to share is my gift."

"Okay." I was positive he still hid a lot from me.

"I see things, not as images, but as very strong emotions."

"Em internalizes what she feels. It's as if she's experiencing what someone else feels."

"I told you right after I met her she was an empath. That's what they do—feel what others are feeling."

"She sees internal colors too." I glanced at my journal. I needed to think about how Emilie analyzed situations. Something profound lay under the surface, but I didn't know what it was.

Ducks waved a match over the pipe's bowl. He puffed until the tobacco caught the flame. He blew a thin stream of vanilla-

and-brandy-scented smoke skyward. "I'm different, but if someone close to me is upset or happy, I know before anyone says anything."

"I'm glad you understand her."

"That's why I said I could help her, along with Angela Schwartz, of course. I've been studying the subject since I was in my mid-thirties."

"What happened to spark your interest? Did you suddenly discover your gift?"

Ducks blinked again. "Something like that. I accepted a truth about myself."

I hoped for a concrete example, but Ducks wasn't forthcoming. Questions elbowed each other behind my tightly closed lips. One look at the teacher's face was enough to shut me up. Not the time or place for prying. I tried a different approach.

"Are you the feather?"

Ducks blinked one more time. I knew better than to probe further. I tried to quiet my thoughts. I'd return to what he said, and didn't say, when I was alone. If I were ever truly alone again. I felt a wash of warmth.

CHAPTER TWENTY-SIX

Mississippi, week of October 17

EMILIE HELPED WITH dinner. She chattered about how she liked painting the new house, how nice it was to work with the single mother who'd be living there, how tired she was, and how this was going to be an early evening. "My arms ache from the roller."

"Mine too." I stirred the beef stew I'd put in the slow cooker before we left for Hope Village. "I hope your dad and Alex get home soon."

"They can always eat leftovers."

Alex and Whip raised a commotion by returning from a day at the beach. Alex shouted to Johnny and a couple of men who were playing catch outside the chain-link fence.

"We had so much fun, Uncle Johnny. We met a man whose house disappeared. It was, like, so cool."

"Cool? Losing your house is cool?" Emilie rolled her eyes at her brother's insensitivity.

I let her get away with it because I agreed. One of these days, maybe, just maybe, Alex would think before putting his mouth in gear.

"Okay, guys. Dinner in ten."

"Set a place for Ducks. He didn't go to New Orleans after all."
I called to Emilie, who went to fetch large soup bowls from the
boys' dorm.

"I know."

I slipped into the bus to hand Ducks a paper sack. He peeked
inside. "Do you have one?"

"You bet. I'll text you when I'm ready."

Emilie and I carried food to the table. I was last out of the
dorm because I needed to freshen my look. I texted Ducks to
arrive at the same time I did. We both wore Groucho Marx
glasses, complete with bushy black eyebrows and mustaches.
Alex's attention was all on the glasses and not at all on Ducks's
new semi-bald look.

"Why the Groucho glasses?" Johnny laughed.

"Why not?"

Before Alex could dominate the conversation, Johnny
wanted to know if Whip had had any luck finding more crews
and supervisors. With more men going missing every payday,
we needed to backfill and add another supervisor or two just to
keep even with the leakage.

"Called Tops. He can't spare anyone. All our guys are booked.
He'll call around, though, and see what he can scare up." Whip
ladled stew into his bowl. "Don't get your hopes up."

"I had no idea how hard it would be to keep people working."
Ducks pushed the Groucho mustache aside. "Of course, it doesn't
help with our menacing quartet prowling the roadways."

"I put both pastors on alert this week. They'll spread the
word, as will the Care-A-Vanners." I didn't mention a sheriff's
car tailing me.

"Did you find anyone?" Johnny knew how shorthanded we
were. "We gotta have more people."

"Don't know. I left a lot of messages and talked to about a
dozen supervisors. One will be down next week with as many
men as he can bring." Whip ate a few bites of his dinner. "Hell,
I got desperate enough to call Charlie to see if her company had
anyone."

"Wow! Is Charlie coming?" Alex turned up the volume.

I couldn't pounce on him about using his outside voice. He
was outside, after all.

"I'm sitting right here, Alex." Whip reminded his son. "I'm not deaf yet."

"And?" Johnny sopped up gravy with a second biscuit. "Can she send anyone?"

"Her company's headquartered in Texas. Most of her crews are rebuilding in Texas after Hurricane Rita hit less than a month after Katrina. It's the pits when two hurricanes hit so close together in both time and space. I left about a dozen other messages. If we don't find more people, the job will take longer."

The family fell silent. The only sound around the table was chewing.

"Tops will be pleased." Johnny was the first to take up the conversation thread.

"With either solution. Both additional crews and longer time earn us more money," Whip said.

"It's a start. We still haven't attracted enough locals to make a difference." Johnny dug into the stew. "Yummy, Max."

Even though I'd spoken to both pastors, none of the residents who had returned had applied for jobs. Only at Hope Village had people turned out. Part of that was Habitat's rule: You had to invest sweat equity in a house to own it after completion. Roads didn't require the same kind of participation.

"What if we ask the families who'll get houses to call their fathers and brothers?" Emilie's idea was sound.

"Great idea. We'll do that." I patted her shoulder.

Alex was too excited to sit quietly any longer. "Mad Max, we met a guy whose house washed away. There's nothing left but some supports poking out of the sand."

"Supports? What kind of supports?"

Whip described a beachfront community of stilts where houses once stood. Most of the houses had towered fifteen or twenty feet above the sand. They'd had open spaces between steel supports for parked cars and storage.

"Water was supposed to flow under the houses and not damage them."

"That worked well, didn't it?" Ducks told us he'd ridden his bike to the end of the strip several times.

"They build them like that in the Outer Banks too. I remember seeing them when you took us on vacation last year." Emilie dug into an enormous bowl of stew. We went a few weeks before her mother was murdered. "It didn't work there either."

"It all depends on the tidal surge. No one engineered buildings to withstand what roared ashore with Katrina."

"Dad parked under this guy's living room. He thought we were his neighbors." Following Johnny's lead, Alex dunked a biscuit in his gravy until it dripped from his fingers. "He was taking pictures for his insurance company. Not much to photograph, though. A bunch of steel supports. Not even any junk."

"It's like a ghetto. Instead of gangs taking over a neighborhood, the sea is hell-bent on reclaiming the land." Whip joined Alex and Johnny in biscuit dunking.

"After the man left, I swam and played with my Boogie board. Dad ran along the waterline."

Emilie told the men about her day. She yawned. "I'm so tired."

"The convicts in the truck followed us. Goth Boy was in the back, but Spot wasn't." Alex refused to believe the black men weren't convicts. He needed the thrill of danger, real or imagined.

"I know. We see them every time we go out. They must cruise the roads and shoreline trying to intimidate the workers." I finished my dinner and pushed my bowl aside.

"And us," Emilie said.

"They still tail me when I'm out on my bike." Ducks filled in another bit of the puzzle.

I looked west where Ducks had had his initial encounter and where birds circled. The vultures were back. More of them than before. Lots more. Two columns, offset by a quarter of a mile, rose in shattered blackness.

That now-familiar brush of something stroked my cheek. I looked up. Ducks blinked once to let me know he was sensing trouble. More bodies.

CHAPTER TWENTY-SEVEN

Mississippi, week of October 17

MY CELL PHONE rang about nine. I'd rousted Alex out of bed to start his classes. Emilie was in the school bus having a lesson on economics with Ducks. All the men were at work. I checked caller ID. Johnny.

"Hello, funny man. Slacking off?" I poured a cup of coffee and was ready for a chat.

"No, pretty lady. I need something from my trailer."

"Sure."

I pulled a light jacket from a peg by the door and trotted over to Johnny's trailer. None of us locked our doors because there was always someone in the compound keeping an eye out for strangers. Besides, Sampson was on guard duty. With his concealed handgun.

"I'm in. What am I looking for?" I stepped over piles of dirty, smelly clothes Johnny and the worker who slept in the trailer had tossed on the floor.

"I left a card from the Highway Patrol on the counter. I need the name and phone number."

"I didn't know you met anyone other than our Dodge Boy." I found the card and read off the information.

"This corporal from over near Gulfport dropped by a week

or so ago. Getting acquainted, he said. He was sniffing around to see if we'd had any trouble." Johnny covered the phone and spoke to someone nearby. He was back in a second. "We told him about the missing workers and Sheriff Hardy's lack of interest in doing anything to discover who killed our worker."

"Where are you? You're not at the worksite." My senses went on high alert. I knew, just knew, Johnny was on the hunt of our missing persons' mystery. I wrote "clean me" in the dust on the tabletop before returning to the dorm.

"I'm out by the bayou with Ducks."

"With Ducks? I thought he was teaching in the bus."

"We drove over this morning because the buzzards were thicker than ever."

"And?" I puttered around the kitchen, putting away breakfast dishes and wiping the never-ending film of grit from kitchen surfaces.

"And I need someone other than Sheriff Hardy. We'll tell you all about it when we get back." Johnny disconnected.

I wanted answers, now. I stamped my foot.

I stopped by the school bus where Emilie was reading a text on economics in French. Alex walked in to find no teacher. He tried to wiggle out of work until he found a note from Ducks with his study assignment.

"Math. Yuck. I hate math." Alex sulked.

"Without math, you wouldn't have the Internet or any of your games." School teacher mode kicked in. "Sit."

"They're both all right," Emilie said, "but they found more trouble."

Just what we didn't need. More trouble.

"Did they find bodies? I want to go see." Alex bolted out the bus door before I could grab him. "Come on."

Emilie and I shot glances at each other. Had the situation not been so serious, we probably would have laughed. As it was, we watched Alex race toward the girls' dorm where the keys to the Rover hung on a hook. I called him back to his math assignment.

I wanted to hop in the Rover and drive to the bayou, but I didn't. I had nothing to offer but ghoulish curiosity. I carried a cup of coffee to the gate and had a quiet word with Sampson about watching out for strangers outside the perimeter. I gave him a good description of the men in the stolen truck.

"Yes, Abeulita. I know what they look like. They drive by but never stop. Like they're watching us as much as we're watching them. Oh, and a policeman cruises by several times a week too."

A cop, huh? Was it the same cop who followed me from the AME tent to Hope Village? Could Sheriff Hardy be taking the threats seriously? Or could he be releasing his deputies to intimidate us?

"He has a rifle and a baseball bat with him."

A bat? That didn't sound like protection.

"How do you know?"

"I could see them through the rear window. He wants us to know he's armed."

Could it be the same weapon used to bash in the dead men's skulls? "Do Mr. Pugh and Mr. Medina think the men should leave in pairs? Alex and Em aren't allowed to go anywhere alone."

"They haven't said anything about that. I'll ask Mr. Medina when he gets back." Sampson waved a worker through and relocked the gate. "Mr. Ducks says it's all right for him to ride alone."

I didn't like that, but no one could keep up with Ducks. When he was in his zone, the man was a veritable biking machine.

By mid-afternoon, each of the kids had talked with their teacher at least twice, and I'd had three more calls from Johnny.

Boots scraped on metal steps. Johnny and Ducks dragged in and threw themselves into chairs. I pulled beers from the fridge without asking. Johnny drank most of his before taking a breath. Ducks poured his into a tall glass, the sides of which barely got wet before the beer was gone. I fetched two more.

"Five more bodies." Johnny rubbed worried eyes. "Two in the same place as the first group."

"Three a quarter of a mile away." Ducks took a measured swallow.

"All highway workers?" I was sick in the pit of my stomach. The situation had spiraled out of control.

"One wasn't." Ducks was pale under his sunburned cheeks. He blinked once.

Four were laborers. Johnny knew three from other crews. "The last, or should I say first, was a man named Angel. I met him when I came down alone. All of us thought he'd gone home to be with his wife, because she's expecting their first child."

"Why do you say first body?"

"His body was the oldest. Birds had been at it more than the others." Johnny went to the bathroom. If it had been me, I'd be puking my guts out. Instead, he pissed and flushed. A minute later, he returned, hair and face damp from a quick wash.

Ducks hadn't moved, except to raise his glass to drink.

"What about the last body?" I didn't want to know, but the men needed to talk.

"Gay," Ducks said. "Very well groomed even in the chaos we're living in."

"That would fit. If the predators don't like greasers, they don't like queers, either." Johnny held up a hand to stop my spluttering. "Sheriff Hardy's word choice, not mine."

Bigot. Maybe Johnny was right. The sheriff hated everyone not from these parts or who looked different.

Johnny drank a long swallow of beer. Ducks looked out the front window, his jaw clenching and unclenching. One hand tugged at his beard.

"Don't tell me he was there." I paced the small open space. "Sheriff Hardy, I mean."

"Oh, he sure was. Showed us how he viewed undesirables polluting his county with dead bodies."

"Pastor Taylor called him as mean as a snake and twice as wily. Pastor Washington doesn't trust him. Neither do I."

"I called the Highway Patrol guy on his cell. He and three other men got to the dump site first. Hardy showed up late to the party. He must have been listening to the police radio, because he roared up, lights flashing and siren screaming. The Highway Patrol didn't come out with sirens." Johnny rubbed the cold can across his brow. "When I called them, I told them I found dead bodies, not injured people."

"Hardy got right in the Highway Patrol corporal's face, screaming at him for trying to take his case." Ducks smiled for the first time. "He really threw his stomach around."

"Let me guess, the corporal wasn't intimidated." The image

of the corpulent red-faced sheriff made me smile in spite of the seriousness of the situation.

"Not in the least." Ducks slid down on his spine, stretched long legs across our compact living area and rested his head on the chair back.

"After about ten minutes of posturing and making unveiled threats, Hardy lumbered to his patrol car. His belt had so many tools on it he nearly lost his pants when he climbed in the driver's seat." Johnny almost, but not quite, smiled. "Roared away with sirens screaming."

"Ass," was Ducks's final analysis.

Johnny told the corporal about our first conversation with Hardy at the station. The corporal assured him Highway Patrol wouldn't ignore what was going on. "They don't give a crap about jurisdiction."

"Don't forget, I have Hardy's threats on my cell." I'd listened to the recording. Scratchy but distinct enough to hold up in court, if necessary.

"Well, that will help. At least the state authorities know."

My neck and shoulder muscles knotted up. I had no intention of sitting down until I was sure neither of these two men had done anything stupid. I so did not need these complications.

"You didn't wade into the muck again, did you?" I planted fists on hips. I dared Johnny to tell me he did.

"Didn't have to. Angel was on the bank. The others were scattered close to the bank as well." Johnny came over and hugged me. I wasn't having any of it.

"At least we're no longer alone. The corporal promised to come to a meeting the general contractor called. We need him on our side since it's clear Hardy won't do squat." Ducks stood.

"What I don't get is why these guys were dumped close to the construction site."

"Intimidation." Johnny released me when I refused to relax into his hug. "Dump them where we'd find them. Maybe it would scare us off."

"I wouldn't have disposed of the bodies like that. I'd have taken them into New Orleans." Ducks moved toward the door.

"Funny, that's what Sheriff Hardy said when we found the first ones."

CHAPTER TWENTY-EIGHT

Mississippi, week of October 17

I DECIDED TO spend more time at Hope Village than just Saturdays with Emilie. With way too much idle time on my hands, I built a schedule of two midweek paint days, one shopping day and two days trying to find ways to help the pastors. They'd call it meddling into their secrets, if they knew.

Ducks dropped by the manse more than once when he was out riding. Finally, Mrs. Sanchez opened the door.

"I asked when the next mass would be and if it would be in Spanish. She all but slammed the door in my face."

"Weird behavior. I wonder what's behind it." I had yet to unravel the Sanchezes' secrets. Their borderline hostility was downright eerie.

When I showed up the first midweek painting day, I was in the same house with Val, who was rolling a ceiling and dripping paint from her elbow.

"I'm such a klutz. I can't paint overhead without splattering every inch of me."

Valerie added paint to her roller, shook off the extra blobs and proved she was right. "Watch out."

A glop fell at my feet. "Want to change with me? You can paint the walls." I poured paint into my pan.

"I don't think you've spent much of your life rolling paint onto ceilings, Max." Valerie looked down from her perch atop a sturdy ladder. She winked.

"You'd be right about that. My decorator won't let me near a bucket of paint." I moved out of range. "By the way, I loved your column about God's Pit Crew in the *Post*."

"How did you know?" The roller hung in midair, paint drips plopping on the subflooring.

"You gave me your card when we first met. Didn't take too much research to verify who Valerie Bysbane and Hank Adams Scott are. Even if I hadn't remembered where I'd heard Hank's name." I winked. "How many people recognize either of you?"

"Very few. My picture's on every column, but it's small and crappy. And old. Although Hank's name may seem vaguely familiar, not many know who he is." Valerie turned her attention to the ceiling.

"Not many would expect the former Secretary of the Treasury to be living in their midst in an RV." I rolled paint.

"No kidding. We get a real charge going around incognito in plain sight, if you will. Now, if we were back in the District, it would be a different matter."

"I'll bet."

We filled silence with the squish and squash of rollers doing their jobs.

"How about you, Max? Does anyone around here know who you are?" Valerie climbed off the ladder and wiped her hands. "Time for more paint."

"My close friends in our compound know, of course." I turned a corner of the room and started on a fresh wall. "It wouldn't make much difference, except some people might come looking for a handout."

"Of course, anyone could find us the same way we checked each other out."

We turned to each other and held up painty thumbs.

"Google!"

On Saturday night, Johnny and I carried hors d'oeuvres and a good bottle of wine to the village. Midway into the evening,

Hank's phone rang.

"I have to take this. It's Ellie." He stepped away from the group for privacy.

Johnny was in the midst of a funny story about being raised on a cattle ranch in New Mexico when Hank returned. He held his cell out to me.

"She wants to talk to you."

"I don't know anyone named Ellie." Puzzled, I took the phone. "Hello?"

"I see you have met my friends Valerie and Henry." Eleanor's voice surprised me.

"Ellie?"

"It's a long story. Henry can tell you about the names." Eleanor needed Hank's expertise for a study for the United Nations on improving the economic status of women in third world countries. They had a kickoff set for two weeks out in Manhattan. "Ask Henry to fly up with you. His meeting overlaps with your board meeting."

I returned the phone to let Hank say his farewells. I was a bit in a daze, but not so much that I didn't attack him as soon as he disconnected.

"Ellie? Henry?"

Knowing Eleanor's dislike of using nicknames, I couldn't imagine anyone getting away with calling her Ellie. Not even the former Secretary of the Treasury.

"We met about thirty years ago. When we were introduced, she called me Henry, not Hank. Drove her nuts when I proved my given name wasn't Henry." He reached for the wine bottle.

Eleanor must have choked when she realized Hank wasn't his nickname.

"How did you prove it?" Johnny tuned into the conversation.

"Showed her my passport. She couldn't bring herself to use my given name. We struck a bargain. She could call me Henry if I could call her Ellie. Been that way ever since."

"How do you know Eleanor?" Val seemed to be bursting with questions.

"She's one of my Great Dames. That's a story for a different night."

Close to midnight, Johnny and I left. A chorus of "see you

next week" followed us to Johnny's truck. Good thing the cops weren't patrolling the road. Neither of us should have driven the few miles back to the compound.

"I didn't realize how starved I was for an evening of conversation and good wine," Johnny said.

"Me too. I've gone back to New York a couple of times, but you've been tied to the work site."

"We'll have to fix that, won't we?"

"Want to go to New York on my next trip home?" I crossed my fingers.

"I was thinking about next weekend in New Orleans."

Phooey. Still no movement on getting Johnny to New York.

"Val and Hank are quite a pair, aren't they?" I leaned against Johnny's shoulder.

"No one knows who they are. What fun they're having." Johnny ruffled my hair.

I looked at him. "How did you know?"

"Well, pretty lady, I can use Google too. How do you think I kept track of you for years?"

For years?

CHAPTER TWENTY-NINE

Mississippi, week of October 24

TWO WEEKS LATER we'd finished a near-silent dinner with everyone sunk into their own black holes of need when we heard a commotion at the main gate. A dusty pickup towing an ancient, battered Airstream waited to come in. The driver opened the truck door.

"Hey, John Wayne, anyone home?"

"Charlie!"

Alex was off the bench and across the compound before anyone else could react. He wiggled around the locked gate and threw himself into Charlie's arms.

"I presume he knows this person." Ducks waved a match over his pipe bowl and blew a thin stream of vanilla-scented smoke upward.

Whip and Emilie ran toward the gate. Whip called to Sampson to let the new arrival in.

"That would be Charlie."

"Somehow I figured it out all by myself. Funny. She seems to be a regular human being. Alex had me thinking she was Wonder Woman." Ducks waved a second match over the reluctant tobacco. He puffed away until he had it lit.

"She is, in more ways than one."

Emilie grabbed Charlie in a bear hug. Our family was complete.

I carried a load of dishes into the bus. Ducks laid his pipe aside and helped clear the table. Johnny directed Charlie to park the Airstream on the far side of the bus.

"Sure you want the Silver Slug next to your fancy digs?"

"Yup." Whip grinned. "The family's all over here."

Charlie beat dust off her jeans, gave me a huge hug and accepted an icy beer.

"Whip, you beast! You never let on that Charlie was coming." I wagged a finger at him and pretended to be angry.

"Man's gotta have some secrets." Whip hugged Charlie before stepping back. "Hope you have extra laborers in that antique."

"No such luck, but I've got a group of guys who'll be here tomorrow. About a dozen with enough dirt on their hands to know what hard work is."

"Great. Gotta tell the general contractor." Whip grabbed his cell. An ear-to-ear grin and a couple of nods from my son-in-law told us the boss was happy with the news.

I introduced Charlie to Ducks and invited everyone to gather around the table under the mosquito netting. Charlie declined anything to eat but allowed as how she might have a beer or two. I pointed toward the ice chests. She should help herself.

"What's in the back window of your truck?" Alex was dying to grab the gun from the cab. He must have remembered the lesson on climbing into the Jag, because all he did was point. Charlie brought the shotgun to the table.

Johnny, Ducks, and Whip drooled over the high-tech twelve-gauge Kel-Tec KSG. The fourteen-shell, pump-action shotgun had enough stopping power to protect anyone.

"Kinda makes our old Mossbergs look as antique as your Airstream." Johnny lusted over the shotgun.

"Glad you like my new toy." Charlie laid the shotgun on the table.

"Trust this woman to outshine us men," Whip said.

#

I stretched out on the couch in our dorm to read. Emilie had gone to bed after chattering with Charlie until both were talked

out. For the moment, at least. Whip and Alex were tucked into
their dorm, and Ducks's door was shut. So was Johnny's. Charlie
had a light on in the Silver Slug. She said she had things to get
ready for the morning. Our part of the camp was down for the
night. Tomorrow was a school day for the kids, shopping day for
me, and work day for the crew.

I stretched out on the couch and lost myself in my first grisly
J.A. Konrath thriller. From the opening page, I loved his new
Jack Daniels character, as flawed a female detective as I'd ever
met. I turned page after page, so deep into the plot I jumped half
off the couch when Emilie flopped in a chair opposite. I hadn't
heard her climb down from her bunk.

"Child, you 'bout scared the life out of me." I affected my
worst deep Southern drawl.

"I'm sorry. I can't sleep. I've been super edgy for days."
Emilie nibbled on a fingernail. She must have remembered she
was trying to break the habit because she folded her fingers into
fists.

I closed my book and got up. "Edgy? How?"

I turned the heat on under the kettle to make cups of herbal
tea, our late night we-have-to-talk beverage of choice.

"I hurt. Not from working and not from the pain caused
by the hurricane. Dr. Schwartz tells me that's cosmic pain. It's
all around us. There's nothing we can do about it. This feels
different."

Emilie padded over and fetched cups from the cupboard. We
were using her mother's good bone china and found we liked it.
I'd brought crystal glassware as well. We had it; why the heck
not use it? If it broke, so what?

"As in localized? Or in one person?" I dropped bags into our
cups and poured boiling water over them. I inhaled the scent of
lemon grass filling the RV.

"I'm not sure. It's like layers of pain. Not mine. Underneath
the pain we know is something darker. Almost dark like Dracula
was dark. I can't find the source, but it's centered around the
Sanchezes."

What lay below the surface of these two strangers? I told her
about Ducks's unsuccessful encounter with Mrs. Sanchez. "Can
I help?"

"Maybe. I'm not sure. I need to get away from Mississippi for a while. You know, put space between me and what's bothering me."

"Do you want to go to New York with me on my next trip? Or back to Richmond with Dad to hang out with Molly and the rest of your friends?" Emilie would help me figure out what she needed.

"I need to hang out with Mollie and my friends. I'm really lonely," said Emilie.

Texting their friends back in Virginia didn't fill in the gap of needing a friend nearby to share secrets, to giggle away the night with on a sleepover, and to play video games with until their thumbs fell off.

"Okay, Richmond. Time with Molly and Dr. Schwartz might be what you need. I'll talk to Dad."

"I want to introduce Mr. Ducks to Dr. Schwartz." She paused. "That way, he'll be able to help more too."

A darned good idea. With two spooky people guided by the same guru, I could feel more at ease. At least I hoped so.

Emilie crossed the narrow room and threw her arms around me. This was no stealth hug. This was a down-deep-thank-you-for-understanding hug.

"The only person we've met close to your age is Marianna. She's a little young."

"She's part of the problem. Like I told you, her center is, like, really dark around the edges. Not as bad as Mom's was, but darker than it should be."

"She has secrets. So does Mrs. Sanchez. They're both terrified of something." I held my cup in both hands. They'd grown quite cold. I stared into the light yellow liquid for answers. "We shouldn't poke too deeply. Like picking a scab won't help a wound heal. Know what I mean?"

"I see what you're saying. If we pry, we might make the situation worse, but we have to do something." Emilie went to a cupboard. Dunking a gingersnap in the tea would be about perfect.

"I'm inclined to step back and watch for a little longer. If we need to intervene, we will. Mr. Ducks will help." My second spook could come in as handy as my main one did.

"It's more than being lonely, like I am. I feel she's in danger."

I leaned over and gave Emilie a kiss on the cheek. When you were thirteen and had no best friend to talk to, lonely was about the worst feeling in the world. "In danger from whom or what? The boys who follow you?"

"Not the feral teens." Emilie bit into a gingersnap.

"Are you sure?"

"Uh huh."

I hugged Emilie until she squeaked. She went back to bed. Her breathing settled into deep sleep within minutes. After her mother died, she developed the habit of telling me what was bothering her and leaving the problems on my shoulders where they belonged. She'd done it again.

I picked up my novel, intending to figure out what Jack Daniels was going to do next. I knew what I was going to do next. I was going to visit Mrs. Sanchez. I was going to send the kids home with Whip for a long weekend. They both needed to get away.

So did I. Johnny and I would go away for a weekend to New Orleans, allergies to big cities be damned.

CHAPTER THIRTY

Mississippi, week of October 24

CHILLY FALL WEATHER alternated with summer, which struggled to hang on regardless of what the calendar said. I pulled out sweaters and jeans; Emilie gave up her Daisy Dukes for jeans and sweatshirts. Alex refused to acknowledge cooler temperatures. I expected him to come down with a head cold sometime soon.

"Rain, heavy at times, will overspread the region after midnight. By this time tomorrow, we should have more than three inches in the old rain gauge. Nothin' like Katrina, but enough to cause localized flooding in low-lying areas. Watch out for ponding on roads and potholes disguised as puddles. Don't drive into running water."

I wanted to throttle the chirpy weathergirl who prevented me from returning to house painting. The map behind her perfectly coiffed hair was overall green, with large blobs of yellow and orange and red where she predicted higher amounts of rain and embedded thunderstorms. Pastor Taylor's church parking lot was smack in the middle of the largest red blob.

Our first serious rain day. How would I handle cabin fever? As if living in the middle of nowhere in an RV didn't qualify for cabin fever on a daily basis.

Since we'd gotten to Mississippi, I'd become even more addicted to exercise than I was at home because there was little else to do. Plus I'd worked out like a fiend when Whip was in jail. Like Ducks, I rode my bike or roller bladed as often as possible. Add Pilates and yoga in the dorm, and I was one fit momma. Rain would restrict my activities to indoor exercise. Or not.

Charlie, Johnny, and Whip left mid-morning for a meeting up at Pastor Taylor's, who had offered yet another use for his multi-purpose building: community center. All the supervisors took advantage of the rain to gather. They could be gone all day.

Emilie was busy in our dorm writing an essay on the current American political system in French, iPod earphones feeding music straight into her brain; Alex was tucked away in the boys' dorm where he was taking an algebra test. He also had to finish a novel for English, with an essay on one of the main themes in the book to follow.

Time to go visiting. I threw on a yellow slicker, pulled the hood over my hair, slipped my feet into Wellingtons and sloshed my way through puddles to the bus. I jumped in a couple, resulting in muddy splashes on the bottom of my jeans. Served me right, but it was fun to be a kid again for few seconds.

Even though the inner door was open, I knocked. The first day here, Ducks established a rule regarding the bus. If the door was open, you could enter. If it wasn't, knock and wait. I knocked anyway.

"Come on in," came a voice from the rear.

I hung my dripping slicker on a hook outside under the awning and slipped out of my wet boots.

"Heads up."

Too late. A towel hit me in the chest.

"You might need this."

"Caught me, huh?" I toweled off my jeans and tried in vain to wipe the mud from the hem of my right leg.

"I'd rather ride through puddles than jump in them."

"Same result, though. Wet, muddy pants." I gave up wiping. The mud would brush off better after it dried. "We've all done stupid pet tricks we wish no one had seen, haven't we?"

"Indeed. Want a cuppa?"

"Please."

Even though I wanted to tuck my legs underneath me, my pants were too wet. I stretched them out, ankles crossed.

"What have you been doing today?" Ducks busied himself with making the tea.

"Being loudly and ridiculously bored. How about you?"

"No lemons in the fridge to make lemonade on a rainy day, but I had plenty of dust and dirty clothes. I became a cleaning and washing dervish." Ducks put the kettle on to boil. "I'm not a neat freak, but I don't tolerate dust. It's hard to keep it under control in a construction zone. I don't have enough space for clutter."

"I agree. Em and I put away everything as soon as we're done with it. On the other hand, the boys' dorm is messy and distinctly funky. Whip and Alex are responsible for corralling their dirty clothes and keeping the RV clean. A less-than-gentle reminder is past due."

When the water came to a boil, Ducks set two mugs of tea and plates on the table between a pair of leather captain's chairs. He took two steps back to the counter and produced a plate of scones.

"I'm afraid they're from a mix."

"I love scones. What a treat."

"A little early for tea, but who cares."

Ducks and I hadn't had much time to just be friends because we talked about the kids most of the time. Our schedules were full during the day, and the extended family was always around in the evening. We chatted about the kids' progress for a while. Ducks must have thought that was why I stopped by. It wasn't.

"Today reminds me of being caught in a four-day deluge off the coast of South Africa." I nibbled on one of the most delicious scones I'd ever tasted.

"Off the coast implies you were on a ship. Were you on a cruise?"

"Sailboat, actually. Reggie and I left for six months and sailed along the west coast of Africa."

"Do you still have her?'

"I do. The Direct Deposit is in Key West. After Reggie died, I let our captain use her to run charters in the Caribbean. I haven't been on her in a couple of years. Might be time to float around for a week or two." I sipped Earl Grey. "Do you sail?"

"I used to race at university, but nothing bigger than a Sunfish." Ducks bit into a scone, crumbs dropping onto his plate. None escaped to his clean floor. "Does Johnny sail?"

"You know, I've never asked. In fact, I've never seen him get in the ocean." Did my funny man dislike water as much as he disliked large cities? "Anyway, Reggie introduced me to blue-water sailing. I love it. Watching the sun rise off Port Elizabeth on Christmas Day was a once-in-a-lifetime event."

"Did Reggie sail the boat himself?"

"Reggie did everything himself. We kept a crew of two, a captain with all the necessary licenses and an engineer in case the emergency engine broke down. We went under wind power whenever we could and used the engine to keep from getting becalmed." I drained my tea.

Ducks turned up the heat under the kettle for refills.

"Reggie hated anything that kept him waiting, including wind. He was the most restless soul. He hated to waste even a second of life."

"Young souls are too often impatient. They miss much of the quiet between the noisy parts."

"That was Reggie to a T. Even when he wasn't talking, his mind churned with ideas to save the world."

"And did he?" Ducks refilled our mugs.

"No, but his last project has potential."

"What is it?"

Since Ducks told me he'd followed Reggie's public exploits, he had to know about the crash in the experimental plane. Papers all over the world covered his death. The propulsion system he was testing wouldn't work for planes, but it might in cars.

"It doesn't run on petrochemical fuels."

"Brilliant."

I took a break and went to the bathroom. On my way back, I stopped in front of a picture of a much younger Ducks with a child of maybe twelve fitted out in soccer gear. It hung on the wall in the short hallway between the schoolroom and bathroom.

"Who's this lovely girl?"

"My daughter, Carole." Ducks blinked once in what I had almost, but not quite, learned was his warning of "don't go there." I went anyway.

"I'd love to know more about her, if you want to talk."

Ducks shook himself. He added two sugar cubes to his tea, along with some milk.

"I married quite young. Nicole and I met in my third year at university. Lust at first sight. When she became pregnant at the end of my final undergraduate year, we married. Same story many of us tell."

Ducks crossed the small space to stop before the photo. "Carole came along in due course. We were happy for many years but, in the end, Nicole went her own way and Carole went with her."

"Do you see your daughter often?"

"I haven't seen her in almost a quarter of a century. Her choice, not mine. The divorce hit her hard, and she never forgave me for betraying her mother."

"You had an affair?"

"Neither of us did. We grew apart. I did something Nicole could never forgive. I married her under false pretenses. She turned Carole against me."

False pretenses? The door slammed shut. For now. I'd find out more later, I was positive.

"Where's Carole?"

"Somewhere in Surrey. I keep track of her as best as I can through the Internet and friends. I've had no contact with either her or her mother since the divorce, so it's damned hard." Ducks rubbed his temples and tugged at this beard. Another sign of discomfort. "She's all grown up. In her forties, married with two children. I keep hoping she'll forgive me, but she hasn't."

"Merry never forgave me for ruining her childhood." I couldn't keep the bitterness out of my voice.

"When we divorced, Carole called me some damned nasty names. I can forgive her because I was the one who wronged her mother." Ducks stared at the wall, his eyes glazed over. "I can't forget what she said, though."

"She was very young and very angry. She was protecting her mother. Have you reached out lately?"

"No. The last time I called, she asked me to respect her wishes and never call her again. I have done so."

"I tried to repair my relationship with Merry, but her brain injury exacerbated the bad feelings between us. We ran out of time. Eleanor gave me a do-over with Alex and Emilie. I won't blow it this time."

"I wish I could have a do-over with Carole." Ducks washed his mug before setting it in the drainer.

"Perhaps in time you will. She didn't come around when you remarried?" I washed and added my mug to the clean collection.

"How did you know?"

"Well, it was a no brainer. You were Stuart Duxworth in England. Now you have a hyphenated last name. Doesn't take a genius to figure out you married a Ross."

"Lesley and I married in Canada a year after I immigrated. Of all the crazy, impulsive things to do, we got married in Niagara Falls."

I never assumed impulsive was part of Ducks's DNA.

"Lesley's a lovely name. You don't hear it very often. Where is she?" I recalled one of the references mentioned an inheritance. Ah shoot. I stepped into the shallow end of Ducks's private wading pool.

"Lesley died." One slow blink.

Saved by Alex pulling the door open, scattering raindrops everywhere and thrusting his algebra test into Ducks's hands, I left and returned to my dorm. Who was Lesley?

Could I find the woman born Carole Duxworth? Too bad I was a recovering Catholic and not a Jewish mother. Perfect job for a yenta. Or for my favorite private investigator, Tony Ferraiolli. I didn't need anyone tailed like I did when we were gathering evidence to trap the man who murdered Merry, but I wanted information I was sure he could get. I called.

CHAPTER THIRTY-ONE

Mississippi, week of October 24

ALEX LACKED A project. I reached out to Pastor Taylor, who happened to be free in the late morning. He invited me for lunch.

"Come on in, Miz Davies. You're a lot calmer than the last time you were here." Pastor Taylor waved me into the multi-use building where a new floor fan circulated stale air. "I haven't had much company since before the storm. I hope you like tuna salad and lemonade. Variety's kinda scarce."

He'd sent his wife and children up north before the hurricane made landfall and wouldn't let them come home until he had more than an industrial building for a house. His forced bachelorhood hadn't left him with much time or opportunity to entertain.

"How are the Habitat houses coming?" Pastor Taylor handed me a plate.

I rattled on about how rewarding it was for both Emilie and me to help provide housing for the dispossessed.

"Dispossessed. Good description. Most of my parishioners still have nothin' they didn't take with them. Pastor Washington doesn't even know where most of his have landed—or how many died." He poured lemonade over ice. "I thought, Miz Davies, you'd enjoy home-squeezed lemonade."

"I would indeed, Pastor Taylor." I sipped the tart beverage.

"I may not have hundreds of people over for lunch, but I remember my momma's and wife's training."

I raised an eyebrow.

"Serve something your guest will like."

I nodded before taking another sip.

"I spend most of my time on the phone, hassling with the insurance company and trying to track down where my families went. I wish I knew a better way to find them than old church records and a poor memory."

"Maybe they need something to look forward to, Pastor." I speared a chunk of celery. "Wouldn't coming home be that something?"

"It very well could be."

"Or jobs?"

"And jobs." Pastor Taylor gazed across the recreation building. Was he seeing it filled with his missing parishioners? Or was he seeing chairs that would be empty for a long time?

All of a sudden, Alex had a project. He had proven himself quite the forensic Internet investigator when he tracked the movements of his mother's killer. I told Pastor Taylor about his skills—as well as what developed them.

"I'm a dinosaur around computers. I keep the church financials up to date and send e-mail, but nothing else. I'd be grateful for any help."

I promised to drop Alex off soon so the pastor could get to know him. Then I moved to another Alex-related topic. I wanted him to be able to give something tangible to the community when the roadwork was done. Emilie and I had Hope Village; Alex needed something.

"Well, we used to have a park of sorts between St. Anna's and Hope Village. After the storm, we piled everything in the space, thinkin' we'd haul the debris to the dump. We saved some things, but mostly we had a huge bonfire."

"That junk heap was once a park and playground?"

"More junk there now than anything. I hated to burn people's belongings, but once they were soaked, they began to rot. It was the best way to prevent disease." Pastor Taylor selected a slice of bread from the basket and spread butter across it.

"Now don't you go tellin' my wife I'm eatin' butter. She'd have way too much to say about it. I'm not supposed to have butter or mayonnaise, or anything with a lot of fat." Hanging his head in mock guilt, Pastor Taylor helped himself to another scoop of tuna salad. "Of course, I did use the best Southern mayonnaise in my tuna salad—Duke's."

"It's delicious. Your secret's safe." I buttered a piece of bread. "You're going to need someplace for children to play when Hope Village is complete. Do you think we could rebuild the park together?"

I could write a check for everything, but I didn't want to. Not enough of a lesson for Alex. If Ducks and Whip helped him apply for a grant, he could design the park, select the playground equipment, and feel ownership of its outcome.

"Let me think on that. We don't have much money, you know."

"Let's get the idea of a park going before we talk about what it will cost." I ate more salad. When I looked up, doubt registered in the pastor's eyes. "What?"

"How are you going to fund it?" Was that a hint of suspicion or curiosity in his voice?

"Let's let Alex figure it out, shall we?"

"Isn't he a bit young for such a task?"

"He'll have help. He's proven to be resourceful beyond his chronological years more than once." When he wasn't being holy-crap boy-child.

"What else is on your mind, Miz Davies?" Pastor Taylor's twinkling blue eyes bored into mine.

"The feral teens."

"Ah yes. Mind you, I can't prove anythin', but I think they're behind the petty crimes we've been experiencin' of late."

"With all due respect, Pastor Taylor, murder and intimidation aren't petty crimes."

"You're right, Miz Davies. I was thinkin' more about the boys stealin' anythin' that's not nailed down."

"Do you know if more strays have arrived?" Did we have a combination of locals and those who'd drifted here from other places wrecked by the storm?

"Well, I've counted eleven up to now. I know seven of them. The others are strangers."

"Are they dangerous?" My favorite worry of late.

"Not one-on-one, but in a pack, I'd be very wary."

Pastor Taylor pushed his empty plate aside and walked to the window. He pointed to a battered copse of trees, behind which was a pile of rubble and a nearly destroyed shack, the same shack we watched from the compound daily.

"That used to be a house, although the health department should have condemned it long before Katrina destroyed it. Jake Montgomery lived there with two sisters and his momma. I don't know if she and her girls survived or not. We haven't found their bodies."

Pastor Taylor's concern for the loss of this family, both to the storm and to the grinding poverty endemic in this section of rural Mississippi, was palpable. I joined him at the window. A fleeting shape darted behind the rubble pile.

"That's Jake. He can out-hide just about anyone around."

"Em says he's harmless. Is he?" Much as I wanted to rely on her special gift, I couldn't. Not without substantiation.

"She's right, but Jake can be manipulated. He wants so badly to belong. Be careful. He's much stronger than he looks."

I filed the warning away.

"I keep thinking that bringin' your grandchildren into this wasteland took a lot of courage, Miz Davies."

I'd have called it flippin' stupidity had I known what to expect.

"Why didn't you take them to New York?"

Hmm, another one who knew more about me than I realized. My license plate told the world I was from New York State. The vanity *Reggie* might have given the pastor a clue about my identity. Being Mrs. Reginold Davies didn't seem to matter to Pastor Taylor, though. I let his comment slide.

"They need to be with their father. I made a decision last year after my daughter's murder to keep the family together. I hadn't thought what message the fancy RVs might give down here."

Not for the first time I questioned their ostentation. To me they were an expedient way of providing roofs over our heads. To others they could be seen as flaunting wealth. And to even more, they could be glaring examples of outsiders coming in and throwing their weight around.

"Don't worry. I won't tell anyone."

I helped clear the table and stacked the dishes in the sink. I thanked Pastor Taylor for his information as well as his ideas about the park. I promised to have Alex meet with him about finding his parishioners.

"Go see Pastor Washington. He was over at the tent earlier this morning. He's most likely still there."

I thanked him again for lunch and headed off for the AME tent.

Hey, wait a minute. Tell anyone what about me? Who would Pastor Taylor tell? And why would anyone care? The only other local man I'd met was Pastor Washington. He wouldn't see a rich white bitch butting in. He'd see a plain old white bitch butting in. Money didn't seem to be a key differentiator in his dislike for pesky Northerners.

CHAPTER THIRTY-TWO

Mississippi, week of October 24

I SAT IN my favorite folding chair under Pastor Washington's tent. When I told him what Alex would be doing to help Pastor Taylor, Pastor Washington said his church building, all its records, and most of its members disappeared during or right after Katrina blew ashore. As far as he was concerned, nothing could be salvaged that wasn't already stacked under the tent.

"Look around, Miz Davies. There's precious little of anything left."

"I understand, but I came to ask for your support for a different project. Alex wants to rebuild the rundown park so it'll be ready when children move into Hope Village."

"You just hold on." Pastor Washington held up a hand. "We got nothin' left. Can't give you anythin'."

"That's the point. You don't have anything, but you have worshipers moving into the village, don't you? They have children, don't they? The community will be mixed, with blacks and whites living side by side, won't it?"

"Likely as not. You have to remember, the law desegregated the South. That don't mean we're integrated."

"I'm hoping we find a way to rebuild the park together. Children will need some place to play."

"Why you harpin' on somethin' as silly as a park? We got bigger problems than that." Pastor Washington stared at me, eyebrows drawn into a foreboding straight line, as if I hadn't a clue about what was important. "This area's been hurt in a deep-down, gut-wrenching sort of way."

"You think a park is frivolous when you need everything." I wanted to peel away the layers of the onion to get this distrustful man on my side.

The pastor nodded but remained silent, arms crossed across his broad stomach.

"It's small, I agree, but if there're a lot of children, where'll they play? In the street? In the construction zone?"

Pastor Washington didn't have to like me, but that wouldn't stop me from finding a way for children to be children. Playing together without regard to age, sex, or race. Free range without restrictions or parents hovering and stifling creativity. Staying healthy through outdoor exercise.

"You don't belong here, Miz Davies. What's a rich lady like you doin' livin' in a trailer?"

"My son-in-law lost his wife last year. I'm here to help raise my grandchildren and see they learn something from their loss and this disaster."

"I'm sorry. Hard to lose a wife. Illness or accident?"

Time to take the gloves off. "Neither. She was murdered."

"Hard to lose a child. I'm sorry, but Miz Davies, we lost hundreds in the storm. You got no imagination what it was like."

"Pastor Washington, you don't much like me. You find me nosy and pushy. You think I'm meddling in your affairs." I waited.

"Well, you're all that. And more." He pushed himself off his folding chair and paced the concrete slab that was once his church's foundation. His worn shoes slapped. "You got no experience watchin' people die. People screamin' for help even when they were bein' washed away."

"You went through hell and came out the other side."

"Mebbe."

Now for the sucker punch.

"May I tell you a story?"

"Can't stop you if I tried."

"I have an office in lower Manhattan. On September eleventh, we were meeting when the first plane hit the World Trade Center. Before we could react, the second plane came in. I watched nearly three thousand people die horribly. I got out, but I'll never forget the sound of bodies hitting the pavement. I had friends in those towers. They're all dead."

My cheeks burned. I knew from experience they were bright red with emotion. My eyes filled with unshed tears. I would never be able to unsee or unhear what I witnessed on 9/11.

"Don't you dare judge me. I've been through hell too. I survived."

Pastor Washington walked over and wrapped arthritic, work-hardened fingers around my hands. Neither of us said a word.

"We both got a heap of pain and tired built up in us." The pastor swallowed hard to clear his throat. "I forget I'm not alone. I'm sorry I doubted you."

"Do you think we can put aside our differences and build something nice for the people who will come home?"

"You are a vexin' woman. I suppose we can try to work together, if it don't kill us both." Pastor Washington looked toward the bare expanse that once held a bare-bones park. Other than a huge pile of rubble, the single identifiable item from the original playground area was a twisted, rusting swing set. Chains banged in the breeze. Even removing the reminders of the storm would be a huge improvement.

"We can. Where'll we get money for the equipment? None of us got two dimes to rub together. Hell, I got a tent for a church." The pastor waved his hand.

"Let my grandson worry about that. Will you help us? Maybe some of your flock as well?"

"Don't have much flock left. Even fewer than Hodge does." Pastor Washington hung his head. He paced the tent. Four poles held up the canvas—not much of a church but his nonetheless.

"At least one of your members is back. Mrs. Jordan's working on a house in Hope Village. I helped her paint her living room last week. Let's ask her when her husband's coming home. She talks about him and their children all the time. If he wants to work on the road project, he'll earn good money."

Pastor Washington studied me. He didn't trust me, but he

was having difficulty finding nonexistent ulterior motives or holes in my argument.

"Pastor Taylor has a few worshipers who've returned. You know, a little sweat equity goes a long way in any community project."

"You don't understand. White churches and black churches never work together. It might be different up north where you're from, but we're really separate."

I laughed. "My family priest back in Richmond used to say the most segregated time in the world was at eleven on a Sunday morning."

"He's right. Mebbe it's time to change. Hell, if everything washed away, why not some of our outdated practices? I'll give Hodge a call. If no one else comes out, I will." We shook hands again. His calloused mitt told me Pastor Washington was no stranger to physical work. In a thinner, younger time.

I had a deal. "So will Pastor Taylor. He's already agreed."

"I was right about you. You meddled me right into what you wanted me to do."

"I surely did." I winked and went back to the Rover.

While Emilie put the final touches on dinner, I disappeared into my bedroom, where I found clown face makeup and painted my face. With a rainbow Afro wig, I was ready for dinner.

Emilie fell all over herself howling. I painted her face too. She texted Johnny and Charlie to come to the girls' dorm. They weren't spared attacks from the face paint. When we emerged, Alex demanded to be painted next; Whip and Ducks looked relieved to be spared.

"Charlie, Mad Max always says you're never too old to have a happy childhood." Alex got over his hurt feelings of being left out of a grand joke. "Do you agree?"

"You can't do much about your first childhood." Charlie pushed a red rubber nose more firmly on her face. "You're in control of your second. How you decide to live it is up to you."

"Mad Max decided to live it by being goofy." Johnny twitched a black fright wig into a better fit. Too large, it slid down over his eyes. "Would any of you want to go back and relive your youth?"

"No way. That would mean I'd have to take algebra with the Wicked Witch again." Ducks made it seem this would be a fate worse than death.

"We all have closets full of people we don't want to meet again," Whip said, "like schoolyard bullies."

"Or ex-bosses." Charlie added.

"My ninth grade English teacher," I said.

"Mr. Ducks," said Alex.

As a group we pounced on him and tickled Alex half to death.

CHAPTER THIRTY-THREE

Mississippi, week of October 24

I REHEARSED MY pitch before I called on Mrs. Sanchez to invite her and Marianna to a last-of-the-year picnic on the beach on Saturday. I wondered if she'd feel less uncomfortable in a larger group than two on two. They'd get to know my extended family and still time themselves out when we became too intense and noisy.

After much wheedling, Mrs. Sanchez met us at the compound and rode with Emilie and me. Johnny and Ducks left an hour earlier to erect a volleyball net between two support pillars from a vanished house. I put several hampers of food and baskets of paper plates in the Rover; Charlie, Alex, and Whip had coolers of soft drinks and beer in Whip's truck. Mrs. Sanchez insisted on bringing something sweet.

We lucked out. The sun was strong, but the humidity had retreated. We no longer faced late summer's blowtorch heat. I invited those workers who stayed in camp rather than go home for the weekend. Several accepted.

While I wanted to get better acquainted with Marianna, I was afraid to ask too many questions. Having Charlie there with Emilie and Alex would help. No one could stay shy around Charlie. She put anyone at ease as quickly as I set people on edge.

We decided the language *du jour* would be Spanish, since Emilie and Alex were fluent. Ducks's plan to teach in the language paid off.

We set up games, blankets, and food and settled in to celebrate the day. A battered pickup with a rotten muffler cruised by on the partially destroyed barrier island road. I didn't have to look up to know who was in it. At least everyone on the beach would be safe for the afternoon and evening. I looked at the way the truck had come. A police car blocked the entrance to the beach.

"He's not here to protect us." Johnny walked up behind me. He leaned over and whispered in my ear. "He's here to watch what we do."

"Well, he's not going to ruin our day. Neither is the gang in the pickup."

Charlie chased three kids into the water, which had cooled from summer's peak and was still pleasant. We had an exuberant splashing contest with lots of belly flops and whoops from Alex on his boogie board. At first Marianna refused to go near the water, but coaxing from Emilie and Charlie's offer to hold her hand helped overcome her fear. Ducks swam, while Johnny fussed with a volleyball net that needed no such fussing. Although he was barefoot in the sand, he didn't even wade in the spent waves.

I lay in one of the lounge chairs and sipped iced tea with Mrs. Sanchez. Soon, Marianna was squealing along with my two wild children in a game of chase and splash. She even tried Alex's boogie board with limited success. Emilie and Alex flanked her and helped her get one good ride. Charlie couldn't get her to go more than waist deep, but a shelf of sand meant you had to go far out before dropping off in deeper water. Ducks ended his swim and toweled off. He threw on a T-shirt, his swim jams doubling as shorts.

"Your daughter's beautiful. How old is she?"

Mrs. Sanchez smiled. "She's almost thirteen."

She didn't look almost thirteen. When I observed her in her chaste, one-piece bathing suit, instead of the ill-fitting T-shirts or baggy dresses she wore, though, her budding breasts and lack of baby fat looked like she was well into puberty.

"She's very mature."

"I don't want her to grow up," Mrs. Sanchez whispered. Her eyes darted around the beach, ever vigilant against unseen danger. "Life is better if she doesn't."

Of course life should be easy for a child, but it wasn't always. Emilie and Alex had faced a murdered mother, for God's sake. Besides, Mrs. Sanchez couldn't hold back time, no matter how hard she wished it.

"She's ready for a bra." I hadn't seen any sign of the child wearing one the first couple of times I'd seen her.

"No!" Mrs. Sanchez's response was disproportionate to the reality of the situation. This child was already an A-cup, perhaps a B.

The men fired up a charcoal grill before they played volleyball. Eventually, the children tired of the ocean. Marianna watched the volleyball game for a few minutes before she wandered back to the blankets and stood behind her mother.

"Do you know how to play, Marianna?" I tossed her a towel from the pile.

The child shook her head.

"Would you like to learn?"

Marianna nodded. She wrapped the towel around her shoulders.

"Maybe your mother will let you come back when it's just us girls. Charlie and I can teach you. Next time we have a picnic you can play too. Would you like that?"

Marianna looked at her mother. "Yes, ma'am."

I waved Marianna to my side and toweled her hard enough to make her giggle. Her mother handed her a T-shirt.

Marianna didn't speak to the men, although she and Charlie chattered away like old friends. When it was time to eat, I bustled around, setting out piles of plates, plastic-ware and napkins. I had a carry basket with condiments for the burgers and hot dogs.

"Who's cooking?" I called out. "The coals are ready. I'm starving!"

Johnny and Whip raced each other to the grill, Whip winning by half a step.

"Hey, old man," Whip said, "looks like I can still beat you in a race."

Johnny laughed and kicked sand in his direction. "I'll open the beer. Ducks, you ready for a cold one?"

Ducks slammed the volleyball over the net for a winning point before shouting he was. Two more points and the men, Alex and Ducks, had beaten the women, Emilie and Charlie.

The work crew sat on various blankets and towels.

"This is my baby." Pete, the cook, showed us pictures of his five-year-old daughter. "She's at home with her mother in Texas."

Like magic, men produced pictures of their families. Even Charlie showed photos of her sisters, nieces, and nephews. Funny how pictures of children and puppies were such great icebreakers.

When Mrs. Sanchez produced a basket of empanadas and churros for dessert, Johnny grabbed some of the sugary treats before anyone else could get close.

"You're making me homesick, Mrs. Sanchez." He had a different sweet in each hand. He leaned over and kissed Mrs. Sanchez on the cheek. Seemed he surprised both of them. "My mother and sisters make these all the time."

"Will you show me how? That way Johnny can have them between trips home." I pointed at the powdered sugar on his upper lip and laughed.

She nodded.

We relaxed and ate until it grew dark. Under a river of stars, Whip built a fire with hurricane debris and driftwood; Johnny, Ducks, and four workers brought out guitars. Mrs. Sanchez had a beautiful contralto voice. She, Charlie, and Johnny formed a trio and sang several old Mexican folk songs as well as some popular numbers, including the perennial favorite, La Bamba. Workers played and lifted their voices. Homesickness tinged the lyrics.

The noise of the battered truck arrived before the truck itself did. Even in the dark I could see two people in the cab and three in the back. My first impression of the new guy was hulking. Huge and dark, but beyond that, nothing. One in the cab pointed what looked like a baseball bat at us. Were we being stalked? The truck continued toward the end of the road. It didn't return. The cop car had vanished.

Mrs. Sanchez followed my gaze. "Those are bad boys. They do not like us. They want us to go away."

I looked across the campfire at Johnny. He, too, had taken note of the men in the pickup. He shot a glance at Ducks who nodded.

CHAPTER THIRTY-FOUR

Mississippi, week of October 31

A WEEK AFTER the picnic, Emilie sought me out for another almost-midnight talk. "Have you ever felt out of place?"

Where the heck had that come from? The question had multiple layers. "Often. How about you?"

What a stupid question. The expression on her face was a pronounced "du-uh."

"I can't imagine you not fitting in ever."

I smiled and told her about my first visit to Davies Enterprises' boardroom after Reggie died. Awkward was an understatement. One board member didn't recognize me. He told me to fetch coffee for the group. I did. When it was time for the meeting to begin, I sat at the head of the table. The man who mistook me for an administrative assistant didn't have time to feel out of place. He resigned from the board a day later. I neither knew nor cared about his reason.

"If I said I was never uncomfortable, I would either be super human or super stupid. Remember, the girl who grew up on a farm outside Richmond is the head of an international company. It makes for uncomfortable moments."

"I thought you were raised in a suburb like Riverbend."

"I lived in an old farmhouse down the road from my grandmother and across from your aunt and uncle. About as far away from your old suburb as possible."

My family had farmed a plot of land since the mid-1750s. Although the original farm had shrunk to a couple hundred acres, we had a working enterprise with milk cows, beef cattle, and a clucking-good egg business.

"Your uncle Carl runs the place. He and my brother Sam own it together."

"Why not you? Don't you have part of it?" Emilie didn't know anything about grandparents' generation or how property might be divided.

"No. When I married, I agreed to give up any interest in the farm. Seemed fitting since I moved away and set up life with your grandfather. My brother Dan made a career in the marines. He gave up his interest as well."

Emilie smiled. "Yes, it was fitting."

The current house was built in the 1840s. Never a *Gone with the Wind* plantation, the two-story brick dwelling had been remodeled and expanded over the years. The bones of the house were unbroken, though; dependencies grew outward like wings from the original foursquare structure.

"I was often the pickee from the snobby in-crowd."

"But you're rich." Emilie protested.

"Now. Not then. I remarried well. It was rather a giggle, you know. Grandfather Frank's mother taught me how to behave in society in Richmond. Confused the heck out of a lot of people who remembered me from high school."

Time to get back to why Emilie asked the question in the first place. "Now what has prompted this midnight chat, dear child?"

"I don't feel right around Marianna. She's afraid of men."

I moved over on the couch to let Emilie snuggle close. "At the picnic she had fun with Charlie and Alex until they began playing volleyball. She fled to the blanket near her mother. She didn't say anything to Dad except 'thank you' when he handed her a hot dog. Did she talk to any of the workers?"

"Only after Pete showed her his daughter's picture."

"That's right. I remember."

"She doesn't like being here."

"You mean, she didn't like being at the picnic?" I was lost, as I often was when Emilie was struggling to grasp what she was feeling.

"Not that. She doesn't like being here. In Mississippi. Something at the church terrifies her." Emilie worried a hangnail on her thumb.

"Have you talked to Dr. Schwartz about this? Or Mr. Ducks?"

"Dr. Schwartz doesn't have all the answers. Mr. Ducks feels the same as I do, but he doesn't know why. I have to think about this some more." Emilie pushed off the couch and walked barefoot down our hall toward the bath.

"Don't think too hard, please. It'll all become clear if we watch and wait."

I might as well have been blowing smoke. Or, more correctly, whistling Dixie, since we were in the South, after all. She wouldn't stop thinking. Neither would I.

CHAPTER THIRTY-FIVE

Mississippi, week of October 31

SINCE I WAS often awake long after the camp settled down for the night, I remained amazed at how quiet everything was. The emptiness was tangible and more than a little discomforting. A single car traveling along the partially completed highway was enough to wake me from the deepest sleep. Crickets, which sang arias celebrating autumn, overpowered most road sounds.

I needed a transfusion of city noise: horns and traffic and people's voices. I was itchy to get home. If my monthly board meeting wasn't coming up soon, I'd be downright snarky. We'd reached a point in our school year where the kids had a week off. Whip invited them to go to Richmond with him.

"You bet!" Alex was always ready for an adventure, especially if it got him out of the school bus.

"Me too. I want to see Molly," Emilie said, "even though she'll be in school most of the time. We can visit in the afternoon. I'll let Dr. Schwartz know I'm coming. I want time with her."

With the kids settled, I turned to Ducks. Did he have any plans? Maybe he'd like some time at home. Johnny and Charlie would push ahead with the construction. Once again, Johnny wiggled out of going to Manhattan.

"I don't think so. Thanks anyway, Max, but it's a long drive for a few days." Ducks had no reason to stay around the school bus if the kids weren't there. "Maybe I'll hang out over in the French Quarter. Sit in on some jam sessions."

"You fly, don't you?" I straightened the kitchen in our dorm. We alternated between the girls' dorm and the school bus when the weather turned blustery.

"I do, but tickets from New Orleans are pretty steep. I'll pass."

"Can you be ready day after tomorrow at seven in the morning?"

"Yes, but I just…"

"Did you think I've been taking puddle jumpers home every month?" Had I never told Ducks about my plane?

"Yes, actually."

"My corporate jet will pick us up at the Gulfport-Biloxi airport."

When the local commuter and general aviation airport reopened about a week after the storm, it made my monthly commute doable. I wasn't about to take three planes and spend an entire day each way to get home. The airport handled a full component of scheduled flights and serviced private planes.

"In that case, I'll be ready before seven."

Hank Scott met us at the general aviation terminal. I'd taken Eleanor's advice and invited him to fly up with us. He carried a laptop and small overnight bag.

"Ellie sent a huge preliminary dossier last night." Hank chose a seat and flipped open his laptop. "I hope I can get through it before we land."

Ducks and I buckled into facing leather seats. We were barely airborne when he fell asleep. I poured myself and Hank cups of coffee, opened my own laptop and got to work. Dozens of e-mails awaited. I dispensed with them as quickly as possible and sent messages to Raney and Eleanor about dinner later in the week. Hank disappeared into Eleanor's report.

Bored with the endless drone of the engines, I poked around the Internet and did some research on park equipment. I found what Alex wanted, did a quick mental tally and decided his grant request was enough. The Wellington Foundation, which I set up with the help of my second husband's children to manage his fortune, could spare a few thousand dollars to help children stay healthy.

Ducks slept soundlessly. On a whim, I Googled his name. I'd done this when I was checking him out before I hired him, but I didn't read all of the stories. This time I did, including an obituary. For one Leslie Ross.

Leslie? I opened the story.

No, Ducks, it didn't matter.

CHAPTER THIRTY-SIX

New York, week of November 7

COREY, MY DECORATOR, warned me to expect major changes in my apartment because he'd been a very busy boy. He arranged to meet me there. If I hated it, he could revive me.

My doorman, George, notified me Mr. Corey waited upstairs. I rang the doorbell. After he relieved me of my two small bags, Corey told me to close my eyes. I let myself be led into the living room. He was all about presentation. I knew the drapes would be open, sunlight dancing across the new room. I breathed in clean odors of fresh paint.

"Okay, Mrs. Davies, you can open your eyes." Corey stepped back, giving me an unobstructed view. "Remember, it's still a work in progress."

I opened my eyes. Instead of a formal room with dark walls and creamy-white woodwork, warm earth tones adorned the walls, with a darker brown on the ceiling, pale adobe-colored carpeting and much more modern furniture than the earlier Queen Anne high style I'd loved with Reggie.

I spun in a circle to take in the whole room. Then I walked around, fingering the furniture and the art objects Corey had placed on some of the hard surfaces. The constant stream of photos Corey had sent didn't do justice to the new look.

"Poor Reggie must be turning in his grave, seeing what you've done to his perfect apartment."

"You don't have to live with Ben. He began whimpering when the first can of paint arrived. After all, I destroyed his masterpiece." Corey laughed.

"Major hissy fits?"

"You have no idea." Corey held my hand. "As you can see, the living room's coming along, although it's far from finished. Look at the two facing couches."

After a moment, I smiled. "You re-covered the love seat from the den and the old camelback couch from the living room. I love it."

I barely recognized them in their new dresses.

"Slipcovers can be changed, as can throws and pillows. Come look at the kitchen. I made the greatest changes there."

Walls that had been white were brick red. Oak cabinets were off-white with an antique yellow over-glaze. All the appliances were a matte stainless steel. And, best of all, I had a huge stove where once I had a tiny range.

"Wonderful! I love the Mexican tiles on the backsplash behind the stove." They picked up the colors of the kitchen and carried forward the warm tans and ochre of the living room.

"You'd better. Hand painted to order. They cost you a small fortune."

I'd all but given Corey a blank check to redo the apartment like Reggie had done after we married. I knew what each item cost because I had itemized invoices. Corey was right. The tiles cost more than all the new appliances combined.

The rest of the tour lasted a few seconds. Corey had removed the wall between the old kitchen and the dining room, opening up the space, while separating it with floor cabinets and a marble worktop. The backside of the worktop was a bar with a built-in wine chiller. I could cook while I chatted with friends. The dining room was two shades darker than the living room walls but otherwise employed the same color scheme.

The apartment had a way to go, but I was more than satisfied. "It's getting there. You translated my ideas better than I could have imagined."

"I'm glad you like it. I haven't started on the den yet, but I

have some exciting ideas. I don't think we need to do much to
your bedroom other than strip the wallpaper, paint the walls
and put different linens on the bed. Guess we're almost in the
home stretch."

We spent another hour talking about what to hang on the
walls and put on shelves to decorate the living and dining rooms.
Over half a bottle of wine, Corey showed me paintings he liked.
He wanted to reframe a couple of the modern pieces and had
hung an unusual oval mirror on one wall between new built-in
bookcases.

"Where's *Blue Dog #3* going to go?" I'd been adamant about
hanging the kitschy oil Reggie despised.

"I'm not sure, but it will have a place of honor. By the way,
you need to go shopping. Be impulsive and buy what appeals.
Don't worry about where to put stuff. We'll figure it out."

Carte blanche to shop until I dropped. I was in heaven.
Of course, it was my money, but still. Corey refused to stay
for dinner. I rang Raney. We agreed to meet at a little Italian
trattoria halfway between her apartment and mine.

###

Over cards and martinis at Eleanor's brownstone on Saturday
afternoon, I brought Raney, Eleanor, Rose, and Grace, my Great
Dames, up to date on life in the disaster zone. I regaled them
with stories about shopping at Walmart. Grace was horrified.

"I still can't understand how you can look so happy." Rose
patted her white curls and bid two diamonds.

"It's simple." I passed. "I'm needed."

"We need you. Couldn't you get the same satisfaction writing
a check for this park of yours?" Grace held her cards close to her
face. She had forgotten her reading glasses again. "Why do you
have to get physically involved?"

"Writing a check isn't enough. When Emilie and I are
painting, side by side, with a woman who is about to move into
the first house she's ever owned, well, I can't tell you how good
it makes us feel." I laid down my cards. "We have eight families
in their first homes."

Eleanor headed off an argument by asking if I had run into
any more mysteries. I couldn't tell the Great Dames about the

feral teens. To put the fear of God in them, Eleanor would send down our private investigator, Tony Ferraiolli, or Joe the PI, who proved Merry was having an affair and later protected Emilie. Rose would demand I come home to Manhattan where life was safe. Grace would say, "I told you so."

"I've had all the mysteries I need, thank you very much."

Since I'd kept Raney informed about the ominous threats from the gang, she knew I wasn't telling the whole truth, but she let me get away with it. Soon we were gossiping about a new tenant at the Dakota, Yoko Ono's latest failed effort to have the building renamed after her husband, what that runty little mayor was doing, and how the garbage union threatened yet another strike. Ah yes, home again.

I missed New York when I was in the war zone. After being back for three days, I missed my grandchildren, Whip, and Charlie. And I sorely missed Johnny.

I headed to Teterboro for our return flight to Gulfport. Hank was staying on another week. Ducks arrived with what looked like a huge book bag. I'd already stashed cases of wine and several large bags of food. I hit a toy store for new things to relieve the tedium of no movie theaters or forms of entertainment outside of our compound. I even found a small espresso machine. If Emilie couldn't go to Starbucks, I could turn the dorm into a coffeehouse.

"I figured we could stow this somewhere."

"No problem."

"I could get used to this lifestyle." He settled back in his seat and buckled the belt.

"As long as we're in a disaster zone, this is the most sensible way to get back and forth."

"Indeed."

CHAPTER THIRTY-SEVEN

Mississippi, week of November 7

ON SATURDAY AFTER my return, Whip and I had barely finished an early breakfast when a couple I knew from Hope Village called. They'd passed an ATM on their way into Gulfport and witnessed several young men dragging a man from his truck.

"They beat the crap out of him." Traffic noises came across a static-filled phone connection. "I called nine-one-one while my wife took a bunch of photos with her cell. The victim fell after a huge black guy hit him in the head with a bat. Then, four or five other guys kicked him while he was down. We have clear images of three—two black men and one white boy who looked like he was wearing black makeup."

"We know them," I told the Habitat volunteer.

Whip leaped to his feet, prepared to race to his truck to go... Where? We didn't have enough information.

"Whip, wait." I pointed to the table. Wonder of wonders, Whip sat.

"The sheriff arrived ten minutes later. By then, the gang was gone. The victim lay on the ground bleeding and semi-conscious. We told the sheriff what we witnessed and that we had photos of the attack."

"What did he do?"

"Not a damned thing. He said he'd handle it his way. Then he got back in his cruiser and drove off."

"He didn't call an ambulance?" I pointed toward Whip's truck. He ran. I followed, cell stuck to my ear.

"No. Guess his way is to let a man die."

"Is he dead?" Did we have another soon-to-be murder on our hands?

"No, but he's bad. He's in our car. We're taking him to the hospital in Gulfport. Can you meet us?"

"On our way."

Charlie came up beside the driver's door. Once she had the lowdown on the attack, she scrambled into the backseat. I called Johnny and filled him in on what we knew. He promised to feed the kids when they woke up, since Ducks had left the night before for New Orleans.

"Why'd they call you?" Charlie buckled her seat belt. Samson swung the gate open and locked it behind us.

"I keep the volunteers up to date on the danger. They don't know anyone else from the camps."

"Gotcha."

The emergency room was boiling over with men and women in a state of panic. The nurse in charge stopped us when we asked for information. We wanted to check on our injured friend.

"Are you his relatives?"

"He works with us. We came to help." Whip ran his hand along the back of his neck.

"You can't go in if you're not family." The nurse waved us toward the raucous waiting room.

"Can you at least give us his name? We'd like to call his family." I stepped sideways and blocked her escape.

"Victor Hernandez." She checked a list of patients.

"Thank you."

Whip and Charlie huddled in the waiting room where I caught up with them. The room throbbed with the chaos of too many people in too small an area, all shouting at each other in excited Spanish. Antiseptic and alcohol mixed with dirt, sweat and blood. I sneezed.

Victor, one of Charlie's men, came in two days after she did. "He's from out Midland way. I'll call his wife."

Whip pulled out his cell and called the general contractor. "We don't know much. Got his name...

"Eyewitnesses said he's hurt pretty bad...

"Yeah, same gang...

"Sheriff drove off without even calling an ambulance."

Pneumatic doors whooshed open, permitting two more gurneys to enter. EMTs shouted for a doctor and recited vital signs.

Whip hung up after a few more words. "Prick."

Charlie stared at him.

"What?" Whip scratched a mosquito bite on his forearm. "Oh, not the contractor. The sheriff."

"Oh."

I pestered the nurse into letting us go back to Victor's area. The nurse, harried and not in the mood to argue, pointed us toward a curtained space at the back of the emergency room.

Victor had tubes and monitors plugged into his arms, head, and chest. We sat beside his bed for well over an hour until a different nurse came in to check his vital signs. He was unconscious with a severe concussion.

"The doctor's reading his X-rays. He'll be in soon."

I'd been through this when Merry was injured. I had nothing but bad feelings this time as well.

After a long time, a weary-looking doctor arrived wearing a stained surgical tunic and jeans. "You his friends?"

"Yeah." Whip held out his hand. He introduced us.

The doctor looked dead on his feet.

"Thanks for letting us stay with him. I understand regulations..."

"Screw HIPAA. I don't have time for that shit right now."

"Busy day?" I asked.

"You can say that again. Big pile-up over on the highway. Six people in critical condition—and we're only a level two trauma center. Their friends are in the waiting room. I'm the only doctor around. And this real stupid beating. Terrible."

Victor had a fractured skull, broken ribs, a broken arm and a bruised kidney. A catheter released a steady drip of blood-tinged urine.

"Aren't all beatings stupid?" I asked.

"Some are worse than others. Looks like he was attacked with a baseball bat and heavy shoes. Got stomped sumpin' fierce."

"The couple who brought him in took pictures of the attack. More important, they have pictures of the attackers." I wanted this documented. "Did you call the highway patrol?"

"I did, but Sheriff Asshole got here first. I gave him the details, showed him the X-rays and photos we snapped of the bruises."

"The attack was in Gulfport jurisdiction. Why did the sheriff butt in?" I didn't like the way Sheriff dumber-than-a-box-of-rocks Hardy kept materializing wherever a worker was attacked or killed.

"Said he'd caught the original call and wanted to see if the guy was alive."

"Well, he is." Whip ground his teeth. "No thanks to him."

"Mildew has a higher IQ than that sheriff." The doctor expended little energy on our Dodge Boy. "I'll do everything I can to keep this guy alive."

"Please do," Charlie said.

"No promises." The doctor walked through a pair of doors.

"Holy shit. What next?" Whip rubbed the back of his neck again.

I sent Whip and Charlie back to the compound, promising to stay until they picked me up at the end of the day. Maybe Victor would regain consciousness. Maybe not, but at least he wouldn't be alone.

Late afternoon, a loud argument broke out at the reception desk. I poked my head through a gap in the curtains in time to see two women demanding immediate treatment. One held the other up.

"She was raped by several men alongside Gulfport Pike."

Gulfport Pike? Our main artery into Gulfport. I drove it every week for supplies. I eavesdropped. From what I could gather, the younger woman went to retrieve some tools she'd left behind at the work site and was close to her camp when a truck forced her off the road. Fragments of sentences and single words came through: battered truck, beaten, raped, spic.

The younger woman followed a nurse into another examination area. I touched Victor's shoulder and whispered I'd be right back. Zero response. I slipped away and approached the older woman who had taken a seat in the waiting room.

"My name is Max Davies." I held out my hand.

"Caren Reynolds."

We shook hands.

I fitted my body into another unyielding molded chair. "I'm here with a worker who was attacked and beaten by two black men and two white boys."

"I brought my friend Olivia in." She tugged at a scrunchie holding back her graying ponytail. "She got gang raped."

"Did you see the attack?"

Caren shook her head. "Olivia came back late and wouldn't talk about it. I caught her crying in our tent, figured out from her clothes what had happened, and forced her to come here before she could shower."

"You did the right thing."

"I want to kill those guys." Caren bit off her words, her face tight with anger.

"Get in line."

Since the attack happened in Gulfport jurisdiction, two highway patrol officers arrived to take a report. From outside the curtained-off area, we overheard Olivia described her attackers and the attack itself.

"The assholes didn't even bother to wear masks." Olivia's voice shook with humiliation. "Like they thought they'd get away with it."

"They have so far." I whispered to Caren, as angry as the woman in the exam area.

"They won't this time," Caren promised.

"I raked the black bald guy across the face." She held up her hands. "See, traces of skin."

A patrolman told the nurse to scrape her nails and put the evidence in a baggie.

"Did they wear condoms, miss?" The older patrolman took notes.

When Olivia said no, he ordered a rape kit workup. At least

they would have DNA if the men were ever caught. Not if. When. These guys were toast.

I stopped the patrolmen when they emerged from behind Olivia's curtain. I all but dragged them to the Victor's bed.

"I know who beat him. We have eye witnesses and photos of the attack. The eyewitness called nine-one-one, but the sheriff didn't do anything. Left Victor bleeding on the ground."

"Idiot. He wouldn't arrest someone if a murder was committed under his very nose. This guy was attacked at the ATM?"

"Yes."

"Only one out your way is working. It's in our jurisdiction. Shoulda called us."

"You're right. I would have, but the Habitat volunteers automatically called nine-one-one. Can you come out to our compound? I'll get pictures of Victor's assault." Maybe this would be stopped once and for all.

"Better you come into the station. Talk with Lieutenant Ellsworth."

I promised to do so, shook hands with each patrolman, and watched them settle their flat-brimmed campaign hats snuggly on high-and-tight haircuts.

Johnny and Charlie arrived around six. I gave them an update on Victor and told them about the rape victim. With nothing much more we could do, we went back to the compound. This time, the attackers and the sheriff made huge mistakes. This time we had a witness. Or rather, witnesses. This time, we weren't going to be blown off.

CHAPTER THIRTY-EIGHT

Mississippi, week of November 7

THE NURSE CALLED Whip at three thirty in the morning to say Victor had thrown a pulmonary embolism. Even though the emergency room doctor tried to resuscitate him, death was instantaneous. Whip woke Charlie and me for a strategy session. We met in the Silver Slug, since it was out of earshot of two curious children. Johnny joined us with a pot of coffee. We were unshowered but done with sleep for the night.

"I have to call Victor's wife again." Charlie's thumbs worked her cell.

Johnny reached out before she could punch the dial button. "Let her sleep. No use giving her bad news that can't wait a few hours. She can't change anything."

Ducks returned very early in the morning. "Not much happening in the Quarter." He covered the Jag and joined us in the Slug. "Besides, I'm needed here."

Whip brought him up to speed. While Ducks lacked specific details, he knew the situation had grown worse since he left.

Charlie made the call to the new widow later in the morning. No one from the hospital or the police had told Victor's wife he was dead. Charlie tried to console her as she sobbed. She let the newly minted widow talk about their life together, their two children, and their plans for the future, now changed forever. She hung up and sat with her arms folded in her lap for a few moments. She shook herself.

"No matter how many times you give someone the bad news, you never get used to it." Ducks reached out to take her hand. A brief flash of warmth told me Emilie was awake and tuned into her secret place.

"Odd, how easy it is to fall into television clichés—'I'm sorry for your loss,' 'I know how you feel.' I am sorry for her loss. I do know how she feels, but as the words left my lips, though, I realized how inane they sounded." Charlie raised her half-empty cup to her lips, hands trembling.

"Indeed. When Leslie died, I said the same thing." Ducks rubbed his hand across his eyes.

"Leslie's father lost a son, which you couldn't understand. But you lost your wife, which I doubt his father could understand either." I didn't blink when Ducks stared at me. I kept a neutral expression, but I didn't look away. The feather touched my cheek.

"You know."

"It doesn't matter."

"That's what Em said."

"When we flew to New York, I got bored and Googled your name, like I did before you joined our family. I found Leslie's obituary."

"Old man Ross hated me from the day he met me." Ducks blinked before looking past me.

"Ass. Will you tell me how Leslie died?"

"He had bone cancer."

"He?" Whip asked.

"Ducks's wife," Johnny said.

Whip was silent.

"His death was as ugly as you can imagine. I spent night and day at the hospital at the end, even after Mr. Ross tried to have me thrown out. Fortunately, Leslie and I had taken care of everything before he got sick. We had legal documents filed with the hospital, because he wanted me to make the final decision." The pain in Ducks's eyes brought tears to Charlie's and mine. "His old man threw terrible scenes. Hospital security was forced to ban him. Before he left, he gave me an earful of vitriol. It was my fault Leslie was gay. It was my fault we were a couple. It was my fault Leslie had cancer. He implied I'd given him AIDS, which caused the cancer, and we were covering it up."

"But you didn't."

"It didn't matter. In his eyes, I was a monster who'd corrupted his son." Ducks stared out over the compound. "After Mr. Ross left, I realized I hadn't a frigging clue about what he was going through. After all, he'd lost a son—twice."

"When Frank, my second husband, died, I was pretty certain I knew everything about grief. When Reggie died, I learned something different. Losing three husbands was bad enough, but when Merry died, I was unprepared to wrestle with the loss of a child."

When we rose from the table, Charlie and I put our arms around Ducks's waist. The hug I received in return helped all of us stand straighter. The men put their hands on his shoulders.

By noon the day had turned nasty. Dark, dreary clouds mirrored our collective moods. Work shut down when the rain blew in sideways. Whip paced the schoolroom; Johnny glowered in a corner, a mug of coffee clenched between his large hands. Charlie rubbed her jean-covered thighs.

"Victor's death is a game changer," Ducks said. "We have proof they killed him. The highway patrol will have to do something."

"They're the only ones I trust. They're not elected." Johnny growled. The muscle in his jaw jumped. "The sheriff is."

"What does being elected have to do with upholding the law?" Ducks wiped a spotless countertop with a clean cloth. "Aren't sheriffs bound by the same set of laws as police?"

"They are, but they don't act like police in cities do," Johnny said.

"Sometimes they're great, really fair and balanced in their approach to the law," Charlie said. "Other times they're like that cop in Jack Nicholson's *Chinatown.*"

"Who?" Whip was lost.

"The Nicholson character accused the cops of doing as little as possible to solve crimes when they happened in Chinatown."

"That fits our dear Sheriff Hardy." Johnny set his empty cup on the sink shelf.

"Remember, we gave him the names of the feral teens and the black guys. He didn't do anything. Hell, these guys may be doing the sheriff's dirty work for him." Whip refilled his and Johnny's cups. "In any case, he may be more worried about re-election than putting these thugs in jail."

CHAPTER THIRTY-NINE

Mississippi, week of November 14

WE TOOK A Few days off. I escaped to New York; Whip took the kids to Richmond. We all needed a break. All but Johnny, Charlie, and Ducks. Charlie and Johnny stayed to keep the crews working; Ducks went back to the French Quarter. I returned a day before Whip and the kids.

Even though I was used to the stillness in Mississippi, I couldn't sleep. I missed Emilie's normal night sounds. No pages turning when she read in her bunk, no gentle breaths when she slept on her back. The refrigerator cycling on and off provided a familiar refrain, though, as did the crickets singing merrily away, oblivious to the pain and destruction around them.

Unrecognizable insects offered love songs, crows cawed near dawn, and motorcycles buzzed along on the distant highway like furious bumblebees. They harmonized in a now-familiar background symphony. Traffic on the ancillary roads, like the one where we lived, was local cars and construction vehicles.

And one battered truck with its rotten muffler.

I glanced at my clock the first time I heard the truck travelling westward. Two thirty. That couldn't be good. I rolled over and dozed, my deep sleep shattered for the night. Around four, the truck reversed itself and rolled eastward through pitch-blackness toward the shack where the feral teens hung out. At five thirty, before dawn but not before I was wide awake, the truck backfired its way to the front of our compound, slowed and roared away. I swung my legs out of bed. My cell vibrated with an incoming call.

"Mad Max, something bad has happened," Emilie whispered into the phone.

"If you mean here, I know about the truck. I'm going to look." I pulled on jeans and threw a sweatshirt over my pajama top. I grabbed the flashlight that hung inside the RV's door.

"Don't go alone." Emilie's concern from Richmond rattled me.

"I won't. I'll wake up Johnny and Mr. Ducks."

"Mr. Ducks is already on the move."

I opened the dorm door and stepped into foggy darkness. "I'll call you later."

Lights were on in the school bus. Ducks clattered down the steps and joined me by the Land Rover. I called Johnny, who was on his way.

"I heard the truck stop," was all Ducks had to say.

Even though I pulled the hood up over my head, within seconds, my face and bangs were damp with fog droplets. I shivered as much from anxiety as from feeling clammy.

Three of us, armed with flashlights and one gun tucked in Johnny's waistband, gathered in front of the Rover. I didn't want to waste time returning to the dorm for my revolver. By the time we were halfway to the gate, Charlie and Samson caught up with us. We spread out. Twenty yards outside the gate a dark lump lay at the edge of the road. Johnny reached it first. A body face-down. When it moaned, Johnny rolled it over.

"Shit. It's just a kid." He ran his hands over limbs to see if anything was broken. "Looks like a broken arm."

Ducks knelt in the dust, pulled back an eyelid and shone his flashlight. The boy lashed out and struggled to sit up, but with two men holding him, he couldn't. When Ducks examined the back of the boy's head, his hand came away bloody.

"He's been beaten." Charlie stared at the kid's face which was covered with blood and bruises.

"Does anyone know him?"

This boy, not one of the feral teens, was a light-skinned black. "I've never seen him."

My cell buzzed. I flipped it open and spoke to Emilie while I trotted back to the dorm. I told her what we knew, which was precious little.

"You're going to take him to the hospital, aren't you?" Emilie was worried.

"Yes. I'm not going to call nine-one-one. Sheriff Hardy's not going to waylay us. We'll take the kid to the emergency room before we call the highway patrol."

"You don't know him, do you?"

"No. It's not Spot or Goth Boy. He's black."

"Call Pastor Washington." Emilie ended the call.

I pulled keys off the peg and ran to the Rover. Sampson swung the gate open to let me through. Lights popped on in the tents; men tumbled out of bed. We waved them away before loading the boy into the backseat and wrapping him in a blanket. Charlie climbed in beside him and Ducks sat in front. Johnny stayed behind to talk to the men. I asked him to call Pastor Washington.

Three hours later my two pastors walked into the emergency room. Pastor Washington gripped my hand. "I called Hodge after Mr. Medina called. I thought we should both be here."

"Thank you. The boy's been able to talk a little." I consulted a piece of paper. "His name's Antwan Biggs. Do either of you know him?"

"Antwan's never been in no trouble," said Pastor Washington, "but his brother's the tattooed hulk you seen running around. LeRoy Biggs. LeRoy got hisself kicked out of our local school. He lit out for Biloxi a few years back. Mean as hog spit. You don't want to mess with him."

"Can Antwan tell us what happened?" Pastor Taylor sat on the ubiquitous hard plastic chair.

"He didn't want to do something his brother and some other guys wanted him to do." I folded the paper and put it in my handbag. "He didn't want to kill someone, so they taught him a lesson."

"Some goddamned lesson." Pastor Washington's face darkened. He waved a dismissive hand. "Yes, I know. I swore. Make good with my Lord later."

Pastor Taylor tried and failed to hide a smile. "How bad's he injured?"

All I knew was a broken arm, serious bruising on his torso and face, cracked skull, maybe a concussion. "He said they beat him with a bat."

"Isn't that the same weapon you think was used on the workers? The ones you've found dead?" Pastor Taylor asked.

"Yes. The highway patrol will investigate." I paced the waiting room. "This has gotten out of control. More people are going to get hurt or killed. I don't know how to stop the violence."

"Maybe it's not your job to stop it, Miz Davies." Pastor Taylor watched me pace the emergency room. "Maybe we're all in this together."

"Why did you get up and go lookin' for Antwan? Did someone tip you off?" Pastor Washington lowered himself into a chair beside Pastor Taylor, his bulk overflowing the narrow seat.

"Two things. I heard the battered truck cruise by three times. Once around two thirty, once later, around four. At five thirty, the truck returned, slowed, stopped, and left." I wasn't sure how to explain Emilie's call.

"That's one thing," said Pastor Washington. "What's the other?"

"You may not believe me, but my granddaughter called me from Richmond. She felt something was wrong."

"Felt?"

"Felt. She has a gift where she can sense things happening around her and to the people she loves. I was alone. She sensed danger. She told me to be careful and to call you." I perched on the edge of a chair opposite the two pastors.

"Looks like she was right," Pastor Washington said. "I don't put much truck in all that weird stuff, but if you say it works, I can't say it don't."

"I'm glad Mr. Medina called," Pastor Taylor said. "Maybe we can get Antwan to a safe place. He sure can't stay with his brother any longer."

"Where are his parents? Or, is he another kid who was left

behind and forgotten?" With the social safety nets disrupted by Katrina, could either man find an agency to help?

"More likely the latter, Miz Davies. I ain't seen his momma since before the storm. His daddy's in prison up north somewhere. Been there a long time. Bad family all around." Pastor Washington stood. "Can we see him?"

"He's in the back. They set his arm after they moved him out of the emergency room."

"Is he alone?" Pastor Taylor looked down the hall toward the curtained-off beds.

"Mr. Ducks and Ms. Lopez-Garcia are with him. We didn't want him to wake up from the anesthesia and see nothing but curtains and equipment."

"That was right nice of them." Pastor Washington grunted and pushed himself to his feet.

"One of us has to take charge of this boy, Roland. He can sleep at my place until we find his parents or other relatives."

"Thanks, Hodge. I'll start lookin' for his kin. Maybe young Alex can help." Pastor Washington turned to me. "You're one meddlesome woman, Miz Davies, but your heart's in the right place. I'm in your debt."

"Nothing anyone else wouldn't do." I swallowed hard.

"Kindness can be hard to come by 'round here," Pastor Taylor said. "'Specially from a stranger."

The Mutt-and-Jeff pastors moved down the hall. At least they were talking and working together. It was the tiniest step in the right direction. I flipped open my phone and called Emilie.

I went hunting for Johnny as soon as Ducks, Charlie, and I got back to camp. When I found him lounging under the mosquito netting, I planted myself in front of him, fists on hips.

"What?" Mr. Innocent asked.

"The gun. What gives?" I didn't see it, but I had this morning.

"It's legal, and so am I." Johnny wrapped his arms around me and pulled me onto his lap. "When all this shit started, I went to the highway patrol to see about extending my Virginia concealed carry permit."

"Don't you have to be a state resident?"

"These are extraordinary times. The Department of Public Safety isn't too bothered about residency requirements just now." He hugged me tighter and kissed the tip of my nose. "Besides, someone other than Captain Chaos has to protect you."

CHAPTER FORTY

Mississippi, week of November 14

"AS PASTOR WASHINGTON might say, we got us a mess of trouble here." I walked around the school bus, fingering a couple of Ducks's books. "It's gone way beyond the gang attacking our road crews and beating up a kid. Murder and rape change the entire dynamic."

"It's been bad all along. Did the rape get to you?" Ducks marked a page in his book, set it on a table and laced his fingers behind his head. Joseph Conrad's *Heart of Darkness*. Appropriate choice given the semi-lawless region we lived in.

I fumbled around the bus. I couldn't sit.

"I don't know what's set me off, the rape or the boy's beating. For some reason, the attacks on the workers didn't have the same impact. Even the ones that ended with death." Because I'd seen murder, I compartmentalized it.

"Rape's the most personal attack possible. Women feel stronger about it than men do." Ducks put on the tea kettle to boil. Tea with Ducks at any hour of the day replaced kitchen conversations with Whip. "When one woman is violated, all women are violated."

I sat on the edge of a chair, ready to spring up and pace, given the right impetus. "I admit the attacks spooked me, but the rape more so."

Ducks washed his hands. Symbolic? No, Ducks wouldn't turn away from someone in trouble.

I returned to my dorm to start dinner.

What the heck happened to my dream of sitting back and relaxing and raising my grandchildren without danger? Why couldn't I have peace and quiet? Why couldn't I have a vacation from drama? As I often reminded Alex, life wasn't fair.

###

Johnny and Charlie left together as soon as they cleaned up at the end of the workday. I was busy in the RV when Johnny's truck pulled out of the compound. I looked up in time to see the truck turn toward Gulfport, chased by a billowing dust cloud.

I rubbed each piece of chicken with Cajun spices and piled them on a platter. Emilie was napping when I walked the chicken over to the dinner tent. Ducks and Whip talked next to the grill. I didn't see Alex. Was he in the men's dorm working on his computer or playing a video game?

"Where's Alex?"

"In his dorm, sulking if I guess right." Ducks pulled the tab on a beer.

"What did holy-crap boy-child do this time?" I waved aside the silent offer of a beer. I'd have wine later. I put the tray on the table after pulling the netting closed.

"He decided he doesn't want to study algebra any longer. I reminded him my classroom wasn't a democracy."

Whip laughed. "I'd have paid money to see that confrontation. He loved that, I'll bet."

"Indeed. He called me a dictator." Ducks brought the beer can to his lips but didn't drink. "I gave him a double lesson to finish before classes tomorrow morning."

"All hail the education tyrant." I bowed in mock salute.

"I can't seem to knock it into his head that studying to pass a test isn't education. I want him to learn the material, internalize it. He can't know when something he learns today will be of value tomorrow." Ducks smoothed his beard.

"I, like, totally agree with you." I used one of Alex's favorite phrases.

"Brilliant." Whip borrowed one of Ducks's favorite expressions.

"Where did Johnny and Charlie go?"

"To talk to several road crews." Whip fiddled with the cooking fork before laying it alongside the grill.

"There's more to that statement than meets the eye, Whip Pugh. Give." I planted myself in front of the two men.

"We found a body this morning by the road where we've been working."

"A body? Not another worker." Alarm bells rang in my head. Dumping a corpse near the road was a direct message. The killer didn't worry about getting caught. "Not over in the bayou?"

"Not a worker and not in the bayou. The dead man was a huge black guy with tattoos, but not the one we see all the time." Whip rubbed the back of his neck. "I didn't recognize him."

"Pastor Taylor mentioned a few weeks ago that more men were drifting around the county."

When Whip called the highway patrol instead of nine-one-one, his favorite corporal told him about a group of convicts that escaped while being transferred to a jail out of the hurricane's path.

"Several guys are still on the loose."

"Alex may be right," Ducks said. "The men with the feral teens could have broken out of jail."

I held up one finger.

"I won't mention it," Ducks said.

Whip drained his beer. "No one expected the gang to be this bold."

"My gut tells me they're not afraid of the sheriff," I said.

I opened the hood of the grill and tested the temperature. Almost ready. I put the cooking fork in Whip's hand and returned to the RV to fetch plates and other eating utensils. I made sure Emilie was awake and making the salad. I then checked the kitchen in the men's dorm where potatoes were roasting in the oven.

"Alex, keep an eye on these potatoes, okay?"

No answer.

"Okay?"

I walked over to Alex's desk and shook his shoulder. He jumped half a foot.

"Concentrating on something interesting?" He hadn't heard a word.

"Sorry, Mad Max. I was reading a bunch of news stories about crime in New Orleans and Gulfport. The cops can't stop anything." Alex pointed to a list of headlines from local papers. "Why won't Sheriff Hardy help us?"

"He doesn't want to. We'll make sure everyone's safe." I turned to go. "Hey, weren't you supposed to be studying algebra?"

"Stupid old Mr. Ducks ratted me out, huh?" Alex thrust his chin out.

"You watch your mouth, young man. Mr. Ducks is neither stupid nor old. As your teacher, he deserves your respect. Got it?"

Alex stared at the computer screen. "If you say so."

"I do."

"I liked you better when you were a plain grandmother."

"Huh?" I hadn't been a plain anything since my first husband died. Alex lost me in synapses firing along paths I couldn't follow.

"You used to be fun all the time."

"Since I'm kinda a parent, I'm no longer a Disney World grandmother?" Being a parent again sucked.

"Yup."

"Too late." I ruffled Alex's hair, earning a shrug of annoyance. He hated having his hair messed up, but I always got his attention when I did it.

"I don't want you to think we are living in the Wild West. We talked with the highway patrol. They're monitoring the situation the best they can."

"But if they don't have enough men, what happens if someone else gets hurt?" Alex turned worry-darkened eyes upward. I met his with a conviction I wasn't certain I believed. Unspoken was "what if Charlie gets hurt?"

"We'll be careful."

"Uncle Johnny's carrying his gun. Why can't Dad carry his?"

"Ask him."

I left the boys' dorm and headed back to mine. We needed something goofy to lighten the mood. I ducked into my bedroom, pulled out a Tina Turner T-shirt and a silver wig made from old-fashioned crinkly tinsel. Emilie almost dropped the pitcher of iced tea and glass of wine she was holding.

"When did you start drinking wine, dear child?" I reached for my glass.

"About the time you started wearing goofy wigs. Why should the grownups have all the fun?" Emilie carried the iced tea outside. I followed.

Alex sneaked up behind me. I jumped half out of my skin when he tapped my shoulder. Payback.

"These creeps keep hanging around. I wish they'd go away so I can ride my bike to the park." Alex blew a large bubble and managed to suck it back into his mouth without popping it on his nose.

"I don't want any of us to run around scared, but we should all be extra watchful."

"I bet you could take them all down, Dad." Alex looked at his father with worshipful eyes. If his father was armed, he could shoot the bad guys if they got close.

"I don't know about that, Alex. I'm sure as hell not going to run around waving a gun. Doesn't help." Whip, the man with a large collection of handguns back in Richmond, was reluctant to go around armed in Mississippi.

"Uncle Johnny carries a gun. Why don't you?"

"Would you feel better if I did?" Whip sat on the bench beside his son.

Alex nodded.

"I'll apply for a permit. Okay with you?"

Alex turned to me. "What about you, Mad Max? You're one hell—oops, heck—of a shot."

I hadn't considered applying for a concealed carry permit. "I'll have to think about it. I'm not sure I want to pack heat." Other than in my handbag, that is.

"Don't look at me." Ducks raised his hands in mock surrender. "I know nothing about handguns, but I could protect you from a rabid skeet."

CHAPTER FORTY-ONE

Mississippi, week of November 17

WE WERE HALFWAY through dinner when Johnny and Charlie returned. Charlie sniffed. "Yum, Cajun."

"Any of that left?" Rubbing his hands together, Johnny headed first to the drink cooler and snagged a couple of beers. He tossed one to Charlie.

"Plenty of chicken on the grill."

"Salad's on the table." I pointed to the bowl. "Potatoes are keeping warm in the oven in the boys' dorm."

Whip leaned on his elbows. "So, what did you learn?"

"Do we know if these guys have guns?" Alex butted in, all excited by the prospect of a real-life shootout at the OK Corral. "So far, all they've used is baseball bats."

"Alex! That's enough!" My parent-teacher voice came through loud and clear. "Let them eat first."

"But..."

I raised one finger then folded my hand like a clamshell. Alex shut up. He glared at me and reached for another chicken leg. If he couldn't talk, he could eat.

Johnny put away a beer and a couple of pieces of chicken before he took a deep breath. Charlie wiped her fingers on a napkin and reached for an open wine bottle.

"Okay, this is bigger than we realized. We went to four different camps and talked with several men, as well as with the crew supervisors. Each has men who've been harassed," Johnny said. "Several have been beaten."

Charlie threw her napkin on her plate, her face as red as her Irish hair. "Several groups of black men have been hanging around the work sites and camps. They carry baseball bats, laugh at the men, and talk trash. One even tossed a noose at a bunch of laborers as they finished work."

I topped off my glass before passing the bottle of wine to Johnny. "Pastor Washington's sure the sheriff won't do anything as long as it's Hispanics being targeted. Driving all of us away suits his grand scheme, whatever the heck that is."

"The highway patrol will respond to our calls." Whip shoved his empty plate aside. "They won't tolerate people getting hurt because of their race."

"I don't know, Whip. Racism's deeply ingrained here," Johnny said.

People being targeted because of their heritage reminded me of Rose and her bigotry. I couldn't fix stupid, but I didn't have to turn a blind eye to people breaking the law. Emilie's eyes were on my face. I looked up. She nodded. I was right. She nodded again.

Charlie frowned. "I don't give a shit. I'm going to carry my gun. Let Sheriff Hardy arrest me. Don't think I won't use it if someone's in danger."

Alex grinned. With both Charlie and his dad armed, the bad guys wouldn't stand a chance.

"Have you finished your homework?" I looked for any excuse to get the kids away from the table. I didn't want them overly stimulated.

"We aren't leaving." Emilie Velcroed her butt to the chair. "You'll have to chase us away with a cattle prod."

"Note to self. Buy cattle prod," I pretended to add to a shopping list.

"So, how many missing men?"

Johnny counted on his fingers. "At least eleven."

"That we know about. Again, if we went farther along the highway, we'd find others." Charlie piled her dishes on a tray. "Even the blonds and redheads could be mistaken for Hispanic under hard hats."

"And bike helmets," Ducks added.

"We should assume the missing men are dead, shouldn't we?" Emilie escaped into her secret place.

"Are these hate crimes?" Alex must have been doing a lot of research lately. What did an almost twelve-year-old know about hate crimes?

"Most likely." Whip looked at his son. "They use racial slurs and target a specific demographic."

"Men in my family get stopped all the time just because," Charlie said. "They're not doing anything wrong, but cops pull them over in Texas and Arizona mostly. Check their IDs, bust their chops. and accuse them of having false driver's licenses. Anything they want."

"That is so, like, not fair."

Ah, to have a crush on an older woman. I met Charlie's amused look and smiled.

"Don't worry, Alex. They don't stop me. My red hair's too much of a warning to mess with this angry chick."

"I'd pay good money to see your next run-in with the law." Johnny swung his legs around and leaned against the table.

"So not going to be one. Sometimes, though, they can be downright funny." A few years earlier Charlie had pulled a muscle in her lower back. The doctor told her to use ice packs several times a day. She'd stopped at a convenience store outside Waco for gas and food. Before she got back in her truck, she tucked an ice pack in the back of her pants. About ten miles down the highway a cop pulled her over and demanded to see her concealed carry permit.

"The idiot thought I'd stuck a gun in my waistband. You can't imagine how furious he was when I didn't have a Glock."

"I love it." Johnny howled. "A concealed carry permit for an ice pack."

"His partner will never let him live it down." Charlie stretched, her back creaking in protest.

"How do we stop this?" I wanted the gang broken up, the ringleaders jailed and the rest sent away where they'd be out of our lives. I didn't care what happened to them. I wanted them gone.

"The crew leaders will file complaints with the highway patrol." Johnny twirled his wineglass, the Zinfandel forming delicate spider legs on the sides of his glass.

"Olivia, the woman who was gang-raped, will file charges." I'd stayed in contact with Olivia's friend Caren. "She wants justice."

"*J'accuse.*" Ducks pointed a finger at a phantom only he could see.

"Huh?" Alex said.

"I'll teach you later. After you finish your algebra homework."

"Ah, gee."

"To Alex's point, if these are hate crimes, we need proof for the highway patrol."

"Hate crimes are federal, aren't they?" Alex muttered.

How the heck did he know that?

"Indeed, they are, Alex," Ducks replied.

Shortly thereafter, an extended silence broke the party up. Emilie and Alex divided the dishes and carried trays into the two dorms to fill the dishwashers. Johnny, Ducks, Charlie, and I retired to the bus to continue our discussion, while Whip roamed over to the cook tent to talk with the men. Ducks produced a bottle of sherry for a nightcap.

We talked late into the night, thinking of ways to compile a portfolio of evidence. When I grew tired, I washed my sherry glass. I needed sleep and quiet time, and not in that order. Johnny walked me to the girls' dorm. He held me for a few seconds before kissing me good night.

CHAPTER FORTY-TWO

Mississippi, week of November 21

MORE FREQUENT ATTACKS on the workers, the beating of young Antwan Briggs, Olivia's rape and the murdered black man renewed our urgency in getting the state highway patrol involved. At dinner the following evening, we discussed how to approach the upcoming appointment with the highway patrol. Whip and Johnny wanted a show of force, so Charlie and I worked the phones. We harped on how important it was for everyone with eyewitness facts to join us in Gulfport.

I badgered Olivia. It was harder for her, because she'd have to tell a room full of men about the attack and gang rape. Charlie and I promised to pick her up, drive her to the meeting and bring her home. She wouldn't be the only woman present. Ducks would stay behind with Emilie and Alex, even though he'd been challenged early on by the gang.

###

At Olivia's camp, I used every ounce of persuasion up to and beyond coercion to get her into the Rover. She climbed in the back; her friend, Caren, whom I'd met at the hospital, came along for moral support.

"What's all this?" The desk sergeant glared over a pair of half glasses at the growing assemblage of men and women in clean work clothes standing in front of his desk.

Whip stepped forward and pulled out a battered business card. "We'd like to see Lieutenant Ellsworth, please."

"You got an appointment?" The desk sergeant acted like he had a bad case of indigestion and wasn't in the mood to be hassled. He half-turned away as if to infer we should leave.

"We have an appointment with Officer Kittridge, but I think it would be better if we met with the lieutenant." Johnny moved up beside Whip.

"I just bet you would. I'll call Kittridge." The dyspeptic sergeant picked up a phone and punched in four numbers.

I stood near the back of the group. After an interminable wait, Officer Kittridge opened a door to the left of the desk and stared at us.

"They say they have an appointment with you but want to see the lieutenant. I told them no way."

Officer Kittridge counted the crowd. The door opened and three more men entered. "You'd better call him. We'll use the main conference room."

"He's busy. Said he didn't want to be disturbed."

"Disturb him."

Officer Kittridge led us to a room with a central table and about a dozen chairs. We filed in and settled into chairs or leaned against the wall. I tried to get Olivia to sit, but she preferred to stand next to me. I held one hand and Caren held the other. Olivia trembled. I was afraid she might bolt, but when I shot a glance at her face, her stony expression was adamant. She'd see this through, no matter what.

After a couple of minutes, two men entered the conference room. A tall man with a military haircut led the way, followed by a younger, shorter man in a dark business suit. The tall man looked around, meeting each person's gaze. He paused at Olivia and later at a man I didn't know who stood across the room from me. A flicker of recognition passed between the two. Marines. The stark high-and-tight haircuts were an instant giveaway.

"I'm Lieutenant Evan Ellsworth. This gentleman is Special Agent Kevin Pace from the FBI." The lieutenant turned toward

Whip, who stood in the center of the group a little in front of the rest.

Special agent, huh? Guess we wouldn't have to ask the FBI to get involved. Special Agent Pace could tell us if this was a hate crime. If it was, jurisdiction would pass to the Feds.

"Do you have a spokesman, or should I go around the room?"

"I'll start," Whip began, "since two of my men have been murdered. One is unaccounted for."

"One of my men is dead, three missing."

"Two and two of mine."

"Two and four of mine."

Voices raised around the room. The final count was fourteen dead, nine missing.

"And one gang rape." Olivia's voice cut through the silence like a hot blade through whipped cream.

Whip introduced himself, Johnny, and the general contractor before describing the missing men and the gang responsible for the attacks. He mentioned Antwan's beating and the dead black man. When he finished, Lieutenant Ellsworth looked at Special Agent Pace then back at the group.

"You called Sheriff Hardy first?" The lieutenant asked.

"Fat lot of good that did," said the marine who was standing ramrod straight next to Johnny. "He's glad greasers are getting the hell out of Dodge one way or another."

"Did Sheriff Hardy do anything?" Lieutenant Ellsworth asked.

"Said the men's deaths were accidental, even though their heads had been bashed in. They'd been beaten, too, before being dumped out in the bayou." Johnny supplied details of finding some of the bodies. "I haven't spoken to him since we discovered the second pile of bodies. He left one guy to bleed out after a savage beating out by the ATM."

Other supervisors added more information. The sheriff told all of them to take their dead greasers away before he threw them out for the crows. Two guys in the truck with the rotten muffler threatened several workers.

"The truck belongs to the widow of our first dead worker," Johnny said. "No plates on it, but I guarantee the vehicle identification number will leave no doubt about ownership."

"If these guys are killing your men, they could be dumping bodies anywhere. Hell, we have swamps, bayous, gators, piles of rubble—about every way you can think of to dump a body." Lieutenant Ellsworth said. "All of the missing haven't been found, have they? Why do you presume they've been killed?"

"Plenty of work and good pay. No reason for them to leave without telling us." The marine spoke with a voice full of authority.

"Can you identify them?" Special Agent Pace spoke for the first time. His voice was deeper than I expected because he looked like a round-faced Charlie Brown. "The men in the gang, I mean."

Whip turned to me. "She can."

"Who are you?"

"Maxine Davies, Whip's mother-in-law. They've been hanging around our camp, following us when we go out, and tried to run our teacher off the road."

"Your teacher?"

"My children are with us," Whip said. "Our homeschool teacher was out riding his bike. They asked if he was Mexican and told him to go home. Funny thing is, they left him alone when they found out he was a Brit."

"How did you identify them?" Lieutenant Ellsworth shot a glance to Special Agent Pace.

"Two local ministers, Roland Washington and Hodge Taylor, recognized the leader, a bald black man, with lots of tattoos, as LeRoy Biggs. The older man is J'Marquis Baptiste. Two white boys, Jake Montgomery and Danny Ray, are followers."

"I knew Baptiste was back." Lieutenant Ellsworth shook his head. "He's plain bad news."

"In what way?" Special Agent Pace asked.

"Involved in just about every type of petty crime as a juvie. No sense of right and wrong. Takes whatever he wants from whoever has it. Usually calls the shots, but lets a dupe like Biggs think he's the leader." Lieutenant Ellsworth walked back and forth at the front of the room for a few moments. "A real piece of work is our J'Marquis Baptiste."

"LeRoy beat the crap out of his younger brother Antwan when he refused to take part in an attack and killing." I told the law enforcement officers about driving Biggs to the hospital, where he identified his attackers as his brother and J'Marquis.

"Where's the kid?" asked Lieutenant Ellsworth.

"He's staying with Pastor Taylor until we can find a safe place." I edged forward. "We're certain his brother will come looking for him. No way can he go home."

"Right now, it's your word—or rather, multiple words—against theirs."

"We have photos," I held up my cell phone. Seven more hands lifted cells into the air. "I have copies of photos of the attack on our friend who died in the hospital."

"And DNA," said Olivia.

"I illegally recorded Sheriff Hardy threaten us when we went to claim the first body." I added one more piece of data.

"Illegally? How did you do that?" Special Agent Pace smiled as if he knew the answer.

"Let's say my butt turned on my phone." For a moment, I was downright proud I'd had the sense to record the encounter.

"Doesn't sound illegal to me." Lieutenant Ellsworth brushed aside any concern I might have had. "How about you, Kevin? Anything in the statutes about butt dialing?"

"No, sir." Charlie Brown grinned.

"Kittridge, take these cells and dump them. I want to see what they have. Tell the sergeant to bring in coffee. We're going to be here a while."

The overcrowded room was thick with sweat and dust, but no one seemed to mind. A little discomfort was worth it if the attacks stopped. The desk sergeant brought a coffee urn and a tray of cups. We stood around chatting until Officer Kittridge returned with the photos on a laptop. He projected the images on the least dirty wall. We had multiple pictures of the four I'd identified, including those I'd already seen of Victor's beating. I watched the lieutenant and the FBI agent. I was curious about the picture of the five men I hadn't seen before.

"You're right about their identities, Mrs. Davies." The lieutenant nodded. "I know these boys, except Jake Montgomery. He looks like he's retarded or something."

"Pastor Taylor thinks he has Asperger's." My heart went out to Spot. "He's one of the lost children who roam the outskirts of our camp."

"Lost children, huh? Good description, but I don't see him

with a bat or anything," Special Agent Pace said. "More likely he's a bystander."

"Except, he was there and did nothing to stop the others." The lieutenant was a law-and-order cop.

Could Spot have done anything?

"Corporal, will you go back to the picture of the five men?" Johnny walked closer to the wall. He pointed to one. "Whip, this is the body we found next to the road, isn't it?"

Lieutenant Ellsworth jotted a note. "Not sorry he's dead. He escaped when the storm blew in. Nasty creature. Violent as hell."

Alex was right after all.

"Where are the rest of them?" Johnny asked.

"Back in a different jail," said the lieutenant.

At least we didn't have four more unknown convicts on the loose.

"You mentioned the boys called you names." Special Agent Pace looked around the room.

Voices called out slurs—spic, greaser, Chicano, illegal.

"I don't mind 'Chicano,' but spic and illegal, man, those are offensive," another worker said.

"They told me to go back where I belong," Olivia spoke up.

"Where's that?" Lieutenant Ellsworth added more notes.

"They meant Mexico. I'm from Oklahoma." Many in the room laughed.

"Someone mentioned a rape." Special Agent Pace said.

"I did." Olivia identified Biggs and Baptiste as her rapists. "The nurse did a rape kit and gave it to one of your men who came by to get my statement. They didn't use condoms. You have DNA."

I knew how hard it was for Olivia to speak up in front of about fifteen men. Could I have done it? I hoped so, but I couldn't be sure.

"I have it all on voice mail." Olivia raised her cell. "I called my home number when I realized I couldn't get away."

"Why would you do that?" Special Agent Pace looked skeptical.

"So people like you would believe me." Olivia crossed her arms in defiance.

Special Agent Pace had the decency to look away. His face

reddened. Olivia dialed her number, punched in her code, switched the phone to speaker and glared around the room. Two voices came through clearly.

"Let's do the bitch. She's hot, even though she's a spic."

"Me first."

"Nah. Me first. You get sloppy seconds."

The voices turned into grunts and pants as the two men took turns.

"That's enough." Lieutenant Ellsworth looked sick.

Olivia killed the connection. She handed the phone to the corporal who left to make a copy of the recording. He took my cell as well. Might as well have a copy of my butt dial.

"Your case or mine, Kevin?"

"If I take it, we get them on hate crimes, murder and rape. If you take it, you get them on murder and rape," Special Agent Pace said.

The lieutenant nodded. "Yours. Let's see how those men survive in the federal system. We might have been too soft on them in our local prisons."

"What about the sheriff?" Johnny asked. "We told him about the crimes. Don't forget Max's butt recorded his earliest threats."

"Sheriff Forrest Hardy is one mean polecat." The lieutenant stood, signaling the end of our meeting. "Kevin, time we paid a call on Forrest."

Charlie and I walked Olivia and Caren back to the Rover. "I can't tell you how proud I am of you, Olivia. I don't know if I could have done what you did."

"Hell, I want to castrate the bastards." Olivia climbed in the back with Caren. "I want an HIV test. If I got anything from them, they'll disappear as surely as several of our friends have."

"If they do, no one'll give much of a crap, either." Charlie glared at the bare brick building housing the highway-patrol offices.

CHAPTER FORTY-THREE

New Orleans, week of November 27

JOHNNY AND I went to New Orleans for a weekend. I had to get out of the war zone, eat something I hadn't cooked, and have some us time. Before this adventure began, Raney warned it would be difficult to find privacy when all of us, the kids, Whip and the crew, lived in close quarters. Turned out she was right. Still, Johnny and I got away to Florida or New Orleans for a few weekends.

We checked into the Hotel Monteleone a block off Bourbon Street. It was quieter than the Royal Sonesta, yet it maintained a similar French ambience. The hurricane hadn't damaged the Quarter. Getting rooms was easy because the crowds that normally filled every available bed had yet to return. The front desk staff was almost painfully happy to see us. Even though the rest of the city was a charnel house, the Quarter partied on.

Johnny and I walked along the riverfront and stopped in a small bar for a drink before deciding where to eat.

"I've never had a bad meal here." Johnny sipped a local craft beer.

"Me neither. Let's find an out-of-the-way place tonight. I don't feel like putting up with even the limited crowds at the tourist restaurants." A deep-seated fatigue took over my mind and body.

We found a tiny storefront that served great gumbo in a back alley. Over the spicy stew and cold white wine, we talked about everything except the woes back in the camp. Later, we walked down a side street in the Quarter to a small bar with live music, where Ducks sat in with a group of local blues musicians. We waved, found a table in back, and listened for an hour or so.

We slept late on Sunday, relishing the sun pouring through lacy curtains on our third-floor windows. I stretched my arms over my head, all relaxed and satisfied.

"You know, you used to scare the pants off me." Johnny rolled over, his arm across my bare stomach.

"I must still."

"What do you mean?" He propped himself up on one elbow.

"You're not wearing pants." I kissed his nose.

"You know I love you, pretty lady." Johnny had never said the words, but I had no doubt about his feelings.

"I love you, funny man."

More than liking to be around someone who made me laugh, Johnny was the most comfortable man I'd ever met. We fit together.

"I'm old school. I want to ask you to marry me, but I'm not sure I should." Johnny sat cross-legged on the bed.

"I've always told Eleanor and Raney I was bad luck for husbands." I pushed myself up against the headboard. I pulled the crisp sheet up to my breasts. "I don't want to jinx our relationship by changing it."

"You don't?" He almost, but not quite, looked relieved.

I laughed. "Not every woman needs to be married to enjoy being with her man. Can we stay as we are?"

"If it's all right with you."

"Oh, funny man, did you think I'd dump you if you didn't put a ring on my finger?"

"Well..."

I hit him with a pillow. In an eye blink, we waged a furious pillow fight around the room. We collapsed, laughing too hard to take another swing at each other.

CHAPTER FORTY-FOUR

Mississippi, week of January 9

WORK SLOWED DOWN over the Christmas and New Year's holidays. I spent Christmas with Whip and the kids in Richmond, where we arrived early enough to decorate the house. Johnny joined my family before he flew to New Mexico to see his. Ducks drove to New York, and Charlie went to visit family in Texas. After the holidays, I took the train to New York to hang out with the Great Dames for a few days.

I'd finished unpacking when my cell chirped. Incoming text message. I assumed it was from Emilie since she, Alex, and Whip were on their way back from Richmond.

"Can you come to the Silver Slug?"

Charlie. I texted back and walked over to her Airstream. Johnny opened the door.

"Is there something I should know?" I kissed him on the cheek.

"Yeah." Johnny closed the door behind me.

"I stopped by the manse the day I returned," Charlie said. "I kept feeling edgy all the time I was away."

"Not you, too." Did I have more spooks running around?

"Not like Em, but I couldn't shake the feeling something wasn't right."

"Me too, Max." Johnny held up a bottle of Jack Daniels. I nodded.

They went to the manse together, but Mrs. Sanchez wouldn't open the door. "When we drove off, I could see Marianna peeking out at us. I went back alone the next evening after work. This time, Marianna answered the door and let me in."

I was fairly certain I didn't like where this was going. I steeled myself for the worst.

"It took some wheedling, but Mrs. Sanchez finally told me she and Marianna are virtual hostages. Father Alvarado controls their money. If he finds they've overspent their budget, he cuts it. If he calls and they aren't there, he threatens them."

"Wait a minute. One thing at a time, please." I held up one finger. "He keeps them hostage?"

Johnny had been watching the house. He'd never seen Marianna outside, with or without her mother. Charlie's new information indicated the family lived under threats of punishment.

"Go on." I sipped the whisky, hardly tasting it. I took no pleasure in what was normally my favorite drink.

Charlie wormed her way into Mrs. Sanchez's trust. "Not only does he keep them hostage, he beats and rapes Mrs. Sanchez."

Charlie's trailer was small, but I found room to pace. Was the pastoral and physical abuse what Emilie and I sensed? I wished both she and Ducks were here to substantiate my suspicions. A rush of warmth flowed through me. The feather stroked my cheek.

"What can we do?" I didn't see how we could step in. After all, Mrs. Sanchez was an adult. If she wanted help, she'd have to ask for it.

"Not much for now. We watch and wait." Johnny pulled me into his lap.

"Besides," Charlie said, "we can't intervene. We have no authority."

I wasn't much bothered about lack of authority. I needed to talk with Mrs. Sanchez, though. I'd find a way to help if it were legally and humanly possible. Even if it weren't legally possible. I wouldn't be able to live with myself if anything bad happened to either of them.

"One more thing. We have a convergence of the gang in the truck with the rotten muffler and the Sanchezes." According to Mrs. Sanchez, three days after we left, she heard noises late at night outside the manse. She and Marianna hunkered down in her bedroom. The next morning she found a black man's body on the porch. She called nine-one-one.

"He'd been shot." Charlie finished the recap.

I shivered. Bats and guns, hostages and rapists—it was too much to comprehend. Johnny walked me back to the dorm.

"Stay the night. I don't want to be alone." I leaned against his sturdy chest.

Emilie had no sooner entered the dorm than she demanded to go and see Marianna. If she could spend some time with her, I could ask Mrs. Sanchez if they were all right.

I pulled into the drive in front of the manse behind a dusty Cadillac. Odd. I hadn't seen any cars besides Mrs. Sanchez's ancient beat-up Toyota. She always parked behind the church. I rang the bell. Footsteps approached the door. A man answered.

"What do you want?"

Heck of a greeting. Was this the missing Father Alvarado? He wasn't wearing his collar, so I wasn't certain. He compromised my personal space by looming over me, but I refused to retreat. I matched his attempt at intimidation with determination.

Emilie stepped between us, stubborn chin thrust forward. "I'd like to see Marianna, please."

"Who are you?"

I introduced Emilie.

"She's busy. Go away."

Before he shut the door, Mrs. Sanchez appeared in the background. She shook her head, pleading with me to leave without asking any questions. I nodded ever so slightly. I put my hand on Emilie's shoulder when the door slammed behind us and steered her toward the Rover.

"Yuck," Emilie whispered.

I gripped her shoulder a little tighter. It didn't take a psychic or a sensitive to see something was wrong. Even dense old me understood.

"Mrs. Sanchez and Marianna are terrified. If that's the priest, he's not nice. I don't like him."

"Me neither."

"It's a good thing you didn't shake his hand." Emilie hopped into the front seat and stared out the window.

"Why?" I gunned the engine and pulled to the end of the drive. The man who killed my daughter had a clammy handshake. I'd ignored the signs when he began manipulating her. Similar neon warnings flashed in front of me. This man, too, was evil.

"He's ice cold. You could've gotten frostbite."

Before I turned into the road, I glanced over my shoulder at the house and glimpsed Marianna's pale face peeping from a side window. She looked scared to death. Painful memories pushed into my brain even though I wanted them to stay gone.

CHAPTER FORTY-FIVE

Mississippi, week of January 9

MY PHONE RANG late one afternoon. Caller ID revealed Pastor Taylor's name.

"Hello?" I'd learned the hard way not to open with "Hi, Pastor Taylor." He considered it rude. I was rude enough without trying.

"Miz Davies, it's Hodge Taylor."

"How are you this afternoon, Pastor?"

"I'm fine. And you?"

"I'm well. What can I do for you?"

Outside the kitchen window pickup trucks returned from a day's work, brown-gray dust clouds enveloping the scattered convoy. Between six and six thirty, workers trickled back to line up for showers first, dinner second. I wiped grit from the countertops in my never-ending battle to keep the kitchen clean. Flat dust smells blended with tomato and garlic from the chicken cacciatore bubbling in the slow cooker.

"It's more what I can do for you. Thought you'd like to know Father Alvarado drove off."

I had mentioned my concerns about the manse. Not that I really knew anything at the time, but my gut churned whenever I recalled my encounter with Father Ice Cube. I couldn't tell Pastor Taylor about my gut, so I asked him to let me know if he saw the priest leave.

"I don't rightly know the man," Pastor Taylor said. "I may have spoken to him a time or two."

Odd that the three religious leaders didn't interact. I said as much.

"I've watched him off and on for four years, ever since he came to St. Anna's. As far as the woman and child are concerned, I've only seen them together in a car."

Could I reach out to Mrs. Sanchez? "Are you certain he's not running errands?"

"I don't think Father Alvarado runs errands. Besides, he went north. When he leaves for a month, he always heads north. Must have another congregation up there, if you Catholics have congregations." Pastor Taylor chuckled.

"We do."

"Why are you worried about that family?" Pastor Taylor had never asked before.

"Trouble's brewing." I folded the towel and laid it next to the sink. "Emilie feels it too."

I told him about the dead man on the porch.

"I heard sirens right around Christmas. I'm ashamed to say I never checked up to see if they needed help. Do you know I've never spoken to either the mother or the child?" Pastor Taylor sounded as puzzled as I was. "I'm not sure when they moved here."

"That doesn't surprise me. They aren't allowed to leave the manse except to go to the store." I rubbed the back of my neck like Whip did when he was worried or stressed.

"What do you mean, not allowed to leave?"

"The priest controls their movements, even when he's not here. Ms. Lopez-Garcia met with Mrs. Sanchez who confirmed they are practically hostages."

"That's not right. That poor child never gets outside. I'd like to see her at the park once it's done."

"Pastor Taylor, the Sanchezes may have problems the park can't fix."

"I've never been comfortable around Father Alvarado. I tried to be friendly, but my efforts were rebuffed." The pastor sounded sad. "Are most priests as, how do I say this politely, unfriendly to pastors?"

"Not at all. My family priest had dinner every week with local ministers and rabbis to see how they could work together to help the greater Richmond community. Father Alvarado's an exception." I gazed outside, no longer able to focus on billowing dust clouds. Warmth flooded me, and a feather brushed my cheek. I wasn't alone.

"Please let me know how I can help."

My hand hurt from clenching my cell. I hoped I didn't crack it. My next mission was to find out what the heck was going on. Emilie, Ducks, and I knew something was wrong. We didn't have a name for it. Yet.

At mid-morning the next day, I presented myself at the manse. All fancied up in one of the three dresses I'd brought with me from New York and with some of Ducks's scones on a plate, I went a callin'. The porch was unchanged. Still no sign of life, but someone had updated the church message board with information about the next service four weeks off. Outside of that, the place looked abandoned.

I steeled myself and rang the doorbell. I waited. And waited. And waited. The door opened a crack. Marianna's frightened eyes widened as she peered around me. She wadded the hem of her T-shirt.

"I'm alone."

She started to close the door but changed her mind and opened it wide enough to let me slip inside. She locked the dead bolt behind me.

I'd been in the living room once before, but much was different. A throw pillow lay on the floor, its innards strewn across the messed-up rug. A chair was tipped on its side next to a table. The contents of an ashtray had spilled across an end table and onto the floor. Drapes shut out most of the light, except for a three-inch sliver in which dust motes swirled and danced. Darkness failed to disguise the room's disarray.

"Is—is Father Alvarado back?" Mrs. Sanchez called down the hall, her voice tight.

When she realized it was me, she stopped mid-step; her shoulders sagged. She walked into the living room, set the chair upright and slumped into it. Even though she ducked her head, I saw a fresh bruise on her cheek that stood out like an overripe plum. One eye was half-shut.

I handed Marianna the scones and nudged her toward the kitchen. She went without protest. I sat for several long silent minutes opposite Mrs. Sanchez.

"Do you trust me?"

Her eyes filled with tears. "Yes."

She turned toward the window. The sun didn't penetrate the gloom indoors. Like the coverings on the window, Isabella had pulled drapes across her heart.

"He hit you, didn't he?"

Isabella nodded.

"Why?"

"I refused to do something he wanted."

"What?"

Isabella's voice was so soft I almost missed what she said next. "He told me to send Marianna to his room. I couldn't."

I leaned forward, my elbows on my knees. I reached out and held her trembling hands. She didn't pull them back like Merry had after her accident. Deep finger prints on her upper arms left leopard-like spots on the delicate skin. She'd been restrained by someone much stronger than she was.

"I hoped he'd wait until Marianna was older, but he's so insistent." Tears filled Isabella's eyes. "I don't know if I can protect her much longer."

"Wait for what?"

A specter from my past wavered in front of me. Junie. I tried to chase her back where she belonged, but she refused.

"I'm linked to what's happening to Marianna," the memory whispered before the image faded.

"Do you remember when you said Marianna needed a bra? That she was growing into a beautiful young lady?" Isabella stared at her stained, wrinkled skirt.

"I do. And she is." I stroked the back of her right hand. Two knuckles displayed fresh scrapes. Had she fought Father Alvarado? "You said you didn't want her to grow up. What did you mean?"

"Father Alvarado wants her. He came back early and caught

us going through her clothes. I tried to make him think she wasn't, um, ready."

"Ready?"

"She's a woman. She started her monthlies. That's why I can't protect her anymore."

"He wants her? Sexually?" I tasted bile and swallowed hard. Heat burned my face.

"He was very angry. He tore the shirt off her back. She didn't have a bra on. He could see how developed she is."

"He has no right to look at your daughter, naked or not. He's a priest, for God's sake." My voice rose. I released Isabella hands, afraid I'd hurt them. I tucked a lock of long, dark hair behind her ear. "No man has that right."

"He does. It's our way."

Isabella's family had long sent excess girls to the Church when there wasn't enough food. Several generations back, they became nuns. Somewhere along the line, some girls became servants of the Church instead. Most were normal household servants, cooking and cleaning for the priests. Others, like Isabella, became sexual servants. Her mother and grandmother lived in the church, doing whatever they were told and bearing children. Boys were adopted out; girls weren't. The priest wanted to initiate Marianna into the same kind of service.

"What he wants to do is illegal and immoral. He should go to prison for a long time." I forced myself to sit still. My natural inclination was to pace and rant, but if I moved, I'd spook Isabella.

"It's not a sin in our world."

"It is in any world. He can't touch you against your will. He can't touch Marianna."

Charlie was right about the priest keeping her hostage. Priests having sex wasn't a shock. It had been going on since the beginning of time. But enslaving a woman? Weeks earlier, Ducks and Johnny speculated about the "de Jesus" extension of Isabella's last name. Did the "child of Jesus" contain a darker connotation than illegitimacy?

"Are you free to leave? Go someplace where Father Alvarado can't find you."

Isabella shook her head. "I have no place to go."

"If you did, would Father Alvarado let you leave?"

Isabella shook her head again.

Father Alvarado committed at least two major crimes: rape and slavery. Keeping a woman against her will was slavery. The mere fact Isabella wasn't free to leave would keep the bastard in prison for a very long time. He'd struck the mother. He raped her. With the child now his target, who knew how many more crimes he'd commit? If the church hierarchy knew...

I wasn't going down that rabbit hole.

"How long has this been going on?"

"With Father Alvarado?"

The question shocked me almost, but not quite, into silence. "Have other priests done this to you?"

"Marianna's father is a priest."

"This has to stop before anything happens to Marianna."

"I don't know what to do."

"Do you want to move into the compound?"

"He'll just find me. It would be worse than ever."

"Well, he won't be back for a month. I promise to find a way to protect both of you. I don't know how, but I will."

I hugged her at the door. When she looked up, a familiar pleading filled her eyes. I knew that look. I'd seen it too often. Years earlier when I was a child, I'd seen that same look in my younger sister's eyes. I hadn't been able to help Junie then, but I could help Isabella now. She leaned into me for support. She would trust me to stop the abuse. I was sick by the time I reached the car. How could this ice-cold man of the cloth keep a woman for sexual gratification? I gulped, stopped the car, and left my breakfast steaming in the dust beside the roadway.

CHAPTER FORTY-SIX

Mississippi, week of January 9

I SPENT DAYS in a whirlwind of activity. I worked out, rode my bike with Emilie, cooked and cleaned the dorms. I meditated for calmness and over-caffeinated myself to keep going. No matter how much energy I expended, I couldn't shake the revolving images of Junie and Marianna. Like a spinning disco ball, two faces danced at the periphery of my vision. Three, if you counted Emilie, who never uttered a word.

Part of me wanted to beat the crap out of Father Alvarado. Part of me wanted to smuggle Isabella and Marianna out of the manse under the cover of night and get them out of Dodge. But where would they be safe? Not in the compound. Even with an armed guard, we weren't going to shoot a priest.

Had I made a promise I couldn't keep? I was adrift. I needed a witness protection program.

I peeled an apple, took half to Emilie in the school bus and walked outside. Caws pierced the empty air. Not one had the answer. Ducks walked from the boys' dorm to the bus. He raised an eyebrow in passing. I shook my head ever so slightly. The feather brushed my cheek.

#

During the following nights, I wrestled with nightmares and thrashed myself awake. Too often I awoke drenched in icy sweat. If this didn't stop soon, I'd be washing sheets and pajamas every day.

I fussed with calling the highway patrol and turning Father Alvarado in, but I had no proof. I was fairly certain Isabella would deny she was raped and abused. No way would I turn to the church. Who knew if it hadn't moved him from parish to parish like it had during the pedophile scandals? It could have known about his exploits but kept them quiet to avoid more notoriety.

I couldn't take Isabella and Marianna to New York. The city alone would leave them quaking on the curb, the target of passing bicycle messengers and self-important pedestrians. Besides, they didn't have two quarters to rub together.

I prayed the nightmares would end. They didn't. One night after a particularly terrifying dream, I lay twisted in my sheets, panting as if I'd biked twenty miles uphill. A tiny tap sounded at my door.

"Yes?" I tried to keep my voice steady. I needn't have bothered. If I'd woken Emilie, she would know I wasn't normal.

"It's me. May I come in?"

No matter how much I wanted to say "no," I couldn't. "Come on in, dear child."

Emilie climbed into bed and pushed pillows around until she was comfortable. She rested her head on my shoulder, her arm across my stomach.

"Don't you feel well?" I put a hand to her forehead. Cool.

"I'm fine. You're not."

Well, what did I expect? I lived with a sensitive. The stronger my emotions were, the more she felt. Why I thought I could hide from her, I'd never know. I wanted to protect her, but I must have been broadcasting at ear-splitting decibels to wake her.

"You're right. I feel rotten." Sometimes it was nice to have someone with her special gift to help make sense of the monsters under the bed. Other times it was downright spooky.

"You've been having nightmares since you talked with Mrs. Sanchez."

Emilie picked at a speck of lint on the coverlet, rolled away from me and dropped it into a trash basket.

"I'm sorry I woke you. I try to be quiet." I didn't like depriving Emilie of sleep any more than I liked showing my weakness.

"As if you could keep me from knowing." Emilie wiggled deeper into the pillows.

"I haven't talked about it, because I don't have a clue what to do." I sighed.

"It's about Marianna and Mrs. Sanchez, isn't it?"

"Kinda."

"So, it's not totally about them." Emilie had a tiny bead of sweat on her upper lip. She'd slipped into her secret place where I couldn't follow. "Father Alvarado's dangerous. He's had sex with Mrs. Sanchez and Marianna."

"Not yet. Not with Marianna. I have to get them away before he can touch her."

"Can you?" Emilie's muscles tensed. "Get them away?"

"I'm not sure how."

"We can help."

"Who's we?"

"Mr. Ducks, Dad, Uncle Johnny, and me. That's the 'we.' Oh, I almost forgot Charlie."

"Not Alex?"

"Holy-crap boy-child would send Dad and Charlie in with guns blazing."

My lips twisted in a grin I didn't feel. "Might not be such a bad idea."

"Might not work, either. Let us help. Please."

I wanted to cry. My thirteen-year-old granddaughter was wise beyond her chronological age. After Merry's funeral ended and the mourners departed, Eleanor reminded me I had a family and a community of friends to lean on. I didn't have to do everything myself. I had the same family plus a new group of local supporters. I needed their help.

"Okay."

"Pinky swear?" Emilie held up her little finger. Time for our age old unbreakable oath.

I hooked mine around hers. "Pinky swear."

Emilie disentangled herself from the pillows. "I'll go back to bed now."

I kissed her.

She turned around in the doorway.
"Who's Junie?"

CHAPTER FORTY-SEVEN

Mississippi, week of January 9

NO SOONER HAD Emilie closed my bedroom door than the parade of monsters began. Marianna and Junie rolled over and over until one superimposed herself on the other. Father Alvarado high-fived Uncle Phil. Mother and Mrs. Sanchez wrung their hands and wept. Other observers, Pastors Washington and Taylor, my brothers Sam, Carl, and Dan, hovered in the periphery of my vision, neither acting nor reacting to the maelstrom at the foot of my bed.

For Emilie to get a good night's rest anytime soon, I had to double-dog dare the monsters to leave us alone. The only way to do that was to face the truth. I'd buried what happened to us so deep it would take a magnitude-nine earthquake to shake my memories loose. Marianna's terrified expression morphed into Junie's silent pleas for help.

I turned on the reading lamp. Better confront what gave me nightmares in the light. Not that I couldn't do it in the darkness, but light robbed the monsters of their ability to lie. I pushed myself up on the pillows Emilie had so thoughtfully plumped and reached for my pen and my journal. I began at the beginning with my baby sister, Junie, and the bad things that happened to her and to me.

Ours was a normal sized farm family, five brothers before me, two of whom died in infancy. I was four when Junie showed up. To say she surprised my parents was an understatement. Mother already had too much work to do with four children, a husband and a farm to help run. Much as she loved her last child, she'd rather not have had the responsibility.

As soon as the boys were old enough, they worked with Daddy around the farm. We all had chores. I gathered eggs from the hen house daily. I hated it because one old biddy was downright mean. She pecked the heck out of my hand when I reached in the nest. Wouldn't you know it? She was the best layer of all.

Once we had a new baby in the house, my responsibility was to feed her. I loved my sister from the moment Mother and Daddy brought her home. She was so tiny.

"You're a big sister." Mother told me it was my job to protect Junie and keep her safe.

I took my new role as seriously as only a four-year-old could.

Junie delighted in life itself. Oh, sure, she did all the normal baby things. She cried when she was hungry or wet. She spit up on all of us, but she never fussed "just because." Junie was born to be adored, and we were her willing fan club.

When I was ten and Junie six, Daddy was out plowing the upper pasture when his tractor hit a hidden root and flipped over backward. He landed on his head and was never normal again. At first, he couldn't stand, walk, or talk. Mother made me feed him when he couldn't even raise his arm.

"Why do I have to feed him?"

"Because I'm too busy." Mother was a perpetual motion machine moving around the kitchen.

My oldest brother, Sam, tried to run the farm, but an eighteen year old couldn't do all the work himself and stay in high school. Even with my other two brothers, Carl and Dan, he needed help in the fields. We faced selling our milk cows when Daddy's sister, Helena, and her husband, Phil, moved into my grandparents' house half a mile down the road. Grandpa worked the adjacent farm; Uncle Phil helped Sam, Carl, and Dan with ours.

After a year, things got better. With Uncle Phil's hard work, we increased the size of our herd and sold milk and eggs for extra cash. Daddy improved a little and recognized his family, but he couldn't walk from his bed in the living room to the front porch without help. He never spoke, but I knew he understood what was going on around him. When I asked him a question, he blinked once for "yes" and twice for "no." His facial muscles regained some movement, too, so he could change his expression a little.

"He's getting better," I told Mother one day.

"No, he's not. He's never going to get better. Stop fooling yourself."

Mother had to be wrong, because sometimes he gave a flicker of interest when I tied his bib around his neck, fed him dinner, and chattered about my classes. Even though I was still a child, I knew he'd never be like he'd been, but inside he was still Daddy.

Once Uncle Phil handled the heavy work with Sam, Mother helped me care for Daddy. When she was old enough, Junie had her chores. She fetched the eggs and got pecked by one of the offspring of the original old biddy.

Junie and I shared a bedroom, like my three brothers. Right before the accident, I talked Daddy into painting the walls a buttercup yellow and the woodwork creamy white, the same color as our beds and chests of drawers. Wrapped up in flower petals, our bedroom was our private haven until one night when we had a big barbecue.

Uncle Phil and my brothers finished baling and stacking the last of the summer's hay. We'd have enough to feed the herd all winter. My whole family came over to celebrate. Grandpa roasted a pig in a pit, and we ate until we were stuffed. The men drank too much beer.

Late that night, Uncle Phil staggered down the hall. I thought he was lost because he lived down the road with my grandparents. I started to ask him why he was in our room when he shushed me. He shut the door behind him, knelt beside my bed, and put his hand under the covers. I shrank away, but when his hand touched me between my legs, I squealed and thrashed hard enough to throw the covers on the floor.

Uncle Phil tried to pin me down by putting his rough hand over my mouth and climbing on top. His breath stank of stale cigarettes and beer. I squirmed and tried to wiggle out from under him. He wouldn't let me go, so I kicked as hard as I could between his legs. He gasped and slapped me. I kicked at him until he jumped off my bed and left the room, hands between his legs.

I had to do something, tell somebody. The next night Mother and I were alone in the kitchen while we cleaned up after dinner. I wiped a plate and told her what Uncle Phil tried to do to me.

"Don't you dare lie about your uncle." Mother's face turned dark red. She slapped me. "He's helping us. I need him."

I put the plate away, tears running down my face. I turned my back on my mother, even though she continued to yell at me. She grabbed my arm, spun me around and shook me as hard as she could, all the time whispering, "Don't you dare tell anyone. If you do, I'll make sure no one believes you."

I ran through the living room where Daddy lay on the couch. He must have heard the argument, because tears soaked his cheeks and drool bib. I didn't stop. He couldn't comfort me any more than he could prevent what Uncle Phil did to me. I hid in my room with Junie.

For weeks, strange night sounds woke me. The creaking screen door sounded nothing like crickets. Neither did the stealthy footsteps in the hallway that continued to Mother's bedroom. One night thumping came from her bedroom. After a groan, the thumping stopped. Uncle Phil was in the bedroom with Mother. I ran to the bathroom and threw up.

I set my pen aside. My hand cramped to my shoulder. I looked at the monster mob. Junie and Marianna separated, one relieved her story was known, the other terrified because hers had yet to play out.

"I couldn't protect you, Junie," I whispered. "I'm so sorry."

"But you can protect Marianna," the ghost of childhood past said.

Junie smiled and faded into the shadows. Marianna followed, glancing over her shoulder, her eyes pleading.

"I will protect you, Marianna. I promise."

CHAPTER FORTY-EIGHT

Mississippi, week of January 9

I READ WHAT I'd written, hoping to find an excuse to stop. No such luck. No matter how much I wanted to sleep, the monsters were in control. I swung my legs out of bed and stared at the creatures waiting to be banished. Or to win if I quit.

"Don't you dare go anywhere. I'll be back after I pee."

I returned to bed with an empty bladder, a glass of water and two of Emilie's peanut butter cookies.

On Junie's birthday, Uncle Phil came into our room and went to Junie. He stood next to Junie's bed and unzipped his pants.

"You leave her alone."

"Don't say anything." Junie turned her face toward the wall.

"How are you going to stop me? If you say anything, I promise I'll hurt her."

After he left, I crawled into Junie's bed and held her while she cried herself to sleep. He'd ruined her birthday.

I sought out Sam in the milking barn the next afternoon. Under normal circumstances, I loved the barn. The cows smelled warm and grassy; the barn smelled of fresh milk and cow poop. This day I didn't pay any attention. I couldn't keep the fear inside any longer. I told Sam what Uncle Phil did to Junie, but he didn't believe me. He knew about Mother and Uncle Phil.

"You don't know how badly Mother needs Uncle Phil to run the farm." Sam pushed a cow toward the opening that led to the back pasture.

"Bad enough to let him touch Junie where he shouldn't?" My anger rose along with my voice.

"You're lying. Mother warned me you were spreading tales about him." Sam released the last cows from the automatic milkers. He walked past me without looking at my tear-streaked face.

When Daddy died, I had no one but myself to rely on. I'd told my family, but no one would do anything to stop Uncle Phil. I comforted my baby sister as best I could.

Two weeks after my fifteenth birthday, Uncle Phil came in from the barn and wanted a glass of cold water. I got up from the kitchen table where I did my homework, too afraid to study alone in my room. When I handed him a glass of water from the pitcher in the refrigerator, he grabbed me with a grimy, nicotine-stained hand.

"I warned you if you told anyone, I'd hurt Junie. You told your mother. She believed me over you. Time for Junie to pay." He shook his fist before he went back outside.

I promised myself if he ever touched Junie again, I'd stop him. I didn't know at the time Aunt Helena had thrown him out of Grandma's house because of his relationship with Mother. I begged her and Grandma for help, but Aunt Helena cried and Grandma pressed a knuckle to her lips.

The last time Uncle Phil tried to have sex with Junie was the last time he tried it with anyone in our family. I hid a kitchen knife under my mattress in case I needed it. Mother went to bed early with a migraine.

Uncle Phil came into our bedroom wearing nothing but underpants, stripped them off and threw them on the floor. He tore at Junie's sheet, pushed her nightgown up to her chin and climbed on top. I could smell his rank sweat across the room.

He clamped a rough hand over Junie's mouth and tried to push himself inside. I reached under the mattress and grabbed the knife. Before he could penetrate Junie, I stabbed him in the butt. Uncle Phil bellowed.

Sam threw the door open and switched on the overhead

light. The blood on Junie's face, the knife in Uncle Phil's ass, and the blood on the sheets proved I hadn't been lying. Mother came in, screamed, and fell to the floor.

Sam dragged Uncle Phil outdoors. In the front yard, the two men, one naked and bleeding, the other in pajamas, slugged it out. I ran at Uncle Phil and head-butted him in the stomach. The knife was no longer in his butt, but I didn't care. I hit him where I'd stabbed him hard enough to make him scream.

Sam pounded the older, larger man, leaving his face swollen and bloody. Uncle Phil yelled loud enough to bring the neighbors at a run. He fell face down in the dirt. Sam and I kicked him in the ribs, our bare feet adding to Uncle Phil's humiliation. The neighbors ran him out of town that very night.

"Now you've done it. Who's going to work the farm?" Mother blamed me for Uncle Phil's behavior.

Sam loomed over Mother. "She told you what he was doing to Junie. She told me too. We didn't want to believe her."

Sam balled his fists. Dan and Carl pushed him into the house to calm down. They left me with Mother and the neighbors. One by one, the neighbors drifted home.

"I hope you're satisfied, young lady. If we lose the farm, it'll be your fault." Mother hissed accusations as she dragged me into the living room. She slammed the door and turned the dead bolt for the first time in my life, locking me in, not Uncle Phil out.

Junie withdrew. The bubbly little girl who'd clapped at sunbeams and danced with dandelion pompoms stopped smiling. Maybe she'd stopped earlier, and I hadn't noticed. Over the next few weeks, she lost weight. Her collarbones and shoulder blades almost poked through her skin. When I held her, I could count every vertebra, every rib.

The walls of our once-safe yellow room had faded to an ugly tan, blotched with brown water spots from the leaky roof over the window. Even with Uncle Phil gone, I hated our room.

I tried to talk to Junie, but she refused to say anything for the longest time. When she could no longer keep the poison inside, she confessed Uncle Phil had hurt her down there when he climbed on top of her. I'd promised to protect her, but I hadn't.

That year flu struck harder and lasted longer than anyone could remember. All of us got it. We ran fevers, ached horribly and coughed our lungs out. Junie was the sickest. She went from flu to pneumonia. Within two weeks, Junie slipped away in the middle of the night. I held her when she left. I kissed her forehead and prayed to God to take care of her. That was the last time I prayed to anyone.

That was Junie's story.

Uncle Phil and Mother were gone.

"Isabella, we'll find a way out. I promise. I'm older than when Junie died. I can do much more to protect you and Marianna."

Isabella faded into a dark corner of the room.

A derisive snort got my attention. Father Alvarado's alter ego sneered.

"You've pissed off the wrong woman, you bastard."

I dragged myself out of bed around four and turned on a pot of coffee. Within minutes, Emilie jumped down from her bunk, poured, and sat opposite me at the breakfast table.

"Well?"

I handed her my journal and went to take a shower.

CHAPTER FORTY-NINE

Mississippi, week of January 9

"LET ME SEE if I have this right. You blame yourself for what happened to Junie." Emilie sat with my journal open on the table in front of her. She tapped a page.

"I do." I walked barefoot into the kitchen, a towel wrapped around my head. "I've never forgiven myself for not being able to protect her.

"You were a kid. You tried to help, but no one would listen." Emilie leaned back, arms folded across her chest.

"I wish I could have figured out how to get Junie away. Maybe she would have been okay." What was my center color?

"Darker pinky-orange than usual."

"Okay."

"You told your mother, right?" Emilie sipped her coffee, steam rising around her face. "When she called you a liar, she betrayed you."

"Mother couldn't admit to what was going on inside her house. She sold us out when she began sleeping with Uncle Phil."

I stared at the clock on the microwave. Could I make it run backward? Could I make things right for Junie at last? The second light mocked me by blinking; the minute number moved relentlessly ahead. Guess not.

"Now I get why you're worried about Marianna. She reminds you of Junie." Emilie walked to the counter to refill our coffee cups. She poured a glass of orange juice. Too early for either of us to want breakfast. My throat was so tight I couldn't have eaten anything solid if I tried.

"She does."

"Is this what you meant last year about schizophrenic childhoods?" Emilie peeled a banana and broke off a bite.

"Partly. My childhood was great until Daddy got hurt. When Uncle Phil showed up, it turned dreadful." I stole a bit of Emilie's banana. "It was never good again, even after Sam ran Uncle Phil off. I couldn't trust my mother."

"Mine was great until Mom's accident, then it stunk after she was murdered." Emilie handed me more of her fruit.

"And now?"

"Now it's great. I love being here with you." We finished the banana in silence.

Emilie flipped to a page in the journal. She pointed to a pair of monsters. "Why do you link Mrs. Sanchez with your mother? She's frantic to protect Marianna. Could she be a victim like Junie, just older?"

Was Emilie right? Was Mrs. Sanchez a victim or a monster?

"If she does nothing and allows evil to happen, like your mother did when you warned her about your uncle, I'd agree, but I don't think she knows what to do." Emilie was way too serious for her age. Again. "Stop beating yourself up. You can't change what happened in the past. What can we do to protect Marianna? And Mrs. Sanchez?"

Why had Emilie added Mrs. Sanchez almost as an afterthought instead of including her in her first statement? I got up to top off our cups, killing the pot. I held it up in a silent question: should I make more? Emilie held out hands that shook from a caffeine high. Better not.

"You have some ideas, don't you?"

"Not yet. But I'm working on it." I hugged Emilie.

"Let me know when you figure out what you've already decided."

"I wish I knew what you think I've decided."

#

I carried my last cup of coffee into my bedroom and shut the door. I was too exhausted to think straight and too wired to sleep. No one liked confronting failure. Nothing Emilie said could ease my belief I hadn't protected Junie. In spite of the caffeine burning through my body, I lay on the bed and closed my eyes.

The last thing I heard was Emilie whispering into her cell in the hall outside my door. "She's totally broken." A long pause. "I'll leave her to heal."

CHAPTER FIFTY

Mississippi, week of January 9

WHEN I WOKE again around noon, Emilie hummed in the kitchen where she fried bacon for BLTs. I was totally trashed, my mind too fatigued to work, my body toxic from too little sleep and too much caffeine.

"Smells yummy." I sniffed, surprised at how hungry I was.

"Sit."

Emilie set glasses of milk and orange juice on the table. I snatched a piece of bacon and did as I was told.

"Aren't you out of class early?" I found time to be the disciplinarian, even if I didn't feel like it. I inhaled the bacon in three bites.

"I started class at six, remember. Mr. Ducks let me out." She slid a plate onto the table. "He drilled us on English grammar all morning."

"Sounds dull."

"It wasn't, really. He makes even routine stuff fun." Emilie shook her head. "My brain feels like it's had a double shot of espresso, though."

"Still wired?"

"Du-uh."

We bit into sandwiches and chewed in silence. Halfway through lunch, Emilie said she'd shared some of what I told her with Mr. Ducks—"Not your journal, though. It's on my bunk."

"He already knew most of it, didn't he?" I bit into a spear of dill pickle. Juice trickled down my chin.

"Some. He doesn't know the details, but he gets the connection between Junie and Marianna better after last night."

"He didn't sleep much either, did he?"

"Nope."

Having a second spook around comforted me. I hesitated to tell Johnny things Ducks and Emilie knew because I didn't know how he'd handle them. Besides, what happened to Junie was ancient history, but I'd need Ducks's support before this mess worked itself out. I'd need Johnny and Whip and Charlie too.

"Anyway, I'm done for the day." Emilie slugged back half a glass of milk. "We're going to do a makeover."

"You just streaked your hair purple. What color do you want to add?" I loved Emilie's ever-changing hair color, even if her father didn't. I never knew what she'd do on any given day.

"Not me. You."

"Me?"

Since I'd been overwhelmed by my monster attack the night before, I could be forgiven for forgetting the two pastors were coming over late in the afternoon for an update on the park. Wiped my memory card completely clean. I was shocked when Pastor Taylor called to say they were on their way. Emilie carried fresh-squeezed lemonade and cookies to the bus. Pastor Washington pulled into the compound seconds before Pastor Taylor.

"Hodge." Pastor Washington held out his hand.

"Roland." Pastor Taylor gripped his colleague's hand.

"You have blue stripes in your hair, Miz Davies." Pastor Washington stared at my makeover.

"It's a long story, Pastor. Maybe I'll tell you one day."

I led the way into the bus, where Ducks gave them the grand tour. I remained uncomfortable with our ostentatious display when the pastors had next to nothing. Too late to rethink the bus and the RVs.

"This really was John Madden's bus?" Pastor Taylor could hardly believe it.

"It was. I was lucky to get it. Mr. Madden had taken delivery on a new one. I grabbed this on lease for as long as we need it." The bus worked out better than I could have imagined. "I wish I'd had the bus company paint it yellow, though."

"I never seen anything like this." Pastor Washington was the proverbial kid in a candy shop.

"When Max hired me to teach the kids, I thought I'd be roughing it," Ducks said with a shrug.

"If this is roughing it, I can be packed and ready to move in within the hour." Pastor Taylor relaxed in a padded leather chair. "Sure beats our folding chairs, doesn't it, Roland?"

Emilie poured lemonade and put the plate of cookies on the table. I texted Alex to join us; he was studying in his dorm. Emilie went back to ours to give her brain a rest. She'd take a nap or read or both. My money was on read first, nap second.

Alex clomped up the bus steps. He walked over to a side table and returned with a folder. Since I hadn't seen its contents lately, my normally disorganized grandson's organization of the park project surprised me. Alex laid pictures of the equipment and a detailed drawing of the park's layout on the table, along with an estimate of the number of people he needed and what construction equipment, supplies, and labor he wanted donated.

"I've spoken to several members of my congregation and should have five or six ready when you are." Pastor Taylor reached for a cookie.

"I don't have many folks back yet, but I'll be out." Pastor Washington said. "May not seem like I'm good for much, but I can use a shovel and carry trash."

"I've been working with one of your families at Hope Village, Pastor Washington," I said. "Mrs. Jordan and her two older children are more than willing to help. I don't know where her husband is yet, but I'll put this woman up against anyone. She dug in to finish her house. And she has five children, three of whom will be playing in the park."

Ducks and Alex had promises from the road crews to donate their time and equipment. After the mounds of trash were removed, the crew would come in with small rollers to flatten the area.

"What's this?" Pastor Washington pointed to a wide rectangle outside the park boundary.

"Um, well, we're hoping Pastor Taylor would let us put in a basketball court between the park and his rec hall. Maybe you two could start a sports league to give some of these kids something to do." Alex barreled on, ideas bubbling out of his overactive brain.

"Don't know about that." Pastor Washington scowled. "Mightn't be a good idea."

"Why not? Everyone likes basketball." Ducks reached for the lemonade pitcher.

Sports were necessary for healthy minds and bodies. If the feral teens got involved, maybe they could break the cycle of idleness that foreshadowed their futures.

"Don't know if my folks would play with Hodge's."

"It wouldn't hurt to try, Roland. Don't you have that retired coach in your church? What was his name?" Pastor Taylor scratched his head. He snapped his fingers. "Stephen Adams. Coached high school and up at State for a while, didn't he?"

"Ain't seen him lately. Mighta stayed up north with his daughter in Tuscaloosa."

"I'll do what I can to find him," Alex said.

"If there's something worthwhile coming back for, he'll be back. His house's pretty damaged, but it's standing, isn't it?" Pastor Taylor had inventoried the damaged houses in order to let his congregants know what to expect when they returned.

"Maybe we could help him fix up his house." Alex bulldozed from one idea to another. Nothing stopped him once he got his mind wrapped around a goal.

"Y'all are movin' too fast for this ol' country preacher. Let's get this here park goin' first." We'd pushed Pastor Washington as far as we could. "We'll see about the basketball stuff later. Who owns the land anyway?"

"The county, I think. It isn't part of my holdings," Pastor Taylor said.

"Um, I kinda went to the county clerk's office, what there is of it, and badgered them into selling me the parcel." I dared Pastor Washington to object.

"You bought the land? Yourself?" Pastor Washington removed his smudged glasses and wiped them on the tail of his shirt, smudging them worse. He frowned.

"I said I badgered them. They sold the land for one dollar. I have a proper deed, bill of sale and everything. It's all legal. I'm the proud owner of two acres of trash."

Pastor Washington's belly shook with laughter. He settled his glasses on his nose. "I don't know what to make of you, Miz Davies. You're obviously rich. You meddle in our affairs, yet here you are worryin' about five children." He shook his head, tut-tut-tutting.

"Pastor Washington, rich has nothing to do with it. It's seeing something I can help fix and then finding a way to do it. Writing a check for any amount, even for a dollar, was insignificant. More important is getting the community, black and white, together to clear the land and build the playground."

"Woman, you're one wearyin' person. You know I can't say no."

I clapped my hands. Alex would have his park, and I would have my basketball court. "We even have room for a volleyball pit."

"All this park stuff costs a lot of money. Young Alex, you say you got a grant? How's a kid like you go about gettin' this much money?" Pastor Washington prodded.

"Oh, he's very resourceful." Ducks finished his first cookie.

"I wrote a letter to a foundation that supports education and healthy bodies. I asked for funds, sent pictures of the destruction, presented my plans and talked the director's ear off about how this would help promote community togetherness." Alex grinned like an idiot.

"A place to play outside with the likelihood of organized sports was what the foundation wanted to hear." Ducks picked a bit of walnut shell from his second cookie.

"He can be most persuasive when he wants to be." I reached for a cookie. Time to celebrate.

"Guess he gets it from his grandmama, huh?" Pastor Washington winked at me. Actually winked.

"It's part of the Davies-Pugh family DNA. Alex couldn't escape his fate if he tried." I winked back.

"One thing you haven't considered. You need a fence around the park." Pastor Taylor studied the drawings. "The higher the better. With that gang on the loose, I'd hate to see them wreck it for the fun of it."

I loathed the idea of fencing the park off from the community. It sent the wrong message, but I could see the point. While the teens were attacking Hispanic workers, they could just as easily get bored or drunk one night and trash the park. Their unpredictability had to be factored into our plans.

"We'll put a fence up. Please don't say it has to be chain link with a locked gate and razor wire on top." Post and rails would keep with the park's rugged look and feel.

"Wouldn't keep them out if they wanted to bust in. Fence'd be more like a warnin'—stay away, 'cuz this space's for babies and mamas."

"Speaking of babies and mamas," Ducks said, "we forgot picnic tables and benches."

"But I already spent all the grant money." Alex chewed his lower lip.

Ducks lifted a sweat-stained ball cap. "We'll take up a collection. A couple of hundred dollars should do it."

Pastor Taylor reached into his pocket and pulled out a five dollar bill. Pastor Washington did the same. When I reached for my wallet, Pastor Washington stopped me.

"You've done more than enough, you vexin' woman." Another big smile took the sting out of his words.

We agreed to meet under the remaining battered live oak on Saturday morning at nine, ready to work. I worried about Pastor Washington, though. I wasn't sure he would keep his promise. More, I wasn't sure he should, because he was seriously overweight and looked to be in poor health.

The two men departed. Pastor Taylor cast a last envious look at the compound before climbing into his old truck and heading back to his makeshift home in the steel rec center.

"They'll both show up. Neither is going to give the other an inch." Ducks said after Alex retreated to his dorm to search for Stephen Adams, the errant coach.

"I agree. They don't dislike each other, but the separateness we all feel down here is generations deep. At least they're

cordial, and a little sweat equity in the park will go a long way."
I returned to my dorm where Emilie was crashed in her bunk,
noisily asleep.

#

I changed my mind about telling Johnny everything. I
remained shaken by the nightmare. Plus, I had to explain the
blue stripes in my hair.

We drove out to the beach, spread a blanket on the hood of
the truck and lay back to watch the stars spin their way through
the skies.

"Something happened, didn't it? Are the Sanchezes all
right?" Johnny pulled me tight against his solid body.

"They are for now. It's me." I told him what upset me: Junie
and Marianna, multiple monsters, the collision of past and
present. I was crying by the time I finished.

"Not all monsters live under our beds, pretty lady. Some
walk among us." Johnny squeezed me before laying his cheek
on the top of my head. "We need special intuition to recognize
and neutralize them."

"I've made so many mistakes." I snuffled.

"We all have. Don't beat yourself up." Johnny kissed my wet
cheek.

"Em said I should tell you." Well, she hadn't actually said
that. Warmth spread through me.

Johnny held me until my tears stopped. "Pretty lady, I'm glad
you did. Em's right. You can't change the past, but we can change
the future. Don't you worry. The men are protecting you and the
kids. Our extended family will watch over the Sanchezes too."

"I didn't want to tell you what happened to Junie when I was
a kid." I blew my nose. Twice.

"What's important to me is this guy can never hurt her again,
just like Dracula can never hurt Em." Johnny tucked my head
into his shoulder. His chin propped itself on the top of my head.
"You're safe with me."

Fresh tears slipped down my cheeks. "Em said much the
same thing just before she did my makeover."

"That explains the blue hair."

CHAPTER FIFTY-ONE

Mississippi, week of January 16

WE WOKE UP Saturday morning to find the remnants of a cold front had blown in overnight. Maybe we could get through the bulk of the trash clearing without anyone, especially Pastor Washington, collapsing.

I fixed a hot breakfast before bundling everyone into various trucks. Johnny, Emilie and I rode together, Ducks rode in Whip's truck, and Charlie and Alex followed. The men loaded the truck beds with tools and trash bags for the cleanup. By the time we arrived, one road crew was already there with a small skip loader.

"Figured it would come in handy for piling up trash." The driver waved at dump trucks pulling in. He was as excited about de-trashing the land and turning it into a playground as Alex.

Habitat volunteers, including Val, Hank, and Gayle, drifted in when more pickup trucks arrived. Pastor Taylor had called to say he'd be late because he needed to visit a sick church member first. Pastor Washington hadn't called, but he'd promised to work with us. His parishioner Mrs. Jordan had moved into her house.

"I have a stove," she said. "I'll make cookies."

We unloaded tools and stood around getting our work assignments from Alex. Emilie, Val, Hank, and I drew one corner of the lot filled with rubble.

"Go figure out what can be burned. Throw the rest to the side."

Johnny, Charlie, Gayle, and Ducks moved to the opposite side of the lot with similar instructions.

Toward the middle of the morning, two pickups arrived. I glanced up when one tooted its horn. Five men and two women crammed into the cabs. Pastor Washington leaned out the driver's window when I walked over.

"Think I wasn't comin'?"

"Never crossed my mind." I removed my glove and shook his hand.

The men scattered to fill in gaps, while the women unfolded a couple of card tables and set coolers under them. The camp cook would bring in lunch, but it looked like the women had more food and drinks.

We broke at noon, not quite halfway finished. Our cook brought piles of sandwiches and potato salad. The women from Pastor Washington's church had platters of fried chicken and hush puppies. Mrs. Jordan contributed a few dozen chocolate chip cookies.

We rested and chatted for about an hour. The intermingling of the men from both parishes with the Habitat volunteers pleased me. Hank, our incognito former Secretary of the Treasury, sat with two wizened black farmers who told him how much they looked forward to planting crops next year.

"Nothin' like homegrown food to make a dinner right tasty."

"Couldn't agree more." Hank listened intently to everything the old men said

The women were a little shier until Emilie asked about their children. Both had sent the little ones to relatives in Georgia until things settled down.

Mrs. Jordan shared her excitement at having a home of her own. "My husband and kids will be in later this week."

"Be sure you send your husband over to the compound," Johnny called from across the park. "We have plenty of work for him."

Mrs. Jordan grinned. "We're right grateful for that. Thank you."

"What with this here park goin' in and talk of one school openin' next fall, might think about bringin' the family back. Not much to look at, but this here's our home," the older of the two women said.

Val stored quotes for future editorials.

We finished cleaning up when Mrs. Sanchez and Marianna drove by. Emilie called out, but Mrs. Sanchez didn't stop. Marianna stared straight ahead as if she hadn't seen us.

"Strange folk," Pastor Washington said. "Sumpin' ain't right with that family."

What more could I add?

The day passed into late afternoon when we lit the first bonfire. Within minutes we had four roaring. We made two enormous piles of plastics and metal that couldn't be burned. The skip loader driver filled two dump trucks with debris. The drivers and a couple of local men headed to a municipal dump that accepted hurricane debris. Whip invited everyone back to the compound for a barbecue. The Habitat people declined, and Pastor Washington was torn. I walked over and took him aside.

"We've all worked hard today and gotten along well." I put a rather dirty hand on his arm. "Let's end with sharing a meal. It would be an honor if you and your group joined us. Besides, after a day like today most of the men will break out guitars."

After pausing to look at the men and women talking and laughing, Pastor Washington nodded. "Woman, you don't give up, do you?"

"What do you think?"

CHAPTER FIFTY-TWO

Mississippi, week of January 16

"I HAVE TO see Marianna," Emilie announced. She was ready for bed and came into our living area to kiss me good night. "When Mrs. Sanchez drove past us at the park, they ignored us. I want to know why."

"So do I. Pastor Washington knows something isn't right with them."

"Let's drop in tomorrow unannounced."

"If Father Ice Cube isn't there, we'll make a stealth attack after school." I kissed Emilie. "Scoot. Time for bed."

I drove to the Catholic Church late the next afternoon.

"Father Alvarado's not there, but he did something bad." Emilie had a familiar bead of perspiration on her upper lip.

We pulled into the drive, walked up the path, climbed the steps and rang the bell. And rang the bell. And rang the bell.

"They're not home." To ring again would have annoyed the heck out of someone who didn't want to answer the door.

"They're home," Emilie stared off into space. "They're hiding."

"From us?" Had we done something to damage a relationship that seemed promising a couple of weeks earlier?

"From everyone. Mrs. Sanchez's ashamed. I don't know why."

A small creak from the other side of the door told us someone had crept to the peephole.

"I guess they're not home," I said rather loudly. Emilie frowned. She stood off to the side of the door, out of sight of the peephole peeper. "We'll come back another time."

With my hand on her shoulder, I steered Emilie toward the Rover. She stiffened but didn't pull away. I backed out of the drive.

"Marianna was on the other side of the door." I shot a glance sideways. Emilie's face was grave; another drop of sweat sat on her lip.

"I'm pretty sure Mrs. Sanchez was hiding in the back of the house." I wrestled the car out of a pothole like I wrestled with emotions.

"Why would Marianna peek at us?" Emilie didn't like rejection any more than I did. "We just wanted to be sure they're all right. She couldn't know why we were there without talking to us."

I waited a few moments. "I think Marianna was hoping we wouldn't go away. That we would camp on the front porch until her mother had to open the door."

"Why didn't we?" Emilie became more agitated.

"Because Mrs. Sanchez doesn't want to be seen."

"She told you Father Alvarado hit her." Emilie looked over her shoulder at the manse disappearing into a dust cloud.

"She did."

"The crisis is coming sooner than we thought."

"Indeed." I jammed on the brakes when the first large stray mutt I'd seen ran across the road. "Sorry about that. Missed him."

Emilie rearranged herself in the seat. Thank goodness for seat belts. Without her being buckled in, she would have struck the dash hard. As it was, the only bad thing was my purse spilling in the back. Well, on second thought, a spilled handbag, especially one the size of mine, was a disaster, since all my stuff rattled around unrestrained on the floor.

Our conversation lapsed. I had too much thinking to do. When Marianna refused to return Emilie's wave, I knew they were running out of time. Pastor Washington didn't know how right he was. Something was rotten in the state of Mississippi. Sorry, Shakespeare.

"We have to do something to protect them, you know." Emilie returned from her secret place.

"What?" I ground my teeth. "I don't like this any more than you do, but I'm powerless. If Mrs. Sanchez won't let us help, we can hardly kidnap them."

"I know. I talked with Charlie and Mr. Ducks. He's watching them like we do. He rides past the manse every day. Charlie promised to visit. Maybe she can convince Mrs. Sanchez to take Marianna away."

Emilie hopped out of the car as soon as we stopped in the compound. She helped me round up the stuff that spilled from my handbag.

"Don't want to pack heat, huh?" She held my gun out to me.

"Nope, but it's necessary." I tucked the revolver away.

"Don't worry. I won't tell holy-crap boy-child."

CHAPTER FIFTY-THREE

New York, week of January 16

WITH ALL THE trouble going on around us, I didn't want to go back to New York. My monthly board meeting fell at a most inopportune time, but leave I must. I couldn't phone this one in.

Emilie went with me. "I want to talk with Auntie Eleanor and Auntie Raney about Marianna."

Charlie, Johnny, and Ducks promised to watch the Sanchezes to be sure they were safe. If Father Alvarado returned unexpectedly, they'd gather the men and storm the bastions if necessary.

Emilie and I flew off on a Thursday. She would spend Friday with Eleanor and Raney while I was at my board meeting. I would join them for dinner. Corey wanted to get together on Saturday. We'd scoot back to Mississippi on Sunday.

The board meeting seemed to stretch out interminably. In reality, we covered the agenda in record time, yet I was distracted. Johnny's text that all was quiet didn't help.

"Maxine, you are very perplexed. Talk to us." Eleanor wasn't fooled by my feigned nonchalance.

I figured Emilie had told both women about the mess we faced back in Mississippi. Warmth spread through me.

"You have two problems you can't resolve, don't you?" Raney asked.

"We do, but I'm less frightened by the gang." Whip, Charlie and Johnny, along with the highway patrol, could deal with the guys in the battered truck with the rotten muffler. "I'm terrified I won't find a solution in time to help the Sanchezes."

"We have to get them to safety, Auntie Raney." Emilie played with her food. This child with a robust appetite wasn't interested in what was on her plate. "We don't have a place to put them."

"This priest has you spooked, doesn't he, Max?" Raney said.

I copied Emilie by playing with a pasta shell. Eleanor's dining room was safe, normal, and peaceful, yet my emotions refused to be still. "I don't go looking for trouble, if that's what you're thinking. It finds me."

"She's right, Auntie Raney. She went looking for kids Alex's and my ages," Emilie poked at a bit of broccoli. "She found a child with more problems than I had last year."

"Mysteries will always fall in your lap." Eleanor ate a last bite of pasta. "You are a magnet for people in need."

"I never looked at myself that way, but life has a way of changing who we are when we least expect it."

The four of us kicked around ideas for helping the Sanchezes. All boiled down to the same thing: getting them away from Father Alvarado. Heck, I knew that. We came up with no new ideas, but I had more people on my team once again.

"No matter what you decide to do, you will rescue this child before she can be injured in a profound way." Eleanor rang for her maid to clear the table.

"How to do it is driving me batty-whacko." I folded my napkin before laying it beside my plate.

Emilie and I stayed at the apartment Thursday and Friday nights under a strict promise to Corey not to peek in the den. Corey had finished it but wanted to be there when I went inside for the first time. He'd even sealed it with a made-up crime scene sticker. On Saturday we ran errands and shopped for necessities. When we returned, George, my doorman, greeted us.

"Mr. Corey's upstairs."

Another big reveal, the final one of my redecorating, was due. I rang the bell. Instead of Corey opening the door, Ben stood inside, arms crossed across his chest.

"Well, you ruined my masterpiece." He turned on his heel and marched down the hall.

Emilie raised an eyebrow and bit her lips. We stowed our purchases in the closet and walked to the living room. Corey waited on the couch. He waved his hand around the room. Artwork hung on the walls. We had space for more paintings and prints, but for now the sparse decorations satisfied me. Emilie walked from painting to bookshelf and back.

"It's so warm and comfortable, Mad Max." She stopped before the head of a Cambodian Buddha. "I could live here forever."

"Well, I can't," came a cutting remark from the kitchen. "Go ahead, put the knife in my heart. We eat soon."

"Eat?" My raised eyebrow was directed toward Corey.

"Ben offered to fix us a celebratory dinner." Corey raised his eyes toward the ceiling.

"Will he poison us?" Emilie whispered.

"I heard that." Ben called from the kitchen. "I won't poison you, but I might spill the salt in the *coq au vin.*"

Ben might have gotten over his snit, but he wanted to rub my nose in my choices.

"Come see the den. Ben helped with it."

Oh, dear God. Ben could have painted the walls purple to get even. Corey led the way.

"Break the seal and open the door." Corey moved toward the den. Ben walked up behind him. I did as told.

Ben had transformed the den from a man's lair to a place for me to read, write, and watch television. The walls, once hunter green, were washed with pale wheat paint striated to look like grass. A sisal carpet covered the floor. Two reading chairs and a small couch wore soft green patterned fabric. The focal point was the bookshelves. Painted creamy white with the original dark green paint on the wall behind, the facing edges of each shelf were burnished brass. Ben and Corey alternated shelves of books with family photos, small art works and sculptures. At the far end of the room was a large white cabinet.

"Look at this, Mrs. Davies." Ben pushed past us in his rush to show off the cabinet. A complete entertainment system, flat screen television, multiple speakers, iPod docking station, and CD and DVD players were tucked away.

"It all folds out of sight," Emilie said.

"There's more. In that smaller one on the opposite wall is your messy desk." Ben rolled his eyes. "Nothing says tacky quicker than a computer screen and printer."

"Thank you, Ben. I can see your fine hand everywhere." I walked over and hugged him.

"The original was much better." He sniffed. "Dinner's in ten minutes."

When we returned to the hall, I looked at a sheet hiding something at the end. I looked back at Corey, who walked over and swept the sheet away. I gave him a thumbs-up.

"You found the perfect place for *Blue Dog #3.*"

At the end of the hall, with nothing on the walls leading up to it, the bright kitschy oil hung in solitary splendor, all but winking at us for its cheekiness.

"What about your bedroom, Em? What do you want it to look like?" Corey asked.

From the startled expression on my granddaughter's face, she'd never considered having her own room in my apartment. "Can I really decorate my own room?"

"May I."

CHAPTER FIFTY-FOUR

Mississippi, week of January 30

NO SOONER HAD Emilie and I returned from New York than I ran off to visit my pastors to share updates I'd learned from Charlie and Whip. While I was gone, Pastor Washington had graduated from camping in the tent to living in a small travel trailer. Coupled with a Johnny-on-the-Spot and an outdoor shower, he had more comforts of home.

Pastor Taylor had located the rundown but serviceable trailer languishing behind a demolished building about fifty miles inland and bought it for one hundred dollars, intending to live in it himself. When he towed it back, he remembered Pastor Washington was living in a tent. He dropped the trailer off and returned to his home in a corner of the metal recreation center.

I tooted the horn before I reached the turnout. The pastor was setting up folding chairs in the tent in anticipation of a Sunday service. So far, a handful of his flock had returned, but at least he joked about it.

"Like Tom Bodett, I leave the light on for them."

In addition to his park project, Alex had posted several queries on various boards on the Internet used to track the displaced. He found half a dozen AME church members. I had three more to report on, including the former coach, who agreed to be down soon. Others were safe but living out of state. No one knew if or when they'd return to their homes. Which, of course, didn't exist. Living with relatives won out over waiting for one of the oft-promised-but-long-delayed FEMA trailers. We told them about Hope Village and jobs rebuilding the highways. Perhaps it would be enough to encourage more families to return home.

Pastor Taylor climbed out of the Rover and walked over to help set up chairs. I still seemed to make Pastor Washington uncomfortable, although our relationship had improved since we started working on the park. I meddled, but more often got a humorous rather than hostile response. Pastor Washington went into his trailer and emerged with bottles of icy cold lemonade.

"At the very least I can offer something cold to drink." Pastor Washington motioned us to chairs.

"Right warm for so early in the year," Pastor Taylor said.

The two pastors compared notes on their congregations, while I struggled to be patient. When they ran out of small talk, I gave them my news. Most of it was bad. More men had been attacked by LeRoy Biggs and J'Marquis Baptiste.

"Danny Ray's getting more aggressive, but I'm not sure what role Jake Montgomery plays." I tapped the side of my lemonade bottle with my nails. My newest bad habit and one as annoying as Emilie's nail biting.

"Knew Biggs and Baptiste was gonna be trouble. Neither has a lick a sense. Started in trouble as early as eight or ten." Pastor Washington stared into the distance.

"The highway patrol is looking at these as hate crimes, because Hispanics are the victims. For the most part, anyway." I sat up straight. "They're bypassing Sheriff Hardy."

"Sheriff Hardy's as worthless as tits on a bull. Hate crimes, huh?" Fault lines deepened across Pastor Washington's forehead. "Mebbe. Mebbe."

I stared toward the shack where the Montgomery boy hung out. "We gave them enough evidence to arrest the gang."

"A lot of crews identified Baptiste and Biggs?" Pastor Taylor knew the answer but wanted me to say it anyway.

The photographic and audio evidence, plus DNA, should be enough to arrest the men. I leaned forward, my elbows on my knees, twisting my lemonade bottle in my hands. I rolled the bottle across my forehead, delighting in the coolness on my overheated skin. "Special Agent Pace will assume control soon."

"Special Agent Pace? Who's he?"

"FBI. You'll recognize him when you meet him. Typical dark suit, tie, and polished shoes. Looks like Howdy Doody channeling Clint Eastwood."

Both pastors laughed.

"Hate crimes fall under federal jurisdiction."

Pastor Taylor watched my face. "Do you have some problem with that?"

"I'm torn. Baptiste and Biggs belong in federal detention. They moved from being bullies to being rapists and murderers, in addition to mouthing racial slurs. I wouldn't be sad to see them go for a long time."

"Killin' folks for no reason 'cept their skin color or the language they speak should be enough to get them sent back to prison." Pastor Taylor glanced sideways at Pastor Washington.

"You'd think with all the racial crap that happened to my people, those two black men would have learned from history." Pastor Washington levered himself out of his chair, his face darker than ever with anger and frustration. "Guess they don't think the past has any effect on them."

"They're too young to remember how it was. History doesn't apply to people like them." Pastor Taylor watched his friend pace in front of us. "All they care about is getting what they want. If people get hurt in the process, they don't care."

"Well, I care. I remember stories of what happened. Pops was nothin' but a kid when he found his daddy's lynched body two counties over. Must have been about nineteen ten or so." Pastor Washington caught my shocked expression. "Pops was my granddaddy. He told us kids stories about oppression. Part of the reason why he moved the family north to Chicago."

"Chicago? You weren't born here, Roland?" Pastor Taylor asked.

Pastor Washington shook his head. His parents had followed jobs north. His father worked the factories until he got religion and enrolled in the seminary. He became an AME preacher late in life. When crime got too bad in the city, the family returned to Mississippi.

"It's where my roots are, Miz Davies. I may have been born up north, but I'm a son of the South. I went back north to my daddy's seminary. After I graduated, I came home for good."

"I see."

"I know you think I don't talk as good as you do. I don't, but I can speak proper English when the mood suits me. It's just my flock doesn't. If I spoke like you, or if I dressed like I had money, I'd be disrespecting them. I can't do that." Pastor Washington shrugged. "My daddy knew that. He set a good example. Don't talk down to your flock, and don't make fun of them."

I'd chalked his substandard English up to his background. I changed my mind. He understood more about human nature than I'd given him credit.

"What's bothering me is the Montgomery boy. I'm not sure what to do about him." I didn't want Spot to slip through any more cracks. My gut told me he wasn't culpable. As Emilie said, he wanted friends.

"I know what you mean. I've fussed about Jake for years." Pastor Taylor walked around the tent. Like Pastor Washington, he seemed too agitated to sit still. "He's a sheep looking for a herd."

"Picked the wrong damned one this time, Hodge."

"I don't think he had many friends in school. He left in the ninth grade. His momma was happy, because he got a job sweeping floors at the local market. She drank his wages."

"Lovely."

"I doubt you've run into people like the Montgomerys." Did Pastor Washington think I grew up in a bubble?

"Don't bet on it. I've met my share of bottom feeders too."

The Gaffneys, a family poorer than we were, had no idea how important education was. The first five kids, all boys, dropped out at the end of what was then junior high to go to work. The dad was a drunk, and the mother, with seven children and no work skills, lived off welfare. I wondered what had happened to the two Gaffney girls.

"I guess everyone does. So, when do you think the authorities will act?"

"Soon." Each passing day gave the pack a chance to harm more people. I stood and made ready to leave.

Pastor Taylor stopped me. "If the gang thinks it's getting away with murder, literally, what's to stop it from extending its intimidation to Hope Village?"

"And the Sanchez family at the Catholic Church."

"That their names?" Pastor Washington asked. "Never met them."

"I'm not surprised. They're terrified."

"Of who?" Pastor Washington frowned his now-familiar frown once again.

"Father Alvarado." I couldn't say more without breaking my promise.

"How do you know this, Miz Davies? Did they tell you, or did your granddaughter feel something?" Pastor Washington had come around to giving Emilie's gift the benefit of the doubt.

"Yes." One word and the expression I was sure was on my face betrayed how deep my anxiety was. "I know Father Alvarado is keeping them against their will."

"We have laws preventing that, Miz Davies." Pastor Taylor placed his hand on my shoulder to reassure me.

"Ain't you jumpin' from A to B to Z without anythin' in between? Just because they ain't friendly and keep to themselves don't mean they're bein' held hostage." Pastor Washington returned to my side.

I was flanked by my two pastors. "All I can tell you is I'm going to need your help sooner rather than later. Will you be there for them? For me?"

The pastors glanced at each other. One black and one white head nodded.

Pastor Taylor stayed at the tent to talk with Pastor Washington.

"Don't you worry about me. I can walk home," he said. "The gang won't fuss with me."

"I'll see Hodge home, Miz Davies. Now you git."

CHAPTER FIFTY-FIVE

Mississippi, week of January 30

BACK AT THE compound, Spot lurked in the distance, watching. What would happen to him when the FBI arrested the gang? Would he be jailed for not preventing the crimes? Would someone take pity on him and get him some help? Would he be turned back into the outlands? Would he continue to stalk Emilie?

We'd been stalked before, Emilie and I, by Dracula. I wasn't going to let it happen again. I met Emilie outside the girls' dorm.

"Spot won't do anything. He just wants to be friends and doesn't know how. He's creepy but kinda sweet."

"We'll see." My heart skipped when LeRoy walked over to Spot. Both stared at us from their vantage point near a pile of debris. Did LeRoy know we'd been to the highway patrol? I hoped not. He grabbed the younger boy's arm and yanked him back behind the shack.

"They've been there most of the morning. They were there late yesterday too. They show up around dinnertime." Alex watched the gang.

I went off in search of Johnny and Whip, who were still out on the highway. I knocked on the bus door and entered when Ducks called out a welcome. He was stretched out in a chair, a book propped in his lap.

"What are you reading?" I sat opposite him.

"*Lord of the Flies.* It seems appropriate with those feral teens roaming the countryside." Ducks pulled his long legs in and straightened his spine to sit more upright.

"Yes. Perhaps *Lord of the Flies* meets *Animal Farm.* LeRoy Biggs is the ringleader, according to Pastor Washington. By the way, Spot was with him at the edge of the rubble pile a few minutes ago."

"Right. I saw Spot earlier when Alex and I rode our bikes over to the park to measure the playground area." Ducks put aside his book. "What's troubling you?"

"Father Alvarado. Pastor Washington calls him the coldest damned man of the cloth he's ever seen."

Ducks walked to the stove and put the teakettle on to boil. "If we're going to do some serious thinking, we need tea."

After the water boiled, Ducks filled two mugs and carried them into the seating area. The bus smelled of cleaning solutions, Windex, Earl Grey and the faintest whiff of vanilla pipe tobacco. "Em told me about Marianna not answering the door."

"She's worried about the priest. If he gets even a hint I'm plotting against him, he could steal them away in the middle of the night." I wrapped chilled hands around the mug.

"He's not going to give up his property without a fight." Ducks glanced sideways at me. "Do you want to expose him for what he is?"

"I don't know. Too many ramifications in exposing him. None of them good. We have to protect Mrs. Sanchez, first of all. If we go to the police, they'd probably arrest her for child neglect. She knows what will happen to Marianna." I stared into my cup. "Do you have anything sweet? I need something sinfully chocolaty right about now."

Ducks fetched his secret stash of Ghirardelli chocolate, hidden in the drawer next to the knives. I opened a dark square and all but purred.

"We can't have anyone separating mother and daughter." While my vivid imagination and strong sense of justice wanted Father Alvarado strung up by his balls and flogged in public, I couldn't risk the authorities taking Marianna into protective custody.

"You don't want to turn him over to the church. After the pedophile scandals in several archdioceses, imagine the feeding frenzy the media would have over a priest keeping a woman in virtual slavery so he can molest her teenage daughter."

Ducks shared my distrust of organized religion.

"Even if he were removed from this parish, the church might shuffle the deck chairs on the Titanic and place him where he could find his next victim. I can't risk it." I gave in to my nervousness and roamed around the bus, but not before snagging another dark chocolate square.

"You were raised in the church, weren't you? What about your old priest? Could he help?"

I smacked my forehead with the palm of my hand. I stopped and stared out the window.

Ducks picked up his book. Something faint brushed my cheek to reassure me.

"Father Bernardo was old when I was a kid. If he's still alive, he's most likely living in a retirement home." What was the answer hiding in plain sight in my brainstem? Every synapse went on high alert.

"Start with your old church and see where it leads. Someone has to be able to help."

I paused in mid-step. I had the answer. It'd been there all along.

"Bug."

I ran out of the bus before Ducks could ask any more questions. His last words chased me back to my dorm.

"Well, I'm glad I was able to solve your problem. What the hell is bug?"

CHAPTER FIFTY-SIX

Mississippi, week of January 30

ALEX REMAINED BUSY coordinating the building of the park, and waiting for the equipment to arrive. Every night at dinner he gave us an update.

"I'm tracking the progress online."

"How are you doing that?"

"The shipping company sent me a tracking number." Alex looked smug.

"Is that new?" It made sense. After all, big rigs and smaller delivery trucks had GPS units built in.

"Yeah. It's way cool. I know where the truck is every day. I know when it'll get here." Alex took a long swig of milk.

"And that will be when?" Whip looked over at Johnny. They'd soon have work to do on the park on weekends.

"Next week."

#

Emilie walked around in a semi-fog. She threw herself into studying while she waited for me to find some way of helping Marianna. She reminded me of me when Junie was being molested. Why shouldn't she? She'd read my journal, for God's sake.

"I feel, like, totally helpless." She fidgeted at the breakfast table before bouncing up to pour orange juice. "I want to do something, but we don't dare call Marianna to see if she's okay."

"I agree." I put two bowls of oatmeal on the table. "As long as Father Alvarado isn't around, we have a little time to get it right."

"Is this part of what Auntie Eleanor meant at Mom's funeral?"

My hand paused midway to the brown sugar bowl. What had Eleanor said that resonated with Emilie?

"You know. About your doo-wop."

"Auntie Eleanor and Auntie Raney gave me the doo-wop to help me improve my relationship with your mother, but we ran out of time. They extended it to cover raising you and Alex." My hand finished its journey to fetch brown sugar.

"I'm sure they'd extend it to cover Marianna and Junie, don'tcha think?"

Marianna and Junie were part of my doo-wop. I handed her my phone, "Why don't you call Auntie Eleanor and ask?"

I hadn't told Emilie I'd reached out to my second husband's foundation, the same one that gave Alex the park grant, to see if it could do anything to help the Sanchezes. I couldn't offer charity, because Isabella's pride wouldn't let her accept it. If I located a potential job in Richmond, however, that would be different.

"You're in luck, Mrs. Davies." The foundation's executive director was looking for a replacement for a clerk who was relocating to Tucson for her husband's new teaching job at the university. "They'll be closer to their grandkids in Phoenix."

I wanted to do a happy Snoopy dance around the dorm.

"I have someone who needs sanctuary and a job. She's in trouble."

I gave the briefest disclosure about Isabella's plight as I could.

"She's a US citizen and needs to get out of Mississippi, right now.

"No, she's not running from a jealous husband or from the law. She's been abused, though. Once I get her out of the situation she's in, I guarantee she'll never see her tormentor again. I wish I could tell you more, but I'd be breaking a confidence.

"Yes, I believe her."

"Does she have the skills we need?" Susan clicked computer keys.

"Not a one, but she's smart, and she can learn."

"I don't know," the director said. "The job's not high stress, but we need someone we can rely on."

"She's reliable. I'll underwrite her salary and training if it'll make you feel better. She can't know, though." I'd do about anything to get this family away from Father Alvarado. I had to take baby steps, though, in spite of my growing concern that time was running out.

A long pause stretched into silence. I listened to computer keys. Was she answering e-mail?

"Sorry about the clicking, but I was checking our training schedule. We have a work-skills program starting in April. We'll teach her how to use the software she'll need for the job."

"I should be able to extract her before the workshop begins." I smiled at a blurry monster hovering over my bed.

"You don't need to underwrite her salary. You do enough as it is."

I thanked Susan. My second husband's fortune might have funded the foundation, but I had nothing to say about its daily operation. Even so, I was grateful the director would give Isabella a chance. Okay, job found. I needed a safe place for her and Marianna to live.

My e-mail chirped with an incoming message. My favorite private investigator, Tony, left a phone number and an e-mail address. I sent a message to Ducks's daughter.

CHAPTER FIFTY-SEVEN

Mississippi, week of January 30

AFTER A FEW phone calls, I discovered my childhood priest had retired, but a grade-school buddy, Sean Regan, had entered the priesthood. I tracked him to my old parish.

"You'll never guess who this is," I said when Father Sean came on the phone. "It's a voice from your distant past."

"I'm not so old to have a distant past. A past, maybe." Father Sean's voice was warm. "Do you want to tell me who you are, or should we play twenty questions?"

"Much as I'd like to see if you could remember me after all these years, I won't torture you. You used to call me Mouse." That was dumb. How many Mouses was he likely to know?

"Mouse? Oh my God. Max. How the hell are you? Where the hell are you?" Father Sean's unrestrained joy lifted me out of my funk.

"I'm well. I'm living in a trailer park of sorts in southern Mississippi." It was the truth after all.

"Last time I heard you were living large in New York. Don't tell me you lost your husband's fortune and are reduced to a single wide."

At least the wicked sense of humor I remembered hadn't been beaten out of Father Sean by the strict discipline of the priesthood.

"Nothing like that." I caught him up on the recent events in my life. Father Sean stopped me when I mentioned Merry's murder.

"I read about that. I'm sorry. Are you doing all right?"

"I'm stronger. Something about raising grandchildren full-time puts bad memories into perspective. I'm loving being with my family, but I have a problem." I laid out the Sanchez situation in no uncertain terms. "I don't know what to do."

"I'm absolutely shocked. To think such practices have been allowed to continue into this day and age. I mean, they were prevalent in Central and South America decades ago, but here? In Mississippi?"

"Are you being sarcastic, Bug?"

"No one's called me Bug in a very long time." Sean got the nickname because he wore thick glasses. "I'm not being sarcastic. I'm being honest. I'm revolted."

"You can't imagine how sick I was when I realized what was happening." I clasped the cell to my ear and swallowed hard.

"I thought we'd cleared out the bad priests during the purge following the pedophilia scandals."

"Well, you missed one." I said. "Or maybe no one knew what was going on. Maybe no one ratted this bastard out. Mrs. Sanchez told me her family tradition goes back at least five generations."

"There are always options, but if her family has a history of bearing illegitimate children under the secrecy of the church, I can understand why she'd see no alternatives. Hard as it is to accept, at least a girl child had a chance to grow up and grow old. It lifted a burden from the family."

"So would becoming a nun." My bitterness came through.

"Still the same old Mouse, huh?" Father Sean laughed. "If you'd been a man, you'd have been Don Quixote, tilting at windmills of injustice."

That fit. "You think I'm not tilting at windmills? Get real. Why did you call me Mouse back in school anyway? Was it because I was small or because you didn't think I had any backbone?"

"You had more steel in you than most of us realized. So, Mouse because you were vertically challenged." Sean laughed.

"Steel? What do you mean?" Hadn't I hidden my fears throughout school? Was Bug telling me my acting was for naught?

"You pretended everything was right at home, even when I

could see it wasn't."

"I didn't realize it showed."

When Junie died, I grew quieter, even more studious. I lost weight. We weren't as attuned in those days to what behavioral changes meant. Today, someone would have diagnosed me as clinically depressed or having post-traumatic stress disorder.

"It did, but I didn't know how to intrude."

"I have more means to help people than I did when we were in school." I set thoughts of Junie aside.

"I've followed your path over the years, Mouse. You've done well. You give back to your communities. You make me proud to have grown up with you."

"Thanks, Bug. That means more than you can imagine." I choked and blinked away stinging tears.

"Back to the trouble at hand. You want this priest stopped. Let's look at options." Father Sean recited the list Ducks and I'd already discussed.

"I know the police drill. Rape kit, statements, photos. We went through this with a young woman who was gang-raped. Isabella wouldn't be able to endure it. She's not strong enough."

"You're worried this priest will rape Marianna next."

"Yes. I can't live with that."

"None of us can, so we must prevent it."

Tears spread across my face. I wiped my nose. Blowing would have to wait.

Father Sean put on his counselor's voice. "If you go to the police, what would happen to Mrs. Sanchez?"

"That's a question Ducks asked." I picked at a loose thread on my sleeve. It came off between my fingers and found a new home in the wastebasket.

"Ducks?"

"Our homeschool teacher. He's become a great friend and confidant since we moved to Mississippi after Katrina. I'll tell you more about what we're doing later."

"If you allege child abuse in a house where the mother knew what was going on, she could be charged. The child would be taken away and turned over to protective services." Father Sean continued down the list of options.

"Shit! Sorry—"

"I've heard the word before."

"Almost worse than the potential of abuse is the risk of losing her mother. Marianna knows no one except her, my family, and Father Alvarado."

"We could report him to his bishop and let the church deal with it."

"Hah!"

"I figured you'd say that." Father Sean remembered me well, perhaps too well. At least he believed me. "Remember, his bishop might not know what's going on. However, if he's from a similar ethnic background, he may be covering up Father Alvarado's actions."

"My fear is Father Alvarado's behavior has been institutionalized. After all the scandal-filled headlines over the past few years, can I trust the new church to clean up this mess?" I couldn't focus on anything outside of the problem at hand.

"Give me a day to locate his bishop and speak with him. Where can I call you?"

We exchanged cell numbers.

"Don't take too much time, Bug. Marianna needs our help. Now." I hung up.

My right hand was cramped. Looking at it, I realized I had crossed my fingers for good luck. Maybe a prayer, too, would be appropriate. I knelt by my bed and prayed to a god I wasn't sure I believed in to protect Isabella and Marianna.

CHAPTER FIFTY-EIGHT

Mississippi, week of January 30

I KNOCKED SEVERAL times before Isabella came to the door. I'd checked the back of the church to be certain her car was the only one in the lot. I wouldn't put it past Father Alvarado to sneak in and hide his car. When Isabella told me Marianna was napping, we walked outside. We headed across the road toward the empty clearing that would become the park. The breeze blew from the south, bringing salty reminders of the nearby Gulf.

"How are you?"

"Better." Isabella stared off into the distance. "I wish he'd leave us alone."

"Do you think there's any chance he won't come for Marianna?" Much as I wanted to spirit the Sanchezes away in the middle of the night, all cloak and daggerish, I could do nothing without her cooperation.

"No. I try to protect her, but he won't let me. There must be something I can do, but I don't know what." Tears on Isabella's cheek gave me an opening.

"If you could do anything, what would you do?" I directed the conversation to the end I desired. I clasped my hands behind my back.

"I'd take Marianna away." Isabella wiped her face with her palms. She squared her shoulders.

Her change of posture was what I needed. "What if you could get away from him? I mean, really get away? Never see him again. If I help find you a safe place, will you leave?"

Isabella stared at me. "Please understand. Women in my family have served the priests of the church for five generations. It's all I know."

"It doesn't make it right." It made it prostitution. Or indentured servitude. Or slavery. At the very least, it made it immoral. "Let's say we find a way to get you and Marianna away. Will you go?"

"You can do something? My mother cried when I became a woman and was sent to a different church. I had my first baby when I was fifteen. I don't want it to happen to Marianna."

Her first baby?

"How many children have you had?" I had only seen Marianna.

"Six. Four boys, two girls. Marianna is the last." Isabella turned toward me. "When I was in the hospital, I told the doctor to make sure I couldn't have any more. It's a sin, but I didn't want any more children."

"Let God sort out the sin part. What happened to your other children?" I wasn't sure I wanted to know.

"The boys were sent for adoption after they were born. I never even got to hold them. Rosa stayed with me until she was seven. She was taken to a church in Mexico, but we aren't Mexican. We're from Colombia. I don't know what happened to her." The empty park reflected the emptiness of Isabella's life.

"I'm so sorry. I had no idea." I put my hand on her shoulder.

"You know, you're my first friend. I've never talked to anyone outside of the church or my family."

I was warmed by Isabella's confidence in me. "I have some ideas to get you to safety. When does Father Alvarado come back? I don't want you in danger."

"He's not supposed to be back for three more weeks. He called yesterday to check on us. You know, making sure we were obeying his orders. I don't trust him. He's dropped in without warning several times lately. He could do it again." She shook her thin shoulders.

"What do you want to happen to Father Alvarado?"

We walked to an area where the park gates would be. We'd cleared enough debris to eradicate the smell of decay. On this sunny day salt-tinged Gulf air surrounded us. For the first time, I could imagine how beautiful this place must have been pre-Katrina. Poor, to be sure, but with its own brand of beauty.

"I don't know what you mean, happen to him?"

"How do you want him punished?"

"Oh, I don't want him punished. I just want to get away." Isabella's eyes opened wide.

"Think about it. Has he abused more women and girls like you and Marianna? Could he have another woman in a different church? If we don't stop him, could he order another girl to serve his needs?"

Isabella stared at me. "Others? I never thought about that."

"Look, you need to protect Marianna. I'd like you to think about sending her to stay in the compound with us. We have plenty of room."

The words hadn't left my lips when Isabella shook her head. Even I knew this wouldn't work. "He'll only beat me harder."

"Mama, can I come over?" Marianna stood on the empty front porch.

"Of course," Isabella called to her daughter. She wiped tears away.

I chatted with Marianna about the park we'd build in a couple of weeks. I told Isabella I'd see her soon. I was drained by the events of the day. I wanted to build a blanket fort and crawl inside with crayons and a coloring book. I settled for a power nap before dinner.

CHAPTER FIFTY-NINE

Mississippi, week of January 30

WHERE THE HELL was the bishop? Why hadn't he called? Didn't he believe me? When my cell buzzed, it was Bug.

"Imagine my surprise when I learned Father Alvarado's bishop was my old seminary friend." Father Sean's high spirits were infectious. "He was two years ahead of me."

"You know him?" Could it be the stroke of luck I waited for?

"I sure do. Joseph Spellman's one of the good guys, Mouse."

"Bishop Spellman? He doesn't sound Hispanic."

"He isn't."

"How soon can I talk to him?" The Sanchezes could run out of time if he didn't hurry.

If Bug knew the bishop, why the heck hadn't he called me? How hard was it to punch in my cell number and set aside some time to talk? Obviously, harder than I thought. Nothing in my mind was more important than stopping a priest from abusing a child.

"Don't worry. He'll call. Try to be objective, Mouse. Okay?" Father Sean wanted me to do something I wasn't ready to do yet.

"Me? Not objective? Get real."

I jumped a foot when my cell buzzed again hours later. Although I had willed it to ring, I wasn't prepared when it did.

I checked caller ID. An unfamiliar number. Not one of the kids, Whip, or any of my friends. Not my two pastors either. I flipped up the top.

"Hello."

"Mrs. Davies? This is Bishop Spellman. I understand Father Sean Regan told you to expect my call." A very rich, deep voice. Someone who sounded like James Earl Jones.

"He did."

No matter what Father Sean said, I was on guard. I wasn't sure I could trust this stranger. I carried the phone into my bedroom and shut the door. I didn't want to be interrupted if Emilie decided to bip-bop into the dorm for something she'd left behind.

"Father Sean said you suspect a parishioner near Gulfport is being abused. Is that true?"

I sat down on the edge of the bed. "I hope you have some time, Bishop Spellman."

"I do. Tell me what I need to know."

"Two people, a woman and her child, are being kept in virtual servitude. The woman is being physically and sexually abused by Father Alvarado at St. Anna's. I've seen the bruises from his beatings myself. Mrs. Sanchez says Father Alvarado is after her thirteen-year-old daughter next."

"Why don't you tell me the whole story?"

I detected a wariness similar to mine in Bishop Spellman's tone. Neither of us fully trusted the other, but neither had any alternative. I put my concerns on the line before I gave him any details about the Sanchezes.

"Bug said I can trust you. Can I?"

"Bug?"

"I'm sorry. Father Sean. Bug was his name when we were in school together."

"Ah."

Oh dear, not one of those priests who went "ah" or "oh" no matter what you told him. Funny, older priests usually fell back on such noncommittal responses. Since the bishop was only two years ahead of Father Sean at the seminary, he couldn't be one of the older priests.

"Can I? Trust you, I mean?"

"You can."

This warm yet skeptical voice on the other end of my cell was my last chance. It was him or the police. The police were out.

I looked out my bedroom window. The skies were partly sunny with wind pushing clouds into fabulous shapes. Light and shadows changed on my wall. A fly landed on the window sill. I took a deep breath and talked. And talked. And talked.

"You saw bruises, Mrs. Davies?" Bishop Spellman let me go on for nearly a quarter of an hour without interruption.

"Yes, but I don't have pictures." I described where they were: face, arms, and wrists.

I hit my forehead with my free hand. In this age of ubiquitous cell phone cameras, why hadn't I recorded the abuse? "I have no proof."

"I wouldn't worry. We won't be taking this to a court of law. Do you think Mrs. Sanchez will meet with me?"

"I don't know. Her only experience with Catholic clergy has been one of oppression." I mentioned her other children and being the fifth generation to endure indentured servitude.

Bishop Spellman said nothing. I wasn't about to break in; silence was more powerful than empty chatter. Pages flipped.

"I can't get down to Gulfport for a couple of weeks. I have church business I can't avoid."

I shouldn't have been disappointed, but I was. I wanted, hoped, the bishop would drop everything, rush down to protect the Sanchezes, and sweep Father Alvarado away.

I couldn't keep my disappointment from my voice. "If you can't make it sooner, you can't. I'll watch the Sanchezes. Father Alvarado isn't due back for three weeks, but since he's started pursuing Marianna, well, he's been dropping in unannounced."

"Take my cell number. If you see Father Alvarado, call me. I'll come as soon as I can. If he touches them, take pictures."

It was less than I wanted, but all I was going to get for the moment.

I walked outside the compound, ground my teeth, and tried to calm down. I moved on autopilot, my attention inward. I dodged impediments without seeing them. Lucky for me, I didn't trip and fall. I tried to regain my inner calm, to live in the moment. When I returned to camp an hour later, Emilie met me on the step of the dorm, fists on hips.

"Well?"

I couldn't pretend I didn't know what she meant. I told her about my conversation with the bishop.

"You aren't sure you can trust him, are you?" My darned granddaughter always cut to the chase.

"I didn't at first, but we don't have a choice. We have to put our faith in him."

"He'll help. So will I."

Ducks rounded the end of the school bus. "Count me in."

I leaned over and kissed Emilie on the cheek. "I know you will."

"Now about going for a walkabout alone..." Ducks planted himself in front of me, shaking a finger in my face.

"Oh, shut up." I dodged around him and went into the dorm.

CHAPTER SIXTY

Mississippi, week of February 3

THE CLOSER THE playground equipment came to arrival, even with an unexpected delay, the more overbearing Alex became. Even when he'd help track down other victims of his mother's killer, he hadn't been this wired. The park tsar lorded it over one and all.

"Are you sure we'll have enough volunteers?" Alex dug into a baked potato half the size of Alabama. "I don't want to be short-handed."

Whip beamed at his son's perseverance. Emilie rolled her eyes. Charlie grinned.

"Haven't you had plenty of help up to now?"

"Well, yeah, but I want to be sure the equipment is set up right." Alex smashed a third slab of butter into the potato.

My turn to roll my eyes. Charlie did too.

Alex looked up. "We're going to have a party when it's done, aren't we?"

"Do you think we could get away without one?" Charlie reached across the table to chuck Alex's smeary chin.

###

Three days after this exchange, I returned from my weekly

food run and backed the Rover into its parking place. Ducks emerged from the school bus.

"Have you seen Alex?"

"No. I just got back from shopping. Help me get the food out of the Rover. We'll go look for him."

We unloaded in record time, stopping long enough to put the cold food in the fridges. All else could wait.

"I'll check with Samson. If he left without permission, Whip's going to be pissed." Ducks's long legs ate up the distance between the RVs and the gate.

"I'll check with the cook." I turned toward the tent. "He sometimes hangs out there after his lessons."

"That's the point." Ducks called over his shoulder. "I left him writing an essay in the dorm. The unfinished paper's there. Alex isn't."

"What about Em?"

We wheeled as one and dashed to the girls' dorm. Empty. No Emilie.

"Bugger. Where are they?"

According to Samson and the cook, a loaded flatbed truck pulled up to the gate about an hour or two earlier. It drove off up the road toward the park. Neither knew if Alex went with it.

"It has to be the equipment. Alex's been so antsy he probably forgot to tell you where he was going." I leaped to the only conclusion that made sense. I opened the Rover's door.

Ducks jumped in. "Let's go."

I looked back at the dorm. "No bike. Em followed him."

"I don't have a good feeling about this," Ducks said. "Something's not right."

"Me too." Fear caused my stomach to churn.

We drove as fast as we dared. Up ahead, the battered truck with the rotten muffler blocked the road. Piles of crates lay stacked around the park. The flatbed was gone.

"Uh oh."

"Not good."

I turned off the engine and let the Rover coast to a halt behind the pickup.

"I wish you hadn't left your handbag in the dorm," Ducks whispered.

"You got that right." My revolver would feel real comforting.

"We have no weapons but our hands and the element of surprise."

"They'll have to do."

I sucked in my gut and walked around the front of the truck; Ducks crept around the back. J'Marquis Baptiste, LeRoy Biggs, Jake Montgomery, and Danny Ray formed a half-circle around Alex and Emilie. I froze. This can't be happening. Not to Alex and Emilie.

"Well, will you looky at what we got here? Two of them little Mexican lovers." J'Marquis loomed over Alex.

Alex stood his ground. LeRoy prodded him with the end of a baseball bat. He lost his balance and fell in the dust on his butt. Alex glared at his tormentor as if willing his superhero persona to fly to the rescue.

"Time to teach this brat a lesson." J'Marquis raised his fist.

"Yeah. We don't want your kind around here. Get the hell out and never come back." Proximity to J'Marquis and being armed gave LeRoy a false sense of power. He slapped his palm with the bat.

"You leave him alone." Emilie shoved her way between LeRoy and Alex.

"Aren't you the brave little bitch? I can't believe our luck, can you, LeRoy?" J'Marquis licked his lips.

"Let's give her the same good time we gave that old bitch the other day." LeRoy pulled at his crotch.

"Don't you dare touch me!" Emilie glared at LeRoy.

Danny Ray sneaked around behind Emilie and threw her to the ground. J'Marquis unzipped his pants and exposed his erect penis.

"You leave her alone," Jake, aka Spot, pushed forward. "She's my girlfriend."

"Oooh, our retard has a girlfriend," LeRoy taunted.

"You don't have any friends 'ceptn us," Danny taunted. "How can this bitch be your girlfriend?"

"She is. She won't tell on us. Leave her alone." Jake tried to pull J'Marquis off, but he was no match for the older man in lust-heat. The larger man kicked him aside like a worrisome pup. The boy landed in the dirt next to Alex.

"If you fight, bitch, it'll make it better for me." J'Marquis knelt between Emilie's legs. He reached for the waistband of her jeans when he flew off to the side.

We rushed the boys as one. Ducks clasped his hands, swung them like a club, and hit J'Marquis right on his ear. I knelt beside Emilie and pulled her away. She was trembling but maintained her composure. Shaken, to be sure, but in full control. Alex regained enough presence of mind to pull his cell out of his pocket and punch in nine-one-one.

I threw him my phone. "Call Lieutenant Ellsworth."

Ducks pinned J'Marquis to the ground with a foot on his chest. "Don't even think about moving. I'd like nothing better than to pound the shit out of you, you little turd."

In what seemed like an hour, but was no more than a couple of minutes, Sheriff Hardy pulled up, lights flashing, siren off.

"What the hell's going on?" The sheriff hefted his bulk out of his cruiser.

"We have attempted rape and attempted assault and battery." Ducks kept a tight grip on his anger. None of the boys moved, not even J'Marquis who was still unzipped but no longer excited. His flaccid penis lay limp on his thigh.

"I see four boys being assaulted by one man." Sheriff Hardy yanked on his gun belt and strutted toward Ducks. He spat on the ground, barely missing Ducks's left foot.

"You see one man protecting two children from harm," Ducks corrected. His face turned dark red, a color that should have warned the sheriff not to mess with him. "You see one man exposed. You see one woman comforting and protecting her granddaughter."

"Nah, don't see nothing like that." Sheriff Hardy tried to shove Ducks out of his way. When he failed, he reached for his service pistol.

"Are you going to shoot me, Sheriff?"

Ducks had never sounded menacing before, but he did this time. If the situation deteriorated, Ducks was going to take the sheriff on, gun or no gun.

"Stop right there, Forrest." Lieutenant Ellsworth walked around the front of the truck, while Special Agent Pace came around the back. The sheriff and the teens were surrounded.

Additional cruisers pulled up as other officers arrived in response to the nine-one-one call.

"You've done it this time. What were you planning to do? Shoot the man standing in front of you? Let these boys go?" Lieutenant Ellsworth relieved the sheriff of his gun and handed it to one of his officers.

"This here's county territory, Ellsworth. You ain't got no authority," Sheriff Hardy blustered and hitched at his belt again. Nothing weighed more than his ego.

"I do." Special Agent Pace flashed his ID and FBI shield. "We'll take you in along with these four boys."

My muscles shook harder than Emilie's. She was safe, but all I could think about was how close she'd come to being raped. I swallowed the bile that burned the back of my throat.

"You ain't got the balls to run me in." Hardy's challenge sounded so hollow it rang like an empty dish.

"Oh, yes, I do. It's pretty clear what was going to happen," Lieutenant Ellsworth said. "J'Marquis, zip up your damn pants. Your limp dick makes you look like a fool. You aren't raping anyone today or any other day, unless it's in prison. It'll probably be the other way around in federal detention."

Ducks removed his foot from J'Marquis's chest. The man rolled away and zipped his pants. He stood shakily and pleaded with Sheriff Hardy for help.

"Hey man, do something. You promised to protect us," J'Marquis whined.

"Yeah," LeRoy said. "We been doing your dirty work, so you gotta help us."

"What kind of dirty work is that?" Lieutenant Ellsworth asked.

"Shut the fuck up." The sheriff's face turned a dangerous shade of red, but he couldn't do anything. He had problems of his own.

"We'll take these boys in and book them. Sheriff, you too. You've turned a blind eye to their crimes. You know the law. This makes you an accessory." Lieutenant Ellsworth waved at his men. "Cuff them and take them to my office."

Special Agent Pace turned to Alex and Emilie. "Are you kids all right? They didn't do anything, did they?"

Alex shook his head. Emilie, paler than usual, confirmed Danny had pushed her to the ground, but nothing else had happened.

"Can you take it easy on Spot? He tried to protect me." Emilie looked at Jake, who let a police officer lead him toward a cruiser.

"Spot?" Special Agent Pace frowned.

"Jake Montgomery. The one with acne."

"I don't know. We'll go as easy on him as we can, but he participated in several of the attacks." Lieutenant Ellsworth looked at the boy.

"You want a couple of tow trucks out here, Lieutenant?" An officer called. "We gotta impound this heap. Guess you want the sheriff's car as well."

"Yes. Have someone with crime scene experience go through both." Special Agent Pace took charge. "I'm sure we'll find plenty for a host of charges. Oh, and impound their phones. I suspect they called each other frequently."

"You got here pretty fast. You must have been close by." I couldn't think of any other answer to their near-instantaneous arrival.

"We were over at the bayou looking at more bodies." Special Agent Pace wiped sweat from his forehead, in spite of the cool, windy day.

"And?"

"Three more. We'll need your help identifying them." Like the wicked witch, Howdy Doody was green.

"Do any of you need a ride back?" Lieutenant Ellsworth nodded toward his car.

I helped Emilie to her feet and dusted her backside. Alex scrambled up, too, but paid no attention to the dirt ground into his jeans.

"No. We'll see the kids get home. Thanks."

Ducks put his arm around Emilie, who leaned against his chest. I hugged Alex. He was rigid. The police moved the truck to the side of the road. The cruisers left with their respective prisoners in back.

Emilie picked up her bike and pushed it down the road. Alex walked beside her. Ducks and I drove alongside the chastened children. A nice long walk in the chilly sunlight would give them time to think before Whip laid into them.

"Oh man, just wait until Dad gets home." With the danger past, Alex was afraid of what his father was going to do.

"We are so, like, busted."

CHAPTER SIXTY-ONE

Mississippi, week of February 6

"LET ME GET this straight. Alex, you ran off without telling anyone. You broke the cardinal rule designed to keep you safe." Whip's voice was low, which made it more menacing than if he'd shouted. "Your sister followed because she worried you might get into trouble. Again, without telling anyone. That about right?"

Whip paced in front of his frightened children. Charlie, Ducks, Johnny, and I sat at the picnic tables. We didn't want to be there, but Whip insisted. We were going to deal with this family problem as a family. No hiding in dorms and getting yelled at. A public dressing down would mean more in the long run. Alex and Emilie stood in front of their father under the mosquito netting, heads hanging.

"What were you thinking, Captain Chaos?" Cold sweat dripped from Whip's chin. He'd come close to losing his children.

"I was thinking about the park. When the equipment came, all I wanted to do was show the men where to put it." Alex looked up, a bit hopeful he might escape punishment.

"You could have been killed. You know the gang murders people." Whip stopped in front of his daughter and pointed at her until she flinched. "And you, Em, you know they raped a woman. Still, you both ran off without a lick of caution or a word to anyone."

Whip stepped back and clasped his hands behind his back, knuckles bloodless from tension.

Cars and trucks hummed along the reopened stretch of repaired highway; tires swishing on new pavement provided a soft symphony. Missing was the battered truck with its rotten muffler. We'd never hear it again.

"Alex, you're a crisis magnet. Everywhere you go, you put yourself or someone else in danger."

Charlie squirmed. I fought the impulse to jump in, because this wasn't the time to get between parent and child, even though I naturally wanted to protect Alex and Emilie. Johnny, Ducks, and I sat as still as we could. If I fidgeted, I could provoke Whip into a deeper anger. He hadn't been this close to rage since the day he confronted Merry with proof of her infidelity.

"Okay, for your punishment."

Whip unclasped his hands from behind his back. Alex looked up. Would he get off with a scolding? Emilie kept her eyes downcast and held her breath.

"I could ground you both, but that would have no effect." Whip paced. "First thing, loss of privileges. No Internet except when school-related, no IMing, no cell phones, and no texting until I say so."

Emilie exhaled.

"Alex, you'll write a letter of apology to Lieutenant Ellsworth and Special Agent Pace for dragging them all the way from Gulfport."

"But, Dad, they caught the bad guys and put them in jail. That should count for something, shouldn't it?"

Charlie and I exchanged looks of despair.

"Oh, it does, Alex, but they'd have caught them anyway. They had all the proof they needed. Instead, they sent four cruisers, plus the lieutenant's car, to the scene. And two tow trucks." When Alex started to protest, Whip held up a hand. "Not another word. Do you understand me? You'll think about what you did and what it cost to protect you. You'll write the letter. I'll approve it before you deliver it in person to the lieutenant."

"Geez."

"That was a word. Silence!"

Whip's voice rose. Under more normal circumstances, he'd have started off shouting and grown quieter. The reverse showed how terrified he was.

"Have it ready by Friday when I get back from work. You have plenty of time to work on it after you finish your homework. Start it tonight. And don't even think about asking Mr. Ducks for help. He's not part of this."

Alex nodded.

"And now you, Em."

Emilie looked up.

"You didn't think. You knew the boys were hanging around, but you left without telling anyone. Did you think you were going to rescue Alex if there was trouble?"

"I don't know. He's my little brother. I didn't think."

"I agree. You tried to help him, but you put yourself in terrible harm. Those two men were intent on raping you." Whip swallowed hard.

"I know, Dad."

"You'll write an essay on safety. Think about everything that happened, what you did, and what you should have done differently."

"Yes, Dad."

"What happened to your gift? Did you feel Alex was in trouble?"

"No. That's what's odd. I didn't feel anything." Emilie's face was a study in confusion. She should have been able to feel Alex's emotions.

"Are you going to talk with Dr. Schwartz about this?"

"Yes, Dad."

"Go back to your dorm, Emilie."

Alex started to move toward the boys' dorm.

"You, sit. Work on your letter right here at the table. I don't want you near your laptop."

We all walked a little way off to give Alex privacy to regain his composure.

"Man, cutting Alex off from his PC will be torture," Charlie whispered. "Great object lesson."

"Not the first time. Won't be the last." Whip went to the cook tent.

After dinner I walked over to visit the workers. They already knew what had almost happened to Alex and Emilie. They surrounded me, providing strength to my still-shaky self.

"Abuelita, we're glad the children are safe," Pete said, "but our job isn't done yet."

I must have looked puzzled because Pete added that they were watching the Sanchezes too.

I wasn't certain they knew about Father Alvarado. Maybe they knew the woman and child were in trouble. I couldn't speak, so I settled for touching each man.

Johnny collected me. "Let's go for a walk."

We left the compound for the first time on foot. Neither of us said anything. We held hands and walked along the road. Stars filled the sky. A lone meteor streaked overhead.

"The truth is out there." Johnny stared at the fading shooting star.

"Huh?"

"*X-Files.*"

"*Ya gotta believe.*"

"*Yogi Berra?*"

"*Tug McGraw.*"

CHAPTER SIXTY-TWO

Mississippi, week of February 6

MY INSIDES STOPPED shaking somewhere north of midnight when the adrenaline rush wore off. The gang was in jail. Emilie and Alex were safe. Chastened to be sure, but safe. So were the workers.

The next morning, over a cup of coffee at Hope Village, I gave Gayle, the Habitat manager, a detailed description of the attempted attack and the ensuing arrest.

"Thank God the FBI agent was there. The guys in the gang must have shit themselves sideways when they realized Sheriff Hardy could no longer protect them."

"They did. Special Agent Pace will prosecute him and the others for hate crimes, as well as rape, attempted rape, assault, and murder." I picked up my oversized handbag. I had two more calls to make. "Gayle, you should have seen the look on the ring leader's face. He knew he was toast."

I pulled in front of Pastor Taylor's metal building. He was outside working on his old car. He wiped grease from his hands. I sat on the bumper.

"What's happened?"

In seconds, the pastor knew all the details.

"I'm sorry, Miz Davies. Are your grandchildren all right? Really all right?" Pastor Taylor put his hand on my shoulder before sitting.

"They will be. Em has more resilience than you'd think to look at her. She's very connected to living in the moment. She goes deep inside to find her strength. That's where she gains her perspective on the world."

She'd retreated after dinner. Back in the dorm, she'd pulled her curtains across her bunk.

Pastor Taylor smiled. "I don't know your granddaughter all that well, but she's a rare child."

"Spooky, too."

"Just like you, Miz Davies. Just like you."

My next stop was the AME tent. I planned to check the Catholic church on the way back. I had to be sure Father Alvarado hadn't slipped in unnoticed.

Pastor Washington wallowed in his cranky persona. When I parked the Rover, he growled at me. "Whatchu want this time?"

I'd learned not to round back on him, much as my nature would have dictated. "I don't want anything, Pastor Washington, except to give you some news."

He didn't receive the retelling of the previous day's events as I had hoped.

"You sayin' J'Marquis and LeRoy are guilty of murderin' those workers?"

What had his nose out of joint? Wasn't he relieved the gang was in jail? I was happy the men were out of circulation, even if he wasn't.

"Not at all. Highway Patrol and the FBI agent arrested them for attempted rape and assault on my grandchildren."

"Attempted?"

"They didn't rape Em, but J'Marquis's penis was exposed and ready. We stopped him in time."

Pastor Washington glowered at me.

"What have I done to offend you this time?" I sighed.

The black pastor stared. Was I supposed to guess? Play twenty questions? If so, I wasn't in the mood. I had neither the time nor the inclination to pick away at his anger. Time for me to get the heck away from him. Pastor Washington stopped me before I could get into the Rover.

"Ever since I came back to Mississippi, I seen white folks blame blacks for all sorts of crimes with no more proof than skin color."

"That's not what's happening this time. We have enough evidence to put the gang away for a long time for crimes they committed and for two they attempted. No matter what you think, being black had nothing to do with it. Committing crimes did."

I climbed into the Rover and reached for the key.

"They tried to rape that pink-haired child?"

"Purple."

"What?"

"Her hair's purple today. And yes, they tried. J'Marquis was going to go first."

"Oh, my." The man put a work-roughed paw on my car door.

"Pastor Washington, I wouldn't care if these men were orange and green aliens." I started the car. "They tried to rape my granddaughter. They were lucky I didn't have my gun on me."

I shifted my handbag slightly on the passenger seat. My Smith & Wesson was a welcome weight in the bottom.

The pastor stepped back. I drove away from the tent. Before I turned onto the state road, I glanced in my rearview mirror. He sat on a chair in a narrow strip of sunlight, face in hands. Was he praying or crying?

CHAPTER SIXTY-THREE

Mississippi, week of February 6

WITH THE MURDERERS behind bars, I slept in relative peace. One problem solved, one to go.

I wanted to dance to rock and roll, but I was too keyed up. Instead, I fiddled around the dorm all morning. I wiped ever-present grit from countertops and put books on their shelf, changed beds, emptied the dryer, and folded clothes. I waited for the phone to ring. When it did, I jumped half out of my skin. Could Bishop Spellman be coming down sooner than expected?

"Hello?"

"Mouse?"

"Hi, Bug."

"Joe Spellman called. You talked to him."

"Joe, huh?" I grabbed my coffee and settled into a living area chair.

"I knew him as Joe long before he became Bishop Spellman. He's a good guy, even if he is a priest."

I kept reminding myself to keep an open mind about the church being able to handle this mess without turning it into a public scandal.

"He has street cred. He headed the group that investigated the pedophilia scandal in Boston because he was an outsider.

He's continued to root out problem priests after his official role ended." Father Sean gave me several examples of the types of problems he'd handled. "He's on our side."

"And that side would be, what, Bug?" I refused to relax my guard after years of being a recovering Catholic.

"The side of the good guys, of course." Father Sean laughed.

"I told him what I knew about the family. Like you, he didn't really believe me."

"I never said I didn't believe you, but you have to admit the story's lurid. Anyone but you, Mouse, and I'd have sworn you were making it up. You have such a high bullshit meter, I have to believe you."

"Thanks. I wouldn't have believed me either. Let's see what Bishop Spellman does." I topped off my coffee cup and turned off the empty pot.

"What happens to the Sanchezes after Joe handles Father Alvarado?"

"Well, I found Mrs. Sanchez a job." I told him about the offer from my foundation.

"I hear a 'but' in your voice."

"Your ears are as sharp as ever. The 'but' is the pay's not enough to support her and Marianna. She'll have to start at the bottom." I didn't want the foundation to pay anyone a higher wage than they qualified for. I would have to find some other way for Isabella to support herself.

"I may have a place where she can stay. The rent's cheap."

"Is the neighborhood safe?"

"It's not in the drug-infested area of town, if that's what you're thinking."

"It was. Isabella and Marianna are the original innocents abroad. Put them in a drug world, and they'd die."

I closed my eyes. Images of two poorly socialized females becoming prey to those much less innocent played out on the back of my eyelids.

"Not a worry. They'll be as safe there as anywhere in Richmond. Anyway, the woman I need to speak with has been away for a couple of months, but she's due back in two or three days. I'll know soon."

"I don't know how to thank you, Bug."

Father Sean's concern for a total stranger renewed my faith in the clergy. A little, anyway.

"You might try returning to the fold, Mouse."

"And give up my favorite line of being a recovering Catholic?" My laugh was genuine.

"Give it some thought. The church misses you."

"Don't lose any sleep over this errant soul."

We rang off. I found my journal and spent the rest of the morning filling in blank pages. When I finished, I found Kool and the Gang on my iPod and danced.

Emilie wheedled me into inviting Marianna to a sleepover. I had to be ultra-persuasive with Isabella, but eventually she agreed it would be good for both girls.

"It should be safe, because Father Alvarado won't be back for two weeks."

We set it up for the following Friday.

CHAPTER SIXTY-FOUR

Mississippi, week of February 13

ALEX, EVER RESILIENT, rebounded from the gang episode in a day. Because Whip restricted him from using anything electronic without supervision, he concentrated on finishing the park.

"I didn't buy picnic tables and fencing. What are we going to do?"

"I'll get them in Gulfport or Biloxi." Johnny pulled out a pad and jotted some notes. "What else do we need?"

"What about mulch or landscaping?" Charlie sat next to Alex and looked over his list.

"Landscaping?"

Alex learned two important lessons. One, projects always ran over budget. Two, no matter how carefully you planned, you overlooked something.

"We need mulch. Plus some bushes and grass." Charlie pulled out a notebook and began making a shopping list. "You can't expect children to play on bare dirt, can you?"

Alex hadn't gone beyond the picnic table, the slides and swings and other playground toys and the surrounding fence. He thrust out his stubborn chin. "I don't have any more money."

"Mulch won't be expensive. Neither will grass seed or sod, fertilizer, and bushes. We'll pass the hat." Charlie removed her ball cap, threw it on the table, and dropped a twenty in it. "Ante up, boys."

Whip and Johnny each dropped a twenty on top of Charlie's. I added mine.

"I'll call some nurseries in Hattiesburg or Mobile. I'd like to get stuff delivered, but if I have to take a couple of our trucks and drivers, I will."

"Plan on a dump truck. We'll need yards of mulch." Whip calculated how much we'd need. "Maybe two trucks."

"Too bad we don't have chipper/shredders." Charlie pointed at piles of rubble. "We could make a layer."

Johnny looked out at the wasteland surrounding our camp. The air was dry and clear. A slight Gulf breeze controlled the whining mosquitoes, which were around regardless of the season.

"It wouldn't be sanitized though."

"We're not going to find sanitized mulch within a two-hundred-mile radius. Let's see if anyone has a chipper. That'll save money." Charlie agreed to ask the other crews. "Maybe someone has one or has seen one in the area."

"Sure. Besides, we should recycle as much as we can. Turning the dead trees and bushes into something useful, not just firewood, is one way to do it. It sets a good example as well," Johnny said.

Charlie nodded. "How's that, Alex? Sound like a plan?"

Ducks ambled over, a lit pipe between his teeth, and scanned the lists scattered across the table. "Collection hat?"

"We need money for plants and stuff."

Ducks added his twenty to the cap. He pointed at an old tree on the plans. "Will that tree survive? It's pretty battered."

"Pastor Taylor says it's been there for at least two hundred years. It should make it."

"Brilliant. What do you need me to do?"

"Most likely help assemble the fort or rake mulch. There'll be areas where we can't get the equipment in because it's too big for this small a job." Whip studied the drawings Ducks had helped Alex make. He pointed. "Here. And here. We'll need an old-fashioned shovel crew."

"Can do. Nice evening for a short ride, isn't it? No more worries about our safety." Ducks rolled his bike out of the gate and headed toward the park.

"Have you been up there in the last couple of days, Dad?" Alex tucked his plans in a folder.

"No. Why?"

"Ducks and I rode up yesterday. Someone's staked out the big lot next door to my park." Alex was very territorial.

"The basketball court," I said.

"We'll take a look tomorrow," Whip promised.

Alex and Whip stayed at the table, discussing what equipment and how many people they'd need on each Saturday. Charlie walked back to her Airstream to make some calls. Johnny and I walked along the road. It was nice to go where and when we wanted.

"Look." I pointed to a spot a few yards in front of us.

"What?" Johnny wasn't sure what caught my attention.

"That small patch of green with tiny white flowers. A definite sign of rebirth."

Johnny squeezed my hand.

For the Friday night sleepover, I laid in a supply of healthy munchies and a couple of videos. The girls slept in my bed while I struggled to find a comfortable position in Emilie's bunk. I heard whispers and giggles until way past my bedtime.

I fed the girls French toast and scrambled eggs for breakfast. Both looked sleepy as was to be expected after a sleepover. Life was normal until I heard angry shouts coming from the gate. I warned the girls to stay inside until I knew what was going on. Marianna's face drained of all color.

"Oh shit," said Emilie.

"Father Alvarado?" Stupid question. No one else's voice could have painted such a look of terror on Marianna's face.

The girls rose as one. Much as I wanted to lock them in the bedroom, I couldn't. I opened the outside door when I heard a tap. Isabella stood alone.

"You must let me take her." She had a fresh bruise on her chin.

"I can't. He'll hurt her," I said.

"It will be worse if she doesn't come with me."

"Come inside. I'll protect you." I reached out to her. She jerked away.

"I can't. Come over after he leaves."

Isabella led Marianna down the steps and out the gate. She helped her into a dirty Cadillac.

"Do something," Emilie pleaded. "He'll hurt both of them."

Charlie and Ducks walked over.

"Bloody hell."

"What do we do now?" Charlie asked.

Emilie handed me my phone. "Call Joe the PI."

I called my private investigator. "Tony, Maxine Davies. I have a job for you. Is Joe available?"

I gave Tony all the information I had about the priest. Joe the PI would pick up Father Alvarado's trail at his next church.

By two o'clock I was ready to lose my mind, when Pete, the cook, knocked at the door.

"Abuelita, the padre left." He'd driven past the manse around one o'clock as he had every day. He saw Father Alvarado drive off.

Emilie grabbed the car keys and camera case.

On the way to St. Anna's, I looked for any sign Father Alvarado had doubled back. I turned into the parking lot and drove around behind the manse. Mrs. Sanchez's old Toyota was parked in its usual spot.

"He's gone. We can go in, but it's not good."

Emilie had beads of sweat on her upper lip, an outward sign she was experiencing someone else's pain. I held her hand. It was ice cold. Another sure sign of how bad things were.

"Are you certain you want to do this?"

"Absolutely. Marianna needs me as much as Mrs. Sanchez needs you." Emilie marched up the steps to the porch and knocked on the door. Loudly. Firmly. She waited a few moments then knocked again. I could tell by the set of her shoulders she was going to keep on knocking until someone answered—or until she wore a hole through the door.

When the door opened a crack, I pushed inside and confronted Marianna in the dusk of the main room. Her pale face was blotched with tears, and a purpling bruise was on her jaw. Emilie was as pale as Marianna. She ran to the girl and held her.

"Where's your mother?"

Marianna trembled under the hand I put on her shoulder. She pointed down the hall toward the bedrooms. She never left the comfort of Emilie's arms.

"You two stay here."

I didn't want Emilie with me until I knew how badly Isabella was hurt. I had no doubt she'd been struck. The twisting in my gut was too persistent to be ignored. I walked down the hall alone. The first bedroom was Marianna's. I listened at the second door and heard weeping. I opened without knocking and walked in.

No matter how much I'd steeled myself, I wasn't prepared for Isabella's misshapen face. One eye was swollen to a slit; she had dark bruises on both cheeks; her nose was bloody. I was pretty certain I'd find other marks on her body.

I opened the door again.

"Marianna, where's the bathroom? I need a washcloth."

"Just beyond my room," came a mumbled response.

"Em, bring me a bowl or pan with warm water, please."

Back in Isabella's bedroom, I turned on the bedside lamp to get a better look at the bruises and blood on her face and hands. She had defensive wounds on her arms. At least one finger looked broken, maybe two.

Emilie knocked. I was across the room to get the water before she could open the door. I didn't want her inside. She handed me a large pan and my camera.

I turned on the camera. My granddaughter had taken several shots of Marianna. She had dark bruises on her face, chest and back. Once again, I wanted to choke the life out of Father Alvarado. Feelings from my childhood rushed back. When I faced such wanton disregard for personal safety, for human dignity, I wanted retribution, real Old Testament retribution.

I shot several pictures of Isabella's face. She tried to turn away. "Isabella, I have to do this."

She was in no position to argue. She lay back and let me photograph her face and hands. I asked her about other injuries.

She removed her stained, bloody nightgown. She had fist marks on her torso and stomach.

"Why did he beat you?" I covered Isabella with a light blanket to protect her modesty, set aside the camera and began sponging the blood from her face.

"I tried to keep him away from Marianna. I told him she had her period, but he didn't believe me. When he tried to drag her into his bedroom, I struck him on the arm and chest until he let her go."

"Is that when he turned on you?" I wrung out the cloth and held it to Isabella's still-seeping nose. Rinse. Wring. Dab. Repeat.

"Yes. He locked me in his bedroom."

"Did she have her period?" Had Isabella lied to protect her daughter?

"No. She'd just finished it."

I held Isabella's unhurt hand.

"We have to get you to the emergency room."

"I can't. I don't want anyone to see me."

"I'm not a doctor, but you may have a couple of broken fingers. You may have injuries that don't show." I helped Isabella sit on the side of the bed and found some loose-fitting clothes. "Pull these on. I'll be right back."

In the living room, Marianna was sobbing in Emilie's arms.

"How bad is she hurt?"

"He hit her."

I knelt next to both girls and peeled Emilie's arms away. Dark bruises on Marianna's arms. A bad one on her face. Some fading bruises on her body.

"Did Father Alvarado do anything else to you?" *Please don't say he raped her.*

Marianna shook her head. "He didn't touch me down there. He threatened to come back after he took care of Momma, but he didn't. He got a phone call and left suddenly. Before he did, though, he said it was my turn next time."

Junie's image floated at the edge of my peripheral vision. She nodded and gave me a thumbs-up before shifting back into the gloom.

I patted the child and went to fetch Isabella. She was dressed, so I helped her to her feet.

"We'll drop Em and Marianna off at my place. They'll be safe. I don't think Marianna's seriously injured."

"I agree. You can't take them both to the emergency room. People will ask too many questions. We don't want that," Emilie said.

"I don't want anyone jumping to conclusions, even though they'd be right. I'll get Isabella checked out. You find some Tylenol to take the pain out of Marianna's bruises. A couple should do the trick."

Isabella was no match for me when I was in my most take charge mood. I explained what we were going to do.

"I called Mr. Ducks, and Charlie's on her way back from the work site. Mr. Ducks is waiting. It's okay to take us right to the bus. He'll make us some soup." Emilie picked up a light jacket and helped Marianna put her sore arms through the sleeves.

"Mr. Ducks will take good care of you." I reassured the terrified child. "Will you stay with Em in the school bus until we get back?"

Marianna shot a frightened glance at Emilie.

"You'll be safe. You can trust Mr. Ducks."

When my granddaughter smiled, Marianna nodded.

I opened the door and hustled Isabella to the Rover, where she settled into the front seat. She pulled the door shut. It locked behind her.

My mind ran faster than my mouth could keep up. I gave disjointed instructions, but I didn't give a damn. Emilie would figure out what was missing and do it. Or Ducks would. Or Charlie.

Four hours later we were back in the compound. Isabella had done well at the hospital, although she'd refused to say how she got her injuries. An attendant took photos, but he could do little if she wouldn't name her assailant. He put the photos in her file in case we needed them later.

Isabella's injuries were superficial, even the blows to the stomach. The doctor found no indication of internal bleeding. The two fingers turned out to be dislocated and were popped back in place. Antiseptic salve on her cuts, a splint on her hand, a prescription for painkillers, and we left.

I called Ducks to see if Isabella could stay in the school bus. No way was she going back to the manse. He assured me Emilie and Charlie had already made up a bed on the couch. Isabella was more than welcome.

Word spread through the compound that the Sanchezes were with us. Pete walked over to say everyone was relieved, but they would stay on guard until we were positive the family would never be in danger again.

Close to midnight, I sat outside, numbed by the magnitude of Father Alvarado's inhumane treatment. Emilie and Marianna were fast asleep, worn out by emotion. I needed a few minutes of quiet and solitude. Even Johnny was tucked into his trailer.

The school bus door squeaked. A whiff of vanilla-scented pipe tobacco preceded Ducks's arrival under the mosquito netting.

"Isabella's resting. What's the word from the PI?" Ducks settled into a folding chair, legs stretched out. "Alex told me what he did to save Em. He called him an absolute wizard. What's he going to do?"

"Follow Father Alvarado. He's the best early warning system outside of you and Em."

"That's good. It's not over, but for right now they're safe."

CHAPTER SIXTY-FIVE

Mississippi, week of February 13

WHILE THE DRAMA with the Sanchezes played out in the dorm, life and the park went on. We arrived early the next Saturday to find the food court set up. Hope Village had hot coffee and iced tea, both sweet and "un." Pastor Taylor's wife, who had returned a couple of days earlier, had made sandwiches, and Pastor Washington's congregation had cookies and other sweets waiting.

"Did you think we couldn't work together?" Pastor Washington walked over to shake my hand. I seemed to be off his bad-girl list. For one day at least.

"Not at all. If nothing more, neither you nor Pastor Taylor will give the other the upper hand."

"That's not very Christian of you, Miz Davies." Pastor Washington's eyes twinkled. Then he winked. "Right, but not very Christian."

I laughed.

"I have to leave. One of my parishioners is near death. I promised I'd help her over the divide." Pastor Washington returned to his truck. "I'll work next week."

We shoved dirt around, graded the site once more, compacted the soil to support the playground equipment and assembled the various forts, swings and climbing bars. A borrowed industrial-strength chipper snarled and snapped its way through piles of debris. Part of the shovel crew, I moved dirt under the ancient oak where the picnic tables would sit.

Emilie and Marianna went off almost before dawn with Charlie and Johnny to bring back plants from outside of Mobile. Isabella had moved back to the manse, but was under loose guard by the men. Johnny drove a huge dump truck for the mulch, because we couldn't chip up enough debris to cover the entire area. I expected them back by dinner.

As project boss, Alex was in his element.

"Hey, Alex. You know where you want the swings?" One of the workers from Olivia's crew walked over. "We don't have enough room. Kids will hit the oak tree if they go too high."

Alex poured over the plans with Whip and Ducks. He pointed at another area.

The worker leaned in, dusty sweat dripping on the paper. "How about here?"

"Still too close. We'll have to put the fencing in, you know."

Ducks pulled off his glove and tapped a place a few feet away from the original spot. "We have space here. It won't spoil your original layout. What do you say, Alex?"

Alex nodded. The worker called to his crew to dig the holes for the footings twelve feet out from the oak tree.

I looked across the park to the area where someone had marked off the basketball court. With the public park, a new basketball court, and the metal building serving as a recreation hall, Pastor Taylor could turn this section of devastation into a welcoming place for returning families. Whip and I walked over to the man who ran the roller.

"I've built basketball courts before. We can pour concrete, if someone wants to donate the materials," the roller operator said.

Whip waved at Pastor Taylor who joined us.

"If you're game, we'll put in the basketball court next weekend." Whip beat dust off his hat before resettling it on his head.

"Okay, if you're up for it." Pastor Taylor grinned at the empty area. "We are."

I didn't say anything. Neither did Whip. Alex was out of earshot, but a glance at Whip told me we'd pass the hat again to build the court.

I pulled off my gloves and fingered the blisters that swelled on both hands. I didn't care. The volunteers, blacks and whites and Hispanics, locals and outsiders, worked side by side, laughing and kidding each other. I smiled at Pastor Taylor, who raised both eyebrows. A different, more united community was taking shape around us. Maybe the basketball hat should be in the food court.

In the weeks we'd been there, I'd seen slow signs of recovery. People who'd argued with insurance companies and won had started repairing their houses. The highways expanded daily, as did the traffic on them. More big rigs growled along, carrying goods from manufacturers in the west to retailers in the east. A few stores reopened, including a small local restaurant out on the Gulfport Pike. I hadn't tried it yet. Seemed to be open for breakfast and lunch. Maybe I'd go Monday. Spend a little money locally.

"It'll be different, but we'll recover. We always do." Pastor Taylor wiped his hands on his jeans. In the food court we poured ourselves glasses of cold tea.

"I'm always amazed at our ability to rise again like a Phoenix." I sipped and removed my sun hat. My blue and blonde hair was plastered to my skull, but I didn't care. I remembered how New York and the entire country came together after 9/11.

"Does that surprise you, Miz Davies? The human being is a resilient creature."

"Whack us down, and we'll get right back up, particularly when we help ourselves."

By the end of the afternoon, we had rolled the basketball court, assembled the main playground equipment and begun digging the post holes for the fence. We'd be ready to set the playground equipment in cement the following weekend.

At the end of the day, Johnny and Charlie pulled up and honked. Johnny's dump truck was piled to the top with mulch. Charlie's truck was full of bushes, bags of grass seed, and hundreds of pounds of fertilizer. We dumped the mulch in several piles to spread another day.

We bid Pastor Taylor farewell and returned to camp, Charlie's truck leading the way, plants and bushes bobbing in the breeze and leading us homeward.

"In two weeks we make the park official." Alex's dream had come to fruition.

We sat around the dinner table mid-week to plan the inauguration party. The two pastors and the Habitat leader had joined us.

Gayle Hollins had conferred with the Hope Villagers. "Leave the food to us."

"I'll load up on soft drinks." Pastor Taylor turned to Pastor Washington. "Want to bring some ice?"

"I surely do. And whatever else is missin'."

"What about beer? We can get the crews to kick in twenty-five dollars each," Whip added.

"I'll throw in twenty-five dollars." Johnny reached into his pocket.

"Not each crew member. Each of the road crews themselves." Charlie appointed herself drinks chairman. "Everyone's invited, even if they didn't work on the park or don't live here."

"You might want to up the amount of money then. These men can drink." Whip pulled out some money and threw it on the table.

"I don't want a lot of money. I'm going to make it clear we're having a family party." Charlie walked over and invaded Whip's personal space, going nose to nose with him in a rare display of mock anger. "They should hold the beer consumption to two each."

"Good luck with that." Johnny laughed.

Whip and I joined in.

"If anyone can enforce such a draconian rule, Charlie can." I imagined our little redheaded firebrand guarding the beer supply and counting how many cans each drinker took. She could change someone's mind about overdrinking with a single glare.

"What's dragons got to do with this?" Johnny tried to look blank.

"Draconian, funny man, not 'dragonian.'"

Ducks went into the school bus and returned with a dictionary. Without a word, he thumped it on the table in front of Johnny. Charlie and I erupted. It wasn't as funny as we thought, but giggles washed away tension from the events of the past several months.

"It's interesting how we've helped create a community," Charlie said. "None of us knew the people here a few months ago."

Johnny and Ducks looked at each other. "We were just talking about this the other night after most of you went to the dorms. This little group has become a family."

"I wouldn't trade any of you for my blood relatives—and I love them all," Ducks said.

"We all want to belong to something. Families stay in the same place for generations, because the sense of belonging wipes out isolation and loneliness." Charlie said.

"You know, when the Sanchezes are uprooted, they're going to need heaps of help to find a new community, a new family." Johnny had apparently been thinking about what the change would mean for them. "You have it under control?"

Johnny gave me more credit than I deserved.

"Almost." I gave my extended family a thumbnail sketch of what I hoped would happen.

"We're here to help. Don't try to do it yourself." Charlie reached across the table and poured the last of the wine. She sounded like Eleanor.

Emilie winked.

"Oh, trust me. I'll take all the help I can get."

Ducks's phone buzzed on the table. We looked at the screen. Unknown number. He punched the speaker button and answered.

"Dad?" A woman's voice floated over the table.

"Carole?" Emotions transformed Ducks's face. He grabbed the phone and turned without a backward glance.

"Who's Carole?" Johnny asked.

"His daughter," I said. "They haven't spoken in a quarter of a century."

"How much meddling have you been doing, pretty lady?" Johnny reached for my hand.

"Just enough to let Carole contact her father if she wanted to, funny man." I silently thanked Tony Ferraiolli.

A warmth spread throughout my body.

"Thank you," a voice whispered in my head.

CHAPTER SIXTY-SIX

Mississippi, week of February 13

I ROAMED THE girls' dorm and tried to plan my next step. I had Marianna with us and Joe the PI tailing Father Alvarado. What I didn't have was any word from the bishop. I called him again. The call went straight to voice mail. Either he had his phone turned off, or he was using it. I left as detailed a message as I could. Frustration set in because I had few details to convey.

A fly followed me around the dorm and landed on the sink shelf.

"If you don't have an answer, stop staring at me." I shooed the fly back into the air. I was mesmerized by its lazy flight

When I couldn't reach the bishop, I called Father Sean. We needed a sanctuary for the Sanchezes immediately. I got his voice mail too. Another message. Another moment of grinding my teeth. What if they were talking to each other? No. That would be way more than I could hope for.

I was fidgeting around the kitchen, putting dinner together, when my cell buzzed. I snatched it up before I looked at caller ID.

"Hello?"

"Mrs. Davies? Joe Spellman. I got your message a few minutes ago. My apologies, but I've been in meetings all day."

Just hearing the bishop's resonant tone made me feel less jumpy.

"Thank you for calling. I know you're busy." Like I was during board meetings.

People talked in the background. Bishop Spellman wasn't alone, but he wasn't on a speakerphone. The call would be private.

My gut cramped. I was afraid I'd throw up or hiccup. One would be nasty; the other embarrassing. I tightened my diaphragm and crossed my fingers.

"Give me an update."

I gave him as much information as I had.

Papers rustled.

"I don't like inaction any more than you do, but I have Father Alvarado under observation.'

"So do I." With Joe the PI on the job, Father Alvarado would be hard pressed to get past him too. "Not to worry. I have about forty rugged construction men in the camp where I live. We can handle him if he shows up."

Even though Johnny and Whip would have been glad to supply the muscle to run the priest out of what was left of the town, he'd probably return and make life worse for the Sanchezes.

Bishop Spellman laughed. "I have this image of men with picks and shovels storming the church."

"It's not like the old days here, but you're close. The men would use intimidation instead of picks and shovels. Or Glocks and shotguns. Still, we don't want a spectacle, do we?"

"No, we don't." The bishop said he had a copy of Father Alvarado's schedule. "Let me find it."

Background noises were muffled; papers shuffled. He must have put the phone down.

"All right, he has a funeral mass tomorrow, another on Wednesday, a baptism on Friday, a wedding on Saturday and mass on Sunday at All Saints up near Hattiesburg. He can't miss any of them."

That might explain the sudden flight from St. Anna's. Marianna's comment about him getting a call and leaving in a rush unsettled me. I didn't know why, but it was out of what little we knew of his character. I wanted the priest snatched off the street and disappeared as surely as Colombian drug cartels did away with their rivals.

"You have pictures of Mrs. Sanchez and Marianna's injuries," I said.

"I saw them. Frankly, they made me ill. I'm freeing my schedule to get over to Mississippi. I'll call you as soon as I have a firm arrival date. I want to meet with you and the Sanchezes."

We clicked off. Beeping in my ear signaled another call coming in.

"Hello?"

"Mouse?"

"Bug! I just spoke with Bishop Spellman." I gave Father Sean the abbreviated version of our conversation.

"Good. Joe will put together a fool-proof case against Father Alvarado. He's assigned a couple of priests to follow him from parish to parish. He's looking for more victims, I think."

"Has he found any?"

"If he has, he hasn't told me. I've left this in his more than capable hands." Father Sean paused.

If he had other women, Joe the PI would find out. So would I.

"Okay, let me tell you how clever I've been."

Just like the old Bug, so pleased with himself. We used to laugh about how self-assured Father Sean was even as far back as his Bug days in kindergarten. "Half a duplex we use for long-term temporary housing for refugees is empty. The last residents were three lost boys from the Sudan. We brought them over, taught them English and helped them get settled into jobs. The place is empty now."

I didn't realize any relocated boys from the Sudan were in Richmond, but then again, I left there a couple of decades ago. It shouldn't surprise me things went on in my hometown I knew nothing about.

"I mentioned the house the last time we spoke. Decent enough neighborhood. Not poor. More lower middle class. Everyone works when there's work to be had. Not much of a drug problem. Not too far from my church and our school."

So far, so good. "You're sure the place is available? If things go as I hope, we'll need to move Isabella and Marianna in a few days. A week at the most."

"It's open and clean. I talked with Hot Pants today."

"Hot Pants? Sue Hamilton? From grade school?" My voice squeaked.

"You wouldn't recognize her. Completely transformed." Father Sean said. "You wouldn't know anything about it. You abandoned us long ago."

"Oh, get real."

"Hot Pants came back several years ago after working for about two decades in a missionary school in Africa. She transferred back when we began providing sanctuary to the lost boys."

"A missionary school? In the Sudan?" My voice squeaked again. Was my hearing going? I scanned the room for a prankster playing tricks.

"Not the Sudan, but close. Eretria."

"Good heavens. What's an evangelical preacher's brat doing in a missionary school?" Sue had about the worst reputation in high school for dating the wrong boys. She wasn't called Hot Pants for nothing.

"Brace yourself, Mouse. Sue is Sister Susan."

"She's a nun?" My voice rose another half decibel.

"She is. She went to Boston College when we went to Virginia Commonwealth. She got religion. Catholic, at that." Father Sean paused as if a solemn thought occurred to him. "Gee, Mouse, you're the only one who escaped."

"Damn straight. I told you I'm recovering. Leave it at that."

We agreed to disagree over my soul, which was fine, thank you very much. It didn't need reinforcing in the restricted confines of organized religion, which I believed was little more than a Ponzi scheme. I went to church on the holidays to keep my name on the good girl list.

"I'll tell Isabella. Bishop Spellman seems pretty confident about Father Alvarado's commitments near Hattiesburg. He's pretty sure he won't be dropping in unannounced."

"Okay. I'll tell Hot Pants to keep the apartment for the Sanchezes. Oh, by the way, Hot Pants lives in the other half of the building, so she'll be there to help your family as much as they need."

"This isn't the old place her grandparents had, is it?"

"My gosh. You remember. Sue inherited it, fixed it up, and leases the other half of the duplex to the Church for one dollar a year. We can almost afford it."

"Bug, thanks for everything. Even for worrying about my soul."

"I can't force you to come back to the church, and you can't stop me from praying for you. Guess it's a stalemate, huh?"

"Going to church doesn't make you a Christian any more than standing in a garage makes you a car."

Father Sean's laughter filled empty air before the phone clicked off.

Charlie and I dropped in on Isabella after dinner. We took Marianna too, because we wanted to tell both of them what we were doing to move them to a safe place.

"I've known Father Sean and Sister Susan since grade school. They're good people."

"I don't want charity. I'll work to repay you for everything you've done for me and Marianna."

"This isn't charity. I found a job where you can learn office skills. Think of it as a starting point. Sister Susan's place is in a decent neighborhood. You'll be safe there."

I was making headway, but we had many obstacles to overcome.

"What about Marianna? All she knows is life in the church." Isabella sat as still as a stone.

"She'll go to Catholic school. I don't know where she'll test, but it'll be below her age. Father Sean's church has tutors. You can work off her tuition by helping in the church office."

"I'm afraid."

"I know you are, but the world has more decent priests who will protect you than bad ones like Father Alvarado who abused you." Charlie put her arm around Isabella's shoulders.

"I've never known anything else." Isabella turned away in shame. "My mother was wrong, wasn't she, when she sent me to serve the church?"

Oh heck. How did I answer that? Her mother was dead wrong.

"Your mother did the only thing she knew. She sent you into service thinking you'd be taken care of. You don't want the same thing for Marianna, do you?"

Isabella put her face in her hands and wept.

CHAPTER SIXTY-SEVEN

Mississippi, week of February 27

ON THE BIG day, Alex ricocheted from the breakfast table to his bunk for jeans and a T-shirt to his dad's truck to "load one more thing."

"Alex, finish your breakfast." I'd had enough of the jumping bean. "We aren't leaving for two hours. Sit."

Alex sulked but planted his butt on the bench and dug into his pancakes. The camp came to life more slowly on Saturdays. Charlie stumbled her way out of her Airstream, a cup of coffee held out like an offering. Johnny emerged from his trailer a few minutes later, shaved and dressed in clean jeans, a fresh polo shirt, and black sneakers, all gussied up for the big party. Whip finished breakfast, picked up his keys and headed over to his truck on an ice run.

"I'm coming too," Alex mumbled through a mouthful of pancakes and syrup.

I caught his attention and raised an eyebrow. "Have you finished eating?"

I looked at Alex's plate. Three bites left. I shuddered when Alex stuffed half a pancake into his mouth. Syrup dribbled down his chin and dripped on the table, just missing his arm. One more gigantic bite, a swipe at his mouth with his napkin, and he ran toward the truck. I shook my head. Charlie howled.

"I shouldn't encourage him, but he's so damned funny when he's focused on something. He was like that a lot in Peru." Charlie helped herself to a piece of bacon and a slice of cold toast. "When he wanted to go riding, it was all Whip and I could do to keep him in his chair long enough to eat. This from the human locust who swallows everything within reach."

"I can't get mad at him. After all, the park was his idea." I smiled at the dissipating dust cloud. "I'm really proud of this village. Everyone is doing a terrific job raising both him and Em."

"When we were moving mulch last weekend, I got to thinking about my childhood. Like most Mexican-American families, we all lived within walking or biking distance from each other."

Johnny strolled over. He'd been talking with several of the men lining up for breakfast at the food tent. He had a plate of eggs and sausage in one hand, a huge mug of coffee in the other.

"Me too. My grandparents lived down the road, and aunts and uncles filled in most of the houses in between. Any adult could tell any child what to do. They shared the same DNA on how to raise kids, so we didn't get mixed signals." Johnny dug into the eggs.

I couldn't watch him tackle the cholesterol load. I finished my single English muffin with marmalade.

"Most of my family lived within a mile of each other." It sounded idyllic even though it wasn't.

"Anyone could swat any child's butt if he acted up." Charlie smiled.

"He? My sisters and girl cousins got their fair share of swats."

"You know what I mean." Charlie stuck out her tongue.

"I worried when we agreed to live in a construction zone, but everyone has been so good with the kids. Ducks is a godsend. He's grounded them in education and instilled a deep love of learning. The workers adopted them as their own."

"Ducks is weird like you and Em." Charlie wrinkled her nose. "I don't have any idea how you do it."

"Neither do I."

"Both kids have developed an appreciation for the importance of civic service." Johnny mopped up remnants of egg with a piece of toast. "Don't I remember Alex asking why you didn't write a check for the park? You didn't. You taught him how to be resourceful if he wanted to put his dream into reality."

"Even though it was my husband's foundation that gave him the money, he had to do all the research, apply for the grant, and win it."

If I'd written a check, this would be my park, not Alex's. Not the community's. With so much sweat equity in the new playground and basketball court, I trusted the community would maintain it long after the road crews moved on to other jobs.

"So right, Max. After all, we aren't going to be here forever. The community has to value the playground and park as much as Alex does. You did the right thing." Johnny gave my hand an eggy squeeze.

CHAPTER SIXTY-EIGHT

Mississippi, week of February 27

WITH ISABELLA ENSCONCED in the manse again and with the private investigator sticking to Father Alvarado like ticks on a hound, I breathed a tiny bit easier. Emilie gave Marianna a cell phone and taught her how to text, which they did all the time. I checked in with Isabella.

"He called to say he was delayed a week and to change the church message board. He said to pack my clothes."

"Why?" I couldn't follow the priest's motive.

"He's moving me to another church without Marianna."

Holy crap. I never dreamed he'd try to separate mother and child. I won't give him time to act on his punitive plan.

Father Alvarado's original schedule would have brought him to St. Anna's the weekend of the park's inauguration, but with him delayed, Isabella could join the community she'd lived in but wasn't a part of.

"Mrs. Sanchez and Marianna need some fun." Emilie said. "The park dedication will be the biggest party this region has seen since before Katrina."

Alex and Charlie were in charge of the festivities. With meetings going on every other night, I figured I'd be running him all over creation. Instead, Charlie drove him, leaving me to work out details for Marianna and Isabella's extraction.

"Bug, Isabella's agreed to come to Richmond, but she's terrified." I stood in the kitchen of the girls' dorm, sipping a cup of tea.

"She should be. After all, we're asking her to leave everything she's ever known, move to a strange part of the country, and put her trust in yet another priest. If I were her, I'd be scared shitless."

"Father Sean! Such language!" I relaxed.

"Give me a break. You've heard it before."

"Said it too." I stirred my tea. "Father Alvarado threatened to separate them. He told Isabella to pack, because he's sending her to another church."

"Not a chance in hell. That's not going to happen," Sean said.

"Do you think you and Hot Pants should talk to her? You know, help her put a voice behind a name."

"Good idea. Give me her number. I'll call her. So will Hot Pants."

Paper rustled. I gave Sean Isabella's phone number.

"Father Alvarado's going to be a week late. It'll be safe if you call her in the next few days."

"But if a man answers, I'll hang up." Sean turned one of the oldest, lamest jokes in the world into a most serious comment.

"That's what I do. They don't have caller ID. The couple of times I called without knowing he was there, I hung up. One rude encounter was enough."

CHAPTER SIXTY-NINE

Mississippi, week of February 27

THE DAY OF the party, I rousted Emilie and Marianna out of bed early. I tidied the kitchen and prepared for the day.

Isabella's face hadn't healed completely, but the bruises were light enough to be covered with a bit of makeup. Marianna's bruise on her face was less noticeable, but her internal pain remained raw. She was shy around everyone but our extended family. She relaxed with us, even with the men, after she spent more time with Ducks and Johnny. Living with Charlie in the Silver Slug helped.

I confirmed that Isabella would be at the park around noon. We'd have plenty of food and planned lots of games. I wanted to see Marianna playing volleyball. She was turning into a tiger at the net, small stature be damned.

Father Sean and Sister Susan had talked with Isabella. "Father Sean said Marianna could qualify for a partial scholarship to the Catholic school. I can't believe it. She's never been to school."

I found that unfathomable. School was a universal right, and parents had an obligation to see that their children attended an accredited institution. It was also the law. I could see how Marianna had fallen through the cracks for so long, since she never left the house. School districts lacked staff to seek out kids who weren't registered. Heck, they had too much to do tracking down delinquents and truants.

"Sister Susan lives in the other half of the house we can use while I get settled. She'll help me make friends in the community. The woman at the Wellington Foundation told me I can start learning how to use a computer as soon as we get there." Her excitement bubbled over.

"That's wonderful." I put bowls of oatmeal on the table for the girls and pointed for them to sit.

"You've done so much for us. I don't know how to thank you."

"Keeping yourself and Marianna safe is enough thanks for me. See you soon."

"When will they move?" Emilie stirred milk into the brown sugar and raisins she added to her oatmeal until it was all dressed up and ready to eat.

"Very soon." I turned toward Marianna. "I found your mother a job and hooked her up with two old friends from school. Father Sean, aka Bug, and Sister Susan, aka—well, never mind—will help you."

"What was Sister Susan's nickname?" Emilie's eyes glinted.

"Better you not know. I don't want you using it by mistake."

"Ooh, it must be something naughty."

Marianna giggled. Emilie chased a raisin that was trying to escape her spoon. She trapped it against the side of the bowl, scooped it up, and popped it in her mouth.

"Let's just say, Sue has done a complete image and spiritual makeover. Her father was the strictest of holy-roller evangelical ministers, and she was as wild as could be. Somewhere along her path in life, she converted to Catholicism and became a nun."

"A 'who'd a thunk it' moment?"

"In triplicate. Now, no more questions."

"One more. What did they call you?"

"Mouse."

"Mouse?'

"As in I was very small and quiet as a church mouse, as Bug used to say." I wiped drops of coffee from the countertop.

"Not any longer." Emilie finished her oatmeal and fetched a

cup of coffee. "You live life out loud."

"Indeed I do, dear child. Indeed I do."

An hour before the party began, Charlie, Emilie and Marianna, Johnny, and I drove to the park to finish setting up. Pastor Taylor dropped off bags of ice and a cooler of soft drinks. Alex, my colossal pain-in-the-ass grandson, ran around checking every last detail and getting on everyone's nerves.

"Holy-crap boy-child's getting like Dad, except Dad doesn't get in the way." Emilie nodded toward her younger brother, who galloped through life with an abundance of curiosity and energy.

"Brat." I tugged a lock of purply-pink hair.

My cell buzzed. An incoming text message sent chills down my spine.

"He's on his way back." Joe the PI.

Charlie, Johnny, Whip, and Ducks anchored the volleyball net and batted a ball back and forth. Marianna watched and waited for her turn. People from Hope Village ambled over. A little before noon, Isabella arrived. I gave her a quick hug and steered her toward Pastor Taylor, who had prepared a flyer announcing a basketball clinic and the opening of the new community recreation hall. He wanted to keep the momentum from the opening of the park going strong. Stephen Adams, the former coach, stood next to the pastor.

"Pastor Taylor, I'd like you to meet Mrs. Sanchez."

Pastor Taylor shook Isabella's hand. "I'm glad you've come to our party. Welcome."

Pastor Washington arrived and joined us. I introduced Isabella and chatted about games and programs for the recreation center. Pastor Taylor envisioned a clean, well-lighted place where children and teens could get some exercise, learn a little about nutrition and improve their overall fitness.

"What do you have in mind for the adults who need similar help?" Pastor Washington's voice rumbled up from an oversized girth. He patted his stomach. "My wife says I do."

"Maybe you could work together. Find someone in the village or in the schools who could help design a nutrition program. Maybe someone over at the hospital could come out." I smiled my most disingenuous smile. "This recreation center could grow into a real community center."

"Woman, will you never stop tryin' to get us to work together?" Pastor Washington's protest was countermanded by the glint of approval in his eyes.

"Nope."

"She is one of the orneriest women I've ever met," agreed Pastor Taylor. "I'll be glad when she's out of our hair, won't you, Roland?"

"Amen to that, brother. Amen to that." Pastor Washington clapped me on the back before moving away to talk with old friends who'd come home.

Cars and trucks arrived from the road crews. Some brought food, even though we'd asked for drink donations. Soon the tables were groaning under the weight of platters of pulled pork, fried chicken, bowls of potato salad, greens and grits, hot dogs and beans, and a variety of other delicacies, some local, some Mexican.

People filled plates and sat on the ground or all over the basketball court. Those who'd brought chairs offered them to mothers and children. Men stood and talked shop. By the time we were nearing the end of lunch, we had more than a hundred people mingling and getting to know each other.

Johnny and Whip organized a pick-up game of basketball and several teens, men. and women joined in. Charlie, as short as she was, played a mean guard position and turned out to have a wicked three point jump shot.

Others began a volleyball game. Alex and Emilie pulled Marianna onto their team, while Ducks and I were on the opposing side. We shouted encouragement, bemoaned a missed spike and encouraged each other with high-fives and slaps on the back. Pastor Taylor and Pastor Washington cheered from the sidelines. For at least one day, the park served its goal.

We'd changed sides when more cars pulled up and parked wherever there was room. I didn't pay any attention. People had been arriving since before noon.

Marianna stood behind the baseline and tossed the ball high into the air. Before it could come down, a hand reached out and grabbed her arm.

"What the hell do you think you're doing?" Father Alvarado shouted. His fingers dug into Marianna's upper arm. He shook her until her head snapped back and forth. "I ordered you never to leave the church."

We froze for what seemed like hours. It was seconds, but it was enough time for the scenario to play out. Father Alvarado tried to drag Marianna away from the base line.

"You belong to me. You will obey me. Do you hear?" Father Alvarado raised his free hand to strike Marianna.

Isabella came running over. Two other people moved in unison. Pastor Taylor stopped Isabella. Pastor Washington lumbered across the volleyball court and gripped Father Alvarado's raised fist.

"No one belongs to anyone. She ain't your property. You... will...not...strike...a...child! Do you understand me?" Pastor Washington was nose to nose with Father Alvarado.

Both men balled their fists, ready to come to blows, when a deep voice rang out across the grounds.

"That will be enough." Silence. "Ramon, release the child."

"Who's that?" Emilie sidled over and whispered to me.

"If I have to guess, I'd say that is Bishop Spellman."

"Perfect timing." Emilie's hand slid into mine. "Did you plan this?"

"As big a surprise to me as it is to Father Alvarado." I hugged my granddaughter before I turned my attention to the ashen-faced priest. "Why don't you go help Mrs. Sanchez?"

A non-descript car cruised by but didn't stop. I caught a glimpse of an unfamiliar profile and a ball cap pulled low but little else. A hand raised and flashed a V-for-victory symbol. Joe the PI.

Emilie joined Pastor Taylor and Mrs. Sanchez. Johnny and Charlie moved into position to create a formidable barrier around the woman. Whip, Ducks, and I edged closer to Father Alvarado and Pastor Washington.

"Bishop Spellman, what are you doing here?" Father Alvarado's face turned a sickly shade of gray-brown.

"I came to talk with you, but I don't have to. I can see what's going on with my own eyes."

Bishop Spellman hadn't taken a single step forward, nor had

he raised his voice, yet he commanded the entire crowd. A baby fussed under the live oak tree, shushed instantly by its mother.

Pastor Washington released Father Alvarado's arm at the same time the priest released Marianna. Pastor Washington gave her a tiny push toward her mother.

"Would anyone mind tellin' me what the hell's going on?" Pastor Washington demanded. "Why's this man claimin' the girl's his property? We ain't had slavery in these parts since my grandpappy was lynched at the beginnin' of the last century. We ain't gonna have it again."

Pastor Washington thrust out his chin and narrowed his eyes. For once, I wasn't on the receiving end of his wrath.

Bishop Spellman scanned the crowd. He looked at a piece of paper in one hand. He called out a few names. "Mrs. Sanchez, Marianna, Mrs. Davies, Emilie Pugh, Pastor Taylor, will you all come with me? You must be Pastor Washington."

Pastor Washington nodded.

"Will you bring Ramon? If you don't mind coming to the church for a while, we can get everything cleared up."

"We won't be long." Pastor Taylor turned to the gawking crowd. "When I get back, I want to know who won the basketball game. Got it?"

Heads nodded. Charlie tossed up a jump shot. Swish. Nothing but net.

Pastor Washington shouldered Father Alvarado toward the church and fell into step behind him. He glanced at me, but I was as much in the dark as he was. I wanted to see what Bishop Spellman would do next.

Several cars filled the small parking area in front of the manse. A Ford sedan with Louisiana plates I thought might be Bishop Spellman's. A large, dusty van with Virginia plates parked next to the sedan. Emilie looked at me. I winked.

CHAPTER SEVENTY

Mississippi, week of February 27

BISHOP SPELLMAN LED the way into the Sunday school room attached to the church.

"If you'll go in here and find seats, I need a moment." The bishop disappeared into the church proper.

"Is this what I hope it is?" Emilie whispered.

"We're about to witness one hell of an intervention." I relaxed for the first time in weeks. Truly relaxed.

We found chairs arranged in a semicircle, like something out of a bad movie, an interrogation by a military tribunal. Except there was no metal table or strong light shining on the prisoner. Pastor Washington led Father Alvarado to a single chair placed so it faced the semi-circle.

"I do believe this is your seat." He placed a big hand on the priest's shoulder and pushed him into the lonely chair. He sat on one side of Isabella, Pastor Taylor on the other.

Emilie placed Marianna between herself and me. Father Alvarado sat alone in the middle of the room, facing the rest of us. His accusers were about to confront him. His reign of abuse was over. I was glad I had a role in it, if only as a whistleblower. The church door opened. Three people entered. Bishop Spellman had put his clerical robe on over his khakis and golf shirt. A man and woman followed.

I swallowed against a lump in my throat. Bug and Hot Pants. My hunch about the dusty van was true; my old friends had come to fetch my new friends and take them to Richmond. I dabbed at an eye. I didn't recognize Hot Pants. No longer the rebellious high school girl with loose morals, she was a stately nun who wore conviction like a layer of fine powder.

Bishop Spellman stood in the middle of the room, his back to Father Alvarado. "I'm Joseph Spellman, Father Alvarado's bishop."

He walked to those of us who were seated and placed his hand on our heads, one at a time. He blessed us for our courage. When he got to the two Baptist preachers, he laid his hand on their shoulders, one at a time, and thanked them for what he was about to ask of them. Then he introduced Father Sean, my Bug, and Sister Susan.

"They have a very important role in Mrs. Sanchez and Marianna's future. I'll tell you about it in a few minutes. First, though, I have something to say to Father Alvarado."

The bishop turned toward the terrified priest.

"You are a disgrace to your collar, Father Alvarado." Gone was the familiarity of Ramon. "You are here before this woman and this child to apologize to them for the way you've treated them."

Apologize? I wanted more than an apology. I looked at Bug, who gestured for me to have patience. Patience, my ass. I wanted to see this man castigated in front of his victims and peers.

"I haven't done anything wrong." Father Alvarado glared at Isabella, as if to silence her with promises of future retaliation.

"Do you deny you struck Mrs. Sanchez and Marianna?" Bishop Spellman's voice had steel underneath it.

"I never hit either of them. Ask anyone. I'm a gentle person, just trying to be the best priest I can." Father Alvarado spread his hands upward as if making a plea for penance, but his expression changed from intimidation to fear.

"Do you deny you had sex with Mrs. Alvarado? And that you were planning to abuse Marianna in the same way?"

Pastor Washington growled. He'd never imagined anything like this going on in his community.

"I took a vow of celibacy. I don't have sex with parishioners." Beads of sweat dripped down Father Alvarado's forehead, even though the Sunday school room was cool.

"Tell me why Mrs. Sanchez ended up in the hospital with two dislocated fingers and deep bruises on her face and body?" Bishop Spellman built his case with the logic of a good trial lawyer.

"It must have happened after I left. Plenty of people could have broken in." Father Alvarado looked around for support. He sat in the loneliest chair in the center of nowhere. No one took his side. "Lots of people are roaming the countryside."

Bishop Spellman walked over to Isabella. He knelt on one knee before her, held her hands in his and asked her if Father Alvarado had beaten and raped her. She nodded, lowering her head in shame.

"And did he also strike Marianna? Did he try to have sex with her?"

Isabella nodded. Tears streamed down her face. She gripped Bishop Spellman's hands tightly. He never flinched.

"This is very difficult for you. You've been very brave to tell me. I promise he'll never hurt you or anyone else again." Bishop Spellman withdrew his hands, laid one on Isabella's head, and made the sign of the cross over her. Pastor Washington put his arm around her and let Isabella cry on his shoulder.

"Father Alvarado, you will accompany me back to New Orleans today, where I will deal with you."

Father Alvarado sagged in his chair. "You have no proof. It's her word against mine. Who are you going to believe, Bishop Spellman? An illiterate woman or me?"

"I believe my eyes. I heard what you said with my ears. I have a stack of pictures"—he gestured toward Bug, who held up an envelope—"taken at the hospital by Mrs. Davies. I don't have to take anyone's word. You're finished. I will deal with you at the archdiocese's office. Wait for me in the church. You might want to pray."

Father Alvarado shuffled out of the room, head hanging, shoulders slumped, all arrogance gone.

Bishop Spellman pulled the newly empty chair over and dropped into it. His café-au-lait face was drawn but calm. I envied him. I wouldn't have been able to face down a child abuser and

rapist with his decorum. I wanted to castrate Father Alvarado like
I should have done to Uncle Phil forty years earlier.

Bishop Spellman suggested I tell the assembled rescuers
what we had in mind for Isabella and Marianna's future. I ran
through the gist of the many conversations I'd had with Father
Sean—couldn't call him Bug in front of strangers—and what
Sister Susan had offered. Couldn't call her Hot Pants. Her high
school nickname was so far from her present reality I drove it
deep into my memory.

"Mrs. Sanchez, is this all right with you?" Bishop Spellman
asked. When Isabella nodded, he turned to Marianna. "You'll
be moving away from everything you know and starting life
over. Sister Susan will help, as will Father Sean. Is this all right
with you?"

No one had to ask the child if life-shaking changes were all
right with her, yet Bishop Spellman did. The child nodded.

"I'll leave you in the good hands of Father Sean and Sister
Susan." Bishop Spellman rose. "You will not hear what happens
to Father Alvarado, but I promise you he will never harm another
person. You'll have to trust me. Can you?"

Isabella and Marianna looked at each other. Relief washed
over them, much as it washed over me, Emilie, and the Baptist
preachers. We all nodded.

"Now, Pastor Taylor and Pastor Washington, I need your
help. I won't be able to send a priest to this parish for a while.
We're short-handed, but Father Alvarado did minister to a
couple of dozen families. When they return, they're going to
need religious support. Can I count on you to welcome them
into your congregations until I can assign someone?"

Silent agreement passed between the two Baptist preachers.
Pastor Washington rose to his feet. He lumbered over until he
was standing next to Bishop Spellman.

"I got somethin' to say to you all. And, in particular, to this
tiresome woman here. Miz Davies, I thought you were makin'
this up."

"That I went from A to B to Z without anything in between?"

"Sumptin' like that." He looked at Isabella and Marianna.
"Believe me, Hodge and I had no idea what was goin' on. I'm
ashamed to say I didn't care. You're Catholics and white. I felt I

had no business buttin' into your lives. I shoulda been a better preacher and extended a hand."

Pastor Taylor also stood and walked over to flank Bishop Spellman on the other side. "I didn't pay any attention either. I knew something wasn't right, but I ignored it. I'm sorry, Mrs. Sanchez, Marianna. If I'd been a better Christian, a better man, I could have given you sanctuary. I stand before you and ask your forgiveness."

Okay, there wasn't a dry eye in the room. Emilie jumped with joy and clapped her hands. We'd won. "Junie is happy," she whispered.

"One more thing, if I might. This nosey woman, this most meddlesome woman, Miz Davies, asked me why the most segregated time of the week was eleven on Sunday morning. I didn't have an answer, but I do now." Pastor Washington turned toward me. "Miz Davies, Father Sean, and Sister Susan, will you join Pastor Taylor and me at the first ever ecumenical church service tomorrow? We'll be meetin' in the rec center. At eleven. We'll both preach our style of preachin' and hope people will be more comfortable around us as they get to know us."

"I'd be honored," Father Sean said.

Hot Pants nodded.

Bishop Spellman led us in prayer, punctuated by a few amens from the Baptists in the room. He left without looking back.

CHAPTER SEVENTY-ONE

Mississippi, week of February 27

I STAYED BEHIND in the Sunday school room. Emilie walked out hand in hand with Marianna. Isabella held Marianna's other hand. I turned to Bug and Hot Pants.

"I had no idea you were coming. I can't thank you enough." I hugged each in turn.

"Joe and I talked it over and decided it best we be here. I had no idea we'd catch Alvarado in the act. We'd planned to confront him in private, remove him from the parish and take the Sanchezes back to Richmond." Bug stopped and shrugged his shoulders. "Maybe this was the better way. At least they know they'll never see him again."

Sister Susan nodded. "Mouse, I can't believe you pulled this off. Where's that timid child who kept her nose buried in a book and rarely joined group activities?"

"Sue, you might say I paid a debt I've owed for forty years. I'll tell you about it sometime."

"Amazing how we've all changed. Even Hot Pants here has found God and the church." Bug had a wicked glint in his eye.

"I hope no one knows my nickname. It could be very embarrassing if they did." Sue didn't look the least put-out.

"I haven't told anyone, although my granddaughter has pestered me to no end about it." I chuckled.

"Oh, she knows. She's a rare child, isn't she?" Sue said.

"You have no idea. When are you heading back to Richmond?"

"Tomorrow after services, if the Sanchezes can be packed and ready."

"I'll go and help them. Where are you staying?"

"We found a place over in Gulfport. Not very fancy, but clean."

"Good. Can we have dinner and catch up? Just the three of us." I wanted to reconnect with my old friends.

"Of course."

We made plans. This was one meal where I didn't want Emilie, Alex, Charlie, Ducks, Johnny, or Whip with me. We had too much of the past and the future to talk about.

The entire community turned out for the joint service. Pastor Taylor began, but Pastor Washington stole the show. His cadence reminded me of Dr. King's *I Have a Dream* speech. I nodded along, amening with the black congregants and praying for peace in my heart as well as for this battered but healing community. When Pastor Washington turned to Father Regan, my dear Bug, to offer the final prayer, it surprised the hell out of everyone.

I waited while the recreation-center-turned-ecumenical church for a day emptied. As a tiresome woman, I wanted to have a last word with Pastor Washington.

"Now what do you want, Miz Davies? You got that look about you." The pastor mopped his brow with a white handkerchief. "You got what you wanted, didn't you?"

"Partly." I had one last request up my sleeve.

"Partly? Today went right well, didn't it? What more do you want?" The black preacher shook his head.

"When are you going to do this again?" I stared him straight in the eye. "After all, none of the churches have all that many parishioners. It seems to me you'd want to combine services, say, monthly?"

"Woman, you're way too meddlesome." Pastor Washington shook his head.

Pastor Taylor walked over. He laughed when he saw the looks on each of our faces. "Is Miz Davies getting on you again, Roland?"

"She got what she wanted. Integration at eleven on a Sunday. She wants even more." Pastor Washington pulled a hangdog expression.

"Like what?" Pastor Taylor acted as if he had a secret, one that didn't involve me.

"Like monthly ecumenical prayer services, for a start." I had a list ready. "And more interaction between the black and white communities, an embracing of the local Hispanic and Catholic communities. It'll move this area one step closer to the twenty-first century."

"We've agreed to joint services on the last Sunday of the month. When the new priest gets here, we may have to adjust to fit his schedule, but we want him too," Pastor Taylor announced.

"You were conning me, Pastor Washington." I lightly slapped his upper arm.

"And why should I let you think you're gettin' your way all the time, Miz Davies? You'll be leavin' when the road's done and will forget all about this backward corner of Mississippi." Pastor Washington sounded like he was both joking and serious.

"I may not get back this way again, but rest assured I'll never forget either of you and what you're trying to do here. You'll do just fine without my meddling."

"That we will, Miz Davies. That we will." Pastor Washington moved away to speak with a family who had been waiting for him.

"Miz Davies." Pastor Taylor moved into the black pastor's place. "The police and the FBI aren't going to charge Jake with anything. J'Marquis and LeRoy are going to be prosecuted in federal court for murder and rape, as well as for hate crimes. Danny Ray will be prosecuted at the local level. He'll serve a minimum sentence."

"What about Jake? Are they going to turn him loose to roam?"

"No. The missus and I are going take him in at least until we can find his kinfolk. I'm going to have him tested and try to get him into some kind of special educational program. He's a good boy, but he's had no chance. Maybe the missus and I can give him one."

I gulped. I never expected Pastor Taylor to take on a mentally challenged youth. I wished him the best of luck.

I had one more stop before I returned to the compound. Emilie had gone ahead with Bug and Hot Pants to help the Sanchezes load the van. I wanted to say good-bye. I caught them as Bug slammed the back door of the van. Isabella's car was packed.

"Will we ever see you again?" Isabella's eyes were red-rimmed.

"Of course. Emilie and Alex and Whip live a few miles from where you'll be. We go back all the time. Don't worry. You haven't seen the last of us." I hugged Isabella and then turned to Marianna.

"Do well in school. It'll make your mother very proud." I kissed the child's tear-stained cheek and helped her into the backseat.

"Bug, thanks for everything. I can't ever repay you." I, too, had tears in my eyes.

"You could always go to Mass…" Bug kissed me on the cheek.

"You never give up, do you?"

"Nope."

I laughed and turned to Sue, who was going to drive Isabella's Toyota. "Take care of them. I can't tell you how much they mean to me."

"You don't have to worry." Sister Susan hugged me. A different sense of peace washed over me.

"Sue, did it cross your mind that sometimes God goes by the name of Max?"

"Oh, no. Don't you go there, Bug. I did what had to be done." I pushed him toward the driver's door.

Emilie and I waved until they were out of sight. I couldn't save Junie, but I helped Isabella and Marianna. I said a tiny prayer it would be enough. I hoped Junie heard me.

"She did." Emilie put her arm around my waist.

"Thanks."

"Um, Hot Pants?" Emilie grinned.

I held up one finger before folding my fingers in a clam shape. "Brat."

Emilie put her finger to her lips, turned an imaginary key, and locked the secret away.

CHAPTER SEVENTY-TWO

New York, April 16

TWO MONTHS LATER, Bug called. I hoped nothing bad had happened. He assured me the Sanchezes settled in nicely. Marianna had tested well below her grade level, as expected, but with tutoring, she was making up ground. Isabella had taken to her job and volunteered to help Sue when she had free time.

"So, why did you call?" I was in New York for the weekend, my monthly board meeting behind me once again. Emilie had come along, but Alex stayed at the camp. We neared the end of phase one of the job. Alex spent as much time with Charlie as she allowed. He hadn't outgrown the crush he'd formed in Peru the previous year.

"Someone put a cashier's check for ten thousand dollars in the collection plate at Mass this morning." Bug acted like he knew I was behind the donation. "You wouldn't have any idea who it was, would you?"

"Did you see me in church?" I played innocent. "I'm in New York."

"I didn't. If you ever find out who gave us the donation, will you thank her for me? We can use the money."

"If I could, I would. Speak again with you soon, Bug."

ACKNOWLEDGMENTS

FIRST, I WANT to thank my husband, Terry Naylor, for reading multiple drafts and being honest in his comments on what I wrote. He has supported my writing life for years without complaint.

To my novel "midwives," I thank Donna Knox, Keith Martin, and John Koelsch for their early support in our Naked Writers critique group. My two writing groups, Lake Writers at Smith Mountain Lake and Valley Writers, the Roanoke chapter of Virginia Writers Club, let me read sections of the novel and provided excellent guidance in strengthening key scenes. Without all of you, this novel would be a mess and stillborn.

To Pastor Philip Bouknight, pastor at Trinity Ecumenical Parish, Moneta, VA, and his Parents Again fellowship group who allowed me to visit their support session to learn what issues grandparents face when they are parents once again. I met so many different grandparents and great-grandparents who went back into the trenches to relearn fifth-grade math, remember where commas belong, and study world history, because the world has changed so much since most of them were in school. They are all my heroes.

The folks at Great American RV Center. Ft. Myers, Florida, let me sit in upscale RVs so that I could get the feel for what the characters were experiencing. Camping World salesmen let me pepper them with questions about how these rolling condos work. I learned more about washers and dryers, refrigerators, electric generators, propane tanks and waste removal than I used in the book. Still I needed to know as much as possible, so that the motor home would feel natural when I wrote about it. I now see why people buy these buses. They're roomy and are rolling homes.

Fortunately, there were many pictures of the Madden Horse Trailer online. I used the real interior until it didn't meet the needs of a certain setting. Then I trashed it and went my own way. For those of you who love and keep alive Airstream trailers, you are special. "Silver Slugs" have a huge universe of fans, many of whom answered questions patiently.

Wayne at Blackwater Guns, my "gun guy," answered countless questions about rifles, shotguns and ammunition. I still don't like handguns, but I could get into the Kel-Tec shotgun.

Habitat for Humanity's Care-a-Vanners and God's Pit Crew from Danville, VA, do great work helping people all the time. Many thanks for letting me hijack your organizations for this book. I hope I presented them in a favorable light.

With heartfelt thanks to Richmond writer, Dean King, who took time to talk to me about a landscape of nothingness when I struggled to describe coastal Mississippi after Katrina. He pointed me toward his *Skeletons of the Zahara: A True Story of Survival*. I drew inspiration from his description of the Sahara, where we mistakenly think nothing is there. There is, and Dean King describes it perfectly.

To Dawn Dowdle, Blue Ridge Literary Agency, for signing me and believing in Mad Max. She's brought so many of us debut writers to the attention of great publishers around the world. To John Koehler, Joe Coccaro and Courtney Davison for their guidance in shaping the characters in this book. Max says she loves them all.